PENGUIN BOOKS

The Pink House

Asda Tickled Pink

30p from the sale of this book will be donated to Tickled Pink.

Asda Tickled Pink is working with Breast Cancer Now and CoppaFeel! to help change the future of breast cancer in the UK. Together we are championing regular boob-checking and educating our community of colleagues, customers and suppliers to be breast aware, alongside raising vital funds for research and support for those affected by the disease.

Since 1996, Asda Tickled Pink has raised a phenomenal £77 million for their charity partners. Through the partnership, Asda has been committed to raising funds and breast-check awareness via in-store fundraising, disruptive awareness campaigns, and products turning pink to support the campaign. The funds have been vital for Breast Cancer Now's world-class research and life-changing support services, such as their Helpline, there for anyone affected by breast cancer to cope with the emotional impact of the disease. Asda Tickled Pink's educational and outreach work with CoppaFeel! aims to empower 600,000 18–24 year olds to adopt regular boob-checking behaviour by 2024. Together we will continue to make a tangible difference to breast cancer in the UK.

Asda Tickled Pink and Penguin Random House have teamed up to bring you Tickled Pink Books. By buying this book and supporting the partnership, you ensure that 30p goes directly to Breast Cancer Now and CoppaFeel!.

Breast cancer is the most common cancer in women in the UK, with one in seven women facing it in their lifetime.

Around 55,000 women and 370 men are diagnosed with breast cancer every year in the UK and nearly 1,000 people still lose their life to the disease each month. This is one person every 45 minutes and this is why your support and the support from Asda Tickled Pink is so important.

A new Tickled Pink Book will go on sale in Asda stores every two weeks – we aim to bring you the best stories of friendship, love, heartbreak and laughter.

To find out more about the Tickled Pink partnership visit www.asda.com/tickled-pink

Penguin
Random House
UK

STAY BREAST AWARE AND CHECK YOURSELF REGULARLY

One in seven women in the UK will be diagnosed with breast cancer in their lifetime

'TOUCH, LOOK, KNOW YOUR NORMAL, REPEAT REGULARLY'

Make sure you stay breast aware

- Get to know what's normal for you
- Look and feel to notice any new or unusual changes early
- The earlier breast cancer is diagnosed, the better the chance of successful treatment
- Check your boobs regularly and see a GP if you notice a change

The Pink House

CATHERINE ALLIOTT

PENGUIN BOOKS

PENGUIN BOOKS

UK | USA | Canada | Ireland | Australia
India | New Zealand | South Africa

Penguin Books is part of the Penguin Random House group of companies
whose addresses can be found at global.penguinrandomhouse.com

First published by Penguin Michael Joseph 2023
Published in Penguin Books 2023
001

Typeset by Jouve (UK), Milton Keynes
Printed and bound in Great Britain by Clays Ltd, Elcograf S.p.A.

The authorized representative in the EEA is Penguin Random House Ireland,
Morrison Chambers, 32 Nassau Street, Dublin D02 YH68

A CIP catalogue record for this book is available from the British Library

ISBN: 978-1-405-94994-1

www.greenpenguin.co.uk

For Bim

I

Tucked away in a drawer in my mother-in-law's London flat, and presumably somewhere equally private in my father-in-law's seaside cottage, I imagine there is a legal document filled with the reasons why the pair of them decided to divorce two months ago, well into their seventies. I wondered, as I finally found the postbox next to the turning and abruptly swerved right, if those irritations might not seem rather petty and inconsequential now? Given the fallout Hugh and I were grappling with? And that if someone had sat them down and explained how divorce would sour what remained of their lives – or if they'd somehow been able to glimpse the future – might they not have reconsidered? Still be together?

As I pulled into the pub car park, half an hour late, grabbing my phone and bag, I realized that some might say that person should have been me, given that the people who by rights should have done it were totally incapable. The family. They'd simply made vague noises about it all being terribly difficult, and Mum and Dad never taking a blind bit of notice of anything they said, then, avoiding my eye and looking awkward, gone back to their books, or their music, or their art, relieved that difficult conversation was over and hopefully Emma was happy.

I hurried on through the panelled bar and into the restaurant where I saw Jane, sitting at a table by the window. She looked only mildly amused as I flew across the room, collapsing dramatically into the seat opposite her. I was dying for a pee but knew this wasn't the moment.

'Ah, the late Emma Petridis,' she drawled.

'Sorry,' I gasped. 'Sorry sorry sorry. That bloody postbox. I swear they move it or something.'

'Oh, they do, every time. They know you're coming, you see, and Postman Pat sneaks out and puts it on the corner of a different lane. Are you drinking?'

'Definitely. Forty minutes on the M3 with my father-in-law on the blower on famously fizzy form would turn anyone to drink. But just a spritzer, please,' I said, looking up with a smile, as our elderly landlord materialized beside us.

Ron greeted me, recognizing me as the other half of the friendship duo who'd been coming here for years, and after much commiserating about the traffic, bustled away to get my drink and 'the usual', a salade Niçoise apiece.

'So.' Jane leaned in, her lips twitching. 'No longer our halfway house, eh? Soon to be abandoned for a pub on the Downs, or even your vast ancestral farmhouse kitchen.' She raised her glass. 'Here's to raiding the Petridis cellar.'

I knew she was pissed off about permanently being kept waiting, but her untypically brittle tone made me anxious.

'Do you think we're acting with indecent haste? Moving in?'

'We?' She raised her eyebrows archly. 'What's Hugh got to do with it? What's Hugh ever got to do with any major decisions in your household?' She must have seen my face fall, and Jane was irritated, but not unkind. 'No, I'm kidding. I actually think it's the most sensible – and incidentally the only – decision under the circumstances. It would be a travesty to let that gorgeous house go up for sale. The only mad decision is to let Sally come with you.'

I relaxed, if that was her only concern. Mine was relieving Hugh's parents of their marital home only weeks after the ink was dry on the decree nisi.

'Sally has to come,' I told her firmly.

'Because it makes you feel better?'

'No-o . . .' I hesitated. 'Well, yes, OK. Of course it makes me feel better. But also, Sally happens to be a good friend of mine, as well as Hugh's sister. Which I know you sometimes find hard to fathom, although I don't know why – she's your friend too.'

'Yes, but she's not my sister-in-law.'

'I know, but honestly, I've got the measure of her now.'

Jane made a disbelieving face. The three of us had been at university together – and the two of them, before that, at school – so she wasn't speaking without intuition, wasn't coming to this blind. Nevertheless, twenty-five years of marriage to Hugh gave me the inside track and I'd come to know exactly what made my sister-in-law tick and how to manage her. There would be no surprises and I told Jane so now.

'And I know what makes *you* tick,' she countered as our order arrived. She waited until the waitress had gone then picked the olives off her salad, lining them up on the side of her plate. 'And keeping everyone in that family happy is high on your list of priorities. And I get that someone has to. But doing that at a distance with Sally on the other side of London, and having her under your roof in Wiltshire, is a very different thing. What do the children think of her having the cottage in the garden?'

'They're cool about it,' I lied blithely, wishing my best friend didn't know quite so much about me. Nico, my eldest, had already told me I was bonkers, down the phone from New York, and Teddy had rolled his eyes in bafflement. 'Good luck with that, Mum,' he'd said.

'The children are fine,' I told her firmly. 'And it's not as if they'll see much of her anyway. They have their own lives to lead.'

'That's not what I meant and you know it.'

'And anyway, of course she should be included,' I

swept on, ignoring her. 'After all, it's her childhood home.'

Jane inclined her head in some slight acknowledgement of this, and I wondered if she was remembering the first time we'd been taken there, as young undergraduates. There'd been quite a few of us. We'd arrived in a couple of beaten-up old cars, music blaring as we drew up to the idyllic pink house, nestling in a deep fold of the rolling Wiltshire hills. All the windows had glinted in the autumn sunshine, as if to welcome us. That evening we'd lit a fire in the field behind the house, and Sally's mother, Clem, now my mother-in-law, had let us help ourselves to bacon, sausages and eggs from the larder to cook on it. I remember being astonished as she'd wafted around the kitchen looking effortlessly gorgeous and bohemian in a long silk kimono, her thick dark hair piled on her head attractively escaping its pins. 'Help yourselves, darlings,' she'd drawled, before drifting back to her poetry reading in the picture-crammed drawing room, a glass of ouzo in one hand, a cigarette trailing in the other. A couple of the boys in the party – Hamish and Tom and some others who came from Scotland – had shown everyone how to do an eightsome reel, and we'd all danced to Sally's tape machine by the fire till dawn. I had a feeling that was where Jane's mind was now, because it was surely the only time she'd been to the Pink House. Whereas I, of course, knew it intimately.

'Well, I must say, I can't wait to go back there,' she admitted wistfully. Ah. Bingo. 'And to have you around the corner will be heaven.'

We beamed at one another delightedly and I knew that, having got any reservations out of the way, it was more than either of us could possibly have hoped for. Jane and I had grown up in very different circumstances but in similarly emotionally distant families and our friendship was intensely valuable to us, in a way, I've noticed, that children from large, happy households don't always require. A sibling is often enough. And neither of us had one. Plus, we had an even stronger bond. Despite being at university together, neither of us had graduated. Jane had left halfway through the third year, six months pregnant with her English professor's child, and I'd left two months later, just before my final exam, when my boyfriend Hamish had died in a boating accident. Jane and I had lived together in London for two years after that, sharing our grief. We'd been loaned a basement flat belonging to her aunt in Sydney Street, where Cassie, Jane's baby, my goddaughter, was born. I'd transferred my grief and guilt about Hamish's death into caring for the baby, whilst Jane mourned the man who'd kept his job and his wife. Sally, meanwhile, had graduated with flying colours, before landing a coveted job at *Vogue*.

Jane and I had stayed extremely close and, notwithstanding the obvious geographical difficulties, this pub in Hampshire had played host to many convivial lunches over the years.

'And your mother? How does she feel about it?'

'The move to the country?' I made a face. 'As you'd imagine. Lots of sardonic smiles and knowing looks – plus the occasional remark about sharp elbows. You'll be delighted to hear I don't rise.'

'Excellent, you're learning.'

'And plenty of references to the lovely Lorraine next door, who looks after her like a daughter, even though she's terribly busy – has a proper job, naturally. Always brings her *The Times* when she goes for her own paper, even asks her round for tea.'

'Lorraine will learn.'

'Except, you know my mother. She can be all things to all people. If she puts her mind to it.' As I said this, I wondered if I could be too. If indeed everyone could, up to a point. Act a part. Be a better person, as Mum was with Lorraine. Except, of course, with those we loved the most. Those that mattered. A lump came to my throat as I recalled our last meeting, my mother's scathing remarks.

As our coffees arrived and we thanked Ron for always remembering exactly how we liked them, extra hot and milky for me and small and black for Jane, I thought, with a pang of relief tinged with guilt, of the impossibility of visiting my mother now, once a week in Hendon. In the gloomy little kitchen, much the same as all her other gloomy kitchens, and enduring her bitter, oh-so-clever barbs. She'd have to come to stay, obviously, but hopefully on my patch she'd have to watch her tongue a bit and relations could improve. Hugh's patch. I wondered if I'd ever feel it was mine.

'Will you change it much?' asked Jane, stirring her coffee, reading my thoughts.

'Not to begin with. But maybe in time.'

'Don't want to look too keen.' Jane grinned at me over the rim of her cup.

'No, but also, Clem's got great taste, so . . .'

'Yes, true,' she conceded. 'In every way, actually.'

My mother-in-law's clothes, jewellery, paintings, eclectic arty house, wild gardens, were always supremely stylish, and she had a seemingly faultless marriage too, which made this latest aberration of hers all the more shocking. It was so unlike her. The sort of thing that would ordinarily make her hoot with derision.

'He's a groom, isn't he?' asked Jane.

I sighed and put my coffee cup down. 'Yes. And she doesn't even like horses. Can't abide the county set who do all that sort of thing, thinks they're all philistines who've never read a book. But she was talked into going to some charity lunch for the local art gallery in some sod-off house, and went outside for a fag because it was so boring. She met him in the stable yard for God's sake! Thirty years her junior, striding around in tight jodhpurs with firm thighs, tousled hair and a sexy grin. I mean, honestly.'

'Sounds terrific.' Jane grinned. 'Very Jilly Cooper.'

'Well, quite, you and I would think so, but not Clem. She sees herself as far more of a Madame Bovary type, trust me. And of course it all went tits up when the groom realized she didn't have any money.' Jane was smirking. 'What?' I frowned.

'Clem. Tits up in the hay barn.'

I giggled. 'God, what a thought.'

'But surely she has *some* money; she can't have been entirely destitute. Hasn't she bought some-where in Ireland?'

'She's renting, actually.'

'Really? Why? They're loaded, aren't they?'

'Apparently it's all in the house. Hugh says they've always presented rich but they're not. And Clem wouldn't have sold Yanni's home just to enable her to live with her toy boy. But now that Yanni says he won't have her back . . .'

'Would she have gone back?'

I shrugged. 'I don't know.'

'And yet he's so bereft, isn't he? He adores her, I thought, always has done.'

'Oh, I agree, got her right up there on a pedestal. But he's so hurt, Jane. And actually –' I thought back to our conversation on the M3, the different tone to his voice – 'he's not quite so bereft now, perhaps.'

9

Her eyes widened. 'What – you think he's met someone? Already?'

'Oh no, I don't know about that . . .' I said quickly, shifting awkwardly in my seat. I always told Jane too much, sometimes before I'd even considered it. Certainly before I'd filtered it. Hugh would be appalled. This was his family, not mine. 'Anyway, we are where we are,' I swept on, changing the subject. 'It's all over bar the shouting now. They've signed the wretched thing.'

'And you'll move in when?'

'Next month.'

'May.' A slow smile spread across her pale face. 'It's beautiful here in May, in our neck of the woods. Cow parsley everywhere, wild garlic, buttercups, vivid greens in the hedgerows. And hardly any tourists either, too early.'

'Exactly,' I said eagerly. 'My favourite month – I can't wait.'

I felt my eyes shine despite myself; I couldn't. That dreamy pink house, the orchard left wild with paths mown through it, leading to beehives dotted about; the smoky-blue rolling hills beyond. I could see myself and Hugh strolling around the grounds in the early-evening light, a drink apiece, stooping to smell the lavender, noting the runner beans which grew, not in a vegetable patch, but amongst the flowers in wide beds, cabbages and carrots too. The children would come down for weekends – well,

Teddy and Ella, and Nico when he was back from New York – and to a place that wouldn't seem strange to them. To their grandparents' house, a place they loved, had called a second home ever since they were children. It wouldn't unsettle them, as I had so often been unsettled as a child, moving from house to house. Not that they were children, of course, well into their twenties now. And Yanni – surely he'd be pleased to have us nearby? Closer to the cottage by the sea he'd decided to call home? Surely he'd come for Sunday lunch, find a way back from his misery, perhaps continue to tend the garden even, the one he'd loved? The one he'd created with Clem, cherished, nurtured, surely that would be hard to give up. And maybe, maybe one day – because I lived in a make-believe world of happy endings – he could get over his pride, which was all it was really, and have Clem back? And they could even one day share the rather decent-sized cottage he'd sent me photos of, down by the harbour, and we could all be in that part of the world together? Polly and Kit, Hugh's other sister and husband, not far away – one big happy family?

I floated this with Jane. She grinned. 'I notice you're not giving the house back.'

'Oh, well, I just thought . . . you know. Getting older, downsizing. They're in their seventies, after all. But obviously –'

'Obviously I'm joking. But yes, who knows, a

happy ending. It could still be on the cards. Never say never. My godparents split up briefly in their seventies – he buggered off – and they got back together again.'

'Really?' I brightened, encouraged. 'Well, there you are!'

We split the bill and as Jane chatted to our waiter, popping her card into the machine, I imagined Clem hastening back to Yanni in floods of tears, flying into his arms. My mother-in-law was haughty and composed, though, so even with my vivid imagination, it was hard to picture. Plus, life had a way of not turning out like that, didn't it? It had a way of wrong-footing one. So that actually, it was a mistake to live a happy fantasy world in one's head, because reality, when it barged in, was therefore all the more brutal.

'What brought them back together?' I asked when the waiter had departed.

'Who?'

'Your godparents.'

'Oh. He got fleeced by some Russian woman he met on a cruise. It slightly curtailed his love action and he came crawling back. So money, basically.'

'Oh, right. Not so romantic then, the reconciliation.'

'Not really. In fact, my godmother told me recently she wished she'd never had him back. She's taken to leaving cruise brochures on his bedside table – budget ones, obviously. She said she's realized she was happier on her own and the next time he meets a gold-digging floozy he can bloody well stay with her.' She grinned, putting her purse away.

You see? I thought as I drove off some time later. Reality always had a way of doing that, didn't it? Bringing one back down to earth with a bump. But something else Jane had said chilled me more. I hadn't even entertained the possibility that Clem might want her house back one day, but now I did. Before I'd even moved into it. The idea of Clem rushing into Yanni's arms and living a reduced life in a cottage by the sea was clearly risible. But striding up what used to be her long gravel drive – which I'd already come to think of as my own – and informing me, with that cold grey eye of hers, that she'd like her house back? That became a terrible possibility.

2

Hugh was at home when I got back; he'd left work early. Central London was so quiet these days, he said; so many people still working remotely, particularly on a Friday. He didn't see the point of sitting there like a lemon, in a suit, with everyone else Zooming.

'Yes, I get that,' I agreed, greeting Scribble, our black Labrador, as Hugh made us both a gin and tonic.

I refrained from saying what all my girlfriends said, that gorgeous though it was to have our husbands around a bit more, we didn't half miss the days when we were masters of our own universes. When we could pop out without someone saying 'Where are you going?' Or not pop out, as we realized someone had taken the bloody car, and we stood fuming on the pavement. Even today I'd had to endure five minutes of Hugh's amused references to the utter madness of driving all the way to Hampshire when there were telephones Jane and I could sit on for hours if we liked, and why anyone would want to do battle with the Friday traffic was beyond him. Despite it being good-humoured it was annoying, because historically I'd pick a day when he was safely in the office and would barely even know I'd gone. But those days were rare now. If they did happen, the two of us had decided when we'd excitedly made the plan about the move to Wiltshire, he'd simply come up to town for a couple of days, and either stay at his club, or with Teddy and Ella, in their spare room in Shepherds Bush.

It was a modus vivendi we'd considered briefly many years ago, when we were raising small children. A country house near his parents for the family as a permanent base, and a pied-à-terre in London for him, the rationale being that I'd have a gorgeous rural time of it, and the boys would have space to roam and ride ponies – idyllic. But in the end we'd decided the boys could make do with a small London garden and count themselves lucky to have that. And not, as one friend had archly asked, because we didn't trust each other and were worried about the slippery slope, but because we liked each other too much, and didn't want to spend most of the week apart. The best bit of my day was Hugh coming in through the front door at about six thirty, perching at the island with me to have a drink, and chewing over the day. Although recently, I realized, as he passed me a strong one and I glanced at the clock, it was more like five forty-five.

'So how was my fantasy woman?' he asked mischievously over the rim of his glass, his eyes, despite their more hooded lids these days, still blue and with a sparkle. His hair was very definitely grey now, though, and receding a bit at the temples, swept back from his high forehead.

'Oh, she sent her love,' I said, grinning.

Once, in a stupid moment in bed, when we'd indulged in what Hugh called 'silly talk' and normally refused to entertain, I'd asked him – obviously in a make-believe world and not the real one – if he had to choose one of my friends, which one it would be.

'Jane,' he'd finally said, when I'd laughingly pressed him for an answer.

'Jane?' I'd sat bolt upright in bed. Stared down at him aghast.

'Yes. She looks like she'd be fun in bed.'

'But you can't say that, it's Jane!' I gasped. Hugh had laughed.

'You asked!'

'But you didn't have to tell. You're supposed to say Penny Lomax or someone.' Penny was a very beautiful friend of mine, but controlled and chilly.

'God no, she'd come to bed in armour. No, Jane looks like she'd roll around in the sack.'

I'd grabbed my pillow and whacked him and we'd dissolved into outraged giggles. I'd told Jane about it too, who'd roared – she and Hugh being the least likely couple to get together, knowing each other, warts and all, for far too long. 'But tell him I'm flattered,' she'd said. I did, which was received with a grin.

'She's very well,' I told him now. 'Lance has got another book coming out, so if they can limp on until he gets the rest of his advance, it looks like they'll be OK.'

'Well, that's a relief. And at least he's realized fiction is where his true talent lies.'

This was generous of Hugh, who found Lance's usual brand of tittle-tattle biography profoundly difficult to read, or at least, to be kind about. But the last one had been a thriller, which was easier.

'Actually it's another biography,' I said with a grin. 'About the princes' bust-up.' I rolled my eyes before looking vainly in the fridge for supper. No. Freezer, then.

'Oh God,' Hugh said weakly. 'Unauthorized?'

'Naturally. But Lance reckons he's got the inside story because someone he fishes with in Cornwall works for the Duchy, and he claims to have got pissed with William last time he was down. It's all bollocks, of course. It's the same guy who hides behind lampposts when he sees a police car in Totnes.'

'Dodgy Derek.'

'Exactly.' I found some frozen Kievs. 'Anyway, they're delighted we're coming to their patch and think you'll go down a storm at their pub quiz nights. Lance is determined to get you on his team; he's told everyone you're the most intelligent man in England.'

Hugh looked nervous. 'I'll obviously have to work quite hard in the evenings.'

I laughed and gave him a hug. 'I'm joking, my love. No one imagines you'll be propping up the bar with the locals. We all know you'll be doing what you do best, getting down and dirty with Søren.'

He smiled ruefully and looked abashed. My husband worshipped Søren Kierkegaard, the Danish philosopher, and read him for pleasure. Most nights. Having spent the day reading and editing military history books at a publishing house in Holborn, more intellectual immersion, it seems, was needed. And to say Søren was heavy was an understatement. But Hugh devoured everything he'd written – and the Dane was prolific – again and again. And everything written about him, too, which was extensive. It was niche, it was unusual, some might say eccentric, but it was harmless, and I loved him for it. Oh, and with Wagner's *Ring Cycle* wafting away in the background. He'd emerge from his study, spectacles gleaming, his usually pale complexion slightly pink, book in hand and say, 'I've got it. I've got the exact sense of the reason behind that obscure text in *Fear and Trembling* that I simply couldn't comprehend.'

And I'd look up from *Bridgerton*, a bar of chocolate in hand and a tablet on my lap, and say: 'Excellent, darling. And I've got the exact shade of ivory Ella was trying to describe for the embroidery on her bodice, and I know precisely where to find it.'

My own particular passion had lasted as long as his, mine being making dresses for brides – I told you I like happy endings. The current one was even more exciting, because I was making it for my darling daughter-in-law-to-be. In the old days I'd forage for my fabric and thread in secret haunts in Wembley or Cricklewood, diving down little-known streets or alleyways, but these days I could source the wherewithal on my tablet, whilst watching period drama. Hugh would nod, but he wouldn't have digested a word I'd said, before hurrying back into his study to read the passage again.

Was that the secret of a happy marriage? I wondered, as I tossed some limp broccoli I'd found lurking damply in the veg drawer into boiling water. Separate interests and hobbies, and the more different the better? We very rarely spent an evening together, and even sometimes ate supper in different rooms if *Casualty* became too much for him. But for some reason, it worked. Maybe my low-brow tastes didn't compete with his very high-brow ones. Early on in our relationship, Hugh had told me the reason he was attracted to me was because I was so natural. I wasn't sure what he'd meant by this.

'What, sort of basic and animalistic?' I'd asked.

He'd looked thoughtful. 'Instinctive, rather than calculative.'

I hadn't been sure how to take this either, but had

decided it was a compliment and let it go. And if you're wondering how this instinctive, non-calculative individual had got into university, I can only tell you it wasn't meant to be. I'd failed my A levels apart from one, textiles, but my mother, a blue stocking to her core, had been so horrified at the idea of a daughter of hers not going to university, she'd driven me, in fury, to the only university on my list of five yet to reply, Kent. She'd screeched to a halt outside the English department, the only one she considered worth attending, and insisted I go in and persuade them to take me.

To this day I wonder at what I did. And I remember little about what I said, or how I said it. I remember exactly what I was wearing though, I always do. It was a heavenly dusty apricot jacket nipped in at the waist with a mandarin collar, and very tight jeans with frayed suede boots. Oh – and a pale green vintage silk shirt that I hoped matched my eyes. I recall going down a long corridor, and I must have knocked on, or pushed open, quite a few empty doors – it was the summer holidays, after all. But eventually I found Lance, Jane's now husband. He was tall, blond and obviously very young, although back then I thought he was ancient. He'd got up from his desk in surprise as I came in, then come round and perched on the edge. Listened. Somehow I talked my way into an interview with the faculty head – he now says I flirted my socks off – and I certainly remember him smiling and looking amused. I suppose there was an element of originality about my approach, which I was in the right department to have appreciated – chutzpah, and all that. Anyway, as luck would have it, the head seemed equally taken and I was able to tell my mother – who'd instructed me not to come back to the car until I'd got a place – that I had indeed got an unconditional offer and could start in September. Off I duly went and started the course, but thereafter my essays were always late if I wrote them at all, my books mostly unread, my seminars embarrassing due to my lack of knowledge, and my chances, frankly, of graduating, remote, even without the horrific events which led to my failure.

I should never have gone to university at all, I reflected, as I took the chicken Kievs from the oven and drained the broccoli. Should never have bumped into Lance and had that stroke of luck – or not, as the case may be. By rights, I should have had a different life. I'd had some vague idea when I was at school about starting a little business – sewing, obviously. Wondered if I'd even design my own clothes. I did that anyway, all over my exercise books, much to the fury of my teachers. And maybe one day even employ others. A start-up, I suppose. I didn't even broach it with my mother, knowing it would have gone down like a cup of cold sick. Which was odd, in a way, because she had a very good eye for fashion, had been a buyer in a department store years ago. But, no, I shouldn't have gone. I drained the veg and slid the chicken from the foil container on to plates. Hugh added a glass of wine to each tray, then we picked them up and took them off to our respective lairs: him to listen to some new arrangement of Bach he'd read a review about, and me to find out if the heavenly Dr Hardy really was seeing that nurse or if it was just a wicked fabrication on the part of his jealous new consultant. I'd never have met Hugh, of course, I realized, as I settled down into my armchair, which would have been awful. I reached for the remote and pressed catchup. But Hugh aside, I mused, as I popped a bit of broccoli in my mouth and watched the familiar credits roll, think how much anguish could have been avoided, if I hadn't gone?

3

It wasn't actually until halfway through the first year that Jane and I met. She and Sally were both right down the other end of the corridor past the staircase, and since I only ventured past the stairs to get to the kitchen and make coffee, or put a bowl of baked beans in the microwave, and never used the common room – no one aside from the geeks did – I was only aware of the two of them when I heard them coming in late at night. They'd clatter back up the stairs to our floor, roaring with laughter and making a great deal of noise. The one time I'd actually seen them was when I too was coming back late. They'd both been wearing jumble sale fur coats, glamorous even as students, and singing drunkenly at the tops of their voices, waving bottles. Someone trying to sleep had yelled 'keep it down!' and they'd dissolved into muffled giggles. Ruth, I think. Ruth had the room next to mine, and played the violin in the university orchestra. She told me they were druggy and had been to Marlborough, which was fast even in those days, so I had a feeling they wouldn't be my scene. And anyway, I had other fish to fry. My particular catch was Hamish MacLeod, a handsome devil, who I'd had the great good fortune of landing a room next to. I was too busy reeling him in to bother about anyone else, although he probably thought it was the other way round.

Hamish was tall, slim and shy, with sandy hair and a high colour from years of fresh air on the Scottish moors. His hazel eyes were flecked with gold, like a tiger's, and they creased right up when he smiled. In those days, gap years were uncommon, unless you were doing Oxbridge, so we'd all come straight from school: in my case a co-ed grammar in London, and in his, some remote boys-only establishment in Angus, where he hadn't had much contact with girls. I say he was shy, but Hamish warmed up. Given a few drinks he was gregarious and funny, and his room became the one where everyone congregated. He could be raucous too, as he stood on the bed and sang Scottish war songs in Gaelic, or mimicked our English professor, with his weird flailing hand gestures and facial tics. The fact that we both did the same subject made it even easier to form a bond since we tended to walk to lectures together, or, invariably, he saved me a place as I ran in late. My clothes, particularly in those days, were eccentric, and as I'd flop down beside him, gasping for breath, never quite beating the lecturer to his podium, Hamish's mouth would twitch with mock amusement at my tartan mini skirt, pink bouclé jacket and velvet beret, all home-made, of course. On one occasion he retrieved the white feather that decorated my beret from the floor where it had floated and handed it to me with counterfeit surprise.

'Yours, I think,' he murmured. 'Sign of cowardice, you know, years ago.'

I smiled right into his eyes. 'I have many problems, but that's not one of them.'

He blushed and turned away. Busied himself with his notes.

At the time, I was actually in the process of winding up a boyfriend in London, but it wasn't a drama. Originally it hadn't been hard to whizz back to Tim at the weekends, or for him to come up to me – he was three years older than me and working in property, so had a car – but now we were both finding the commute a bit of a bore. We parted amicably enough, perhaps with more relief on my side than his, and Hamish and I finally got together at the end of that term. During that time he'd briefly gone out with Sally, whose younger brother he knew from somewhere, but I believe they parted amiably enough too; certainly neither of them ever mentioned it. It was only when I realized I'd done nothing about accommodation for the second year that my path with Sally, and therefore Jane, really crossed properly.

'You haven't got a house?' Hamish had said in some surprise. I was lying on his floor at the time, struggling into my jeans and reaching for the coat hanger I kept under the bed to pull the zip up with.

He was already dressed and ready to go to lectures, standing by the door with his books, waiting.

'No – why, have you?'

'Yes, I told you, I'm going in with Ed and Tom.'

'Did you? Oh God, yes, you did. I'd forgotten. Maybe I'll ask Ruth.'

'She's sharing with Tig and Paula, I think. But don't worry, you'll find somewhere.'

Except, I didn't. The late Emma Baker had left it too late, as usual, so suddenly I had a panic on my hands. My mother was predictably smug on the phone.

'I told you those public-school types would be ahead of the game. You should have stuck with Bridget and Megan from school, instead of running around with that crowd. Well, never mind. Perhaps you could find a bed-sit?'

I replaced the receiver to the payphone in the corridor with a clammy hand. My mother had never recovered from being left by my father when I was young, and for some reason, saw that as being mostly my fault, although what a four-year-old could contribute to the breakdown of a marriage I failed to see. And Hamish came to my rescue. He found out that Sally and Jane were living in the top floor of a professor's house in town, and that there was an extra room available. He took me there to see it, in his ancient white convertible Herald, just as, coincidentally, Jane and Sally were coming out. It was a tall, narrow, yellow terraced house at the top of town, in a residential street of wide avenues and lime trees. A student area, but pretty. The girls looked surprised to see me, but when I breathlessly explained that I was pretty damn desperate, they were sweet.

'Of course you must have it,' Jane urged. 'In fact, Lance's wife, Jess, was just saying that they really need the rent for all three rooms, not just two, and it's vast up there in the attic. We've just been to see; it's got its own bathroom. So yes, take it.'

'Although the actual bedroom itself is tiny,' said Sally, concerned. 'You might want to take a look?'

'No, no, it'll be fine,' I said quickly. 'It's all I've got, if I'm honest, so I'll definitely take it. I can't thank you enough. Are you sure –'

'Of course!' they both cried in unison.

'Couldn't be more thrilled,' said Jane, linking my arm. 'Come on, let's go and drink to it. Our three-some second year.'

And off we all went to the Haunch of Venison to celebrate, Hamish collecting a couple of friends of his along the way.

And it was a happy household, at Lance and Jess's. We had a long, skinny garden with an apple tree at the bottom and two dogs, and we all tended to eat together at the kitchen table, taking it in turns to cook, so that it felt like a family, a home. Looking back it was probably the closest I'd come to either, and although the house was in reality quite small, it was certainly the largest I'd ever lived in. It felt like a palace. Weekends were occasionally spent away, once in Wiltshire, at Sally's parents', and sometimes in Scotland, at Hamish's house. Mostly, though, we were in the pubs and wine bars of that student town, with all our friends around. Hamish lived in the parallel road to ours with Ed and Tom, in a similar house, except with a landlord living below. His brother, Rory, who was at the local art school, was at his house a lot too, principally because he lived with six other art students, and he said you could get high just walking into the house. He told us he hadn't realized the psychedelic route was such a prerequisite for studying art. He was very like Hamish to look at, tall and sweet, but with more of a dry sense of humour, and he and I got on famously. So much so that Hamish accused me of flirting with him one night. I was still at the stage of really wanting his family to like me and had possibly gone a bit overboard, but this was utterly ridiculous. We ended up having a drunken row about it, but then both woke up the next morning feeling silly and sheepish, wondering what on earth that had all been about.

Jane had a car, a beaten-up Cortina, which was a godsend, since the only other way into campus – eight miles away – was a tremulously slow bus, or hitching a lift, which if I'm honest, I found scary. The first time I did it I remember wishing I hadn't worn such a short skirt as I sat in the front beside a balding, forty-something businessman with a sweaty face. I ran from the car with barely a thank-you as he suggested picking me up every morning on his way to work. The second time was when Rory, who also had a car, had picked me up, and for some reason, having got on so brilliantly previously, we were completely tongue-tied. We both sat staring straight ahead, pink-cheeked.

So after that I made sure I was up in time for Jane's lift, which, being the organized girl she was, meant leaving earlier than I would have chosen; she liked to get to campus in time to have a coffee. And of course, as time went by, I kept them waiting, my friends. Jane was mildly irritated at the wheel, but Sally sat fuming beside her.

'Just go!' I heard her shriek one morning as I ran down the path to the car, gasping breathless apologies about searching for my books under my bed. 'Your mascara, more likely,' Sally muttered, barely concealing her not so secret belief that I was possibly a bit shallow.

Jane said nothing as we drove away, but thereafter I made a special effort to get up on time. So much so that when the clocks went forward, I mistakenly got up a whole hour early. Realizing my error on encountering the dark, silent house, I nonetheless crept down the attic stairs in my dressing gown, for a cup of tea to take back to bed.

It was then that I saw Jane appear from Lance and Jess's room on the first-floor landing. She didn't see me, and disappeared into the bathroom opposite. I stopped in my tracks, going cold. Jess was a marketing consultant for L'Oréal, and was often away on business. This particular week, she was in Paris for a conference.

I didn't say anything on the way into campus, even though Sally had a revision day and wasn't with us. But that evening, I went into Jane's bedroom. She was kneeling on the floor sorting out her laundry. I confronted her, quietly and delicately, having had a day to think about it, but knowing I'd be unable to keep it to myself. She broke down and admitted everything: said it had been going on for two months now and that she was in love with him. Her hands were shaking as she wiped her sodden face with the T-shirt she'd been holding.

'I know it's very wrong,' she said, looking up at me with streaming, anguished eyes as I sat on her bed, 'but I just can't help myself.'

I mean, we've all been there, even if it is only in our heads. But hopefully not with a married man.

'And Jess has no idea?'

'No,' she whispered, lowering her voice as we heard Sally's door shut softly next door. 'But I swear to God, I'm going to stop, Emma. This is my wake-up call, you finding out. Enough.'

But, of course, she didn't. Well, she did, for a few

weeks, maybe even a month, and I told her how well she was doing. But then it started again. So I insisted we had to look for somewhere else to live. I told her we absolutely couldn't stay, and Jane agreed. I found a place, in a tiny hamlet out of town, but much closer to the university, and since it was only for the last term, we decided to take it, rural or not. Unfortunately, there were only two bedrooms. Jane and I had become incredibly close by now and Sally spent nearly all her time with her law course friends, Tory and Liv, who lived across the road. So when we gingerly and tremulously asked if she'd mind, telling her we'd already talked it over with Jess, to our surprise, she didn't.

'No, that's fine. To be honest, I've got such a heavy workload with my second-year exams, I just want to be head down for these last few weeks. Plus I quite like being on my own.'

It was gracious of her, albeit not the first time she'd mentioned her second-year exams, which Jane and I didn't have, being on a humanities course, and, Sally would joke, a softer option. So after Jane and I made some excuse to Jess about not wanting to be so far out, and with Jane's trust fund paying the rent we owed her – I know, different world – we moved into a sweet two-bedroom cottage on a farm, with the farmer next door. The fact that the farmer retained a key to the cottage, and whilst we were on campus, came and sat on our beds and looked through our drawers – we laid ingenious traps – was something we decided we had to put up with. We only had six weeks to push.

Hamish and I rowed about Jane, because, yes, of course I told him. We told each other everything. He was appalled.

'But how can she? He's married! And you're fucking living there!'

'Well, not any more, we're not.'

'No, and thank God. But is she still seeing him?'

'I . . . don't know,' I lied. Jane had been absent for the last two nights and she didn't have a boyfriend.

'Shit.' He was aghast. And more aghast than some might be, perhaps. Lance was young, only thirty-ish, and extremely good-looking: a blond god, in fact, plus, as I pointed out to Hamish, there were no children involved.

'Oh, so that's all right then, is it? The sanctity of marriage is only upheld when children tie you to it?'

I knew we were talking about Hamish's family now. His father lived alone, devastated after his wife had left him – claiming she'd only stayed for the children – and now that Hamish and his brother and sister were over eighteen, she'd gone, to her lover of some years. And of course I shouldn't have said anything to that effect, but tempers were frayed.

'This isn't about you, Hamish,' I hissed. 'It's about Jane and Lance.'

'Yes, but it's also about you,' he told me, white-faced. 'Your collusion with adultery, your blithe acceptance of the situation. I thought you were better than that.'

After that it got ugly. I told him that my own father had left when I was barely more than a baby, travelling salesman that he was, having found a comfier bed elsewhere, and however hard I looked for him, which I did at that stage, he'd left no trace, clearly not wanting to be found, and Hamish had no right to lecture me about the sanctity of marriage.

'Which is why I thought you were different,' he said scathingly. 'I thought you'd be on my wavelength, precisely because of that.'

'Oh, so is that why you're going out with me? Two babes in the wood from dysfunctional families, who would never step out of line because they know about the collateral damage? Is it fear, Hamish? Are you afraid of women and their wayward emotions? Real life?'

Ghastly. Horrid. And me, the worst. But I was furious at being cast as the villain here, when I had not had an affair with my poetry lecturer, and had only supported my friend who had. Should I have deserted her? I asked as he made to slam out of the cottage. Gone off on my own and left her to it, or not even have orchestrated the move? Stayed at 42 Hamilton Terrace with it all going on under my nose? Jess's too?

It was a Thursday, and the following day, we were due to drive to Argyllshire, to stay at his father's for the weekend. But of course Hamish went alone. I say 'of course'; I was actually quite surprised we hadn't made up and gone together. But at least there were no mobiles in those days to text, in a fit of pique, when I realized he'd gone without me: 'Fine, fuck off then.' Just silence. And silence thereafter, eternally. Forever.

Because while taking the dinghies out on the loch one evening to fish for mackerel, Hamish in one boat, and the ghillie, I believe he's called, in the other, there was an accident. The ghillie had gone back to shore, to his cottage, to gut the first catch and to mend a lobster pot, he said. But Hamish hadn't returned. And after a bit, the ghillie paused in his work on the beach, stared out at the glassy water. He left his nets and his pots, and he rowed out again. It was a long way, almost to the centre of the loch, which was vast and smooth. He'd found Hamish, dead, drowned, in all his heavy outdoor clothes, face down in the water. The boat was upside down. Apparently it had capsized, the drain valve nowhere to be seen. No life jackets, of course; no one who'd actually grown up there bothered, and miles from shore. Apparently the last person to use the dinghy had put the wrong valve in, it was later discovered, which was why it had come out. Which was odd, because the ghillie always checked the boats. He was distraught. And Hamish was a good sailor; he should have been able to right the boat anyway. But with all that heavy clothing and wellington boots and so far out . . . So there it was, the coroner later said: a terrible accident.

Coincidentally, it was the same weekend, or at least during the following few days, that Jane discovered she was pregnant. I wasn't there, I'd fled home to London, but Jane later told me about it, and about the row that ensued. Jane had told Lance, and they'd agreed she'd have an abortion. She'd even booked herself into a clinic the following week, which Lance, mortified and full of love, she told me, had promised to accompany her to. Somehow Jess found out, though, and chucked him out. Jane didn't go through with the abortion then. Because, surely, she'd thought, now that his marriage had broken up, he'd come to her? Instead, the following week, she came to London. Lance, meanwhile, was staying with a friend near the university, and she kept hoping against hope that he'd come. But he didn't. He didn't show. But still she waited. And after a bit, she got beyond the date advised for a termination, and Cassie was born some months later. By now, Lance had gone back to his wife. We never did find out who told Jess. Although obviously, we had our suspicions.

4

So there we both were, Jane and I: two still very young girls with a great deal of grief to manage, no real prospects, and a baby to care for. One way or another, we'd seen more than our fair share of trauma. Although, the older I've got, the more I've realized that's not true. Scratch the surface and many young people have an abusive father, a depressed mother, a sister who needs care – they just quietly get on with it. And so did we. We looked after Cassie together, cried a lot when she was asleep, and Jane's mother was brilliant. Jane didn't want to go home, and not because her father was tricky and an alcoholic – I don't think that would have stopped her – but because she was convinced Lance was more likely to come if she stayed alone in London. Jane's mother, Margot, provided the tiny flat we lived in – or borrowed, from her sister, Jane's aunt – and made sure Jane had everything she needed. And if she was aghast and upset that all her dreams for her beloved only child seemed to be crashing down around her ears, she didn't show it. Margot would often come by, up from her gorgeous house in Hampshire, to bring armfuls of baby clothes and nutritious food. She'd put a quick wash on and whip a Hoover around, asking, only gently as she was leaving, if Jane wouldn't like to come home? Daddy was quite good, at the moment. It had been a bit of a wake-up call for him, apparently. He only wanted Jane to be happy. Jane would shake her head sadly, hug her mother warmly at the door, and say goodbye.

My own mother was vitriolic. She never came to the flat, but when I did go and see her she'd crow scornfully at my inability to achieve any sort of education, never once mentioning Hamish, except in passing and only to wonder at my getting mixed up with a fast, rich set beyond my station, and saying that if Jane's boyfriend sailed his yacht recklessly, accidents were bound to happen.

'It was a rowing boat,' I'd mutter. 'And he wasn't Jane's boyfriend, he was mine.'

'I don't think so, dear,' she'd said scornfully. 'Not really. Those sort of people don't go out with girls like you, or if they do, only as a passing fancy.'

As I shut my eyes and counted to ten I wondered how I'd managed not to murder her yet, or if I actually would, one day. I got up from the threadbare armchair beside the electric fire and put my coat on, wondering if it was the last time I'd ever come here. The fact that I wondered that every time I left and still came back for more, hoping that one day I'd make her happy – or, no, not make her happy, but just that she'd say something pleasant – did not escape me.

On that particular day, Jane was unusually animated when I got back to the flat. Her eyes were bright as she came down the hall to meet me, Cassie in her arms.

'You just missed Sally,' she told me.

'Oh?' I was surprised. Jane and Sally had somewhat fallen out, over Sally's horror at the affair going on under her nose, and the betrayal of Jess, who was a good friend of hers – of all of ours, actually. She hadn't contacted us for months.

'Yes, she was fine. She said she'd come to realize that people were capable of all sorts of things when they were in love – she's got a new man, by the way.'

'Ah, that's good.'

But I was waiting for more. Jane had been ringing Sally, begging her to forgive her. Yet with a slightly ulterior motive.

'She had news. So much. Wait.' She bustled away to put Cassie down for a sleep and I realized it was the first time I'd seen her make any haste for ages. When she came back she told me that Lance and Jess had parted and that Jess had put the house up for sale. They were getting a divorce. Lance was living with another young professor in town and was still teaching, but had handed in his notice and was working out the year, before deciding what to do next.

'He'll come. Of course he'll come after that, he has to. And it's only natural he'd work out the year, it's the responsible thing to do.'

I nodded, not wanting to burst her bubble, but I knew in my heart he should have come already, at least to visit. Why hadn't he? If he wasn't living with Jess, why had he completely abandoned Jane and Cassie?

'Sally's asked us down for the weekend, you know, to her parents in Wiltshire. They're divine, actually, totally chilled and relaxed. I met them when we were at school, when they came to visit – oh, and of course we went there that weekend, remember?'

'Of course I remember,' I said shortly. 'Hamish was there.'

'Oh. Yes. Sorry.'

'You go,' I went on quickly. I still wasn't up to facing the world with what I felt to be my guilt about Hamish weighing me down. 'I don't think I will.'

'Oh, please, I can't possibly go without you. It would be my first time out of the flat – I haven't even been to Mum's!'

Margot had a pied-à-terre in Marylebone where she stayed when she was in town, and it was true, Jane hadn't even been there. And she adored her mother. This was testament to how much she wanted to go. Sally was her only link with Lance, and she wanted to cultivate it at all costs.

And so we went. Back to Clem and Yanni's

glorious rambling house in the fold of the soft green valley in the rolling countryside: a house painted the pale, muddy pink of Florence, rather than the richer Suffolk pink, I noticed this time, seeing it more forensically, with new eyes, and with a thatched roof, which I hadn't noticed before. But this was no cute little chocolate-box affair. It was large, and it roamed, seemingly endlessly, from one interconnected room to the next, all of which had been brightly painted in shades I'd never seen before on walls – peacock blue, jade green – so that the many paintings and drawings fairly pinged off the coloured walls. It was like an art gallery, I thought. And nearly all the rooms were full of books too, sometimes in stacks on the floor when the shelves were full, and lots of wobbly antique furniture and layered Persian rugs – to cover holes, I was told. I was still too young to see any artifice in it; it looked deeply authentic to me.

To add to the vibe, long-legged, leisurely people were reclining and reading on faded chintz sofas, whilst a lurcher chewed a cushion at their feet. A variety of music played in each room – jazz, classical, pop – and French doors were flung open to the sweeping lawns beyond. It was all very arch and Somerset Maugham. Clem, Sally's mother, drifted about much as I remembered before, coming in with armfuls of flowers and vegetables, asparagus and lettuce to prepare for her children's friends, because, she told us in surprise, when we asked if she minded, or if we could help, she enjoyed it. Enjoyed gardening, enjoyed cooking, enjoyed young people. It could not have been more different to my own home, and to an extent, to Jane's, where her father had to eat on the dot of eight in the morning, one in the afternoon, and eight in the evening, every single day, or he'd start going purple. Throw something.

This time I met all four siblings: Sally, I knew, obviously; Polly, a lot younger and home from school with some friends; and then two older brothers, Tom and Hugh. Tom was attractive and tousled but beefy, with a thick neck and a mouth that hung open when he was listening to you, in a slightly gormless fashion. He was wearing too short shorts, I thought, as he came into the kitchen with a couple of huge trout he'd caught for supper. He slung them dramatically on the table with a wet flop, making Jane and me jump. Clem smiled.

'Don't mind Tom, he's showing off. Trying to look like the hunter gatherer. Stop scaring the girls and take those outside to gut, please,' she told him as he produced a sharp knife. 'Not in here.'

He grinned good-naturedly and retreated with his catch, muttering something about being the only one who helped around here with all these fucking aesthetes about. This was a reference to his brother, Hugh, who'd just appeared in the kitchen holding a book, and was one of the bodies Jane and I had encountered earlier when we'd arrived. He'd been lying on the hall sofa. He was tall, skinny and dark, in complete contrast to his brother. He looked as if his body had grown much too quickly and he was still trying to catch up.

'Take the girls' bags up, would you, Hughie? And show them where they're sleeping. I can't seem to find Sally.'

'She's gone to help Dad in the far meadow; one of the sheep got out. Where are they sleeping?'

'In the green room at the top, and there's a crib for the baby by the window.'

Clem already had Cassie in her arms and was smiling down at her, making gurgling noises. Cassie's eyes were wide and she reached up for Clem's long, dark hair which hung loose around her shoulders and gripped it in her podgy little fist. Clem swayed and hummed with her and I watched, transfixed. I'd never seen a mother wear a long woven skirt with tiny round mirrors on it, or a floor-length, pistachio-green linen waistcoat, or a pair of embroidered pointed slippers. She had a beautiful, serene face, a small part of which each of her children had inherited. In Hugh's case it was the eyes, hooded and pale blue, and looking, as Jane later said, as if they were about to deliver some terribly sad news. Hugh hid his, though, choosing to look everywhere except directly at us. He did as he was told and took our bags, despite Jane and I protesting that we could manage and honestly he didn't need to. Clem assured Jane she'd hang on to Cassie for the minute, and we followed him up one of the rickety oak staircases, which in this case led straight up from the kitchen.

'This is called the Shepherds' Passage, by the way,' he told us over his shoulder, and I could tell he was dutifully going through the motions of the guided tour.

'So-called because hundreds of weary shepherds have traipsed this way to bed?' I asked him.

He smiled back at me. 'No, apparently so called because once, this part of the house was agricultural, and the sheep traipsed their weary way to the hayloft.'

'Stop it. Sheep climbing stairs? Is that something you've gleaned from books, or experience?'

He turned to look at me. 'Mountain goats?'

'Oh. Yes, I suppose . . .' I still couldn't imagine it, though. I forged on to hide my ignorance and lack of country roots. 'So you farm here, do you?'

'Only in an arty farty gentleman farmer type way. Dad has a few sheep and likes to look the part at the weekends, and Mum has chickens and ducks, but don't be fooled. My father works in Fleet Street and Mum worked for Princess Margaret. Here we are, and that's the cot for the baby.'

We'd arrived in an apple-green attic bedroom and Jane went to view the cot, over by the window, but I was still with the Royal Family.

'What – as a lady in waiting or something?'

'No, as a dresser. Seamstress, I suppose. She made a lot of her clothes.'

And that, of course, bonded Clem and me immediately. When I went down, I asked her all about it, and then told her about my own passion for making things. She confessed she'd spotted my home-made skirt when I walked in.

'Home-made in a bad way?'

'No, in a beautiful way. It's cut on the bias, which is so hard with silk, but I could see you'd had a fight with the waistband.'

I twisted the skirt around and undid the zip a bit, so she could see, and she set to work telling me how to incorporate the extra fabric without it bulging so much, so that when Sally appeared, Clem and I were already ensconced in her mother's sewing room, whilst Jane, through the French windows, was on a rug in the garden, showing Polly and a couple of her school friends how to give Cassie a bottle.

Sally looked surprised to find us in there, but she beamed. 'So sorry I wasn't around when you arrived. We had to come back for one of the dogs, to sort the sheep out.'

I got up from the paper patterns we'd spread on the floor to kiss her, pleased to see her after all this time. She looked well and I told her so: brown from the sun, and so tall and lean. I realised now that the full lips had come from her mother. As we chatted we were constantly interrupted by the loud roar of a quad bike, as Tom circled the gravel path in the garden, going around the lawn again and again. His mother put her head out of the window above her sewing machine.

'Tom! In the field with that thing – now!'

He stopped on the far side of the lawn and grinned, revving the throttle aggressively. His huge teeth gleamed at me and I realized it was for my benefit. I also realized his older brother might not have the machismo but was far more civilized than this exuberant, outdoorsy boy. He took off again and stopped the bike outside the window.

'I can't. Dad says it cuts up the fields.'

'Well then, do something else, for heaven's sake.' It wasn't hard to see that her second son annoyed Clem. As his face fell she tried harder. 'And we'll all join in, whatever it is. Organize a game or something. Badminton or whatever. Supper won't be until late.'

Tom slunk off, giving Clem a wordless look, and Sally and her mother rolled their eyes at one another. Sally linked my arm as she led me away to show me the rest of the place.

'He's a pain,' she confided. 'But then brothers often are, lucky you for not having any. But you're clearly a hit – even with Mum. And she doesn't do strangers.'

'Really?' This surprised me. She'd said she liked

young people, and in this seemingly open house a neighbour had already popped in, and Polly had some friends. Plus, her manner was quite engaging, all of which I said.

'It's Dad who has the open-house policy. Mum goes along with it, but she's just content with her own family, really. And her books. She's utterly self-contained. Come on, we'll go and find Jane.'

The day wore on in a convivial fashion. Yanni appeared from his hobby farming, delightfully gregarious, somewhat overweight, but still a very good-looking man with a patrician nose and swept-back dark hair. He had a heavy Greek accent and periodically referred to himself in the third person. He strode across the lawn to meet us, a huge smile on his face which went right up to his eyes.

'Girls! Marvellous! How good it is to see you! Sorry Yanni was not here – welcome!' He greeted us like old friends, with both hands resting on our shoulders, and then he wanted to know exactly what we'd been doing since we'd been here.

'You go for a walk? Then you have tea? Then you play this card game? Marvellous! When you walk, did you go right down to the pond, did you see all my garden? So splendid and glorious today in the sunshine, yes?'

We smiled and agreed that it was indeed splendid, and glorious, and he beamed hugely and clasped our shoulders again. He reminded me of an opera singer, I wasn't sure which one, but any one would do, and I felt that at any moment he might put his hand on his heart, draw himself up to his full height, and belt out an aria.

Having all dutifully played the game of rounders Tom had organized – although I could see Hugh found it tedious to participate – we helped make salads for the barbecue. Yanni had lit this much earlier, a proper fire within a circle of bricks – no John Lewis models for this family. He'd also already marinated the prepared rabbits and home-produced lamb ready to roast, and the trout Tom had caught, he told me, we were having for a starter, with a dill sauce Clem had made.

It was early evening now, and we were all in the meadow behind the garden. We'd gathered in a sunken hollow, a natural windbreak, not that there was any breeze; it was a beautiful day. I watched this family in awe and wonder, having never seen the like. Yanni was loud and funny, with an easy, exuberant laugh, throwing his head back and roaring whenever anyone said anything remotely amusing; in fact, his entire default setting was a roar, and he was as chatty and convivial as Clem was quiet and composed. After telling Tom exactly how to cook the meat – 'Don't cremate it, Tommy boy!' – he came and sat with us, lowering himself down on to the rug with an exaggerated groan. He asked us three girls how we all knew each other. University? School?

I saw Clem shoot him a look, but Sally was doing a good job of blandly explaining that we'd lived together at university, and then was swiftly moving the conversation on, when Polly, who was only fourteen, suddenly realized who we were. She looked up.

'Oh. Was it your boyfriend who killed himself after a quarrel?'

There was a ghastly silence. It was a version of the narrative I'd never heard before and I had neither breath nor words to draw on.

A great deal of angry shushing then erupted, both from her sister and her mother. It caused Polly to wail in anguish and say she just hadn't *thought*, which of course she hadn't. Then a fair amount of flurried activity followed, as Clem issued instructions and everyone busied themselves getting to their feet and getting plates and salads, and slices of meat. But I saw both the boys looking at me as I fought for composure. Sally had looked awkward. Later, when it was dark, and we were all sitting around the fire, along with some family friends who'd joined us, I asked her, quietly, if that was what people had thought? When I'd left? At university?

She said no, it was a ridiculous rumour that had spread after the verdict of accidental death had been announced. It was nothing any of them had taken seriously. Polly had apparently heard it at school, from a friend's older sister.

Four years later, however, when Hugh and I met

up again at a party in London and he asked me out, he told me, over dinner, and only because I asked, that that's what Sally had told them. Up until then I'd always given Sally the benefit of the doubt, and there had been many occasions on which to do so. But it did occur to me to wonder then, what it was about me she didn't like?

5

Over the years, however, Sally softened. To be fair I probably softened too, and despite what I knew about her sharp – and sometimes loose – tongue, she became a good friend. Not as good as Jane, obviously, and Jane had always been closer to me than she was to Sally. By this time Lance had finally made it to London. His divorce had come through – at his instigation, not Jess's, it transpired – and he got a new post in the English department at Gold-smiths and moved in with his parents above their pub, in Peckham. He and Jane married – and subsequently went on to have another daughter – and Hugh and I married the following year. But Sally never did. Most of our friends had weddings at the same time when we were in our late twenties, and Sally always appeared with a man on her arm, fresh from a fashion shoot in Italy or somewhere, looking glamorous, but she never seemed to seal the deal. Or didn't want to. Jane wondered if she was gay; she had a very close relationship with a girl called Annie who definitely was gay, but she never confided in us, so although we saw a lot of her, we never knew. And after Annie, there was nothing. Strangely no relationships at all for the next twenty years or so, which was odd. At least it was to me. She had a very successful career, first at American *Vogue* in New York – a surprise, given that she had a law degree – and then back in London, with English *Vogue*. Her reputation was formidable in fashion circles where I was on the fringes with a small wedding dress business, and clients would blink in awe if I mentioned her name. But no love life at all.

Hugh and I had two boys by now, and periodically I'd ask him about her, about her childhood, wondering if there were any clues there as to why she'd found it difficult to form attachments. Tom and Polly were both married with children. He'd smile at me over his book.

'Why does everything have to have a happy ending, Emma? Or at least, not a happy ending, but a neat little tie-up?'

Coincidentally I'd been neatly tying a double knot which I snipped off efficiently with my scissors; I was hemming an underskirt by the fire at the time.

'I just don't think she's happy, and none of you siblings seem too fussed about it.'

I refrained from saying that neither Clem nor Yanni were fussed either. The more I'd got to know my parents-in-law, the more I'd realized their laissez-faire attitude sprang not from a conviction that this was the way to bring up children, but in Clem's case, from a lack of maternal instinct, which had surprised me. Oh, she cared for them, but not in the way I did my own boys: worrying about their every exam, their friendships, the circles they were excluded from, their worries, their problems. Clem neither knew nor cared. And obviously there's some benefit to that, and some middle ground, too. Some would say I cared too much. Yanni, on the other hand, was much more loving and expressive, but like many men he didn't get involved in their personal lives, and although Clem enjoyed her children's company, she never concerned herself about them. When Polly spent a year in India after university and disappeared, literally went off the radar, I was beside myself with worry, but Clem just shrugged and said – I'm sure she'll turn up. Yanni was in Athens at the time, where his father was dying, but he returned at breakneck speed, and went and found her, in a kibbutz in Delhi. The very same day he brought her home, Clem flew to Spain, to walk the Camino trail, alone.

'I think you've rather idealized family life,' Hugh told me, as we sat reading and sewing by the fire together. 'Growing up the way you did. It would be nice to imagine we spend our time looking out for one another, but we didn't as children and we certainly don't now. It's always been every man for himself. I think you'll find that's quite normal.'

'Until the chips are down.'

'Oh, sure, when that happens we've definitely got each other's backs.'

I wondered again at my allegedly Enid Blyton view of the world some weeks later, as Hugh and I drove down to Branchester in Wiltshire together, following the removal van from London. I decided, as I pondered what he'd said, that in actual fact I was more realistic than that. Yes, my solitary childhood, my absent father and my cold mother had made me long for something different – and determined to recreate it one day, which I surely had – but I was by no means gullible. Clem's relationship with a local groom had surprised me less than it had Hugh and Sally. I can't speak for Tom who we saw less of since he lived in Scotland, but Polly had certainly been shocked when I'd talked to her on the phone. But I'd grown accustomed to Clem's me-first attitude. If she was up in London when my children were small, she might drop in to see them, but only after she'd seen all the exhibitions she wanted to first, and then she'd get their names muddled. The first thing she did on arriving at our house was not to greet her grandchildren, but to look at our walls – Hugh was a keen art collector – and enthuse about our latest painting. She would always be very complimentary about everything, but I'd be left disappointed, and sometimes upset at her lack of interest in a surely more important crayon drawing that Nico had been trying to show her.

Clem was ruled by the aesthetic, and for all the Pink House's seemingly effortless bohemianism, I'd come to realize it was heavily curated. Polly met this aesthetic, being pretty and easy-going, but Sally, despite her clothes and glamour, didn't. Apart from her mouth, she had Yanni's coarser features and I could almost see Clem's eyes turn critical as she looked at her. It had occurred to me over the years that Sally hadn't had a great deal more mothering than I had, and that appearances were deceptive. In a way this had made us closer, and she'd broken down in tears to me once at lunch, as she told me she knew exactly why Polly was the favourite, then Hugh and Tom, both good-looking in different ways. It was why, she told me, she'd tried so hard at *Vogue*, and with her style, to gain her mother's approval, but her heart wasn't really in it.

'So why do it, Sal?' I'd asked as she mopped her eyes with a napkin I'd handed her in the restaurant. 'Why not change tack, do something completely different?' She'd looked up at me sadly. 'Too late, don't you think? Just as it's too late to find someone to love that my mother would approve of.'

'Oh, that's nonsense!' I'd gasped, knowing at the same time that it was true, and the real reason for Sally's disappointing love life. She'd looked at every prospective suitor through the prism of her mother's eyes and found them wanting.

As Hugh and I cruised towards the brow of the hill which heralded the view of the valley below and the wide spread of fields where the village of

Branchester sat, I found myself hoping that Sally's life down here with us would take a turn for the better, with more approval and less censure. She surely had always been the most loving of aunts to the boys and they were very close to her, finding her quick and clever. I realized I was already planning how I could improve the cottage she was having in the garden, my mind's eye making it a haven for her, a sanctuary.

Our first view of the medieval village was always the same: a collection of small stone houses, breathtaking in its ancient beauty, squat, grey and timeless. It had always held me in its thrall, except this time, it had an added intensity: it was mine. Well, you know what I mean. At this time of year the hedgerows surrounding it were frothing with cow parsley and the fields around the May trees were thick with oxeye daisies where sheep grazed, the stream running through the middle glinted in the light, and the spire of the old Norman church peeped out beyond. The whole thing was surely exactly as it had been hundreds of years ago, if one slightly shut one eye and blocked out the wind farm in the distance. Oh, and ignored the cluster of new white bungalows over – way over actually – on the hill beyond. Ted Tucker was responsible for those, I thought grimly, and I determined one of the first things I'd do was join the local residents group clamouring to put a stop to things like that. Obviously affordable housing had to be built, particularly for the young, and to stop an exodus to the cities, but did it have to be so ugly? I'd maybe even join the Parish Council where one had more of a voice. Having never lived in the country and having owned a rather attractive but nonetheless typical Edwardian house in Chiswick, I was looking forward to getting involved in rural life in a way that I knew Clem never had been, dismissing the villagers as parochial, and, as far as I knew, having no proper friends locally at all.

Hugh saw me straighten my spine and smiled. 'Looking forward to being lady of the manor?'

'Of course not!' I said, outraged. He knew me far too well.

'There's an old bicycle in the barn with a basket. I could skin a few rabbits and you can cycle round delivering them to the poorer cottages, perhaps?'

'The idea of you skinning anything more than an orange is laughable,' I told him as we turned into the long lane which led to the house, but I was already wondering if I could clean up said bike to get the paper from the shop in the morning. Waving to all my new friends in their front gardens on the way? And if I did, whether I'd opt for a long dirndl skirt and a home-made jumper, or pedal pushers with brown ankles, canvas shoes and no laces? The latter, obviously. I might be moving into the big house but I wasn't ancient enough to be cycling around in clothes more usually seen on knitting patterns from the fifties.

'But I am looking forward to being part of a community,' I told him firmly. 'London was so anonymous.'

'Well, only because most of our friends had moved out.'

'Exactly. Where they're all now doing their own rural thing – Sarah with her pottery, Alex with her horses, Tam her yoga. Which is why I'm determined to carry on with your mum's gallery.' I didn't look at him when I said this, though. Before Clem had bolted with her lover, she'd been instrumental in organizing an artists' barn, a space where painters could exhibit and show their work. She'd been on the cusp of opening it to the public when she'd fled to Ireland with Fergus.

Hugh groaned predictably beside me. 'You know I think that's a terrible idea. It was bad enough with Mum at the helm, but at least she . . .'

'Knew a bit about art?' I said archly, as he tailed off.

'Well, darling, with the best will in the world, it's not exactly your forte.'

'No, but Ella said she'd help me.'

'In a sweet passing moment. She's far too busy in London.'

Ella, Teddy's girlfriend, who I adored, had an online gallery with a friend and had promised to occasionally lend a hand.

'But it is *your* forte.' Amongst others, I thought.

'I'll be busy!' he exclaimed.

'Yes, but I'll only need you in an advisory capacity. Just to cast an eye over – I don't know. The odd portfolio.'

'Portfolio,' he groaned, hunching miserably over the wheel. 'Who are these artists who don't even have canvases? Just folders?'

'I've told you, I want them all to be local and uncelebrated – unlike your mother who was getting well-known artists from London, which was why the planners were so hot under the collar about her doing it, incidentally. I've looked into it. The main complaint – if she was planning on doing it commercially, which she was – was that she wasn't supporting the local artisans.'

'Artisans,' he whispered, still theatrically hunched. 'Dear God, we're rearing a commune.'

'I just want to encourage local talent, that's all,' I told him, although in my head, some sort of Newlyn School was already emerging, perhaps even taken seriously by the likes of that art dealer chappie Phillip Mould, who'd pop down to check us out wearing one of his snazzy scarves tied like a Frenchman. But there was no way I was mentioning that.

'The Branchester school of painting, perhaps?' Hugh said, so horribly close to the mark, I flushed. 'Why not carry on with the sewing? You're good at that.'

'Because I don't want to have a needle and thread

in my hand for the rest of my life. It's – it's – I don't know – demeaning, somehow.'

He raised his eyebrows. 'How so?'

'Well, you know. The little woman stitching.'

He glanced at me, surprised. 'You've always resisted that stereotype. Been incensed if anyone so much as suggested it. And you've built up a nice little business.'

'I know.' I bit my thumbnail. 'Nice' and 'little' felt slightly damning, though. 'But it's always irked. Other people's idea of what I do.'

'Or you projecting tropes on to them,' he muttered.

I frowned, confused. 'What?'

'Nothing.'

I straightened up. 'Anyway, I've done all that. For ages. I want to do something different. Art is my thing these days,' I said staunchly, nodding firmly. 'After all, I joined the Tate and the V&A in London, went a lot with Liv, plus we went to the lectures, so I know a bit, and why shouldn't I reinvent myself? I've brought up my children, I've grafted away to help with the mortgage and now we don't have one. Well, not so much,' I said hastily as he made a horrified face. 'Surely it's my time?'

'Oh, sure. And when will it be mine?'

I patted his knee. 'Now, darling, you know very well that working from home *does* sort of make it your time, in a sense. Everyone says so.'

Hugh snorted with derision.

'We're *both* very lucky,' I added magnanimously, although I wasn't entirely sure about what. Hugh didn't look convinced either, but happily our bickering was brought to a halt as we turned off the lane through the village, and forked left into the gravel drive.

As we crunched up to the house, I sighed, soothed by its beauty. It was the sort of thing you might gather round a table to put together at Christmas, I'd always thought, and I'd said as much to Clem, but it hadn't gone down very well. Not twee, I'd said quickly, but the damage was done. The sun was low in the sky and the soft light caused the muted pink walls to glow like welcoming beacons as the windows peered out from under the thatch like beady eyes under eyebrows. One of them flashed in a shaft of light.

'It's welcoming us,' I whispered, smiling, as we stopped behind the huge removal van which was already parked outside the front door.

'Hm,' said Hugh with a smile, but his was more knowing and less rapturous than mine. He ran his eyes over the façade. 'Home sweet home.'

I glanced at him, wondering if there was an edge to his voice, but he was already getting out of the car, so I decided, on balance, there wasn't. He was delighted to be back. Of course he was.

6

OK, it has to be said, I'd been keener than Hugh to make the break from London. He'd been perfectly happy there. And it had also been me who'd been determined to buy the Pink House, and not let it go on the open market. Did Hugh want to move back to his roots? I don't know. But I'd reached a certain stage in my life, and in my marriage, and with Hugh's family, where I was determined to please myself. One of the very few pieces of advice my distant mother had given me years ago, when I was a teenager – she was washing up and I'd been drying – was when she turned to me and said: 'Emma, only ever get married if you can't believe your luck.' Her eyes had been strangely soft and faraway at the time, which was rare, but it did happen. Then she'd gone back to the dishes. I'd nodded, surprised. I hadn't said anything because I didn't want to break the moment, but there'd been so much I wanted to ask. Did you feel lucky, Mum, marrying my father? What was he like? How did it all go wrong? I knew better, though. But I took her words to heart, and, truly, I couldn't believe my luck in marrying Hugh. This handsome, shy, literary editor was everything I'd ever wanted – and, yes, I did have a tick list, many girls do. And, yes, I'd fallen in love with his family too. Probably because I didn't have one, if I must be psychoanalysed. But as the years had gone by, and I'd seen them for what they were – surprisingly disparate and often unhappy parts of what looked like a happy, homogeneous whole – I'd become more clear-slighted about my own ambitions. In short, I'd moved on from congratulating myself on my lucky break. I was on to something else.

Now that Nico and Teddy were happy and settled I wanted them to have somewhere to bring their own wives and children, just as we had done when they were small. And I wanted to create a beautiful house and garden in my husband's – ancestral is too strong – family home, and thus far, yes, it sounds as if I'm wanting to be Clem. But I wanted to give back, too, knowing I'd been lucky in a way that Clem never did. She felt herself to be above all that. She'd never volunteered locally even though she'd been asked many times – church flowers, the village school, local charities, the usual rural things – but no. She only really ventured out from her oasis to potter to the now famed Kaplinsky gallery in nearby Breston when she couldn't get to London. She was happy, as Sally had told me years ago, on her own, adding yet more treasures to her house, and more beauty to her garden, which occasionally featured in smart magazines. Nothing wrong with that. But I wanted to do it all differently, on my terms.

After we'd been at the house a few days, though, I realized certain things were going to be harder than I'd thought.

'Are you happy about me putting all those black and white prints of your mother's in the cellar? I thought we might have that large bright gouache of Venice above your desk instead. Cheer it up a bit.'

I'd found my husband under a pear tree at the bottom of the garden in dappled shade, reading an historical tome he was editing. Hugh mostly dealt with military history, and still preferred to read the books in physical, manuscript form; he paused with his pencil poised, smiled kindly at me over his glasses.

'I told you, darling, I'm happy for you to do whatever you like. There's nothing I'm precious about.'

'I know, it's just . . .' I stood on one leg and scratched it, felt awkward. 'I'm worried they might be – you know . . .'

'What?'

'Good.'

He shrugged. 'So what if they are? You want to put your personal stamp on the place, and that's fine. If you're not enamoured by old Beardsley, put him in the cellar.'

'Is that who they're by? Isn't he famous? Or is

that someone else?' He smiled. Didn't answer. I pressed on. 'Actually he can't be famous, they're quite rude.'

'Erotica,' he murmured, going back to his manuscript.

'Sorry?' God, my husband mumbled.

'Nothing.'

'Quite a lot of dicks.'

Hugh looked up, blinked. He hated crude language but at least I'd got his attention. Plus, it might encourage him to take a closer look above his desk, see that the pictures were indeed full of throbbing members. Typical Clem. Always trying to shock.

'But the thing is,' I persevered, 'there's already a lot in the cellar, that's the problem. I'm wondering if we might sell some stuff? And share the money with the others, obviously,' I said quickly.

'Well, I'm sure Polly and Tom would be delighted, they're always strapped for cash, but you don't have to share it. We bought the house and everything in it. I went to the trouble of having the contents valued twice, if you recall. Dewsons and Hardings. Took the highest valuation. Same with the house, too.'

'I know, but I just don't want there to be any – you know. Trouble.'

He went back to his manuscript again. 'There won't be. The fact that my parents abdicated all responsibility and left it to me to broker the deal having left practically their life's belongings here means they can't attach much significance to it. So why should anyone else?'

There was definitely a touch of bitterness in his voice but I knew better than to probe. Hugh hated talking about feelings. Like so many men, he couldn't express his emotions. But it *was* odd that his parents attached so little sentimental value to what was effectively a life's collection. For different reasons, obviously. Yanni, when we'd been to visit him recently at his cottage on the coast, had been understandably furious at my suggestion that he might want something from the house to put on his rather bare walls.

'Why would I want anything of hers!' he'd roared, his face livid. 'Burn it, Emma, for sure, from my heart, do what you like with it. The whole collection makes me *emetós*. I don't want to look at it. Do not want a thing.'

He and I had been sitting in wrought-iron chairs in his tiny front garden overlooking the estuary; Hugh was standing in the foreground by the low wall, his back to us, looking out to sea, hands thrust deep in his trouser pockets. It was only the second time he'd seen his father since the split, and he was finding it hard to cope with Yanni's unhappiness.

'You know, this might just be a midlife crisis, Yanni,' I said gently, touching his arm. He didn't look at me and I watched his piercing dark gaze trained steadfastly on the blue boat bobbing on the water on the horizon. 'She might well be back.'

'Yanni is not wanting her back,' he said fiercely, turning to look at me. '*Me katavaíneis?* You understand me? She has destroyed any scrap of feeling I ever had for her, ever. I never want to see her again. I have no love for her any more.' He gulped and tears began to roll down his weathered old cheeks. Yanni, unlike his son, had no qualms about showing his feelings and I saw Hugh's back hunch in horror. 'And we are divorced for God sake!' he said in a cracked voice into my shoulder as I held him. 'There is no coming back from that, you know? She be marrying some other poor sod soon!'

Personally I wasn't convinced. There'd already been vague rumblings via Polly, whose house we'd dropped into on the way down, that all was not idyllic in her mother's life. She suspected she was putting on a brave face having been deserted by Fergus. Oh yes, despite a brief reconciliation, the groom had well and truly gone. Bolted the stable. The flit to Ireland, for reasons best known to the pair of them, had not been a resounding success, but what we did know was that Clem was now living in a flat in Bloomsbury, having a ball. Or at least, that was the party line. But living the merry divorcee life in London was not, Polly reckoned, quite what it was cracked up to be. Indeed, it had occurred to both of us, over a cup of coffee in her kitchen, whilst Kit, her husband, strolled with Hugh in the garden, that Clem might be back.

'I mean, she's hardly going to tell me, Emma, is she? She's far too proud. But I get the impression the grass is definitely not as green as she thought it would be. In fact, it's distinctly parched.'

'It was always bound to be,' I'd whispered, as we saw the men approach through the kitchen window. 'Life with someone so fundamentally different was never going to live up to her expectations.' I didn't say once the sex had gone, but that's what I meant.

'Once the sex has gone, you mean.'

'Well . . .'

'No, I agree, but she wouldn't listen then, and she won't listen now. But mark my words, she's not entirely happy.'

Which was another reason, I decided, as I left my husband under the pear tree with his manuscript and went uneasily back into the house, that I felt more unsettled at Branchester than I'd imagined I would. More in a state of limbo. Because what the bloody hell would happen if Clem decided she'd made a big mistake? Came back and wooed Yanni – who for all his protestations, adored her and was heartbroken – and wanted her home back? When I'd already painted the dark jade walls Elephant's Breath, and the peacock ones Mouse's Droppings or whatever it's called? Covered them with our jolly paintings from London?

'Well, she can't have it,' Hugh said simply, later that evening, when we were having supper and I'd broached it again. 'She's burnt her bridges. Stop perpetually worrying, Emma. It's wearying.'

But I couldn't help it. Her touch was on everything I encountered: every tablecloth I shook out – antique, darned and beautiful with crochet edges – every jug I filled with flowers – pale blue and white with tiny cracks, no doubt a hundred years old. It was as if she still somehow possessed the whole house. I felt weirdly like the second Mrs de Winter, haunted by Rebecca, as I roamed silently from room to room, wondering how I could rid myself of my mother-in-law and make the house my own, without sacrificing its charm. How I wished the contents sale that had been mooted had gone through, but the siblings had decided against it.

'If you're happy living with it, Emma,' Polly had said, when we'd discussed it, 'we think we'd rather not.' Her huge china-blue eyes had filled up, and at the time, I'd been so excited about living here I'd have agreed to anything. 'OK,' I said quickly. 'It's fine. We'll take it all.'

Now that I was here, though, it was like living with a ghost. Every cupboard I opened, every chair I sat in, I felt Clem. And although I did put some more stuff away, when Polly popped round one day and said, 'Oh God, you've got rid of the Heron!' – and looked appalled at the modern print I'd hung in its place – I'd hastened down to the cellar and put it back again.

I felt paralysed: trapped in a beautiful, eclectic, gilded cage full of charming tatty velvets and chintzes and original drawings by Augustus John and sister Gwen, and although anyone who came enthused and admired, nothing felt like mine.

'So where's all your London furniture then?' asked Jane, gazing around the sitting room on her much anticipated visit. We'd had to wait an agonizing few weeks because Jane was a primary-school teacher and the summer term was the busiest; she'd been up to her eyes in school trips, sports days and parents' meetings.

'Well, most of it's in the stables,' I told her, scratching inside my wrist where my eczema had flared up recently. 'I tried it all, but it looked so odd. Like I'd got terrible taste, or something.'

'Which you haven't,' she said staunchly.

'No, but blue-velvet sofas and lime-washed wooden furniture doesn't work here, trust me. Even a bit of OKA looks weird. Too shiny, somehow.'

She shrugged. 'So live with the Chippendale. Most of it's beautiful anyway. God, look at those curtains,' she went across to the window to finger them. 'Are they tapestry?'

'Bound to be. Seventeenth-century needlework, no doubt. I'll have the British Museum coming round soon.'

Jane turned at the edge to my voice. 'Look, you don't have to do anything in a hurry, you've only just moved in. How long have you been here?'

'Six weeks.'

'Well, that's nothing in the scheme of things. Live with Clem's stuff for a while, and maybe change it bit by bit. That little round table could go, for instance, that's got no real age. And that painting by the window is a Laura Knight copy; it isn't the real McCoy.'

'Isn't it?' Interesting. Jane wasn't even arty. Had just grown up with it. 'OK, I'll move those.'

Later, though, I decided. Not now. You see, I'd lost my confidence. And when I was alone, like now, when Jane had gone, and Hugh was in London seeing an author, I'd find myself wandering from room to room, gazing out at the beautiful view of the cornfields swaying in the breeze, at Scribble lying luxuriantly on the lawn – she'd relocated perfectly – then pressing my forehead to the glass, sighing a bit, wondering what on earth I'd done.

My children were splendid, though, full of bravado. 'Make it your own, Mum,' Teddy insisted when I called him. 'Granny hasn't got the monopoly on good taste, our house was lovely in London.'

'It was, wasn't it?' I agreed, glowing. 'Thank you, darling, I will.'

'Just put it all away and start again. Then get the local auction house to pop along at a later date, when everyone's calmed down a bit. Polly will be fine about it then. I know she felt sad about stuff being sold, but she'll have moved on by then – she's super reasonable. It'll all fall into place. Oh – and if it's OK, Ella and I think we'd like to get married there.'

'Oh!' I was thrilled. Had to sit down for a moment, choked. 'Oh, Teddy, how wonderful, I'd love that! But her parents wouldn't mind? I mean, she is the bride, after all.'

'Not at all, they'd love a country wedding. And we can hardly have it with them, can we? Too much of a hike.'

Ella's parents lived in America, but a lot of their family and friends were in England. They were sweet, generous people and I knew it would work well.

'Perfect,' I purred. 'I'll forget the house for the minute, and plan for a wedding.'

He laughed. 'Well, don't get too excited, we only want family and a few friends. Fifty or sixty at the most, then a big party in London later, so it won't take long to plan. Ella just wants – you know – a hog roast, wild flowers, hay bales and bunting. That sort of thing.'

'Oh yes – *ideal*. Dear Ella!' Not for the first time I blessed my tremendous luck in having her as a daughter-in-law.

'And she says she'll give you a hand with the art

barn when you get it started. Why don't you concentrate on that?'

'I will,' I said warmly. 'Good idea.' God, why hadn't I spoken to Teddy earlier? He always made me feel better. Nico too. They galvanized me. 'I'll park the house and let it – you know, create itself. By osmosis. Gradually.'

'Good plan. You've got years there, after all.'

'Quite,' I whispered as *forever* sprang uneasily to mind.

'She's got a great mate, by the way, from university, Jenny someone or other, at Kaplinsky's. Why don't you pop down and have a chat with her? I'm sure she'll give you some tips. Ella's already rung her and explained what you want to do and she was full of enthusiasm. Said something a bit more accessible and down to earth was just what the area needed.'

'Really? They wouldn't mind?'

'Mum, I think they're pretty established. I reckon they can cope with the competition.'

'Yes, quite,' I said hurriedly, realizing he was laughing at me. I mean, of course. What was I thinking?

'But don't just sit there and stew. Forget the house, get going with the barn, and find out about the local artistic talent, OK?'

'OK. Thanks, Teddy. I will. And thank Ella for me too. Heavenly girl.'

I put the phone down feeling lighter and more clear-headed than I had in weeks. Don't stew. Those words were not casual. I had a habit, you see, of doing just that. Of overthinking things. And Teddy was astute enough to know that without a plan or a project, I would do exactly that, and then the much vaunted move to the country, which I'd bored everyone rigid with in London, would turn to dust and ashes in my mouth. When did children become wiser than their parents? When did the roles reverse? There'd been a subtle shift, surely. Seismic, some might say. It hadn't escaped my notice, either, that Hugh, who hadn't exactly been dragged down here, but let's say led, would be quietly furious if I succumbed to any sort of second thoughts.

Only last night, as we were getting into bed, I'd said lightly – but it hadn't sounded terribly light:

'It's lovely here, isn't it, darling?'

He didn't answer. To be fair, he was brushing his teeth at the time. I was behind him, cleaning my face in the mirror with a cotton wool pad. I rubbed a bit harder.

'But nevertheless, I do wonder what people do all day?'

He'd raised his head slowly in the mirror to look at me, his mouth full of froth, leaned the heels of his hands heavily on the basin.

'I mean, obviously, teach, like Jane, or keep pigs, like that lovely girl up the lane, and then there's me with my gallery. But I mean, if one doesn't have a sort of, rural pursuit – like I do – one does . . . sort of wonder . . .'

Hugh's eyes, which didn't, as a rule, blaze, were beginning to gain a little fire.

'Garden, of course,' I said hastily. 'And keep a few chickens, I expect. Anyone can do that. Even me!' I'd given a slightly hysterical little laugh and left him clutching the porcelain, eyeballing the plughole.

I'd hastened from the bathroom and hopped into bed, quickly turning out my light, but just catching a glimpse, before I did, of all the family portraits on the wall, beside what had been Clem's side of the bed. They'd been drawn by some French artist she'd met in Paris, back in the nineties. All four Petridis children, in round gilt frames, when they were young. Clem in the middle. I'd planned to replace them with my own children, but I didn't have any exquisite drawings – what had I been doing with my life that I hadn't had my children's portraits done? So I'd tried photographs. Lovely black and white ones, but still, it had looked odd. I put the Petridis children back – after all, one was Hugh – but took Clem out of the middle. Which looked like she'd died. Or I hated her. So I replaced it with a water-colour of the house. The colour looked peculiar, though, juxtaposed with the drawings. So I put Clem back. Just for the minute. I shut my eyes tight, so I couldn't see Clem's, mocking me, looking down from the wall. And I couldn't see Hugh, either, as he got heavily into bed. He turned off his side light and neither of us spoke. We didn't even say goodnight, which was unusual.

7

The following morning I hurried to find my husband, already in his habitual position in the garden, continuing to mark up his manuscript. It was a beautiful day, much warmer than yesterday and it made a ridiculously idyllic scene: the learned fellow in his panama hat and deckchair, with the May blossom bobbing prettily overhead, like something out of a Merchant Ivory production. I'd dressed in a floaty summer dress he liked and which I couldn't help but waft in, and had a spot of make-up on. I'd also brought him a coffee.

'I'm off to Kaplinsky's,' I told him merrily. 'Ella's set up a contact for me there, so I'm going to go and introduce myself.'

Hugh moved his pencil to mark his place and looked up. 'Excellent news,' he said dryly.

'Yes, isn't it?' I said, ignoring his tone and his steady eyes over his glasses. 'And then, before you know it, I'll have the art barn up and running, and that'll be my rural thing.'

'Joy unlimited.'

I kept my bright smile going, knowing it wasn't

his way to gush, but I'd show him. I really would. 'I thought I'd called it The Barn Gallery.'

He nodded, but he'd already gone back to the Napoleonic Wars. Lovely, darling, I replied in my head.

'What's Wellington up to?'

'Defending the Portuguese.'

'He's a brick, isn't he?'

He gave a tolerant smile to show I was forgiven and carried on reading.

'We need a supermarket shop at some stage,' he said into his pages, but his tone was more convivial and his pencil was moving again.

'I know, I'll be back in time to do it with you before lunch. Bye, my love.'

'Toodle pip.'

As I drove down the lanes enjoying the red campion which frothed exuberantly from every hedgerow, I thought how stupid I'd been these last few weeks, worrying everyone with my moods, which were only moods, despite what Polly said, who was training to be a counsellor, and who therefore saw an opportunity for therapy at every gloomy corner. 'Areas of concern,' she called my darker moments. But I knew my black dog of old and could shift it myself if needs be; it just took more energy than it used to. In the old days, living with my mother, a night out with friends could shift it. Or moving out, when I was seventeen, to live with a friend's much older sister who had a spare room and a kind heart. That hadn't half shifted it. And then I'd moved back again. But some sort of change of direction was all it took to transition from what I refused to call more than a spell of unhappiness, to happiness. Except these days, it wasn't like tacking a Mirror dinghy, it was more like turning a ruddy great oil tanker. Nonetheless, to stick with the nautical analogy, once the tanker was 'ready about, heave ho', or whatever they said at sea, it was on track for longer. My moods were less mercurial, which was a blessing. I just had to get a grip occasionally, that was all.

As I drove through the pretty market town of Breston, admiring its ancient counting house of mellow, honey-coloured stone, I reflected that, iron-ically, things would improve when Sally was here, too. Despite our differences she always buoyed my spirits, and Hugh's too, on account of her dogged refusal to sink below the water line, whatever life threw at her. And a bit of me knew that when I was with her, a smaller, not very nice part of me, felt blessed, when I considered what my life could have been like, had I not chosen the right path. Had I not married Hugh, and had I instead turned out like Sally, or – the greatest fear of all – my mother. Or her mother, Granny Baker. I shook my head, ban-ishing those terrible demons, and concentrated instead on sweeping out of Breston and embarking on the incredibly narrow lanes that led to . . . where was it now . . . golly, it was twisty – oh yes, here. I almost missed the sign. Kaplinsky's.

I parked in the cleverly designed car park, ostensibly a field, but with gravel spaces for cars amongst the daisies. As I stopped I marvelled, as I always did, at the thought that had gone into this charming gallery. From here, it appeared to be housed in an old farmhouse, but hidden round the back, there was an enormous gleaming glasshouse, filled with room after room of modern art. Or contemporary art. I was never quite sure what the difference was. And perhaps I should be sure, since I was on the point of opening a gallery housing the stuff. Obviously I wasn't planning anything on this scale, but a bit of me hoped for the flavour, if not the grandeur. I had no formal training, of course, but I liked to think I knew what the average Joe would want on their walls, rather than the pretentious sophisticate.

As I skirted a giant iron gate on the way in, stuck in an awkward place where one couldn't avoid it, and at a strange angle, I realized it had a label, so was therefore a sculpture, not a gate, and marked at £42,000. I blinked. I was pretty sure I was OK for gates. It occurred to me too that really, anything could be an exhibit in this place. This heavy glass door, for instance, I thought, as I struggled to open it and make my way to the reception. Years ago, when Jane and I had first visited, we'd spotted a coffee bar at the top of the garden and popped in, only to find it empty and in darkness, with paper cups and napkins strewn about. We'd realized, as we'd crept out, that it wasn't a coffee bar at all, but an installation, as I'd learnt to call these things. Jane had asked a waiter about it at lunch and he'd said no, they'd had a party yesterday and hadn't got round to clearing it up. Perplexing, wasn't it? When one had to constantly wonder what art was.

The girl on reception was a cool blonde with generations of privilege behind her which she hadn't checked for a very long time. She listened inscrutably, with opaque eyes, as I asked for Jenny, and then informed me that she was away for a couple of days, looking at an artist's work in Derbyshire.

'Oh, right, what a shame. I'll come back. I probably should have made an appointment with her.'

The blonde inclined her head as if to suggest this was undoubtedly the case, and turned her gaze back to her computer screen, thus giving me my stage direction to leave the scene. I swallowed. Persevered.

'So . . . perhaps you could book an appointment with her for me? Later this week?'

Her eyes didn't leave her computer. 'It's best if you do it with her. She keeps her own diary.'

'Oh. Right. Can I take her number, then?'

The blonde turned her head back slowly towards me. Blinked. 'You don't have her number?' She was laying the incredulity on thick and I wanted to slap her. She was all of twenty-two.

'No, I don't actually know her. My daughter-in-law – well, daughter-in-law-to-be – suggested I call in. Ella Hamilton? She runs a gallery in London.'

She looked at me blankly. Ridiculously, I realized I was incapable of being quite as rude as her, and so instead, I muttered my thanks, picked up a catalogue and moved away to look at the first room, pretending it was half the reason I'd come. Her cut-glass voice halted me.

'I'm sorry, they're eight pounds. We don't charge for admission, but we do charge for the catalogues.'

I walked back and replaced it. 'I'll do without, then,' I told her crisply, just as, at that moment, a voice at my elbow said: 'Here, have mine. I'm going, so you may as well.'

I turned to see an attractive, pleasant-looking woman with the streaky-blonde hair most of us greying, fifty-something women affect. She was wearing a summer dress identical to mine, but in a different colour. We both clocked it at the same time and laughed.

'Cos,' she affirmed. 'And funnily enough, I nearly bought it in the blue.'

'And I nearly bought the green!'

'Live in it. Throw it on with a pair of trainers.' We each stuck out a foot and then laughed at our pretty much identical white shoes. It occurred to me that the woman herself looked familiar too, but I couldn't place her.

'Sure you don't want to keep it?' I indicated the catalogue, the girl on the desk forgotten now, or actually, pointedly ignored.

'Absolutely not. My brother's exhibiting, so I just wanted to see what he's got here, but he'll have loads of them at home.' She lowered her voice. 'And to be honest, the rest of it is a bit too out-there for me. I'm not sure what I'd do with a model of an elephant's penis, even if I did have a spare eight thousand pounds.' She nodded at the strange grey exhibit on the plinth beside us. I rolled my eyes in solidarity.

We'd moved away from the desk by now, although the girl had straightened up a bit on hearing the artist's sister was present, but she was too late for second chances.

'But how lovely that your brother is exhibiting. Which room?'

'The last one. And he's got a huge room to himself; it looks fab, actually. But you have to go all the way round to get to it.'

'I'll get going then.' I gave her a broad smile and made to move on, when she stopped me, her hand going to my arm.

'You look awfully familiar. Were you at Lizzie Cavendish's fiftieth lunch last week? So many women – twenty-two, apparently – but did I see you in the crowd?'

'No, but funnily enough I was thinking the same about you. I'm Emma Petridis?'

She shook her head. Put a hand to her chest. 'Susie Alexander?'

I shook mine too.

'Perhaps we bumped into each other in the changing room in Cos!'

We laughed and said goodbye, going our separate ways. But actually, I was encouraged. That was just the sort of woman I wanted to come to my barn, and perhaps she could encourage her twenty-two friends to come with her? The sort who liked an outing to a gallery, but found this sort of thing – I moved slowly past a giant plaster cast of a thumb with a rather nasty-looking gash entitled 'Split Digit' – inaccessible, and frankly, bewildering. And who simply wanted – I moved hopefully into the next room where rows and rows of knitted socks had been pinned to the walls – no. Not this sort of thing either. I studied the socks with professional interest. They'd all been knitted by hand, but some had huge holes in the heels and some were very frayed. Why? Perhaps if I stared long enough, I'd understand. Hugh would, I was sure, and Clem, and Sally, and the rest of the family. I took a few paces backwards and made myself concentrate. No. I just wanted to darn them. Either that or chuck them in the bin. I moved on.

The next room at least had paint on canvas, but the pictures were dark and intense, mostly of gnarled tree stumps or pollarded elms which looked stunted and disfigured. A bit too human. Disturbing, somehow. But perhaps that was the point of art these days, to disturb? As if there wasn't enough going on in the world to do that anyway. Another room boasted skeletons in clothes made from bits of stretched cling film, dyed to look like skin – just plain horrid. But the one that led away from it was much more my scene. Vast canvases with billowing skies and enormous hurrying clouds above turbulent seas, or flat marshes tinged with gold.

I stopped in my tracks, right in the middle of the room, and I'd been hurrying along, keen to get away from the skeletons and the gashed digits. Oh, this was much more like it. I turned slowly, taking it all in. These were just heaven. And transporting, too, not just attractive wall coverings. If you stood in front of them – this one, for instance, with the river running through the flat marshlands – you could actually feel the rhythm of the water, rippling down from those high tors beyond. Hear it, too, gurgling towards you. The light was sensational, soft and low, and I almost felt I knew the place – somewhere Scottish, perhaps – from my travels. Years ago . . . I walked forward to peer at the label. 'Obermoray, at dusk.' Of course. I *had* been there once. I felt a glow of self-congratulatory pleasure. I took my victories where I could these days. I straightened my shoulders. Not such a philistine, after all. And it wasn't the *scene* I recognized, you understand, but the very particular *light*, which one only gets in the Highlands. I could almost hear myself talking about it, telling people, in my own gallery. Wafting my hand about artistically as they listened, rapt. I reached in my handbag for the catalogue, which I'd stuffed there in disgust on learning the skeletons were called 'Famine', to discover more, when I heard voices in the next room. So far I'd had the place to myself, it being early, and I realized I'd come full circle, and was about to arrive back in reception again.

'You've just missed your sister,' the receptionist was purring, in very different tones to the ones she'd employed with me. 'She left about ten minutes ago. But we've had *so* much interest in your work,' she gushed.

I heard a familiar voice say something about enthusiasm never quite translating into hard cash, in his experience, but it was said with humour and a laugh. As I listened, I felt my brow furrow as I riffled through the files of my mind to place the speaker. The voices stopped and footsteps came my way. I glanced at another picture and realized, with a jolt, it was a scene I knew well. It was McTannor Bay, in early morning. Indeed I'd sat on that very rock; gazed out to sea. With the owner of that voice. I went very still.

The footsteps came closer, and into the room, older, obviously, and greyer at the temples, perhaps a little thicker around the waist, but still tall and slim, came Hamish's brother, Rory MacLeod. As he entered, he saw me standing alone. He stopped and stared. I'd at least had the benefit – albeit fleetingly – of these scenes I knew well, and also of meeting his sister earlier, who I now placed instantly. It was our surnames and the context that had confused us. But it obviously took him a moment longer. I watched as a startled light flickered in his eyes. We stood there, still feet apart, in that room full of Scottish scenes, of moorland and heather, of rushing seas and skies, gazing in astonishment at one another. As the years fell away, all manner of memories, some wonderful, some horrific, gushed like a torrent into the calm waters of the present.

8

I'd wanted to go to Hamish's funeral, of course I had, but it had coincided with one of my mother's dramas. I'd got up there all right, to the Highlands – or a pregnant Jane and Sally had got me up there, I was pretty distressed – but on the actual day, I'd had to stay at the B&B we'd booked at the foot of the glen, while they went without me. Instead, I'd spent the day in the little telephone kiosk in reception, pouring coins into the box under the plastic hood, trying to talk my mother out of committing suicide. She took the bottle of pills nonetheless, so I had to call an ambulance, and then I had to speak to a doctor at the hospital in London. By which time the funeral had started and it was too late. All of this I wanted to say immediately to Rory as he stood there – I'd written, of course, and tried to ring, but no answer – but his eyes told me, plus the palm of his hand gently rising to stem the flow of my words, that he already knew. He lowered the hand, and looked a little longer. His familiar hazel eyes were flecked with gold. Then he said my name.

'Emma.'

'Rory.'

That was it, for the moment. But it seemed to me his pictures reared up and then closed in, crowding round to listen.

He cleared his throat. 'I should have taken your phone calls. I mean, I knew you were there, in the glen, that you meant to be there . . . and I got your letter.'

I nodded. I felt my eyes fill with tears. I saw his do the same. After a moment he swallowed. 'Was she OK?'

'Who?'

'Your mother.'

'Oh. Yes. She always is.' That no doubt sounded terribly callous and I hastened to retrieve it. 'I mean . . . you know. I'm used to it. She's stopped now, of course. It was for my father's benefit and she no longer cares.'

He nodded and gave a gentle smile. So much ground to cover and we were talking about my mother?

'And . . . your family?' I asked tentatively.

He came closer. 'Better. I mean, they'll never be completely healed, or complete, obviously. But much better than we were. Dad's charity is going well and he soldiers on.'

'Yes, I follow his charity.'

Murray, Hamish's father, had set up a Safety on Loch Loman charity after his son's death, organizing more life guards. I remembered him well: a smiling, charming yet rather reserved man, whose life had been shattered, first by his wife leaving, and then on losing his son. But he'd been so generous to me, when I'd rung to tell him Hamish and I had had a row, and stuttered out my guilt about it being all my fault. He'd refused to even entertain the idea, had told me to put that thought from my mind instantly, that it had just been a terrible accident. But I knew how upset Hamish had been, you see. I too thought it was an accident, and nothing along the lines of my mother's deliberate brush with death, but I also knew that had I been with him, it wouldn't have happened. He'd never have been out on the loch at dusk, because I didn't particularly like fishing. Didn't like killing things. Hated shooting pheasants, as they did up there. Hamish would laugh and tell me I was suburban, because after all, the animals had a much better life than anything commercially bred, and I ate the produce too, which was true, but there we are.

'And Susie's been brilliant.'

I came reeling back to the present. 'She always was.'

I couldn't for the life of me think how I hadn't recognized her just now: the lovely elder sister who'd done her best to take her mother's place. Out of context, I suppose. And to be fair, I'd mostly heard about Susie; we didn't often meet. She'd been in her mid-twenties at the time, and living in

London. Rory and I had seen more of each other, by dint of us all being in the same university town. And not just in Kent, in Scotland too. He loved it up there. Went home at every opportunity. As Hamish and I did too. And there'd been that terrible, fatal attraction, right from the beginning. When I'd leave a room, I'd feel his eyes following me. When the three of us flopped on beanbags in the basement at Drumleeran, watching television, I'd turn to say something and find Rory, sitting behind me on the sofa, already looking at me. And then that evening in the kitchen, when Hamish had gone fishing with his father, which left just the two of us; how strained the atmosphere had been – so difficult just to make a coffee together. How relieved we'd been when Hamish and Murray had come back, loaded down with their catch, so many mackerel. How we were able to laugh and joke and cook them together at the Aga, the three of them teasing me because I couldn't bear to see them wriggling on the hook – but now look at her, wolfing them down with chips and ketchup! I wondered if all this, Rory was remembering too, and if he'd felt the same guilt as me when his brother had died; but none of this could be voiced, after a gap of so many years, facing one another in an art gallery.

'There's a coffee place here, just across the way. Shall we . . . ?' His voice tailed off, his hand waving vaguely outside.

'Oh yes,' I said quickly. 'Let's do that.'

We made our way outside silently. How could we yet speak? Comment on the art, the weather? As we went through reception, however, the blonde's cold eyes were far more lively and alert; I felt them on my back, following us through the main door, down the steps, and outside. We went up the gravel path through the meadow to the café I'd been to with Jane, at the top of the hill; it had been refurbished and was terribly edgy now, with cups made from stone and the coffee ground up in an extraordinary space-age machine behind the bar. We managed to laugh about that, and the strange papier mâché dragons hanging from the ceiling, the giant octopuses with hundreds of tentacles lurking in every corner, so that, by the time we'd taken our coffee outside to the terrace and were sitting down, stirring our cappuccinos, I felt more composed. And foolish, too, for remembering those decidedly teenage days. Life had moved on.

There were quite a few people having coffee on the terrace, which helped, and I chatted away about Hugh and the boys, and why we'd moved down from London. How I hoped to have a wedding here, soon. I mean, obviously I was married with children, why wouldn't I be? But still, it felt strange telling him, and I realized I rushed through it all very quickly, like a train whistling through stations. He listened, smiling and nodding. Then he told me about living back in

Scotland: how he'd gone back there to paint, and loved it, but how Susie had lured him down here with the promise of an exhibition. How she'd got cross with him for never exhibiting, for being too much of a hermit. She'd persuaded the gallery here to show his work.

'I think she browbeat them into submission. Told them the reason they didn't sell anything was because it was all too weird, and not to have at least one room of commercial art, if only to keep the gallery going, was madness. She then brought all her hundreds of friends to the opening night and plied them with booze until they coughed up.'

I smiled. 'I'm not having that. The pictures are beautiful. They'd sell themselves. But I did spot the sea of red stickers.'

'Susie had a fistful of them. No sooner had one of her friends said – well, maybe in the spare room . . . than she'd whip out a red spot, charge forward and stick it on triumphantly, before they had a chance to change their minds.'

I laughed. This was much better. Less awkward. More relaxed.

'She lives round here?'

'Yes, she's married to a lovely local chap. They're about ten minutes away.'

'And you? Are you married? Have children?'

'I did marry, but we divorced soon after. It wasn't right.'

I looked into his steady hazel eyes. Heavens. Divorced. Quickly, too. I wasn't prepared for that. All of a sudden I wasn't quite so relaxed.

'But . . . you have children?' I stuttered, almost hopefully.

'No, it was a very brief liaison. She went on to have some, though. Is happily married now, too.'

'Good, good,' I purred as if that was simply marvellous. The answer to all our prayers.

We both hurriedly and simultaneously picked up our cups and sipped our coffee. It was hot though, and I burned my lips. I'd forgotten his attractive shyness. The way he lowered his eyes abruptly like that mid-sentence. Long lashes. I glanced away from them. The sun was just disappearing behind a cloud which threw a shadow over the nearest statue, a Henry Moore-type figure, a mother perhaps, only more angular than Moore: not such soft curves. Its back was towards us.

'So you're only here for this exhibition?' I turned back. 'You'll go back to Scotland after that?'

'Well, I'll have to at some stage. It's mine, now.'

I glanced up. 'Oh – you mean, your father . . . ?'

'Moved to a cottage on the estate, two years ago.'

I nodded, picturing Murray pottering about, an old man now. 'He was very kind to me,' I said softly.

'He liked you,' he said simply, and then realizing, I think, that we were on unstable ground again, rushed on. 'But you'd probably find him very changed. Not nearly so robust, which annoys him. Can't get about so much, certainly can't get up on the moor. The old ticker gives him gyp, which makes him grouchy.' He tapped his heart, and I saw that he had paint on his fingers.

'You're still painting down here?' I asked, indicating his hand. 'Not just exhibiting? Whereabouts?'

He grinned. 'Can't not paint. It's like breathing. And Susie has a friend with an empty studio, and a cottage to rent too, so she's installed me there. Still the bossy older sister. But to be honest, the studio is not ideal, it's a bit dark, so I'm mostly in the fields. So yes, there I am with an easel and some sandwiches, which never get eaten, just like the old days. I'm fascinated by the change of light down here, it's so different to what I'm used to. I like it and I really didn't think I would.' He grinned sheepishly. '"The soft south", I believe I called it, before I got here. And of course, although the house up there is mine, I don't have to stay in Scotland. Could rent it out if I felt like it. Dad divvied it all up some years ago to avoid tax, and Susie got the London flat. They both turned out to be worth about the same.'

'Stop it. A flat in Earl's Court and that vast house in the glen?'

'Swear to God. Madness, eh?'

'So might you sell it?'

'I might. I don't know. Don't know what I'm going to do yet.'

I glanced away. There was something unsettling about those words. Something temporary. The cloud had thickened and it was getting chilly. The sculpted grey stone back looked more hunched: a little threatening, even. It was as though the world had tilted slightly on its axis, and my heart, which had been sleeping, had been jolted awake.

'You've spilt some coffee on your dress,' Rory said gently.

Driving home later, I decided I was being ridiculous. Of course it was a shock seeing Rory; any crush from the past turning up like that would have a startling effect, especially one that hadn't gone bald, or grown a paunch, or had dribble drains, as Jane called them, down the side of their mouth – was perhaps better looking, even, having grown into himself. Rory had been an incredibly skinny, almost gangly young man, with long limbs that he didn't seem to know what to do with. They almost had a life of their own, slung bonelessly over sofa arms like an old coat, or flung out like a starfish on a rug. The tartan picnic rug, in fact, which we spread at our favourite spot, at the foot of the glen. On the sandy stretch of beach by the loch, where, if we were lucky, we saw the beavers playing, catching fish near the rocks by the shore. We were lucky that day. We watched them ducking and diving, their sleek bodies gliding through the clear water. And Hamish had also spotted a golden eagle, rising high up to perch on a rocky ridge. The three of us had been lying down after lunch, chatting and dozing in the sun, and Hamish sat up, raised his binoculars to get a better look. Rory had glanced across at me, behind his back, as we lay there. Hamish. Had he known? Nothing had happened, ever, but once, and it had indeed been that occasion on the picnic rug, Hamish had turned to report on the eagle, and intercepted our glance. Had he known what it was? Rory and I didn't even know ourselves, so it was unlikely. And we were all so young, and so close. The brothers were inseparable. How could it happen, then? How had even the faintest attraction been possible? It was shameful that the heart could go its own way, irrespective of the head; still felt shameful, even after all these years. I felt myself go hot.

I drove back through the little West Country market town, bustling with people now, so different to Scotland, where even the busy town of Dunleven seemed sleepy in comparison. We'd had so much beauty to ourselves, up there. Those long drives in the Land Rover up the heather-lined tracks to see a herd of roe deer, or a badger sett, or even a white hare – Hamish always knew where the wildlife was. Walking for miles, then driving home at breakneck speed, Rory at the wheel, me in the front beside him because I got car sick, Hamish in the back: music playing, singing along – why always the three of us?

Because life was lonely up there. Or solitary, rather. It would have been strange to leave Rory behind in that huge house, his father off on estate business elsewhere. But it seemed to me the only time Hamish and I were alone in that house was in his bedroom, which, towards the end, hadn't been great. I don't know why. Well, that's not true, I do. Did. Even then. I took a sharp intake of breath, let it out slowly, gripping the steering wheel. If truth be told, I knew I was on the cusp of breaking up with Hamish. I was only twenty. I knew, or was beginning to realize, the relationship had run its course. It probably would have taken a couple more months, because I certainly hadn't mentioned it to anyone, not even Jane; it hadn't even crystallized in my own mind. It was only in retrospect I knew. And of course, to honour his memory, I agreed, after he died, that he'd been my great love. That I was devastated. And I was. But there had been so many other complicated feelings too. Guilt, naturally, but another terrible grief too, for something that, with Hamish dead, could never happen. Neither Rory nor I would do that to his memory. But especially Rory.

As I rounded the last bend and curled down over the brow of the green hill into the valley, the long, low thatch of the Pink House came into view. In the gravel drive at the front of the house, Hugh was getting out of his car. He saw me approach and threw up his hands, exasperated. I'd been much

97

longer than I'd said I would be. He went round to the boot and flung it open theatrically to reveal all the Waitrose bags, full of the shopping I'd said I'd help with. Over the brow of the hill from the other side of the valley, the one that led back to London, came a familiar black convertible BMW. Sally was arriving, as she always did, at every eventful stage of my life, almost as if she took some celestial cue to do so.

9

Had Sally known Rory? I couldn't remember. Certainly he'd been to our house in Clarendon Road a few times, when he was an art student up the road, so they might have met, but I couldn't remember any meaningful evenings, any drunken supper parties when they were both around the table. Sally tended to socialize with her more studious lawyer friends, the ones she shared with in her final year. And it was all so long ago – these days I found it hard enough to remember what happened two weeks ago, let alone thirty-odd years ago. Except that wasn't true, I thought, as I shut the car door, raising my hand in greeting as the tyres of her car crunched in beside me; some snapshots from all those years ago I remembered as if they were yesterday.

'Well done!' I called, as she got out and mopped her brow dramatically. She staggered towards me. 'You made it!'

I knew better than to welcome her to her childhood home, so I kept it neutral.

'Three hours, door to door. A personal best, but obviously I'm dying for a pee,' she said, as we fell into each other's arms.

'Then make haste,' I ordered, as she did just that, pausing briefly to greet Scribble, who'd come out to greet her.

'Need the loo!' I heard her shriek to her brother as she tore past him in the kitchen where he was unpacking the shopping. Bulging plastic bags covered the floor and table.

'She did it in three hours,' I told him in a cheery voice, but he didn't reply, and I realized he wasn't going to let his sister's appearance dilute his irritation with me.

'Why?' he said, exasperated, as he tossed a packet of biscuits into the larder. 'Why are you *always* late?'

'I'm sorry,' I said quickly. 'Really I am, I lost track of time. But I know, I should have texted.' I'd seized my phone at some traffic lights, realized Hugh had messaged: *Where are you?* But by then, the lights had gone green and I was beetling home.

Sally emerged and, sensing the mood music, raised her eyebrows enquiringly, never one to let a drama go to waste. She tiptoed across the kitchen mimicking treading on eggshells and gave her brother a quick hug, then ostentatiously picked up a full bag. She proceeded to unpack it efficiently, knowing, of course, the kitchen intimately but, nevertheless, not our configuration. But actually, it was incredibly helpful, I told myself, grabbing a bag too and joining in, even though she'd just put the jam in the fridge, which we didn't.

'Actually, I ran into Rory MacLeod,' I said bravely, deciding on the spur of the moment to go for full disclosure. I mean, why not? I saw Sally's back stiffen as she reached into the fridge. Ah. She did remember. 'That's why I'm late. We had a quick coffee,' I went on, emboldened. 'He's exhibiting at Kaplinsky's.'

'Good for him,' muttered Hugh. I turned, surprised at his tone. 'No, I mean genuinely, good for him. It's quite a ritzy gallery.'

I realized he meant it; it had just come out terse, a hangover from me being late. Hugh was not one to bear a grudge.

'Very ritzy,' I agreed. 'He's obviously done well. Amazing landscapes he's got, all rushing clouds and windswept moors and things – do you remember him, Sally?'

'Of course I do, he was Hamish's brother.'

Perhaps I was misinterpreting everyone's tone today; perhaps I'd had a bit of a shock. I left the unpacking and went to put the kettle on, although what I really wanted was a drink.

'Oh, come on, let's open some rosé and sit in the garden,' said Sally suddenly, grabbing my arm. 'Hugh, you do the honours, and Emma and I will put the rest of this away later.'

I thanked her with my eyes. There were some very good reasons why she was still more of a friend than a relative, and this taking control of a situation was one of them, I decided, as she gave him a bottle opener and pushed him gently towards the fridge for the wine; although whether I'd welcome such habitual control in my own house was another matter. Except, of course, she wasn't going to be in my house; she was going to be in the cottage at the bottom of the garden, and, after we'd had a drink on the terrace, and she'd admired the herbaceous borders frothing to either side of it, and the extraordinary green of the sunken lawn beyond, and the wild-flower meadow down another level beyond that, and generally been sweet and complimentary about what I'd done in the garden – which was absolutely nothing, incidentally, I hadn't touched it – we went to have a look at her new home.

It was at the far end of a grass path, mown through that very same wild-flower meadow, a dear little brick and flint former outhouse, with a pitched slate roof and a pretty green porch. Clem had converted it years ago to serve as a studio for aspiring artists. To our knowledge no aspiring artist had ever been invited to take up residence, because Clem was more interested in the look and feel of the place than having anyone around. She'd done it up beautifully, though, with walls the colour of yellowing tobacco, a muted fresco of dancers by a friend from London on the far wall, cool slate floors and a spiral staircase leading to an attic bedroom and bathroom. It was furnished in typical Clem style, which I suppose could be described as shabby chic, but was more individual than that. All I'd done to make it more habitable was add a few cushions to the sagging cream sofas at the far end, the same colour as the tobacco walls, and put a rug between the sofas to warm up the floor, where I imagined Sally might flop and watch television. Oh – and I'd put a few things upstairs, like a large cheval mirror I'd had in London, and a chest of drawers for her clothes.

Sally sighed with pleasure as we entered the cool space, a welcome break from the midday sun.

She spun around delightedly. 'It's exactly as I remember it,' she told me, eyes shining. 'And everything I'd hoped for. I haven't actually set foot in here for years.'

'Oh, I'm so pleased!' I realized I was ridiculously heady with relief.

'I suppose the only thing I might do is add my own cushions. I don't remember Mum buying these.' She went across and picked up one of mine. 'I've got some in the car, lovely old velvet ones, you know, with eccentric tassels. These are a bit matchy-matchy with the walls.' She gestured vaguely. 'And the rug's a bit Habitat, but, other than that, it's perfect.' She squeezed my arm.

I blinked, not holding my breath for the cheval mirror and the chest of drawers upstairs.

Sure enough, she decided they were both too Victorian for the artisan feel of the place, but other than that, she couldn't thank me enough. I'd done a splendid job. Well, at least she was pleased, I told myself. And at least I hadn't added curtains as I'd been sorely tempted to do. All the windows had wooden shutters, but it was pretty spare and austere as a home, I thought. When we went downstairs Sally piled the cushions on the floor in the corner. Then she ran a practised eye around the place without my suburban frippery and nodded approvingly. I shrugged inwardly and kept the bright smile going. Oh well.

She'd towed a trailer from London behind her car, full of her stuff, and we walked back up the garden to the drive where I helped her unload it. Hugh, who after our drink had gone back to the kitchen to finish unpacking the shopping, came out to assist, as he saw us struggle with a couple of chairs and a rolled-up rug. We carried it all down to the cottage.

'That's nice,' he said, as we set the rug down inside and it unrolled a bit. Exquisite faded needlework was revealed.

'Isn't it? I found it in a flea market in Paris. Had it sent back.'

'You could put it between the sofas at the far end,' he said, picking it up again, carrying it across and setting it down. He rolled it out and the muted golds, russets and creams melted into their surroundings as if they'd been there for centuries.

'Where's this blue one from?' He kicked the one underneath with his toe.

'I found it in the loft,' I lied, having bought it from Cargo two weeks previously. 'Must be an old one of your mum's.'

I kept my head lowered as I went to put the antique chair I was carrying in the corner of the room, where there was an empty space, but Sally intercepted me.

'Here, under the window. See, they're a pair?' she said indicating the one she'd already placed there, and employing a voice one might to a four-year-old. 'And what happened to the easel that was there?' She glanced in the corner I'd been making for.

'Oh, I put it in the stables. Thought you'd rather have a piece of furniture there, since it's no longer an actual studio?'

Hugh and Sally laughed. 'Well, it never was, as we know. Just Mum embracing the conceit without actually implementing it, but no, she brought that old wooden easel back from Tuscany. It's ancient, cost her a fortune. It definitely stays.'

'Right. I'll get it then,' I said, in the manner of a woman saying 'Oh for fuck's sake.'

They looked at me in surprise. 'I mean – won't an empty easel look a bit odd?' I asked, exasperated.

'It won't be empty, I'll put a painting in it,' Sally explained.

'Ah, right.' I trooped off.

After a bit, Hugh came and found me in the stables. 'Everything all right?'

'Yes, fine.' I turned from struggling with it in a dusty corner. It was huge and much too heavy for one person to move. 'It's just, I added precisely six things to that cottage to make her life more comfortable, and she's found fault with every single one of them.'

He looked awkward. 'I suppose it is going to be her house.'

'Oh, I agree. In retrospect I should have left her to it, but I got a bit excited. Wanted to make her feel at home. Would it have been too much to ask for her to enthuse about them and then discreetly pop them in cupboards at a later date?'

Hugh frowned. 'Would that have been better?'

I hesitated. Would it? If every time I came across I'd see something else disappear? Maybe not. 'I'm not sure,' I answered honestly. 'I just can't help thinking it might have been better manners though, Hugh.'

Hugh's eyes widened meaningfully. He spread his hands despairingly, as if to say – let's not forget who asked her down here.

We lifted the easel together in silence and carried it back to the cottage.

That evening, we had a very pleasant supper outside in the soft, dusky light, on the terrace overlooking the valley. Jane and Lance were there too. I'd rung them on the spur of the moment, thinking a few more non-Petridis personnel might be good, and praise be, they were free. Hugh barbecued a butter-flied leg of lamb he'd marinated, I made a pavlova, and Jane and Sally cobbled together a fishy starter from some smoked salmon Jane had found lurking in her fridge. The wine flowed as did the conversa-tion, and spirits were raised inordinately. None of us had seen Lance for a very long time, chiefly because although Jane and I had our regular halfway house lunches and Sally saw Jane whenever she was in London, Lance rarely accompanied his wife, pre-ferring the country and disliking the city. He was still a very good-looking man: tall, broad-shouldered and with a shock of blond hair and that beaming, boyish smile. As it flashed on greeting, it took me right back to our tutorial days when every single girl in his seminar group sat up straight and bright-eyed and tried to contribute at least something to the dis-cussion on *Beowulf*, instead of quietly dozing off a hangover. Later, his allure waned for me a bit when we all lived together in Clarendon Road and I saw him getting to grips with the more prosaic side of life, like digging spaghetti out of the S-bend under the sink, or clipping his toenails in a deckchair in the garden when he thought he was unobserved. Clearly it hadn't for Jane, though, and I was pleased to see they still looked at each other with the same degree of affection, if not passion, as they did then. But I did wonder, since he was still teaching, if other, much younger girls than Jane, were still sitting up straight and looking perky about *Beowulf*?

'Probably,' she'd said, when I'd had too much to drink one lunchtime in our Hampshire pub and mooted it. 'And don't think I haven't considered it. I've obviously created a vacuum by marrying him. But he was so traumatized by the split from Jess, I honestly don't think he'd go there again.'

Jess had had a nervous breakdown, which had shocked everyone, not least Lance. She'd spent a few months in the Priory and he'd lived with the guilt ever since. And we all know what that can do to you.

'Plus, he loves me,' she'd said simply, with a dazzling smile, and I knew that to be the truth; perhaps even more so now, I thought, watching as he fussed around her, getting her jacket from the car when the evening turned chilly and we were still sitting in the garden trying to make the most of the weather. As the sky turned from dark blue to inky black and filled with stars, I looked at his kind, attentive face with gratitude. It was sad for Jess, obviously, but my goddaughter Cassie and her younger sister Rose had had a wonderful father, and my dearest friend had not been left a single mother. Jess, too, recovered in time.

Sally was talking to Lance, now, about the Shakespeare bookshop in Paris; she couldn't believe he'd never been there, not just to the bookshop, but to Paris, and was teasingly calling him parochial. Hugh had disappeared inside, down to the cellar for another bottle. I turned to Jane beside me, lowering my voice.

'You didn't tell me Hamish's sister lived round here?'

She frowned. 'I didn't know she did. Do I even know her?'

'Susie? You must have met her.'

'Where?'

I thought. Yes, where. 'The funeral?' I suggested, more doubtfully now.

Jane made a face. 'Emma, there were hundreds of people there. And it was hundreds of years ago, too.'

'She's Susie Alexander now.'

Her face cleared. 'Oh – her! She's nice. I've met her at a few charity dos. God, I had no idea.' She sat up a bit. 'She's frightfully smart. But doesn't show it.'

'How d'you mean?'

'Well, she's married to some aristo, possibly the earl of somewhere or other. Lives at Hambledon Manor. Quite a pad. Oh, wait . . .' Her pale blue eyes widened into the distance as something else dawned. 'So the artist brother . . .' She turned back to look at me enquiringly.

'Is Rory, yes,' I said quietly. Jane was, after all, my best friend, and as such, knew a little of the history of my heart.

'He's causing something of a stir.' She blinked. 'With his paintings,' she added quickly. 'Apparently they're amazing.'

'Who's this?' Sally had broken off from Lance, who was talking to Hugh now, about the bottle he'd brought out: a new vineyard he'd discovered in Burgundy.

'Only a woman I met at the gallery today,' I said quickly. 'A potential new best friend,' I added teasingly. They predictably roared in outrage.

'Why would you need one of those when you've got both of us!' Sally demanded.

'Turns out she's rather grand so you can relax.' I grinned. 'I'll stick to my shabby old ones. Now – does anyone want cheese with that rather dusty bottle Hugh's produced?'

'Definitely,' Jane agreed. 'Go fetch it, wench. We haven't come all this way not to have four courses.'

I gladly made to go to the kitchen, but as I stood up, I caught Jane looking at me, her eyes thoughtful. Perhaps wondering why I'd chosen to tell Sally a bit of a lie, when I could so easily have told the truth.

10

As it transpired, Susie wasn't too grand. A week or so later, I was surprised to find her on my doorstep. Well, the barn doorstep, actually. Hugh had gone to London for a meeting with an author so I was having a good clear-out of my future gallery. I'd been up on a stepladder getting rid of all the cobwebs in the corners, then I'd wiped down the walls, and now I was sweeping the floor and generally getting to grips. It was huge and cavernous, with white walls and a lofty, heavily beamed ceiling; an ideal space for an exhibition, I'd decided, even if the vertical beams down the walls might pose a problem or two in the hanging of some of the pictures – one or two of the paintings were quite big. Sally had already found them for me; they were by a local artist who I was quite excited about. Well, that's not entirely true. When she'd shown me his work on Instagram, I hadn't instantly taken to it. But I hadn't said anything, because Sally knew about art. It was mostly portraiture, and I wasn't sure people wanted that unless they knew the sitter, plus they were quite sort of, brutal: lots of thick paint and huge, sweeping brush strokes. I'd asked Jane, later, on the phone to look at the site.

'I mean, I wouldn't hang them,' she'd said, ringing me back later. 'But what do I know?'

'Well, quite.' Jane and I liked pretty much the same thing. Countryside views. Seascapes.

'Sally's got taste,' she told me. 'And she knows her stuff. I'd go with it.'

And the more I'd thought about it, the more I'd decided I didn't want tame, accessible whimsy of the realistic sort. I wanted something a bit more cutting edge, the kind of thing Sally was au fait with, that would put me on the map. Not totally out there like Kaplinsky's, no gold sausages hanging on chains from the ceiling, but not the faux impressionist stuff I secretly liked. That huge nude, for instance, that Sally had told me would look great – I stepped back with my broom to view the space – right in the centre of the main wall, between the two beams. And people loved nudes; I wouldn't class those as portraits, actually. As I narrowed my eyes to imagine it hanging there, I heard a noise behind me. Susie had obviously tried the house, then found me in here. I tended to dress the part for any sort of activity, so I was wearing ancient dungarees and had my hair tied up in a silk scarf. She was in a pretty yellow dress and bearing a small bunch of roses tied with a raffia bow.

'Oh – hi!' I was surprised and not displeased.

Very pleased, actually. I put my broom down and went to greet her.

'Hi.' She smiled, her heart-shaped face clearing, relieved at my enthusiasm. 'I had to pop round, we're so close. And I felt so stupid not realizing who you were the other day.'

Ah. Rory had told her. And she'd have joined the dots locally and realized where we lived. 'Oh God, me too!' I rushed on. 'So stupid of me.' I came out of the barn into the sunlit doorway, wiping my hands on my trousers. 'We met in Scotland once or twice, do you remember?'

'I do. On my rare, fleeting visits back home. In those days I couldn't wait to get back to London.'

Those days. For a moment I think we were both transported back to her father's farmhouse kitchen: Hamish, Rory and I still lounging at the table at midday nursing hangovers and having a late break-fast, Susie, looking gorgeous – I remember her vividly – in white pedal pushers and a blue gingham shirt tied at the waist, perched on the Aga. She was sipping a glass of wine and telling us about the flat she lived in, just off Beaufort Street, with a view of the river: how lucky she'd been to get it, owned, as it was, by parents of a school friend, who let them stay in it for a minuscule rent. Four girls. And what fun they had. The parties, the army balls, the nights in Annabel's and Raffles, her blue eyes dancing in her pretty, fragile face as she'd described it. Probably four years older than me. I'd thought her achingly cool, and vowed, as I'd sat watching her light a cigarette with a gold Ronson lighter, her skinny long legs crossed and swinging, so full of poise and confidence, that one day, I'd be like her.

'I don't know how I forgot you, actually. You were a bit of a role model for me back then, even though I only met you once or twice.'

'Oh, you're kidding!' She looked genuinely surprised. Then pleased. 'I was probably incredibly full of myself.'

'No, you weren't. Just incredibly enthusiastic about London. The bright lights. How we should all get up there after university.'

She rolled her eyes. 'Very early twenties.'

'And . . . I always felt . . .' I hesitated, 'I should have written to you. Later.'

'Why?'

I shrugged miserably. Looked at my feet. 'I don't know. I just . . . I think I should have done. I wrote to your father.'

'Which would have helped him. He kept all the letters. But, Emma, nothing helped anyone, really. There was nothing anyone could have done.'

'No,' I agreed sadly. That delightful family. Another lovely family. Which I hadn't had. Shattered.

'Although his charity work does still help, you know. The safety on the lochs stuff, and I've taken it on; he's getting old now. It's actually one of the

reasons I've called.' She looked at me shyly. 'I wondered if I could rope you in? I gather you're opening
this up as a gallery. Hoped I could introduce you to
an artist?'

'Oh God, with pleasure! Do you know some local
ones? Golly, at the moment I've got the venue but
not the talent – well, one or two. And of course
you'd know what works round here.' My mind raced
eagerly to her well-connected social life, her high-
profile friends, their walls no doubt dripping with
incredibly beautiful art, eager for more. And perhaps she'd like to leave a stack of her charity leaflets
at the door? I suggested it.

'Oh, perfect!' she said eagerly. 'Here, let me show
you some artists.' She pulled a small leather portfolio
out of her bag and glanced about for somewhere to
put it.

'Hang on, let's go up to the terrace, everything's
dusty here.'

We hastened up the garden together then up the
steps to the terrace, and she put it on the wooden
table. Unzipped it. 'So. This is Martin Haversham,
who paints with his mouth.' She'd opened it at a lovely
golden meadow swaying with corn and freckled with
poppies, but I was still digesting what she'd said.

'With his mouth?'

'Yes, he's paralysed.'

'Oh.' I looked up at her. My eyes searched hers. 'A
boating accident?'

'Rugby, actually, but you're right, that's how it all started. I came across a boy who'd lost both his arms in a speedboat accident on Loch Loman. The propeller. He became the most amazing wildlife photographer. Look.'

She flipped the page to a wonderful black and white seascape, with a puffin, far out to sea in the distance, perched on a rock. On the facing page was a hare bolting into a mist. I was still taking it all in though. Loch Loman. And Susie was no fool. And full of sensitivity.

'I know, it's a bit close to home,' she said quietly, shutting the book. 'And I didn't mean to show you Paul. Just Martin. Because he lives literally round the corner.' She gazed away, abstractedly. 'Frida Kahlo had disabilities, I discovered. And Van Gogh. Matisse, later on. Anyway,' she shook herself inwardly, regrouping. 'It's become a bit of a passion. Here, have a few postcards.' She delved in her bag and handed me one of the poppy field, another of the sun streaming like silver through a beech wood. I looked at them in my hands.

'Can I hang on to the portfolio?' I said slowly.

She looked surprised. 'Sure. If you'd like to. But don't . . .' she hesitated. 'You know. Get distracted. By me. You have your own ideas for this place. Anyway. Aside from the art, what I really came to ask is if you and your husband would come for supper?

Maybe Thursday, since the weather's so nice? It's going to break after that, apparently.'

'We'd love to,' I said absently. We really would. And she didn't need to tell me where to come. I'd driven past the house already; it was vast. Hard to miss. Well, the gates and the lodge suggested as much. 'And are they all local?'

She knew where I was. 'Some are. Some are a bit further afield.' Her face collapsed a bit. 'And you want local artists, I get that. Quite a few are Scottish, actually. From the Highlands.' She gave a wan smile. 'I suppose I've used it as a bit of a crutch.'

'Clever you.' She looked perplexed. 'I mean – for finding something,' I explained. I wanted to add – I didn't. But she sensed it anyway.

'We were all so young,' she said softly, her eyes clouding. 'We didn't know how to react. But I felt responsible. Deeply. Felt I'd abdicated responsibility. Buggered off to London.'

'Oh! No – you shouldn't –'

'I'd been a mother to them,' she rushed on, ignoring me. 'Enjoyed it, for a bit. Probably felt a bit grown up. Important. Then I got distracted. Bored, even. And so suddenly I wasn't there. When Hamish needed me. I'd spoken to him the week before, I knew he was upset. I should have gone home that weekend. I knew he was going. That's why he rang, to ask if I was coming. I said I might. But instead, I went to a party.'

My mouth was dry, and my voice, when it came, was tight and unnatural-sounding. 'Oh, you have nothing to blame yourself for. Nothing at all.' We were silent for a moment. Then I picked up the portfolio and held it tight against my chest. 'Thank you for this. Let's chat on Thursday.'

Our eyes communed as we stood facing each other in the garden, hers, pale blue and luminous, but fringed too with lines of worry. It seemed the most natural thing, as she opened her arms, for me to walk into them, still clutching the book. She held me tight.

Hugh, as it turned out, had to stay in London a few more days, to have a meeting with an author on the Friday. When I rang to tell Susie, she said, 'Well, come anyway. I'd love to chat to you, and we'll have you both together another time.' And I'd love to chat to her too, I thought, as I put the phone down. And a little bit of me thought, and not all about art, either.

It put a slight spring in my step that Thursday, as I was going about my business, setting to in the barn, so that when Sally popped her head in, it was because she'd heard me singing. I was at the top of the stepladder down at the far end, trying to sort out the lighting.

'Look at you!' she called.

I turned, wobbling a bit on my ladder, to see her silhouetted in the open doorway. The sun was behind her and she made a statuesque figure: legs apart and hands on hips. Almost manly. Like something out of the O.K. Corral. 'Quite the curator!'

'Is it too bright?' I asked. I was vaguely wondering if I'd overdone it with the spotlights.

'No, it's great. What are you putting in that particular slot?'

I came down the ladder, wondering how to couch this. In the end I went for the truth, telling her about Susie's visit, and showing her just Martin's work to begin with, in the portfolio, on the table by the door. Her face was inscrutable. And hidden slightly as she looked down at the work.

'OK . . .' she said slowly. 'Well, of course, it's entirely up to you.'

'Meaning?' I asked anxiously.

She looked up. 'Well, do you want this to be about the art, or the biography?'

It took me a moment to work out what she meant. I felt myself inhale sharply. 'Can't it be both?'

'Really? A mixture?' She looked incredulous.

'No, no, of course not.' Why not? I thought.

'I mean, don't get me wrong. Martin's work is astonishing. Unbelievable. But . . .'

What? I didn't ask. I'd always been a bit nervous around Sally's intellect.

'Anyway.' She smiled, handed me back the book. 'I must get on. I've got a Zoom conference in half an hour, and I haven't prepared.'

I bet you have, I thought, as I watched her go, deciding that this was one of those occasions when she felt more like a sister-in-law than an old friend.

I decided to walk to dinner that evening; it was a balmy summer's night, positively tropical for England, and then I could walk back, with my torch, via the footpath across the fields. Perfect. I'd already worked out my route on an Ordnance Survey map, scrutinizing it carefully. I'd actually considered walking it first, doing a dummy run with Scribble, but obviously I didn't get round to it, which was a mistake. Because when I finally arrived that evening, on Susie's extremely grand doorstep, up a flight of stone steps to some double doors under a pillared canopy – one pillar of which I had to clutch, breathing hard – I looked a bit like Elizabeth Bennett, having just walked to see Jane at Netherfield. There had been unforeseen circumstances en route – namely a cattle field with a burst pipe that was positively boggy, plus a bramble patch that had completely overgrown the footpath. My metaphorical petticoats were muddy. It had also taken far longer than I'd imagined it would, so I'd speeded up at the end, literally jogged, which meant I was red-faced and sweaty when Susie came to the door. Added to which, of course, her drive was about half a mile long.

'Oh, great – we thought you'd got lost!' she

exclaimed, swinging the door wide. I was taken aback again by her beauty in the lamplight; with a spot of make-up and wearing a cornflower-blue shirt and white jeans she looked radiant.

'I stupidly walked,' I told her breathlessly. 'Thinking I'd like a drink. Took longer than I thought.' I could barely speak and my sentences were truncated into staccato-like utterings.

'Oh, you poor thing!' She ushered me into a huge black and white limestone hall with vast pillars holding it up and a sweeping stone staircase in the distance. 'Oh God, you probably thought you could go across country . . .' She gazed down at my espadrilles which were caked with mud, and I instantly took them off before I went any further in her ancestral hall. 'Did you go by the map? If so you won't be the first one to fall for that footpath ruse. That particular farmer is on our hit list; he's hopeless at clearing it, just lets it flood. Here – put these on.' She'd dashed to a wooden trunk under a portrait and opened it with a creak, pulling out a pair of shoes. 'Size five OK?'

'Perfect,' I agreed with relief, perching on a handy throne to squeeze into the canvas high tops she'd handed me. I was trying to look as if this was perfectly normal behaviour and nothing to be embarrassed about at all, when a very tall man – presumably her husband – appeared under an arch. He was wearing a colourful pink shirt with flamingos on it and was slightly portly – his stomach preceded him – but nevertheless very handsome. His grey hair was swept back off a high, patrician forehead and he had an arched, noble nose. Susie introduced him as Rupert as I grinned up.

'Hi!' I said, still struggling, like a child, to get the second shoe on – I'm actually a size six. Plus my feet were damp with bog water.

Luckily he was one of those men with generations of breeding and perfect manners and he understood my predicament in an instant; he knew exactly what to say to put me at my ease and made a joke of it, complimenting me, in his robust, thousand-acre voice, on 'having a *go* for heaven's sake' and 'being so jolly *plucky*', et cetera, as if I'd just scaled Everest. When I'd finally made it to my feet and held out my hand – but not before I'd wiped it on my skirt – he loomed down with a twinkle. 'And so what if there's a wardrobe malfunction, eh? Takes gumption.'

I began weakly and secretly to giggle. He was straight out of P. G. Wodehouse. I liked him instantly, though. I rolled my eyes. 'Well, it was pretty idiotic. Not a little nip across the fields as I'd stupidly thought.'

'Ah, but you can drink,' he said mischievously, looming again from his great height to tap his nose conspiratorially. 'That's the main thing. And Alan will run you back. He's lamping tonight.' Before I could respond to this enigmatic non sequitur he was genially steering me onwards. 'Come. A glass of cold champagne is called for. *Allons-y!*'

He put his hand on my back to guide me but, aware that my back was wet, I scampered joyfully ahead, so he didn't have to leave it there. This was going well; now I was an over-eager child in borrowed plimsolls who'd never been in a big house before and had broken into a run. Obviously I didn't know where I was going and the possibilities were endless, so I then had to double back as he and Susie went through an arch under the staircase, and then through a huge eau-de-nil drawing room – or possibly just a sitting room? – to emerge through some French windows on to a terrace. It seemed to stretch the entire length of the house and was full of the scent of roses and the sound of bees. Beyond was an immaculate sweeping lawn and the view of the park with peaceful grazing deer stretched away into the distance. I sighed with pleasure and beamed gratefully as Rupert, still chatting heroically, simultaneously poured me a deliciously cool, slim glass, letting me catch my breath and allowing me to ask only the most perfunctory of questions, as he told me about the place he'd inherited.

'It's a bit of a double-edged sword, actually,' he confided, sitting down and crossing his endless legs. 'I mean, obviously we're incredibly lucky to be here, but I had no idea how much work was involved.

Ask Susie, I was totally incompetent when we first got here.'

'Rubbish! You were brilliant!' She was rushing to pull around a large wicker armchair. He got up quickly and helped her.

'Well, hardly.' He sat down again. 'I didn't know an ear of wheat from a grain of barley, or one end of a cow from the other. Don't know what I'd been doing with my childhood,' he said ruefully, 'let alone my adolescence. Aside from racing motorbikes and propping up the bar at the local, obviously,' he twinkled. 'Anyway, I was steeped in ignorance and just thought the whole farming thing would slot into place, come naturally after the army – and my father had warned me it wouldn't. In the end he sat quietly by and watched me cock it up quite comprehensively. He obviously took the view that I'd find out soon enough that I did indeed need to go to agricultural college as he'd bally well told me I should.' He made a face. 'I found out the hard way. After a year of getting it completely wrong – my farm manager with his head in his hands by now – off I finally trotted to Cirencester, trying to ignore my grinning pa. He and Ma moved back in from the Dower House, and Susie and I took another few years before we actually moved in. But we got there in the end, didn't we, darling?' He turned to smile at her. Then leaned forward abruptly. 'Oh, but even *then* it wasn't all plain sailing. Let me tell you what I did with the *pigs*

when we first got here. Did you know they eat literally everything under the sun? No? Well, they do,
and I left my ruddy coat *and* my wallet . . .'

And on he chatted, amusingly, easily, in his bari-
tone voice, letting me sip my champagne and
recover, so that I couldn't help but compare him to
Hugh, who was always a bit ill at ease when people
first arrived. Not later on. And not if he knew them
well, like the other night. But if he didn't, he went a
bit silent. It was me who leapt around making them
feel comfortable, chatting and smiling and generally
doing jazz hands. It was nice to be in the passenger
seat for once.

And it was easy to see how this good-looking
couple had got together, I thought, imagining him
as one of the handsome soldiers Susie had told us
about that day in the kitchen in Scotland, swinging
her emerald-green fake Chanel pumps – which I'd
immediately rushed out and bought – without a
care in the world. I wondered if she'd met him
before or after Hamish died?

'After,' she told me, when Rupert went off to tend
the barbecue on the lawn, swearing loudly about it
being too bloody *hot*, squirting water from a squeezy
bottle on it. 'And I was in a terrible state. I hadn't
wanted to go back to London at all, but Daddy had
made me after a few weeks. He said it would be
good for me. Also there was the small matter of a
job to return to, plus a flat to pay for. But I didn't go

out. Just stayed in the flat every night. Eventually a friend persuaded me to go to a drinks party with her, and Rupert was there. I was rotten company. But for some reason he wasn't put off. I was determined the last thing I needed was to fall in love, but little by little, he persuaded me that actually, it was the very thing I did need. I don't know what I'd have done without him. And there were plenty of much prettier, far more charismatic girls vying for his attention; there was no reason for him to be scraping this misery guts off the floor, making me go out to restaurants with him. Then eventually, persuading me to marry him.'

I smiled. Personally I could think of many reasons. Susie was one of those lovely, warm, open-hearted girls who tell you everything about themselves immediately. The whole shooting match plastered all over her sleeve. Any man would have trouble resisting her.

'And Daddy liked him too. Not that I needed any more persuading, but when I finally took him home, it just sort of worked. Everything just slotted into place. And he couldn't have been more different to Rory – very traditional, which Rory isn't – but funnily enough, they got on like a house on fire too.'

The mention of his name was sufficient to set my heart racing, but if that wasn't enough, the man himself – and don't kid yourself when I'd accepted the invitation I hadn't wondered if he might be there – hove into view. Suddenly I was the one with the house on fire. In the middle distance I could make out Rory, coming through the parkland towards us. He was slowly making his way in that familiar, loose-limbed, easy manner, wearing jeans and a baggy white shirt. I averted my eyes, knowing my face was burning. Rupert was giving his glowing coals another squirt with his water bottle, and as I turned my gaze on to him instead of the mirage appearing like Mr Darcy from the lake, I wondered if before the evening was out, I might need to borrow his bottle?

11

In the event, once I'd relaxed and calmed down a
bit – and actually it took Rory a while to walk
through the park, so time was for once on my side –
we had a very pleasant evening. It was just the four
of us and we ate on the terrace in the golden syrup
of the evening sun, the conversation flowing easily.
There were many things to talk about, after all.
Rory's exhibition for one, my move to the country
from London for another – was it everything I
expected it to be? My art barn was obviously high
on the agenda too. Susie was keen to rope her
brother into telling me that, although one or two of
her artists might sit well amongst the others since
they were from around here, she felt she'd slightly
ambushed me the other day, and I absolutely
shouldn't include the ones who were further afield,
which, as a matter of fact, I'd already decided, rather
eagerly, I might.

'I think Susie's right, actually,' Rory said slowly.
'I'd keep to your original script of local artists, if I
was you. And include those of Susie's who you like
and who fit that brief. Why not just show a couple
whose work you like who live close by?'

The trouble was, I was really excited about doing it the way Susie did it. Since her visit a few days ago, I'd felt a new passion and excitement for the project that took it to another level. It was something I hadn't felt for years. Not since the days of setting up my own little wedding dress business, but I'd slightly grown out of that, unless it was for Ella, of course. And I knew too this new approach was filling a gaping hole as it had done for Susie; that it felt like some kind of atonement. Penitence, perhaps. I also wondered why she hadn't done it already with this vast house.

'I didn't think of it,' she said simply. 'These days artists promote themselves on Instagram, or through online galleries. I hadn't thought of gathering them all together in one space.'

There was a silence and I wondered if there was indeed a need for that sort of gathering, these days. It seemed to hang unspoken in the air.

'It's definitely necessary,' Rory knew what I was thinking. 'To hang art physically, I mean. Just as physical books are necessary. It's a tangible thing, creatively. You don't get the whole experience without all the senses being involved. At least in my view.'

'There speaks the practitioner,' smiled his sister.

'Yes,' I agreed, 'I get that.' I hesitated. 'But on reflection, I think you may be right about not taking all your artists,' I said slowly. 'Because if I'm honest, the thing is, I'd be doing it for me, so . . .' I trailed off.

'There's nothing wrong with that sort of motivation,' said Rupert gently. 'It helped Suze too, which is surely a good thing. And after all, it's your barn. If you want to change tack, why not? But championing local talent is a completely splendid thing to do, you know.'

I gazed into his kind eyes, torn. Finally I nodded. 'Yes, you're right. I'll stick to plan A. And go and see the artists I like who happen to live in the county. Or next door,' I added quickly. I'd pored over the portfolio last night and no way was I giving up that amazing girl in Dorset who painted shadows so beautifully, flitting across the canvas like spirits.

I smiled decisively at them and they smiled back in agreement and I felt relaxed and happy to be amongst these generous people. Rupert was new to me, of course, but I'd forgotten how lovely the rest of Hamish's family were, or tried to forget, for obvious reasons. I didn't think it was my place to know any of them any more. I wondered, rather disloyally, how Hugh would fit in. He was so reserved, kept people at a distance, was less likely to say what he thought, for fear of causing offence. Was offence really the worst thing in the world? Getting him to talk about feelings was like trying to force open a clam, the manifest struggle involved causing physical pain on his face. The little boy at boarding school who'd written to his parents begging them to take him home, saying he'd sat on the steps at lunch time waiting for their car to come up the drive, had put up strong defences since then. Oh, I'd seen the letters. Clem had kept them, laughed as she'd shown them to me.

'What does your husband think about it?' asked Susie, passing me the tomato salad. I came to, aware that Rory was watching me keenly.

'Oh, he's totally up for it. He's away quite a lot, so I think he'd like me to be busy.' Why had I said that? He was away a bit, not a lot. This week was an exception. I felt myself redden as I helped myself to the tomatoes, hoping they didn't clash with my face. But Susie didn't seem to notice.

'Rupert likes me to be busy too. And now I've got the art thing under way, I'm doing flowers – just for friends' parties, the local church – but I love it. I did a floristry course which I adored. It's something different, plus I think change is good. And I need to keep busy or I bother the children too much, empty nest and all that!'

'Oh, me too! I agreed. 'Tell me about it. Or actually, tell me about them. I saw some photos on the way in, how many have you got?'

It turned out they had two boys, like me, and they asked about mine. I told them about my wedding plans – well, Ella's: a bucolic affair, which suited me down to the ground, and they told me their eldest was getting married too, but in London, so they wouldn't have much to do with it. I wondered why they weren't doing it here, in this amazing house, but didn't like to ask.

'I've offered to host it, obviously,' said Susie, and not for the first time I realized I'd missed this sort of frankness. Knowing what I wanted to ask and saying it for me. 'But Annie wants to do it where she grew up, at her parish church in Barnes, and I respect that.'

So did I. And good for Annie, for not being taken over by a rich, grand family, sucked in. Not that the Petridises had done that, but . . . well, yes, a bit. I'd always known that Clem liked the fact I was a bit of a lame duck on the domestic front. That they could envelop me. Incorporate me. Too pejorative, perhaps. Welcome me. And every Christmas was spent with the Petridis family, obviously. Not least because by about September my mother would announce she was spending Christmas with her friend Sheila in Deal. But still, I could have made an exception one year, said we'd come with her, drive her down to Deal, stay nearby in a hotel if needs be. I'd never met Sheila. A science teacher, apparently. Unmarried. Would my mother have wanted that? Probably not, but I could have suggested it. Except, I'd loved the huge, jolly Petridis Christmas, something I'd never had before. Mine had been very quiet, just Mum and me. But she did make an effort; a small tree on a table, one of the many bookshelves cleared of books, and, in their place, the Christmas treats: a bowl of satsumas, a long thin carton of figs which neither of us ate, a round wooden box of Turkish Delight (likewise) and a small bowl of Quality Street. A few presents in a pillow case were at the end of my bed which I opened on my own, then a walk, and then church, which was always a revelation. Church, I mean. My mother seemed to know people. Lots of them. People smiled at her, said Happy Christmas. Only briefly, and she was very brief with her own greetings back, but still. Then a small turkey, crackers, another walk, *The Morecambe and Wise Show* and bed.

At the Petridises there were lots of people round the dining-room table, Tom and Lou down from Scotland, Polly and Kit, all the cousins, games, charades, laughter, a towering Christmas tree cut from the woods and dragged down the hill, and it went on for days. Clem had never asked my mother. Not that she'd have come, of course. But still. Would I still love a Petridis Christmas, even if Clem and Yanni were together? Probably not, I realized with a start.

Susie was clearing plates, chatting away about planting a cutting garden for her flowers, so I got to my feet and went inside to help her with the pudding.

After a delicious panna cotta we had some coffee, and Susie was just pouring out some more, when I put a hand on her arm. It was late, and I really must be getting back. And then of course Rupert got to his feet and said he'd get Alan, who turned out to be the gamekeeper, out in the fields anyway in his Land Rover keeping foxes at bay, and I said, oh no, please don't bother Alan, he's clearly busy, and then, naturally, the inevitable happened and Rory offered to walk me home.

'No, really, I'll be fine,' I laughed, kissing Rupert goodbye as we all got to our feet, not daring to look at Rory.

'I'd run you myself,' Rupert told me, holding my shoulders as he smiled down at me from his great height, 'but I'm far too pissed. It's been far too jolly an evening for me to get behind the wheel. Let Rory walk you. But don't go across country – it's perilous, you'll fall. Go down the lanes.'

So, of course, we did. And luckily it was dark so he couldn't see my cheeks, ridiculously flushed, as we wound our way down the silent lanes in the still, balmy night air, my espadrilles swinging from a bag on my arm, the moon hanging pendulously above us like a great lantern, shimmering, lighting the way, together with the light, we realized, from my own house. It was nestled deep in the adjacent valley, guiding us, like a beacon.

We spoke of Hamish that night, in the dark, and I told him what Susie had said. About her guilt. Which of course he already knew. And I told him of mine for not being there either, and he spoke of his, but neither of us spoke of the real reason for that guilt. Rory said he was actually the one who should have been with him, not Susie, because he'd been home that weekend, at the house. Hamish had asked him to come fishing with him, but it was late, and he couldn't be bothered. There was a football match on the telly. I told him I'd had an argument with him over Jane having a clandestine relationship with Lance, and how he'd disapproved, and at that moment, we did glance at one another in the dark, knowing that we too had been starting an embryonic, deceitful relationship, involving, as it did now, purely eyes and privately wildly beating hearts, but still, it was there. Twenty-eight years on, I thought in amazement as I averted my eyes to my borrowed canvas shoes. Still there, after twenty-eight years. A silence descended like an invisible cloud, floating down from the sky. We walked along under it, enveloped in it. When we finally got to the end of my drive and said goodnight, it was awkward, because neither of us could look at each other. We settled on a bear hug, my eyes wide and wild into his shoulder, and a laugh, but it was forced and cracked. And then he turned and walked away.

It didn't help, of course, I thought, as I slowly climbed the stairs to bed in the empty house, that he was single. I paused on the landing at the window. Stared out at the moon, limpid in the inky sky. Would it have been any different if he'd been there tonight with a beautiful wife? Talking of his own adult children, their marriage plans? I liked to think so but I wasn't certain it would.

The following morning, I realized with a jolt that of course the house wasn't empty. Sally was here. I heard her in the garden, outside my bedroom window. When I got out of bed and looked out, she was weeding the herbaceous border on the other side of the lawn, which I hadn't quite got to yet. I gazed down. Oh, right. I drew my head back sharply. Was that OK? I mean, my border, surely? But actually, it was very helpful, I decided, as I pulled on my dressing gown. And her family home. And the *Alchemilla mollis*, which were my absolute favourite, were about to be swamped by the rather sharp pink geranium I wasn't so fond of. It needed attention.

As I came down the back stairs, the old shepherds' passage, into the kitchen, she was just breezing in through the back door, her cheeks pink, wearing her gardening gloves.

'Morning!' she said cheerily, crossing to the sink. 'I took quite a lot of the *Alchemilla mollis* out,' she told me over her shoulder. 'It was drowning Mum's lovely pink geranium.'

I opened my mouth to protest. Shut it again. Oh. Right. But why was she in my kitchen? Didn't she have one of her own?

'I thought I'd separate some of those Michaelmas

daisies, don't you think? Just came in to borrow a trowel.' She was taking her gloves off at the sink.

'It's in the greenhouse,' I told her.

'No, not that one, the one Mum used to keep under the sink. Ah, here it is.' She'd crouched down, ferreted around in the cupboard and found it. 'She said Bob used to hide it because they both liked its sharp edges. So she kept it in here.' Bob was the gardener who still came once a week. But now she was moving to the coffee machine on the counter, reaching up for a mug in the cupboard and putting it underneath. 'I must remember to buy another one of these. That's the trouble with having two houses, you need to duplicate everything! First-world problem, of course.'

'Of course,' I said as she made a cappuccino.

She turned. 'You don't mind, do you?'

'Not at all! God, help yourself.'

Obviously this should have been my moment to set a few ground rules. To clear my throat and say – well actually, Sally . . .

Instead, we had a pleasant breakfast together. She made toast while I nipped up and got dressed, and when I came down we chatted at the table. And then, at her invitation, I went down to see what she'd done in the cottage. She'd hung a long row of framed silhouettes on the wall above the gallery, put some photos around the place, and filled vases with flowers. She'd also hung a sweep of faded red velvet over the front door, on a pole. It looked cosier and I told her so. And then, I thought, she'd stay there and get on with some work, or whatever it was she had to do, while I went back to my house, but she didn't. She came back with me, and helped herself to another coffee. As she turned away from the machine, she casually asked what I'd got up to last night. Said she'd heard me come in.

'Oh, I went to the Alexanders' for dinner. Susie invited me. Stupidly I walked, thinking it was much closer than it was. Rory walked me back.' Full disclosure. Why not?

She stared at me from across the room. I couldn't read her eyes. Finally she spoke. 'Blimey, look at you. Only been here five minutes and already you're having dinner at the hall!' There was more than an edge to her voice.

'Hardly dinner, it was just a low-key barbecue.'

'Right.' Her eyes danced now but I didn't like the energy or the brightness of them. 'Did you talk about Hamish?'

I felt myself getting angry. This was surely none of her business, and very, very private to me. I never spoke about Hamish.

'No,' I said shortly. 'We didn't.'

She rolled her eyes. 'So-rry. I just thought – you know. It's been so long now and –'

'Sally, I'm really sorry, but I'm going to have to

get on. I've got some artists to ring and I said I'd talk to Ella about flowers for the wedding.'

'Sure,' she said lightly. But it was the lightness of metal. 'And I've got work to do too. I was just going. I just didn't want you to feel lonely here, I know you're not used to the country. But clearly, you're not.'

There was a silence. Sally gathered up her phone and tucked it in her pocket. Then she flashed me a look, turned on her heel, and left.

As I crossed to the sink and watched her walk back to the cottage through the window, it occurred to me that we'd effectively had a row, which was not a good start. I breathed in deeply. Let it out slowly. Then I went to gather the rest of the breakfast things from the table and took them to the sink to wash up. Instead of running the tap, though, I clung on to the edge of the white porcelain Butler sink, the type I'd never seen before I first came to this house when I was young, having grown up with stainless steel. With a plastic bowl inside. I shut my eyes tight. It was a while before I opened them again and, when I did, I realized my knuckles were white.

12

The next time I saw Sally was a couple of days later. Hugh was back by now and they'd both come to find me in the barn. I'd just said goodbye to a lovely artist who was going to exhibit a couple of small oils: a still life of overblown roses in a vase, and some lemons on a blue-and-white-checked tablecloth. He'd lost his right hand in a threshing accident and had learnt to paint with his left. The lemons were beautiful, very Tuscan and bright; I quite wanted them in my bedroom. Sally was smiling as she came in and so was I, thrilled to have secured him.

'Look who I found skulking around in her cottage about to have a solitary lunch,' Hugh said with a grin. 'I told her I'd bought far too much crab so she's joining us for sandwiches.'

'Excellent,' I beamed, pleased that she looked so smiley. 'And a glass of something. I've just had a major coup so I'm determined to celebrate.'

'An artist?' she asked, going across to the far wall to peer at the canvases which were propped against it. She squatted down on her haunches to take a closer look.

'Yes, Josh Malone. He's exhibited at the Saatchi Gallery. Quite a catch.'

She stared at the lemons. 'Online, I presume?'

'Sorry?'

'They have an online gallery. This won't have been in Duke of York Square.'

'Oh. I don't know.'

She straightened up. Smiled. 'You like this figurative stuff, don't you?' Something about her tone suggested I shouldn't.

'Don't you?'

She shrugged. 'Well, if you've only gone for one, that's fine!'

'Two. So far.'

'Come on,' Hugh rubbed his hands together. 'We came to drag you away. I'm starving.'

Back at the house, Hugh made the sandwiches and I found the end of a bottle of rosé in the fridge and we had lunch on the terrace in the sunshine. And as a matter of fact, after giving it some thought, I decided I was grateful to Sally. I'd googled 'figurative' in the loo. 'The type of art where the subject matter is recognizable from the real world.' Initially I'd pocketed my phone with a snort of derision. What – as opposed to having no idea what it is? But then I hesitated; because actually, I must remember not to get too carried away with my accessible art. Be a bit more edgy. As I went back outside and we carried on chatting, I determined I'd ring Oscar

Burnett, an artist who'd sent me his portfolio, but whose very aggressive brush strokes and bold use of colour I'd been rather daunted by. Sally had walked into the barn when I'd been flicking through his work and said he was good. I'd give him a ring. When she got up to go she gave my shoulders a quick squeeze as she walked behind my chair, which pleased me ridiculously. I felt so much tension relax inside me.

'Shall we have a proper lunch next week?' I asked her, turning in my seat. 'You know, go out to a pub, get Jane along?'

'Yes, good idea. Although maybe the following one. Jane and I had lunch on Tuesday, so she may feel she's had enough of me!'

'Oh . . . right.' They'd had lunch? Without me. This felt like being back in the playground. Jane was my best friend and I'd just moved down here. I *was* back in the playground. Do grow up. 'Yes, great. And actually, I've got so much to do – we'll make it later on.'

She shrugged. 'Whenever.'

I watched her go. Realized my breathing was a bit shallow. When had I last felt like this? So full of dread? A bit sick? It was something I was familiar with but hadn't experienced for years. Ah yes. Not since waking up in the morning, opening my eyes in my little attic bedroom and thinking – what's it going to be like today? What's *she* going to be like today? My mother. Someone I couldn't reach. Someone I couldn't reason with. Couldn't break down in tears and plead to – please love me, it'll be fine, honestly. She'd look incredulous. Brush me aside. In the end, I couldn't wait to walk away from that chilly, hostile house. And now I'd walked into another.

Don't ask me why, but the following day, I went to see Yanni. Hugh was working on his manuscript and I popped my head into the study and said I was going to Covington, to see an artist.

He turned from his desk which faced the window. 'Have fun.' He smiled.

'Will do.' And then, on an impulse, I nipped across the room and dropped a kiss on his cheek.

He looked surprised. 'What's that for?'

'Can't I kiss my husband?'

'As much as you like.' He grinned and went back to his work.

The drive to the coast was long and winding and I had to concentrate like mad on my app as it directed me, so I didn't have much time to think, which was a good thing. When I arrived on the outskirts of the little coastal town, the road suddenly plunged down from the top of the hill towards the sea, past the usual cluster of white seaside bungalows, then the more elegant and formal Edwardian villas, and finally, to the tiny cottages around the bay. I realized

I had no idea if Yanni would even be in. Or indeed, if he was, if he'd be pleased to see me. I've never been mad about impromptu visitors myself, but I hadn't wanted to text him because . . . well, because I'd wanted to see him alone. And he might have suggested Hugh came with me. I needn't have worried though, because Yanni was delighted. After I'd parked in one of the streets behind his house and then walked around to the row of Neapolitan ice cream-coloured cottages overlooking the harbour, making for the pale green one on the end, I saw him. He was standing on his front doorstep brushing sand off a pair of deck shoes. He looked around at my approach, stared for a moment as if in disbelief. Then his hand shot up in the air in greeting. He beamed expansively.

'Darling!' he bellowed for all the world to hear. 'How lovely!'

Oh God, I'd forgotten how much I adored Yanni. I hastened towards him along the sea wall. I flew through the garden gate and then we fell into each other's arms, laughing. My darling, emotional, effervescent father-in-law.

'What you doing here? Why you not tell me you come?' he demanded, smothering me in kisses, rubbing my cheeks raw with his sandpaper stubble. He held me at arm's length, the better to see my face, his brown eyes scanning it eagerly. They were still as bright and sparkling as ever.

'Thought I'd surprise you!' I laughed.

'You did! The best surprise. And you look gorgeous as ever.' He was still inspecting me. 'Gorgeous!' he declared. 'Come. Some coffee? Come, inside, while I make it. Then we sit outside and you tell me all – I want to know everything.'

He hastened into his cottage and I followed, plunging from the bright sunlight into the cool shade of the sitting room, which I noticed he'd painted a cheerful primrose yellow, and then into the little kitchen, which had a stable door thrown open to the back garden. He'd painted the kitchen too, a cool modern grey this time, which was divine. I wanted to ask what colour it was, it would look lovely in Hugh's dark red study, brighten it up a bit, but there wasn't the slightest opportunity because Yanni did not draw breath. He was talking in rapid quick-fire sentences as he brewed some typically strong coffee, not waiting for my answers, and indeed answering for me when I tried to respond.

'You in the house? You like it? Of course you do. How could you not? It's a special house. You happy there? Of course you are. You always a happy person. And thank God. Thank God, it's *you* there, the perfect person. Was not nice to think of strangers having it, but family is good. Family is perfect. The best solution – my solution, by the way, if anyone interested. But they not. And Hugh? He happy? He like it?'

Yes, Hugh was happy, I managed to tell him. Enjoying the peace and quiet and the countryside, and managing everything remotely, work wise, with the occasional dart to London.

'Good, good.' He turned from the whirring cacophony of his machine to beam at me, his tanned face seeming to almost crack with delight. 'And you here! You made it! You come to see Yanni today of all days, which is perfect! Come.'

He poured the steaming liquid and bustled past me, carrying the two brimming cups of coffee, leading me back to the front garden which overlooked the bay. He set the cups down on a round wrought-iron table, pulling out a chair for me, then beamed at me again as he waited for me to sit, and I was so pleased, so relieved, because the last time I'd seen Yanni, he'd been crying. It was that time I'd been with Hugh, and as we'd gone inside to collect our things – my handbag, Hugh's car keys – Yanni had sat down on the sofa and burst into tears. He'd really sobbed, with his wet face in his hands, saying his life was over. Ended. That he'd only ever loved one woman, truly, in his whole life, and that she'd broken his heart. His home had gone, his children – even though, as Hugh had pointed out, hovering nervously as I held Yanni tightly, beside him on the sofa, his children were in their fifties and had gone long ago. But, no, he wouldn't listen. No. Everyone had gone. Left him. His life was over. *Tetelestai.*

I think it was why I hadn't been to see him since, I was so scared of his sadness. Scared of being similarly infected? I didn't know, but it had been wrong of me, and wholly untypical. Hugh said I rushed in far too much, where angels feared to tread. That's where Emma goes, he'd tell people with a smile. He said I wanted to fix people, when sometimes they couldn't be fixed. Or needed time to do it on their own, to mend themselves. In some half-formed way I'd think, well, maybe I don't mind being compared to an angel, fluttering in to help, but then one day the rest of the quote had dawned: about fools. So on this particular occasion, I'd held back. And perhaps Hugh had been right. Because now, here Yanni was, positively bouncing around his dear little cottage, not depressed at all, or unable to cope, as he'd told us that day between sobs. In fact, he was decidedly buoyant. He was slimmer, too, and Yanni was a big man – but there was much less of him. Less tummy. As we sat down in the sunshine and he reached to squeeze my hand, I told him so.

'You look great, Yanni, really terrific. What's happened? You're like a new man. I've never seen you so chipper.'

'Chipper? Chipper? I more than chipper. I in seventh, maybe eighth heaven! So beautiful here, you see?' He swept his hand expansively around the bay which was indeed picturesque: the green hills loomed in the background and the harbour bobbed with anchored boats – pink, red and green – some with sails, some motor boats. Yanni was a very good sailor, or had been in his day.

'And all my new friends are here, you see? They here too. All my neighbours, and they all sit out here, looking, admiring the view. And we chat. People!' he exclaimed. 'Not vegetables,' he spat derisively. 'Or sheep, or cows, eh? People!' He waved to his next-door neighbours, a middle-aged couple, who were indeed sitting outside like us, warming their hands on their mugs, enjoying the sunshine. 'Bess, Lennie – you good?' he hollered, half standing up, one hand cupping his mouth.

'Really well thanks, Yanni, and you?' They waved cheerily back.

'Never better! And this my daughter-in-law, Emma. She come to see me, you see? Look how beautiful she is!'

I laughed as they could do nothing other than nod their agreement, laughing as I rolled my eyes in mock embarrassment.

'And Clem, you know?' He sat down, lowering his voice as Bess and Lennie went back to their newspapers and their coffee. 'She no like people. Not really. Except her family. And even then . . .' He made a dubious face. Gave an expansive shrug. 'She like to be on her own, eh? Self-contained, remote. Well, you know that. Of course you do. Why I tell you about her? You know. And all my life, all my married life, I go along with it, because I love her. But it's not me, you know? At heart? Here?' He made a fist and put it to his chest, his brown eyes appealing to me earnestly, searching mine. And it was so exactly what I'd come to talk to him about that it took my breath away for a moment.

'Yes, I do know, Yanni,' I said softly.

'And when I meet her, in London, I so Greek, you know? And proud of it, naturally. But no English in those days. She like that, of course. Yanni was different. Not like her usual crowd. Not that she really had a crowd. She always the cat to walk its own path. And she so cool, and sophisticated and glamorous – I was – how you say? – bowled over by her. In her thrall, as you say. And I stay that way for so many years, I love her so much.' His eyes, for a moment, filled ominously. But then he blinked, and they hardened determinedly. 'But not now,' he said fiercely. 'Now, I know I need to be true to myself, to my own needs and pleasures, eh? And, please God, I haven't left it too late. But I only seventy-eight, you know? We both students when we met, when we had Hugh. I still young now, I reckon!'

He looked it too. About ten years younger than when I last saw him, to be honest. And to complement the weight loss he was wearing a natty pair of navy shorts and a pink polo shirt and he was very brown. He was still a good-looking man with a full head of hair.

'So – you mean, you're not sorry she's gone?'

'Sorry?' He put his mug down in astonishment. 'No, darling, best thing that ever happened. And now it has gone tits up with the jockey, and also –' he lowered his voice conspiratorially – 'I hear, with some young antique dealer in London, you know that? You hear that? Some other chap too?'

'Has it? Gone tits up?' Polly had rung me recently and said she thought there was another man on the scene, and that he was very young. She'd been a bit distressed. About thirty years her mother's junior, she'd thought. I hadn't told Hugh.

'So Polly say. Maybe he too realize she not the lady of the manor? She just come with all the airs and graces, but none of the money.' He made a disgusted face. 'She cold, too, you know?'

I did know. Aloof. Controlled. How I would like to be, I'd once erroneously thought.

'Polly say she come running back soon, after this latest bruising, but Yanni know better. She too proud. And I not have her anyway, even if she did. I won't ever have her back. Polly wish I would, but you know Polly.' He shrugged.

I did. Warm. Emotional. Like her father. And Tom, too, always spilling the beans, sometimes saying things he shouldn't, getting it wrong. Both of them were like Yanni. Sally was definitely like her mother. And Hugh? I'd always known he was like Clem and had admired him for his dignity, his restraint, but as we'd got older, I'd hoped for more of Yanni. Because, of course, the two parents together were the perfect combination. The ultimate melting pot. But Hugh had actually become even more self-contained, even happier in his own skin. Occasionally I was scared for our later life together. The silences. For some reason I didn't like sitting in separate rooms in the country; the rooms were much larger and it was too far away. So I'd forfeit *Bake Off*, or something I'd usually watch, to sit with him. Occasionally I'd look up from sewing Ella's dress, embroidering intricately under the brightest lamp I could find, or feeding yards of tulle through my machine at the table, to glance at him as he read some huge tome on Wellington. Then I'd sigh inwardly and go back to my work.

In London, the children had been around, had often popped in – Sunday lunch, midweek suppers, they'd brought their girlfriends. But now they were about to have their own families. So it was just me and Hugh. With his classical music playing softly in the background, the soundtrack to our lives. No friends down the road, or round the corner as they had been in Chiswick, because there was no road. Just a long drive and a quiet lane. Susie had been kind, but she was very much established, had thousands of friends. Jane, of course. And Sally. I tried not to think about their lunch. Of course they'd talked about me, naturally they had. I licked my lips which were strangely dry, but then that was probably the sea air. The salt. I stared out at a little pink boat, bobbing about in the harbour.

'Sally's like her mother, don't you think?' I asked tentatively.

Yanni looked at me. 'You mean Sally's a bitch.'

'Well, no, I –'

'Yes, she is, for sure. Like her mother.'

'But not Polly and Tom.'

'No. For certain, no. They more like me.'

'Yes.'

The last child hung unspoken in the air. Yanni opened his mouth to speak, never one to hold back, and I longed to hear what he had to say, when suddenly, the shape of his mouth changed; the cipher became a delighted smile and he got to his feet, glowing.

'Larissa!' he boomed into the distance. He waved both arms madly above his head like someone bringing in a plane. I turned in my seat. Coming along the harbour wall on the narrow pavement opposite, was a very attractive dark-haired woman. She was wearing a short navy skirt and had slim, tanned legs. At her heels trotted a tiny Yorkshire Terrier on a lead and she was wearing huge Jackie O sunglasses. Yanni rushed to open the gate and flung it wide.

'You not tell me you were coming!' he roared indignantly.

She laughed, shaking back her mane of hair, and as she took off her sunglasses and gave him a dazzling smile, I saw that she was not as young as I'd imagined. There were laughter lines around her eyes and mouth – she was probably in her late sixties.

'I thought I'd surprise you, but I see you've already got company!' It was said pleasantly, with no edge to her voice, as she turned her smile on me. Yanni steered her into the garden, ushering her in with his arm.

'Larissa,' he said excitedly, 'this my daughter-in-law, Emma, the one I tell you about. The one I adore as if she was my own. Who is married my eldest boy, Hugh. And this, Emma,' he looked at me proudly then puffed out his chest and stood up straight. He turned back to Larissa. 'This my most gorgeous, my most lovely girlfriend, my Larissa.'

He took both her hands in his and gazed at her as she smiled back, and then they kissed briefly, on the lips. Yanni looked as if he was going to burst out of his pink polo shirt as they stood together in the sunshine, like a couple making vows, I thought. Their eyes were dancing, their faces full of happiness.

13

I looked on, amazed. This was a very attractive woman. But then, I was not so amazed. Because actually, Yanni was a very attractive man. Plus, he was great fun, and he was loving, and also – and I know it shouldn't matter – he was solvent. Not rolling in it, but his half share of the house had enabled him to buy this idyllic seaside cottage. And Yanni still worked. He wrote a weekly column and also most of the obituaries for *Kathimerini*, the Greek equivalent of *The Times*, had done for years. In the very early days he'd split his time between London and Athens, but these days, of course, he could be wherever he liked and just file his copy remotely, plus he covered more UK stories, which meant he didn't have to travel so much. He didn't earn a fortune, but it kept him afloat. And, more than that, it kept him vital, busy and interested, which in turn, made him *interesting*. He knew everyone in Greece, or, as he'd tell me mournfully, used to. Now many were dead, or, as he'd add gleefully, recovering his sparkle, dying, which gave him more to write about.

Larissa was sitting down as Yanni rushed to push in her chair, crossing her shiny brown knees which were about the size of my knuckles, and swinging a twinkly white trainer. She had quite a lot of twinkles going on one way or another: rhinestones on her white belt and on her handbag, but also in her eyes, as she took both of my hands in hers and told me she knew all about me.

'You the one Yanni talks about,' she confided softly, as Yanni bustled off to get her a cup of coffee. 'You and Polly, the ones he loves so much.' Her voice was husky, low and heavily accented, and I wondered if she too was Greek.

'No, I'm from Naples,' she told me when I asked. She released my hands and sat back, lighting a cigarette. 'I came over here ten years ago when my husband ran off with my tramp of a best friend and I liked it so much I stayed. I have a boutique in town, you know? Italian clothes only – you know it? Next to the deli, at the top of the hill – Rossa e Verde?'

I said I didn't know it because I didn't know the area but I'd be sure to pay it a visit. I was trying hard not to smile because she reminded me so much of Yanni, her speech, her mannerisms, colouring – everything.

'Do that.' She wagged a finger. 'Visit. You come in, and I make sure you get a bargain.' She winked conspiratorially. 'And I like the people here too,' she went on contemplatively. 'They are friendly on the whole, but I didn't meet anyone I connected with properly until I met Yanni.' She smiled up into his eyes as he delivered her strong black coffee. He gazed adoringly back. 'But then, of course, he's not English, you know?'

I did know. And it didn't surprise me at all that these two open-hearted, hot-blooded – and no doubt hot-tempered – types had made a connection. I had a feeling there might be quite a lot of drinking, smoking and passing out in deckchairs to complement the passion, but nonetheless, love and desire and tenderness clearly dwelt in this house. I suppose it only surprised me now how long Yanni had lasted with Clem. And yet, if you'd asked me a year ago, I'd have lit up and told you they were the ideal couple. That opposites attract and they were the perfect foil for one another. That they were yin and yang. But here were two yangs. I tried not to think of myself again. Knew, in my heart, I was only trying to rationalize something unnamed and dreadful, because I'd met Rory again. That I mustn't try to justify anything I might be feeling because of the juxtaposition of the two people before me. The warmth that was emanating from them, creating more of a greenhouse than a garden, was entirely their business, and nothing to do with me at all. Conclusions should not be drawn.

Larissa was asking me about Hugh, if he was happy, and I answered as I'd answered Yanni, that he liked the peace and the countryside, trying not to say – the silence. Trying not to feel panicky, resentful. I wondered, not for the first time, why he hadn't come to see his father on his own, since our first visit – without the rushing-in fool. Why hadn't I suggested it, you might think? Because, after all these years, I knew what he'd say. Or wouldn't. He'd look pained and uncomfortable and at length stutter something about being sure his father would call and ask him to visit in his own good time. Something so repressed and English and always with the slight suggestion that they weren't that sort of family and when would I understand that? Well, half of them were. And half of them weren't.

I wondered about my own sons. More like me, I decided. Nico, definitely, was full of emotion. Teddy, though, had a touch of Hugh's reserve – less so since he'd met Ella, who I knew made him talk. Larissa was asking me about them now, and so I told her that Nico was in New York, really happy with his new girlfriend and loving the life out there, and Teddy was about to get married. She sat up straight: clasped her heavily jewelled hands on her shiny brown knees with glee.

'A wedding? Really? At home, with you?'

'Yes, because Ella's family live in America.'

'So I help you,' she said determinedly. 'You will need help, for sure. You have lovely country wedding here and I help you with flowers, the food, all sorts.'

Ordinarily, I'd revert to the vocabulary of Hugh's

wife: smile and say how lovely, but it was all in hand, thank you, then change the subject. But there was something intoxicating about her enthusiasm, and I was so grateful for the offer that I looked into her keen, shining brown eyes and thought – why not?

'D'you know, I think I'd love that,' I said slowly. 'Ella doesn't want anything big, only about fifty people, and I'm pretty sure I can do the catering for that myself.'

'Of course! It's no problem at all! We do lots and lots of large platters on long trestle tables – Ottolenghi style – and people help themselves. And we fill vases with wild flowers – boil the stems first – and put candles in jam jars and fairy lights in trees. It's easy, no problem! It will rain, of course, but so what?' She made a lugubrious face and spread her hands in despair.

We all laughed and I thought – yes, why not? I'd love to do it myself, with no caterers, and with Larissa bustling around the kitchen with me. And Polly, possibly, although with four children she was incredibly busy . . .

'And Polly might help too?' she said, interrupting my thought process.

'You've met Polly?' My eyes widened.

'Of course, two – maybe three times! We all had supper last night.'

So why not Hugh? Did he even know, and hadn't told me? Was he aware of Larissa? Perhaps not. I didn't want to look foolish by asking, but some time later, as I stood up to bid them farewell, Yanni said quietly:

'I tell Hugh, but perhaps he need some time to process it?'

I looked at him gratefully. 'Thank you, Yanni. For telling him. And, yes, you're right. Perhaps he does.'

I couldn't help feeling cross and irritated though, as, having popped into a cottage on the outskirts of town and seen the artist Sally had recommended who I thought was excellent, I drove home through the windy lanes. I completely understood why his father having a girlfriend might be painful for Hugh, but surely he could have shared that pain with me?

Stupidly it was the first thing I said when I got home. Hugh was exactly where I'd left him: in the study, making editorial notes in the margins of his manuscript in his small, precise handwriting. An empty plate with crumbs suggested he'd had lunch at his desk.

'Hi, darling!' I breezed in.

He looked up. Smiled. 'Hi.' But he had his finger on the spot where he'd left off reading, which always annoyed me. He was keen to get back.

'I saw your pa, en route to my artist. He sends his love. And I met Larissa! She's lovely.'

'Good.' He smiled thinly. Still the finger.

I hovered in the doorway. 'Don't you want to know about her?'

He shrugged. 'If Dad's happy, I'm happy for him.'

This was genuine. Hugh *was* genuine. But surely . . . I wanted to shake him. 'She's bright, she's sparky, she's open – quite like him, actually.'

No answer. Still the fixed smile. At length I nodded and walked away. I knew, if I approached, hugged his shoulder and said – is it difficult, darling? Do you mind? – he'd look genuinely surprised and say – no, not at all. It wasn't. He didn't. Or – he did, but it was private. And the Peloponnesian War was more important. Or perhaps a displacement activity, if one was a psychologist? Either way, his eyes had gone back to the page before I'd even left the room.

It wasn't that Hugh didn't love me, or his family – his boys, his parents – he did, very much. I knew that. It was just that he loved in a different way. There was a book called something like that, I mused, as I went through the back door and into the garden. I sat on the little wall that separated the terrace from the lawn below and gazed up at the sky. 'A different kind of loving.' Maybe I should read it?

Obviously, I rang Polly later. I'd taken a drink and my phone down the garden to the Lutyens bench by the pond.

'Oh, I know, isn't she heaven?' she enthused. 'I'm so glad you've met her, Emma. I just want Dad to know we're happy *he's* happy if you know what I mean. After all, he was the one who was deserted;

he shouldn't feel it's a big deal to introduce a girl-friend at *all*. Did Hugh go?'

'No, just me. But to be fair, mine was an impromptu visit. I wish he would, though.'

I heard her sigh on the other end. 'Sally hasn't been either. And I can't ask her . . .' Because she was so effing scary. It wasn't hard to see why Polly and I had always gravitated to each other at family gatherings, despite Sally and I being friends, and the two of them being sisters.

'But she will,' we both said loyally at the same time, and laughed.

'Yes, she will,' I repeated. 'And so will Hugh. They just take their time about things. How's your mum?'

'Furious.' She lowered her voice as if her mother was in the room, which I knew she wasn't – a Pav-lovian response. Clem induced the same fear as Sally in both of us. 'Honestly, Emma, I know she lashes out when she's upset – the antique dealer had just buggered off when I rang – I'm sure Dad told you about that – but there's no need to take it out on everyone else. It isn't as if we didn't tell her she was being ridiculous the first time round, and making a – you know . . .' She trailed off, not wanting to sound disloyal.

'Fool of herself.' I finished. And Polly had bravely told Clem so, with Tom adding his support down the telephone too, when it all first happened, with the groom. They'd both told their mother not to be so stupid, but no one else had. The other two siblings, who hated it more than anyone, had pretended it just wasn't happening. Metaphorically put their hands over their ears.

'And these things happen,' Polly had shrieked at her mother on the steps of the groom's caravan having heroically gone to see her. 'I'm not denying that, Mum. People do have affairs. And, OK, you had one too, a midlife crisis or whatever you want to call it. But you don't have to immediately move in with him, literally minutes from your family home! In some seedy caravan!' She'd swept her hand around the camp site. 'You could just have a quiet, inappropriate affair and put it down to hormones and boredom; you certainly don't have to leave Dad and break his heart!'

'I couldn't do that,' Clem had claimed piously, not letting her in, head held high. 'Lie.'

'Seizing the high moral ground,' Polly had hissed to me later. 'As if lying was the worst thing in the world, as opposed to humiliating Dad in his own village and shattering a fifty-year marriage.'

I could imagine the scene: Clem, haughty and aloof in some swirling kaftan, her hair loose around her shoulders; Polly, trembling and a bit out of control, as I would be. She'd even confronted the groom.

'Oh yes, I did. I was shaking with rage. He wasn't at the caravan, but I went on to his yard at Georgina Fordham's house, while I still had my blood up.

Snuck up the back drive to the stables. He was mucking out and he wouldn't let me in, just talked to me over the stable door. Leaned on his pitchfork and lit a cigarette – which I thought was pretty stupid in a stable. He told me they were in love, and I should mind my own business and sod off.'

'How old was he?' I asked now.

'Thankfully not a child, but much younger than her. A sort of wizened forty? And as we know, the antiques chappy was even younger.' She lowered her voice. 'Celia Masters, who lives near his shop in Camberwell, says he's incredibly fit and that Mum must have been decades older.'

'Well, he is an antiques dealer.'

Polly giggled. 'Quite. And think of Joan Collins. Same thing. D'you think they do it?'

'Who, Joan Collins or your mum?'

'Both.'

'Well, they must do, don't you think?'

'Exactly. Otherwise what's the point?'

Of a relationship without sex? Ah well, that was a whole new can of worms. A whole new subject matter, and one that I couldn't possibly cover with Hugh's sister, even if it was Polly.

'And I mean good for her, in a way,' she went on down the phone. Then she went quiet and I could tell she was sad. They were her parents, after all. And I didn't like to say any more. At length she sighed. 'As for Dad. Honestly, Emma, when Kit and

I went round the other day they were all over each other. Larissa even sat on Dad's lap after supper – Kit didn't know where to look. Dad did. He looked like the cat who'd got the cream.'

I smiled, but decided not to mention that when Larissa had taken a call on her mobile in the garden, and I'd taken the cups back to the kitchen with Yanni, he'd turned and breathed excitedly into my face: 'She very tactile, Emma, you know? Very . . . sensual . . . bendy.' His breathing had become quite rapid and he'd looked a little wild around the eyes. A bit giddy.

'Your father says he doesn't want your mum back,' I told her instead.

'And he means it. I've told Mum.'

'Have you? Good for you. And?'

'She says she could never go back to that sort of life anyway, as if living out your twilight years with your husband in your country house was somehow sad and pedestrian. Says she doesn't know how she stood it for so long. Shoreditch is her spiritual home now – she's moved, incidentally, from Bloomsbury – and she's become an activist.'

'*What?*'

'You know, goes on marches. Ban the Bill, ban HS2, Extinction Rebellion, the whole lot. Taken up the cause. Any cause will do as long as it's militant, and preferably involves sticking herself to motor-ways. She also told me she thinks she's probably always been bisexual and is now seeing a Finnish plumber called Anika.'

'Christ.' I spilt my gin down my chin. 'What – since the antique dealer? Fast work. Did you know?'

'That she's bisexual? She probably isn't. She just likes to be cool for the sake of it, you know Mum. Oh, and she's a vegan now, having kept her own sheep for years and taken them to the slaughter-house herself because it's terribly important you know what happens to them and blah blah preach preach. She's sold her car too – carbon emissions – and she and Anika go everywhere on a tandem. When Anika's not inspecting her S-bend, obviously.'

We giggled, but it struck me that Polly was furi-ous with her mother. And very hurt. She was a gentle soul and this was strong language for her.

'And does Hugh know?' I wondered aloud.

'Well, no, obviously not. Or Sally. But I was won-dering if you . . .?'

'Hugh,' I agreed. 'But not Sally.'

'I'll leave that to Tom,' she said firmly. 'Actually, I'll get him to ring Sally *and* Hugh, would that work?'

'Beautifully,' I breathed. 'Thanks, Polly.'

And Tom did promise to ring them both. But actually, he didn't, he emailed – and I don't blame him. A few days later. I know because I crept in and looked at the email in the study. Hugh and I shared a desktop so it wasn't difficult and he'd never mind. He'd look at mine too. If I had an email from the boys I wanted him to see, I'd tell him and leave it up. And there it was. From Tom. Telling his brother and sister exactly – well, no, not exactly, he was less graphic than Polly – what I'd already heard. That after the groom came the antique dealer and now the bisexual plumber. Yet neither of them had ever said anything. Not my old friend Sally, or, more extraordinarily, my husband Hugh. Don't you think that's strange? Or is it me?

14

One thing I did wake up feeling a tiny bit sick about the next morning was the realization that I'd accepted Larissa's offer of help without considering Clem. Teddy's granny. Who would obviously be there in a matriarchal role, whilst her ex-husband's new girl-friend buzzed around looking like she owned the place, and doing the cooking in her old home. I went a bit hot as I lay there under the duvet. Hugh was already up and dressed. I wondered if I'd over-stepped the mark and should unravel it all? But then Larissa would be hurt, and I liked her. No, I decided, throwing off the covers and getting up. I'd keep shtum for the moment and pretend to myself that everything would be fine – a familiar default position of mine. Because after all, by the time the wedding came around Clem would probably appear with activist Anika. Or someone entirely different. Let's be honest, she couldn't care less. I went off to have a shower.

Jane came for a cup of coffee later. I'd tried to get her for lunch, but she'd said she was too busy, she had essays to mark, but she had to go into Malmes-bury and would pop in on her way. I sounded her out.

'Oh, I think you should definitely have consulted the family.'

'Do you?' I was horrified. I'd expected her to side with me.

'Yes, for sure. What did Hugh say?'

'Oh, er, well,' I faltered. 'I haven't told him yet.'

She raised her eyebrows. 'You are sneaking around these days, aren't you?'

My mouth fell open. 'Meaning what?'

'Oh, nothing. Sorry. I didn't mean that.' She went a bit pink. Glanced down at her watch. 'Actually, I must go, I've got an optician's appointment at eleven.'

She got to her feet gathering her phone and keys from the kitchen table. We walked to the back door in silence. I paused a moment.

'Jane, have I offended you in some way?'

'No!' She laughed. 'Of course not.' She hugged me in the doorway and kissed my cheek warmly. But I had. Best not articulated, though, I thought, as I went slowly back to the kitchen. Best not to say things like – is your nose out of joint because you've been here forever and I'm making friends and starting a business on your patch? But I knew it was a bit of that. I'd been dying to show her the barn, I had quite a bit of art in there now, but she said she didn't have time. Maybe she didn't? Maybe I was being uncharitable. Yes, grow up, Emma. She was in a rush. Had things to do. I walked to the barn on my own.

I felt soothed in here, I realized, as my eyes adjusted to the light; great shafts of dusty sunshine were pouring in through the open door, and as I stood in the cavernous space and gazed around, I knew it was because I was making it my own. I still wasn't sure about some of Sally's choices, but Josh and Martin's work shone like bright little beacons down the far end, and Susie had introduced me to another fabulous artist when I'd popped over for coffee the other day: a wonderful girl called Amelia, whose tiny white cottage I'd visited in a deep green fold of a valley. She'd had motor neurone disease ever since she was a teenager, but from her wheel-chair, and with the help of an amazing remote-controlled palette, she painted the most marvellous fantasy scenes of enchanted woodland, full of spir-its and ethereal creatures and mythical figures, all from her imagination. I'd come away with tears in my eyes at her bravery.

'So is it her bravery you admire, or her art?' Sally had asked when I showed her the canvases. Some-times I wanted to slap her.

'Both,' I said finally. 'Is that OK?'

Sally gave an enigmatic smile. 'Of course.' She'd wandered off with an air of superiority about her.

The following day I went to Kaplinsky's to reassure myself I was on the right track and wasn't going too chocolate-boxy. At least, that was the party line. In reality, I'd seen from one of their emails that all of their current artists would be in situ today, if anyone wanted to ask questions or get to know more about what made the artists tick. I definitely wanted to do that. Looking as casual as you like – but my pink neck may have betrayed me – I breezed through the front door, smiled at the frosty receptionist, not waiting to see if she smiled back, then wandered from room to room, noting as I went that the gallery's publicity had worked; the place was more crowded than usual. Quite a few people had turned up and were jostling to chat to the artists in their own particular spaces. The space I was making for – as we well know – was the very last one. And there he was. His back was to me in a crumpled blue shirt and black jeans, and he was alone. I saw a party of recently departed women making their way back to reception. He was gazing reflectively at a seascape before him which they'd clearly been chatting about. Suddenly I felt ridiculous. What to say? I realized I'd hoped he'd be surrounded, which somehow would have made it easier to blend in, and for him to then spot me in the crowd, but now it seemed entirely obvious why I was here. Too late to double back and mingle with some others, he'd turned at my approach. He looked surprised, then smiled immediately, his face creasing up with pleasure.

'Oh good, I hoped you'd come.'

'Did you?' My heart broke into a gallop. It was getting a lot of exercise these days.

'Yes, I was wondering how to get in touch with you without looking an idiot and thought maybe I should invite you to the open house today, but here you are.'

I was unused to such candour and didn't know where to put myself. I decided not to be Hugh's wife. To adopt candour myself.

'I wanted to see you too,' I told him. 'I used it as an excuse.' He'd come across and was smiling down and it seemed to me I bathed in his warm, tigerish eyes, those specks of sparkling gold and amber glinting.

'Come on,' he took my arm. 'Let's go outside.'

Impossible to describe the extraordinary lightness of being I felt as I fell in step beside him, raising my chin, floating rather than walking, every vein fizzing, feeling more alive than I had done for a very long time. We stepped out together, through the French doors of the reception on to the terrace. The receptionist watched us go, her eyes boring into my back.

Along a gravel path we went, through the wild-flower meadow where, amongst the billowing grasses freckled with cornflowers and cowslips, sculptures were dotted about. It was picturesque and pretty but cultivated nonetheless, as if someone from the city had imposed the purists' idea of the country upon it. I could do it better, I decided, around the barn. I wouldn't have gravel, I'd have mown paths, but if I'm honest, I wasn't really thinking about mown paths as I followed Rory to a Henry Moore sort of statue, a huge Goliath, whose lap, a sign told us, we were invited to perch in. Rory told me it was where he sat and had his lunch. I had to jump up a bit to manage it, but strangely, I had a bit of a spring about me at the moment, so it wasn't a problem. As we settled down I realized why Rory sat here; spread out before us was the most glorious view of the Downs. I gazed down into the misty distance and stroked the warm, sun-kissed arm rest absently, wondering what to say, then snatched my hand away realizing I was stroking Goliath's thigh. Goliath was entirely naked by the way, and I wondered, for a moment, where my bottom was. I couldn't help thinking there were more conducive places to have this chat, but here we were.

'Won't the gallery be pissed off that you're not available to the punters in there?'

'Oh, I've done my duty. At least an hour with the housewives of Malmesbury – not that there's anything wrong with that,' he said quickly. 'But there is a bit of a type around here.'

'Large country houses? Not much to do? I suppose I'm one of them myself. And some would say they deserve their culture-vulture moments after years of bringing up children and putting the captain of indus-try's supper on the table every night.'

I watched a couple of well-dressed women pass by; one was bright and perky, chatting away to her friend, delivering a long monologue, but the other, although pretending to listen, was distracted, con-stantly checking her phone, perhaps with an unhappy teenager or ageing parents.

'Is that what you did in London? Children and supper?'

'Well, I always did my wedding-dress thing, but yes, I was at home mostly. Bringing up children. It's different now, of course, all the girls carry on with their careers. Ella, Teddy's girlfriend, certainly intends to do that. But someone's got to do the school run.'

'And were you happy?' He wasn't looking at me. His eyes were narrowed and considered, trained to the smoky-blue hills in the distance which were shrouded in a haze of heat. I gave this some thought.

'Yes,' I said finally, but I didn't elaborate. To be honest, I didn't often stop to think – was I happy? – I just got on with it. Such had been my relief at marrying Hugh, I never considered the alternatives. It was only now, as I sat in this naked man's lap – and, yes, OK, now and again in the last few weeks – that I'd given my life any serious thought.

I cleared my throat. 'And you? Have you been happy?'

'Well, I've painted, so yes. I've done what I enjoy doing most, professionally, for a living. Not many people can say that.'

I dared myself to say it.

'I meant emotionally.'

'I know. I was avoiding it. Like you did.'

I considered this. I'd said Yes. But hadn't elaborated. Because I hadn't wanted to have a My Husband Doesn't Understand Me sort of conversation. Which of course he didn't. I swallowed, tried again.

'Hugh is reserved. And . . . likes to keep his feelings to himself. I sometimes think he's so self-contained he doesn't need another half. Will that do?'

He nodded. 'It gives me a flavour.' I waited for him to respond in kind, which he did. 'Whereas I married someone, briefly, who definitely needed another half. She – Tamara – was very needy. And very beautiful. It lasted two years. I couldn't give her what she wanted.'

'Ah.'

This much I knew already because I'd googled him. Rory was well known enough to have a Wikipedia page, and Tamara Ramsden had been a society girl, daughter of Malcolm Ramsden, a multi-millionaire building contractor, whom I'd googled too. 'I did know that,' I admitted.

'After that, I had an on-off girlfriend in Paris for many years – as no doubt you know too.'

I wondered if she too was a society girl and

somehow I'd missed it in the MailOnline. 'No. And is it on, or off, now?'

'It's off.'

'Right. Well, of course you no longer live in Paris.'

'Well, she didn't live in Paris either.'

'I see.' But I didn't really. All I could see was that he hadn't settled, ever: hadn't married again, had children, made a stable life for himself, as I had. That it was therefore easier for him to be having this conversation, all things considered, than it was for me. I had a lot more to lose. And Rory was a very attractive man. The blonde's eyes on reception hadn't escaped me – predatory – and Tamara and Paris aside, I was sure there had been many other liaisons. I rearranged the hem of my summer dress, a prim little regrouping gesture, designed to remind myself, and the man beside me, of who I was in real life. Wife of Hugh, mother of two boys, about to host my son's wedding. I told him about it, about my plans, keeping my voice light and informal.

'Sounds great,' he said, when I'd finished. 'My nephew's getting married too.'

'Yes, Susie said, the other night.' I hesitated. 'And you don't regret . . . ?'

'Not having children?' He turned right round to look at me, surprised. 'Of course. Hugely. It's the biggest regret of my entire life. I adore children. But I wasn't prepared to have them in a situation that wasn't right. Look at my family. And yours.'

Of course we both knew about each other's abandoned parents, but I was surprised he remembered mine. I thought of what I'd perceived to be that loving, fun Scottish household: no mother, sure, but Susie jumping down from the Aga in her emerald shoes and making a spag bol, the laughter of brothers and sister as they helped chop onions, their smiling, hospitable father coming in from the cold, taking his flat cap off, rubbing his hands, pouring wine and asking what was for supper – it was so much more than I'd ever had. I'd thought them all so happy. But, in actual fact, they can't have been. Their mother had deserted them. And then, of course . . . Some cold dread filled my soul.

'Rory . . . do you know . . . do you think . . . did Hamish . . . ?'

'Kill himself? We'll never know. I like to think not. An accident.'

I nodded hard. 'Yes.'

'Emma . . .' I turned at my name. His eyes were full of anguish. 'I've beaten myself up for years over whether or not Hamish knew we were attracted to each other, and let's not pretend we weren't. But I cannot live the rest of my life atoning. And neither can you. You ran to Hugh, and you say you were happy – great – and I ran to art, and I say I was happy too. But we can't run for ever.'

I felt all the breath leave my body. 'No,' I whispered.

'And call it what you will – fate, chance – but something has seen to it that all these years later, we stumble across each other.'

'Yes,' I managed.

'So are we going to continue as before, staying in our lanes, blinkers firmly on, or are we going to admit that some attraction is still there?'

He was looking directly at me now, his brown eyes soft and gentle. Vulnerable, too. This was going so much faster than I'd ever imagined it would, but – was that really true? I mean, obviously I was safe here, in broad daylight, with people wandering around, looking at the garden sculptures, pausing to bend and smell the wild roses, but I wasn't really, was I? I was hiding in plain sight. My heart was pounding like a drum and he was being so honest and open, it was wrong of me to pretend otherwise, but I was scared. Scared of what I knew I was getting myself into, and what I would suddenly become if I succumbed to what I knew all too well was within me. I hadn't felt as alive as this, as vital as this, for years and I very badly wanted him to kiss me. Where had I heard that recently? Ah yes, not heard, but read. In that romantic novel I'd got out of the mobile library that stopped in the lane. Not my usual thing, I tended to read thrillers, as I'd told the librarian with a shrill little laugh, but something had compelled me to borrow it, and now I was turning into the very same married woman I'd been reading about. I fought for composure. On an impulse I jumped down from Goliath's lap and walked a few yards away. Rory appeared beside me and we fell into step along the gravel path. Walking helped. My heart rate was coming down a bit – not much, though. My skirt brushed the wild grasses, flecked with nodding flowers of purple thyme which filled the air with their scent. I don't know why I'd been so uncharitable about it; it was beautiful – of course it was. The most beautiful cultivated wild-flower meadow I'd ever seen.

'And what happened to your girlfriend?' I asked as, after a while, we approached the plate-glass doors of the entrance. The blonde had left her desk and a little crowd had gathered there. All the artists had assembled too, and the ladies who lunched were looking expectant – perhaps someone was going to make a speech? The blonde saw us approach and beckoned to us eagerly, all smiles now, even to me, clearly wanting Rory to be part of the line-up.

'My girlfriend?'

'Yes, the one in Paris.'

'Well, you know what happened to her.' He turned to me, surprised.

'I do?'

'Of course you do. It's Sally.'

15

'Sally?' I stared at him, astonished. Even as I said her name, I wasn't imagining her. Not that Sally. Someone else, surely? But gradually the penny started to drop. Slowly. Bit by bit. Sally. Who worked a lot in Paris. Went twice a year to the shows – if not more. Who'd known Hamish – and probably Rory, when we were young, although I'd never been aware of that. Or had I? Well, of course, Rory had been at art school in the same town with us . . . but still, I had no firm recollections of us all being together. I shook my head, trying to compute all this, to file it properly. Rory helped me out.

'She was there for Paris Fashion Week one year, and a designer was staging a show in the Musée des Beaux-Arts in the eighth. I had a painting in the gallery next door. It's where all the art is. We bumped into each other in the street.' He shrugged. 'We had lunch, then dinner . . . it started as a casual thing. Just grew from there. Whenever she was across, we'd get together. It was never serious, nothing heavy, which suited both of us really.'

I felt anxious. 'Sally too?'

He laughed. 'Sally most. She's as tough as old boots, as I'm sure you know. Good fun, though.'

I was still incredibly shocked. My heart felt twisted like a wet rag and I realized my breathing was quite shallow. 'Yes. Yes, she is, she's fun,' I said mechanically. Was she? Fun? She used to be. Which was why we were friends. Except I'd met her through Jane, and she'd always been a tiny bit acerbic for me. Dry. Clever. I was still trying to assimilate this. Rory and Sally.

'For how many years?' It didn't sound like my voice.

'Quite a few, on and off. But we haven't been together for at least two.'

'Oh. Because?'

'Because we just drifted apart, really. Neither of us is in Paris any more – well, I'm not; she might be. And for some reason we only ever played away, never at home.'

'So – her family never knew?'

'I suppose not. She didn't really get on with her mother. I'm not sure she was the confiding type.'

'No. Clem isn't.'

He frowned. 'Actually, I think she told her brother.'

'Tom?'

He shrugged. 'Not sure.'

'Well – I'm married to the other one!'

Rory shook his head, smiled helplessly. 'I don't know.'

Hugh. Tom lived and farmed in the Highlands. He had a completely different life and had drifted a bit from the family, although Polly was still very much in touch. I was certain it wouldn't be him. What – Sally ringing the sheep farmer she barely saw to blurt out a confidence? No. So why hadn't Hugh told me? He knew about Hamish, knew Rory was his brother. Why hadn't *Sally* told me? It was just so odd.

'But – there was no reason for the secrecy,' I blurted out. 'Neither of you are married, so . . .'

He looked surprised. 'But not everyone walks around with their heart on their sleeve. Sally certainly doesn't. And I respected that. It was something she kept in Paris. And that suited me, too.' He smiled, amused at my bafflement. My astonishment. 'There are no rules, Emma. Not all love affairs play out the same way.'

'So did you love her?'

He frowned. 'In the moment,' he said finally. 'Is that allowed?'

I thought about this. 'Sounds very male.'

He threw back his head and laughed. 'It probably is!'

'You didn't think about her in your quiet moments? Driving? Painting? Last thing at night?'

He grinned. 'No. I didn't. And I daresay she didn't think about me, either. How often do you think about Hugh?'

'Well, obviously not much, we're married!' I blustered. 'Have been for years!'

'And Sally and I were on and off together for years, too. We rubbed along.'

It was convenient. He was too gentlemanly to say it. But . . . was it for her, too? And why hadn't she said anything? She was my friend and she was also my sister-in-law; we spoke, we chatted, we confided, or so I thought. I'd tell her about the children, their worries, their problems, whatever was concerning me at the time. Or I used to. Surely that was normal? I realized I felt ridiculously betrayed. As if she'd been sneaking around behind my back. After all, it was *Rory*. And yet . . . she didn't know, did she? Couldn't know, about the stolen glances, on a beach. Or by a loch, skimming stones. Our hands brushing as we picked up the same smooth, flat one to throw, then springing apart in alarm. Hamish, in the background. What had he seen?

We were right outside the huge glass gallery doors now and the receptionist had hastened to prop one open with her arm, to glance enquiringly, beseechingly even, at us. There was no escape for Rory. He shot me an apologetic look and made to go inside. As I went the other way, I felt a restraining hand on my arm. I turned.

'Meet me for lunch, next week. I'll text you.'

I swallowed. Nodded.

*

I drove home with a riot of very mixed emotions coursing through my veins. As I wound my way along the narrow lanes, the hedgerow brushing the side of the car in places, it occurred to me that, had I finished that conversation twenty minutes earlier, I'd be rather euphoric now. Rory had never stopped feeling the way he did about me when we were young. He'd never settled for anyone else. That was surely – although guaranteed to cause disruption in my life – something I would nevertheless hug to myself with a small smile of elation as I went about my business, walking the dog, hanging out the washing, cooking the evening meal. But that elation was now tainted by the revelation that the woman he'd got by with, up to now, even loved, up to a point, at least during sex – *sex* – was Sally. I had a sudden horrific vision of her lithe, athletic limbs wound around his, her long legs wrapped round his back. I almost drove into a ditch: had to lurch the car back on to the road.

My eyes, which I'd caught in the rear-view mirror as I'd righted the car, were wild. Why on earth hadn't I known? Why hadn't Sally said, during our regular lunches in London – more than I had with Jane, given our geographic proximity – oh by the way, I'm seeing a bit of Rory MacLeod in Paris? Years ago, when it started. Why? I could see that as time had gone by, it became harder, more of a revelation, but surely friendships were made of confidences like that? Otherwise, what was the point? And I'd thought her life sad, a spinster even – awful word from my mother's lexicon – but it was true. I'd felt sorry for her. Why hadn't she said? That she did indeed have an emotional life? Well, she *had* said. To Hugh. I was convinced it was him she'd told. Why hadn't he told me? These *fucking* Petridises! I banged the steering wheel hard with the heel of my hand in exasperation. So bloody secretive! But even as I stormed, I knew that one reason for my anger was that it put a fly in my ointment. If I had any ointment to speak of. Which obviously I didn't, I decided cravenly, hunching my shoulders as I crunched up the gravel drive to the marital home. The last thing – the very last thing – I needed right now was a crush on an old flame who hadn't lost his looks and was no doubt breaking hearts all over the county, with hot – only in the flushing sense – hormonal women like me. Except somehow . . . I didn't think that was true.

As I went into the house I decided I'd confront Hugh as soon as I saw him. Have it out. There was no reason why I shouldn't. Just say – oh, I bumped into Rory again and he mentioned he'd had a thing with Sally in Paris, did you know? Mentioned? How did anyone mention a thing like that without it being part of an intimate conversation? Nevertheless, the blood was up and I'd manage it somehow; it needed to be done. He'd be in the study. I marched through the kitchen and opened his study door, but his leather chair was empty and the French windows were open, as if he'd stepped outside. Voices were coming from the terrace. I popped my head out. My husband hailed me. As I stepped outside, I saw he had a large jug of Pimm's in his hand.

'Oh, darling, you're back! Good timing. Look who's here!'

I looked beyond him to the lawn, whereupon my face took on the same delighted hue as his. It couldn't help but suffuse it. Teddy and Ella were strolling towards me, coming hand in hand up the lawn, laughing at my face. Sally was with them.

'Hi, Mum!' My darling boy raised his hand in greeting. He came up the terrace steps and gave me a huge hug. 'We were with friends in Devon. Thought we'd drop in on the way back.'

'Oh, how lovely!' It really was. I hugged Ella warmly too. 'I had no idea you were coming down!' And would have been upset if you *hadn't* dropped by was implicit; such visits were precious.

'Neither did we, till a few days ago. We got a surprise invitation from some mates. Looked at the weather and thought – why not? We took off down to see Stephen and Chris in Salcombe for a few days.'

'And you look so tanned!' I stood back and admired their smiling faces, both as tall and good-looking as each other; they could be brother and sister with their wide smiles, heart-shaped faces and straight blonde hair.

'But I've got no food . . .' Instantly I was in mother mode.

'I popped out,' said Sally, smiling. 'Got a quiche, some salads, that sort of thing.'

'Oh, you are a star.' I turned gratefully to her, my gaze going to the table beyond her, already laid on the terrace, with a cloth and flowers, napkins; then my eyes came back to her. The same Sally, skinny and lithe, in a black T-shirt and jeans, a thin silk scarf knotted around her neck. Just the same. What was I expecting?

'Come on, have a drink first, darling, catch your breath. We can wait a bit longer for lunch.' Hugh was putting a glass of Pimm's in my hand and squeezing my shoulders. He planted a quick delighted kiss on my cheek. 'Oh – wait.' He darted to pick some mint for my drink.

I followed him feeling small. This was my life. My real life. Why had I morphed my husband into a monster? In the space of moments? To suit the narrative, perhaps. He was a good man. A kind man. Who adored his boys, his wife, his family. He just wasn't very good at talking about emotions, that was all. Hardly crime of the century. Always I had to exaggerate things. And Sally, who had quietly had an affair in Paris – so what? Wasn't she entitled to a private life? I thought of what Rory had said – no rules.

And suppose she had confided in me; once I'd got over the shock, might I not have constantly asked her about it? Brought it up every time? Wondered, aloud, where it was leading? Whether she loved him? And privately been jealous, which would colour my line of questioning, encourage her perhaps to doubt the relationship. And maybe she didn't want that, to be quizzed. Maybe she wanted to hug it to herself, not to be questioned by me, or Jane – oh, I'd have definitely told Jane, or persuaded Sally to – or any of her other friends, of whom there were many. For Sally was a popular girl. Entertaining. Witty. Sharp. Unusual.

I watched now as Teddy and Ella laughed delightedly; she was telling them how, as something of an art collector herself, she'd thought she'd have to show me the way with the barn.

'But not a bit of it!' she said, eyes wide. 'Your mum showed real flair and imagination right from the start – she just got on with it! Who knew? Emma Petridis the art connoisseur!'

I flashed her a look of pleasure. She was bigging me up. What was wrong with me? Since when had I allowed such sour and angry feelings to overtake me? Ella was asking if the barn could be a wet-weather option for the wedding – Sally had suggested it – and I heard myself saying it absolutely could, and suddenly we were all deciding to go down there with our drinks, to look before lunch, because Hugh said they'd waited to show it off until I got back.

'I can't wait to see, Mum. Dad says it's terrific. And I'm so pleased you've found your stride.'

My son's kind brown eyes were warm, but I knew what lay behind this remark. That if I wasn't occupied, I could get anxious. Brood. Overthink things until they filled the room, blocking out everything else, so that I lost perspective. I hadn't so much when they were younger, I was so busy, but recently, I'd engaged in too much Edge of the Bed Talk, as the boys laughingly called it. When they were young and I'd say goodnight, I'd sometimes linger, perch on the way out, ask questions. Now it was more telephone calls, checking in, worrying about their jobs, Nico's lack of a proper girlfriend – until now – things that didn't concern me. Making wedding dresses hadn't been enough. Or they had, but I'd got bored. They'd gone on too long. I needed this, to stop my gaze forever landing on Teddy and Nico. I've always known children cannot withstand too much scrutiny, and sometimes, perhaps as a reaction to my own mother who gave so little, I gave too much. They liked my eyes to be elsewhere.

We strolled down the garden to the meadow and then through the huge open barn doors. In the dusty, sunlit space, Teddy and Ella spun around in awe, exclaiming. Then they went closer, and admired all the pictures individually, agreeing that the rafters on the white walls worked well as natural frames, that they all looked terrific. Even the huge nude with her back to us – Sally's recommendation and which I'd been so unsure about initially – looked wonderful, they agreed, in pride of place where Sally had kindly hung it for me, on the triangle of wall above the slightly raised floor, which formed a natural stage at one end, and which, Ella was saying, could perhaps double as a dance floor? She approached it contemplatively.

'Or even where you could get married?' Sally mused thoughtfully.

'Oh yes. Say our vows up there,' Teddy agreed, joining Ella in front of it. 'With all the guests assembled here, below us, on chairs? Benches?' He turned and spread his hands to demonstrate a seated congregation.

Ella went up the few steps and he followed. They stood centre stage and faced one another, then held hands and laughed; it was as if they were being wed. I could see they were both charmed by the idea of having at least part of the wedding in here, whatever the weather.

'With maybe drinks and lunch in a tent outside?' Ella considered, turning to gaze through the doors outside. She narrowed her eyes to the wild-flower meadow, a vision forming in her head.

'And keep the pictures, do we think?' asked Teddy, glancing about.

'Definitely,' said Sally. 'They make the place. Makes it more personal, less of a rented wedding venue.'

They nodded, liking this. Invitations, they told us, had gone out, nothing stiff and white, all by email, and some friends were going to play some music. Another friend, Ginnie, with a fabulous voice, had volunteered to sing. I could tell they were eager and excited as they explored all the possibilities. A few trestle tables, covered in floral cloths, not white, and lots of flowers, Ella was saying. No, not wild, she didn't think; a friend had tried that and said it was stressful, because unless they were picked on the actual day they wilted disastrously. But definitely something loose and natural – roses, maybe? Perhaps a bit faded, with lots of greenery? I told her there was a flower farm nearby that did cultivated stuff; that I'd go and check it out.

We wandered back through the field to the house and Ella linked arms with me as we went up the lawn. I told her about Larissa, how lovely she was, and how she wanted to help, to be included.

'Oh, amazing!' Ella stopped for a moment. She turned wide eyes on me. 'Because actually, I thought we'd go a bit Mediterranean with the food. Lots of pretty vegetable salads, aubergines, courgettes and feta, some pulled lamb, don't you think? Which is all very Greek.'

'Exactly,' I agreed. 'And I'm sure that's the sort of thing she had in mind. She'll do it perfectly.'

Sally had joined us and I included her in the conversation, watching her face anxiously. But she didn't turn a hair about her father's girlfriend coming to help. And neither of us mentioned we'd never spoken of Larissa before. She enthused along with us, said what a lovely idea, and I was relieved. I'd been overthinking everyone's emotions, as usual. Getting things out of proportion. Sally was chilled and relaxed, and families moved on, they evolved, morphed into other shapes and sizes, didn't stick to a rigid conformity. They were fluid, everyone knew that. It was just my mother and I who stayed the same.

My mother. She'd come, of course, although she wouldn't stay, she never did. She never stayed away anywhere, not even with Sheila in Kent. She always drove home in her little blue car, stone-cold sober, because she never drank. In the old days maybe a sherry, in a special fluted glass, which she kept in a little antique cupboard in the sitting room, with the single sherry bottle. But for many years, no. My father had liked a drink, apparently. She'd look at me meaningfully when she said that, and I knew she meant – too much. Not that he was ever mentioned. I'm talking about the very old days, when I'd asked. Pleaded with her to know more. I shook myself inwardly and mentally turned away from that old cliff edge. And she'd mellowed, too, my mother, as I always told anyone who asked. Not that many people did. And only out of politeness. How's your mother? Oh, she's fine, she's mellowed, I'd say, and they'd smile, look pleased. The boys knew differently, but she was better with them, and with Ella, who popped in regularly. But not with me. However hard I tried. Although that was less so, these days. The trying.

Lunch went off in a jovial fashion; the sun was strong overhead, so we had to put up two more umbrellas – and drink more rosé, obviously. Everyone erupted as Sally recounted how, outside a fashion show in Milan, she'd been rushing to a meeting and one of her black pumps had come off. The street was crowded with other fashion journalists and she'd slipped her shoe back on and hurried away, only to discover later that she'd got two odd shoes. 'Someone else had lost their black pump and we both had two odd feet!' she told us as Ella collapsed laughing.

'Stop it!' Teddy roared. 'That's a tall story even for you, Sally – I simply don't believe it!'

'Quite true,' she told him, her mouth twitching. 'And I never got it back.'

It could indeed be a tall story, but she was good at telling them. And at playing to the gallery. And the young loved her, always gravitated towards her. Because she was edgy and different, and had a cool job, I thought, as she helped me clear up afterwards even though I told her she'd done enough. Sally had opinions on the economy, climate change, the refugee crisis – you name it she knew about it. As I obviously did too, but her opinions were more informed. She was better read. And the young treated her as one of their own. One of their tribe. And I'd always felt sorry for her, because she'd never married, never had children, had had to forge a career instead, but now, and having spoken to Rory, I realized that had been an absolute life choice. And look at her, in her Sandro jeans and Maje T-shirt. Always youthful, handsome – 'beautiful' – Ella had said to me in surprise when I'd described her thus, and in perhaps, she thought, not glowing enough terms.

'Oh yes, beautiful,' I'd agreed, thinking *really*? That strong jaw, short haircut, piercing blue eyes, androgynous figure? But it was a long race, wasn't it? Life. And looking at her now, through the kitchen window, as she went with a tray to clear more glasses from the table and bring them back to the dishwasher, I thought how lithe and athletic she looked. Fit. She swam in the Serpentine most mornings in London. Walked miles on Richmond Common.

I pulled the bin out and scraped the scant remains of the quiche into it, then, realizing it still had the cardboard base attached and I could recycle it, I retrieved it. As I wiped it down, I saw the pretty logo, in the centre: Kaplinsky's. I stopped for a moment, with my cloth. On an impulse, I went to the recycling bin. No cardboard carton, but as I dug down, underneath newspapers, I found it, right at the bottom, as if it had been hidden. The box had a much bigger blue logo and a ribbon: *Kaplinsky's of Breston, Wiltshire*. I dropped it back. Quickly put the newspapers back on top. Then I raised my eyes and watched, as Sally turned from the table and came back towards the kitchen, a tray of glasses in her hands. Her watchful eyes were on mine.

16

Teddy and Ella went on their way after their pit-stop. Ella was at the wheel having only had one glass, and there was much affectionate waving off in the drive, and promises from the young couple to ring soon and finalize numbers for the big day. As the open-top car disappeared around the end of the drive, Ella's blonde hair flying, I lowered my hand and turned to smile fondly at Hugh, but he was already on his way back to the study. Sally was nowhere to be seen either, having said her goodbyes earlier in the kitchen. I made to go after Hugh, and then abruptly stopped. I'd been so sure I'd have it out with him when I'd returned, but actually, what *would* I say? I ran into Rory MacLeod at the gallery and he tells me you knew he and Sally had been an item for years? Odd conversation to be having – not only with Rory, but with my husband, perhaps. Particularly since I now knew Sally had popped into Kaplinsky's to buy the quiche – the only place locally to get anything decent like that – and the deli was literally opposite the Goliath statue. What had she seen while she was picking up lunch for everyone? And what might she say later if, in time, I confronted her? Asked her why she'd kept her relationship from me all these years? Might she, in turn, ask me what exactly *I'd* been doing, snuggled up so cosily in the giant's lap?

I decided to say nothing. It was so unlike me; indeed it went against every natural instinct in my very being, but for once I decided to become a Petridis. Not to have anything out with anyone. To keep quiet. The fact that this uncharacteristic silence would then not impinge on my ability to have lunch with Rory next week, was neither here nor there, I told myself as I went inside. I was only doing what the rest of the family – with the exception of Yanni – would do. Keep their secrets to themselves.

They hurt, though, both of those secrets. Hugh's from me, all these years, never sharing his sister's life. On the many occasions I'd brought her up – usually after I'd had lunch with her, prattling on as I cooked supper for him, about how I hoped she'd find someone one day – why didn't he say: she has. It was lying by omission. And on the many occasions I'd chatted to Sally, washing up after she'd been to Sunday lunch, driving to a garden centre, and had jokingly said – albeit side by side, never facing her, either at the sink or in the car – 'How's your love life, Sal?' 'Barren,' she'd groan. A lie. And now, here I was, living with the pair of them. Two liars. I felt so angry all of a sudden. Wondered whether to talk to Jane. But Jane and Sally . . . suddenly I went hot. Carrying a pile of laundry up to the airing cupboard I had to sit down on the stairs for a moment. Did Jane know? My best friend? And hadn't said? That, to me, felt like an even worse betrayal than Hugh's, somehow. And I couldn't not ask her, I just couldn't.

I waited until both Hugh and Sally were out of the house. Hugh was strimming nettles in the far field, which was how he relaxed sometimes, got a bit of exercise, and Sally was in her cottage. Jane listened and I could tell she was staggered.

'No, I didn't know,' she said slowly, and I felt so relieved. Knew she was telling the truth.

'Blimey, all these years. Good for Sal.'

I blinked, wrong-footed. 'You don't think it's a bit rich?'

'What?'

'Not to tell us?'

'Not if she had good reason not to.'

'Meaning?'

'Well, the whole sort of Hamish–Rory situation. With you.'

'But that was all over years ago. With Hamish, you mean. Tragically so.'

'No, I meant with Rory. Everyone knew, Em. How you both felt about each other.'

'Did they?' I was appalled. I felt my hand go to my forehead.

'Yes,' she said gently.

I couldn't speak. Didn't ask – did Hamish? But I

197

knew. I shut my eyes. Saw his dear, young, twenty-two-year-old face. In the local pub, where we all drank, in Canterbury. The Fox and Firkin. I saw his brother breeze in through the door from art college. Wearing that huge army greatcoat, dark wavy hair curling over the collar, and an enormous, blowtorch smile. I'd feel my head turn and my eyes light up, his too, then quickly – I'd glance back to Hamish. His eyes were full of fear. Everyone knew. And that included the girl who'd kidded herself for so many years. The one with a not-so-well-kept secret.

'Did everyone hate me for it, Jane?' I whispered. 'Hamish's death?'

'No! Don't be silly. How could that possibly be your fault?'

But her voice wasn't convincing and I knew, at the time, they did. Not now. Too much time had passed, and people had got on with their own lives, but there had undoubtedly been one or two people, at the time, outside my very close circle of friends, who had put their arms around me when they'd met me on campus, or in the street in Canterbury. One girl, Clarissa Jenkins, had whispered: 'You mustn't blame yourself, Emma. You really mustn't.'

Rory had suggested Exeter for our lunch, but I told him I'd rather meet him locally, in town, in the only decent wine bar, the Cricketers. As I parked, I told myself that we hadn't arranged to meet. We'd just bumped into each other and had lunch, on the spur of the moment, as two old friends might. Whereas Exeter would be strange. I rarely went there. It would be too coincidental. I knew I was yet again using normal life as a disguise but I wasn't brave enough for anything different.

The moment I sat down opposite him at a table on the pavement, though, I knew it was a mistake. Not to come had not been an option – I'd never felt so overwhelmed and excited in my life – but we should have gone somewhere else. Somewhere extremely clandestine, like Birmingham, or New York. Anywhere except here, where two pairs of glistening eyes meeting over a bottle of wine he'd ordered could clearly be seen; they blazed like a beacon, in fact: two people who were completely delighted to see each other. My postman walked past and gave me a cheery nod. Rory grinned as I blushed.

'Or inside?' he asked.

'Definitely inside,' I agreed hastily. I quickly gathered up my handbag and got to my feet thinking – in the cellar, if they've got one.

They didn't, but they did have a tiny back room with only a few tables. There were just a few elderly folk having lunch. I was relieved to scuttle to the relative gloom and privacy of a far corner. I glanced furtively about.

'How have you been?' asked Rory, as he poured me a glass of wine.

'Not so good,' I admitted, taking a quick sip. 'Questioning my whole life, as a matter of fact. And examining my increasingly flawed character.'

We both knew what I was talking about. He made a face. 'I think you're being too hard on yourself.'

'I'm really not.' I leaned forward. 'Rory, in a way, I wish we'd faced up to the truth sooner. Got it over and done with back then, behaved like the beasts everyone clearly thought we were.'

'That would never have worked and you know it.' His voice was thin.

'No. I mean – yes, of course, you're right.' I sat back, horrified at what I'd suggested. 'I'm sorry, I wasn't thinking about you . . . that was a really crass thing to say. I was thinking about myself. But this, now – well, it's an impossible situation.'

We paused as the waitress appeared. We ordered a goat's cheese salad apiece. When she'd gone, he leaned forward. Regarded me urgently. 'Nothing's happened, Emma.'

'No, but you being here, in this town. Me living here . . .'

'We know it will,' he finished.

'It won't. It can't.' I glanced at him, scared. 'That's what I came to say. Why I'm here. In person.'

'Right.' For some reason this made him smile.

'What's so funny?'

'In person.'

'Well, I wasn't going to text.'

He inclined his head ironically. 'Thank you, for that.'

I knew he didn't believe me. 'Rory, what are you suggesting? A raging affair? Get it out of our system and just carry on as normal when it's done? You know I can't do that.'

'Oh no. I know that.'

'Well – what, then? Leave Hugh, my family, start a new life with you?'

'Yes, that's it. The life you should have had.'

His candour was astonishing. I sat back, as if blown there by a gust of wind. I stared at him. 'You *know* we can't do that!'

'So why are you here?'

I struggled with the truth. But I couldn't locate it. 'I told you. To tell you it's over.'

He grinned. 'Before it's even begun.'

I swallowed hard. Took a sip of my wine and regrouped as some water and a basket of bread arrived. It gave me a moment to think. 'Rory, was your thing with Sally . . . was it somehow – I don't know how to say this –'

'A way of getting closer to you?'

I looked up, surprised. But then I remembered that this was why I loved him. Because he always told the truth. Always.

'Yes.'

'Yes, I'm sure, in a way, it was. Subconsciously. I mean, I didn't grill her about you or anything.

But obviously you came up in conversation occasionally.'

I imagined them together in cafés in Paris. Les Deux Magots, which I knew quite well. Hugh and I used to go there. I knew Sally liked it too. I saw Rory asking casually what we were up to, over the years. 'Oh, she's having another baby' or: 'Oh, they're off to Italy with the boys, for the holidays, taking my parents.'

'And d'you think she knew that? Sally?'

Rory weighed this up, gazing beyond me for a moment. 'Yes. I think she probably did. She's no fool. But if you're wondering if it was some sort of weird titillation –'

'No, of course not!'

He shrugged. 'Maybe. On both our parts. I don't know. I really don't know the answer to that. Emma, let me ask you something. Would you rather a camera recorded your every single action, or a tape recorded your every single thought?'

I considered this. 'Every single action,' I whispered eventually.

'Quite.' He gave me a penetrating look. 'Don't judge. Life is never that simple.'

'No,' I agreed humbly.

Our food arrived and we ate in silence.

After a while, we managed to talk about normal things, the way the lunch should have started. We talked about my barn, his work, an exhibition he was having in Rome next year, but then, because we'd gone in heavy early on, all conversation seemed to revert to the central issue. I told him, for instance, about visiting Yanni, meeting Larissa, and he asked me if he was happy.

'Very,' I said – too late, recognizing the obvious parallel. 'But who knows if it'll last,' I added quickly, knowing this was a lie. Yanni and Larissa were very similar, both warm, generous souls, and he had looked happier than I'd ever imagined he could. And yet, I'd also imagined he'd been happy with Clem. In the gorgeous Pink House where I now lived, where he liked to gather his family, tend his sheep, make honey from his bees – but those were all just things, weren't they? Things he could live without. As long as his heart . . . Suddenly I realized I felt utterly miserable. I put my fork down and hoped I wasn't going to burst into tears.

Rory put his hand on mine and spoke gently. 'Sorry. I wasn't trying to draw obvious conclusions.'

'I know.'

'And the last thing I want to do is push you into anything.' He moved his plate aside and rested his arms on the table. There was a silence. 'I could go away if you like? I have a house in Umbria, up in the hills. It's where I often go to paint. I bought it after I sold my studio in Paris. It's about time I went there, to build up a body of work for the Rome exhibition.'

I glanced up at him, relieved. 'Yes. I think that would help.'

Neither of us said 'to give us some time'. But I think we both knew it was implicit.

Not a lot more was said after that. We parted, with a brief hug, in the gloom of the now empty back room, the old folk having gone, and I came away shocked.

I walked down the familiar high street in a daze. How had my life somersaulted like this? How, in a matter of days, had I gone from being a happily married mother of two grown-up boys, planning my semi-retirement with my husband of twenty-five years, living the dream in the idyllic country house where I'd always wanted to end up – to this? A ridiculous middle-aged woman, hands a bit sweaty as she opened the car door, so overcome by a stupid, overwhelming emotion that she was encouraging her crush from her twenties to disappear to a foreign country? Why did he have to go to Italy? Because we'd be unable to control ourselves otherwise? I shook my head in disbelief. As I drove away I opened both front windows to let a stiff breeze in and cool my hot cheeks. I caught a glimpse of myself in the rear-view mirror. My eyes were over bright. I looked alive. Vital. And foolish, I told myself firmly as I crossed the little bridge out of town and wound my way back home down the lanes.

I couldn't help wondering what his house in

Umbria was like, though. An ancient stone farm-house, I imagined. With thick, solid walls, set in an olive grove, cypress trees dotted around. Fig trees might grow on the south wall, with grapes dropping pendulously from the vine which covered the ter-race. I'd asked him where it was as we'd paid the bill. Near Orvieto, he'd said. I'd never heard of it, but had googled the town feverishly in the car park, on my own, like a teenager. Beautiful. I'd stared at the pictures. A cathedral city, with cobbled streets, the Umbrian hills beyond. Suddenly I'd tossed my phone on the passenger seat as if it were molten. Oh, he had to go away, he had to. I was a lost cause. A danger to myself.

Hugh was on the telephone as I came into the kit-chen. He rolled his eyes meaningfully at me: grinned as he made polite noises down the phone. He put his hand over the receiver.

'Your mother,' he mouthed.

Oh. I nodded. Only my mother rang the landline, and for once it was not so unwelcome. Right now, perhaps I needed her inimitable blend of sarcasm and bitterness. Perhaps it was all that would bring me back down to level zero. Talk about a sobering influence. I waited for him to sign off and took the phone as he handed it to me.

'Hi, Mum.' I wandered to the open back door.

'Hello, Emma. I was just telling Hugh that my

garden fence has finally collapsed. I did tell you all it was bound to happen.'

I massaged my temple with my fingers. She made it sound as if she regularly held meetings with her family and we all ignored her. And who was all? She had one daughter, and to my knowledge, she had never mentioned her fence.

'Oh dear. Well, not to worry, Mum, I'll have a look online for a replacement for you.'

'Oh no, it doesn't need replacing, that would be a silly expense. Just a new strut in the middle.'

'Right. I thought you said it had collapsed?'

'It's a figure of speech,' she said wearily. 'Must you always overreact? And a new fence is hardly an imperative. It's not as if herds of marauding wildebeest are going to come stampeding across from next door. This is Hendon, not the Highveld.'

'No. Right. Well, perhaps your handyman?'

'That's it, pass the buck. Hugh has already kindly said he'll see to it when he's next in London, which is Thursday week, apparently.'

'Oh, great. Yes, he's up in a couple of weeks.' I turned to look at Hugh, who suppressed a smile. We both knew house maintenance was not his strong point. 'Yes, well, I don't suppose he'll be able to mend it instantly, but he'll certainly have a look, see what needs doing. How kind.'

'Hugh *is* kind.'

There was a silence and I shut my eyes, knowing

full well the insinuation. As I counted to ten, I imagined her horror at the lunch I'd just shared, her terrifying reaction had she been a fly on the wall, witnessing her daughter behaving exactly as my father, her husband, had done. Fear suddenly threatened to overwhelm me. I came back from the door and sat down hard on a kitchen stool.

'He tells me the wedding is on the twenty-third of August.'

'That's right, yes, we've only just –'

'And that I am invited.'

'Well, of course you're invited, Mum!'

'It might have been nice not to have to ask. I shall wear my good navy suit.'

'Excellent,' I said softly.

'And don't buy anything too tight, Emma. That wrap dress you had on the last time I saw you was for someone much younger.'

'Right.'

'And by the way, your mother-in-law called me.'

I frowned, perplexed. 'Clem? She did? Why?'

'Well, she docs stay in touch, occasionally. And after all, she's living in London now. She thought we might have lunch.'

I blinked. 'How extraordinary!'

'Why?'

'Well, I – I don't know,' I stuttered. 'I just . . . I mean, have you *ever* had lunch with her?'

'Given the vast tracts of country separating us,

no. It's never been an option, has it? She says she wants to pick my brains.'

'About what?' I said stupidly, simultaneously going cold. My mother had the power to induce terror in my soul. I felt my heart shrivel like the dry old dishcloth I was gazing at in the sink.

'Well, how should I know? Anyway, I have to go.' She said goodbye abruptly. I stared at the receiver a moment, then clicked the phone off. I turned to look at Hugh.

'Our mothers are having lunch.'

He barked out a laugh. He was separating some semi-frozen bacon rashers to fry for his lunch. 'That's a first, surely?'

'Precisely. Your mum wants to pick her brains. What can it be?' My eyes searched his, frightened. What did she know? My mother knew everything. I mean obviously not, but guilt was making me paranoid.

Hugh shrugged good-naturedly as he put a pan on to heat. 'Probably something to do with the wedding. Maybe Mum wants to tell her what she's going to wear? Oh, by the way, she asked me which church Teddy and Ella were having it in.'

I was appalled. 'No!' I said with a spectacular hiss. 'What did you say?'

'I told her they'd decided to have a minister do it here in the barn. I wasn't quite brave enough to say "notary".' He grinned.

'No *quite*. God, I'm amazed you said that much. Was she horrified?'

'She didn't seem to be. She said she had a feeling it might be the case. Ella had dropped by, apparently, and hinted as much. She said young people had to find their own path these days and do whatever made them happy, and I agreed.'

'My mother said that? Dear God! She's never thought that in her life! Never about *me*, anyway,' I said with feeling.

He looked at me strangely. 'People mellow, Emma.'

It was almost as if he might add – give her a break. And mellowing was what I told other people about her, but it wasn't true. It really wasn't. Except . . . Ella had told me she'd been very kind to her, when she'd popped in. Given her a set of silver apostle spoons that had belonged to her mother. The family Bible for Teddy. That Bible. I could see it now. Small and black with a thin, worn leather cover. On the lowest bookshelf, next to her prayer book. Plucked out every Sunday.

'Weirdly, though, they've always vaguely got on, haven't they?' Hugh said. I glanced back at him. Blinked. I was returning from a long way away.

'Who?'

'Our mothers.'

'Oh. I suppose.' Yes. They had. A couple of intellectual snobs. Although both thought the other slightly inferior. Which was why lunch was odd. Surely it could only be about me? My mouth went dry. Oh, for heaven's sake, Emma, you're behaving like some sort of guilty teenager. Get a grip. I picked the dry J-cloth out of the sink and wiped the tea stains where Hugh had put his mug. I should have rinsed it first, though, because it just moved the tea around and made even more of a mess.

17

Rory sent me a message the following morning to say that he couldn't go to his house in Italy immediately, as he'd forgotten a friend of his was using it as a holiday let. Plus, he was also expected to stay here for a bit longer while his exhibition was on, but he'd meant what he'd said; he'd go as soon as he could. I texted back frantically. In the first place I said I was so sorry, I had completely overreacted, and of course he didn't have to upend his life and rearrange his whole summer on my account, and secondly I begged him to please forget it – that I wished I hadn't suggested it. He didn't reply. However often I looked at my phone there was no glimmer of a response from him, and I realized it was because my own text wasn't quite true. I hadn't suggested the flight to Italy, he had. I also realized I didn't actually want him to go, which was why I'd worded my own message accordingly.

It occurred to me in that moment, as I pocketed my phone, that I wasn't as straightforward as Rory. And my increasingly flawed character got worse. And not just with Rory. The following day, I broached the subject of flowers, with Hugh. He was once again seated in his deckchair in the apple orchard, under the dappled shade of a Cox's Orange Pippin, and he glanced up from dear old Kierkegaard to peer at me from under his panama hat. Understandably, he looked confused.

'The flowers? You want to have them done professionally now? But ... I thought you said you could just order them from the local flower farm, do them yourself. You said that between you, Sally and Jane you could easily decorate the barn. Nothing to it, you said, plonking flowers in vases.'

I rubbed the back of one leg with my other shoe and looked awkward. 'I know, I did say that, but now that I've decided to do the catering myself – well, with Larissa – I honestly think the flowers might be a bridge too far. Too much for me. Do you mind?'

'Of course not, darling. Crikey, this wedding is hardly costing a bean. I've just had a message from Teddy to say he wants to pay for the booze, which I'll fight him for, but I suspect I'll lose. Of course get them done. Who are you going to ask?'

'Susie Alexander. Remember I told you about her?'

'Oh. Yes.'

Ordinarily he'd go straight back to where his finger was resting on his page, and after a moment, he did. But not before his gaze had lingered thoughtfully on me for a second longer than it might. Was he wondering what I was up to or was that my imagination? It was a bit out of control at the moment.

I sped over to Susie's with the radio on loud. What *was* I up to? Manufacturing a connection with the sister of the man I'd just banished to Italy? Surely not. Music blared and the window was wide open too, the wind rushing in, as if to obscure senses and obfuscate cogent thought about my motives.

Susie had sounded surprised on the phone when I'd rung her earlier, but delighted too.

'You do realize I've only just this minute been brave enough to even *call* myself a florist, don't you? I've only been doing it for two months!'

'Yes, I know, but you're bound to know more than I do.'

'Oh – I did do the Covent Garden course,' she said quickly. 'For six weeks. And one in the Cotswolds too. And I've arranged them for other people – but for friends, as a favour. I haven't dared charge!'

'Well, this time, charge,' I told her firmly. 'I'll see you at ten.'

She'd told me to come and find her in her greenhouse, and to ring her if I got lost. She said it was around the back of the house, a long Victorian affair attached to the barn. Apparently I couldn't miss it. When I'd parked the car at the front and scuttled around the vast mansion, admiring the view of the undulating parkland dotted with deer, skirting the kitchen garden encased by neat box hedges, I found her, in situ in the glasshouse.

'I can't believe you want me to do this!' she squeaked when she saw me in the doorway. 'Come in, see for yourself. Look at these disasters.' She was pink and flustered and her hands were shaking slightly as she brushed them over a tray of plant heads yet to flower. As I went down the brick pathway it occurred to me that it didn't matter how pampered and happy anyone's life appeared, they were still prey to the lack of confidence and nerves Susie was displaying now.

'They'll be fine,' I told her reassuringly. But the buds were tight and I felt her fear.

'When is the wedding?' she demanded.

'Not for a while, August the twenty-third,' I assured her.

'That soon!' she exclaimed. 'If only my dahlias were out,' she moaned, bending down and peering anxiously at another tray of tight buds on the floor, as if willing them to open. 'I'll be awash in a month or so, and I love them in late summer. But actually –' she stood up abruptly, remembering – 'I do have plenty of pelargonium and alliums. Come. Come and look at these.'

She led the way, leaving her recalcitrant dahlias, and hurrying out to what she told me, as we hastened along, was actually her main cutting garden. Inside a raised bed encased with railway sleepers, a riot of bright pinks, purples and vivid jewel colours met my eye. Red-hot pokers towered majestically in the middle and I had a sudden horrific vision of Ella going up the aisle politely clutching one, wild-eyed.

'Um, it's gorgeous, it really it is,' I said nervously. 'But I have a feeling Ella might want to go quite pale and frothy?'

'Oh, don't worry,' she laughed. 'This is to be used very sparingly. Just the odd blue or pink one from down here.' She pointed to something small and much less electric. 'No, I just thought I'd show you this, but the crucial bed for us is over here. It's where I'll be doing the majority of the picking.'

I sighed with relief as we moved further along, behind a yew hedge, to a bed full of faded vanilla and cream roses, with white hydrangeas beside them, just about to flower. 'Perfect,' I breathed. 'And presumably in a few weeks' time they'll all be a bit overblown, too, which is gorgeous. She'll be thrilled. I'd originally thought I'd do it myself, but, to be honest, I'm doing the food, so –'

'I think you're mad, by the way,' Susie interrupted.

I turned, surprised. 'Oh no, because the thing is, I'm not, really. Larissa is. And I can't take that away from her. She's Yanni's new girlfriend and she's terribly keen. You must have known the two of them, surely, Yanni and Clem?' I asked curiously, as we wandered back. 'Living so close?'

'Oh, everyone around here knew Clem. Wafting

around the village in her flowing skirts and kaftans – or bicycling. She was so beautiful and ethereal you couldn't miss her. But I certainly didn't know her well. I think she'd find us far too boring and trad. And me too stupid.' She grinned. 'We're not really her type, are we?'

'Oh, well . . .' I knew it to be true, though, and was disarmed. Clem was very dismissive of the county set, withering almost.

'*He* was lovely, though. Always a treat to run into. *So* jolly. But even hearing me say that – *soo jolly*' – she mimicked her own cut-glass accent – 'would bring Clem out in hives.'

I laughed. 'Yes, it would,' I admitted.

'She was super scary. Always carrying a book, or a picture to the framers. I had a horror of her coming here and asking me about the art – can you imagine? I mean, I do know a bit, and can rattle off something Rupert's taught me – he grew up with it all so he's heard it a million times – but it's all totally rehearsed. I'd be stumped if she asked me a question. The only one I truly know about – and adore, actually – is the Gainsborough. Have you seen it?'

'No, why would I –'

'Oh, we ate in the garden, didn't we? We usually show it to people when we go through to eat because they love it so. Oh God, you must see it! Come and have a look.'

She linked my arm in an endearing manner and

I felt ridiculously pleased as she led me back up the lawns and into the house, through the open French windows at the back. We went through a sitting room, then a library, and then into the front hall, scene of my awkward shoe change. Ancestral portraits abounded.

'There.' She pointed above the fireplace.

I stood and stared. A large painting of a beautiful young blonde girl in a frothy pink dress in the middle of some very familiar-looking parkland gazed down at me. She had wide, sparkling blue eyes and a slight smile on her face.

'Lovely,' I said politely. In truth, it was a bit pink and white for me.

'She never used to look like that. When we first came here she was dressed from head to toe in black.'

'Oh!' I swung from the picture to look at Susie.

'But when we took it to be cleaned, the picture restorer rang us to say she was in a pale pink crinoline underneath, and did we want the pink or the widow's weeds?'

'Lord. It was painted over?'

'Exactly, when her husband died. She was only twenty-two at the time. I said – oh, the pink! – and luckily Rupert agreed. And actually, I rang Rory, and he said – *God*, yes, even if it's not such a good picture. Imagine being consigned to be seen like that for ever, in black? When you're so young? There was a veil over her face, too.'

I stared back at the girl with different eyes. Suddenly I was loving the pink and whiteness of her, the glow to her cheeks, the light in her eyes. How incongruous must those eyes have looked with a veil over them.

'What was her name?'

'Gwendolyn Mary.'

'And what happened to her?'

'Well, she did marry again, but it was a disaster. He was much older than her, and very unlike her first husband who she adored – he was only twenty-two when he died, incidentally, same as her. The next one, the old one, was horrid, by all accounts. Had affairs with the entire county. That's her, later on.' She turned and pointed to another, much darker portrait, under the stairs. It was quite unlike the first and of a sallow-looking middle-aged woman in a lace cap. She had a narrow, pinched face. 'Having led the life she shouldn't. The wrong life. Sliding doors and all that. Isn't that sad?'

'Yes, very,' I breathed. All of a sudden I felt the need for fresh air and I began to move away, to go back outside again. Susie fell in beside me. After all, we were here to look at the flowers. We retraced our steps, moving through the house to the French doors. But we walked in silence.

'I don't know why I showed you that,' she said suddenly. 'I just thought . . .' She trailed off.

Perhaps I was overthinking it, but I felt there was

so much left unsaid because there were so many parallels. The brother she'd lost, exactly the same age as Gwendolyn's husband. The other brother who, certainly in a romantic way, hadn't lived his best life. And this woman beside her, for whom she was kindly arranging flowers, the cause of both tragedies. Did she know? Or was I imagining things? Was I reading too much into everything, as usual? My head was swimming. I took a deep breath.

'Susie . . . I heard the other day, well, Rory told me, in fact –' I felt myself blush at the brazenness of admitting Rory and I had had an intimate conversation but I pressed on – after all, it was why I'd come, why I wanted to talk to her – 'Well, he told me that he and Sally, Hugh's sister, were lovers for a time.'

'Yes,' she agreed. 'That's true.'

'So you knew?'

'Yes, Rory's very open.'

'Did you ever see them together?'

'Oh no, he said it was just a Paris thing. I don't think it was serious.'

'Yes, he said that.' So why was I here? Had I doubted him? Maybe I just didn't want any more surprises. I felt foolish, but I also felt relieved I'd done it. My breathing returned to normal.

'Didn't you know?' Susie asked me.

'No, she didn't tell me.'

'Oh.' She looked surprised. Then she shrugged. 'Oh well. No reason why she should, I suppose.

Everyone's different.' She lowered her voice. 'Now she really *isn't* my type, I'm afraid. I mean, she's probably lovely,' she added quickly, suddenly remembering. 'Sorry, I forgot for a moment she's your sister-in-law. But she's just a bit too sharp for me. I get tongue-tied the moment she even says hello. But Rory can probably speak her language. He's such a chameleon.'

'Oh?'

'Oh, not in a bad way. It's just – he can talk to anyone. Make anyone feel comfortable. Which is what we should all do, actually, isn't it? Not pull rank. Intellectually, socially – whatever. Find some common ground. It's just sort of . . . good manners, isn't it?'

Her eyes narrowed into the distance and I thought how wise she was, despite what she might think to the contrary. Wisdom wasn't about knowing about paintings, or books, or having a university degree. It was about making people feel comfortable. At ease. Whatever their race, religion, culture or social standing. I drove away wondering what she knew about me and Rory, and realized, given his penchant for the truth, and for full disclosure, that she probably knew everything.

I'd decided to open the barn that coming Saturday. Given that I'd talked about it for so long and bored everyone rigid, it seemed almost rude not to say – ta-dah! – at some point, and do the deed. I'd also had some brochures printed – pieces of paper, at least, with the date on and a list of pictures – to ensure that there was no going back. When I finally opened the doors with more of a grim 'here goes' to Hugh than a ta-dah, I had a fine, sunny day on which to welcome the public. Well, I say public, there were about fifteen people at the most at the outset, and that included the artists, me and Hugh, Sally, Jane and Lance, and Susie and Rupert, the only people I knew locally. Polly had sweetly rung to say she'd love to come and although Saturday mornings were grim in her house, totally hijacked by ferrying children to rugby or ballet or drama classes, she and Kit were nevertheless determined to be there, but they'd be late. I'd also put a notice in the village shop, and in the post office, and one or two people did saunter up, but I could tell, as I watched them come up the drive, their eyes roving beadily over the house and garden, that it was more to do with the snoop factor than the art. After all, this was where that snooty Clem Petridis had lived. This was the garden they'd heard so much about, but had only ever glimpsed in smart garden magazines at the hair-dressers. And up there was the bedroom where, potentially, the scarlet woman had spent her days with the young stable lad, when that Greek husband of hers was away. He went to Athens a lot.

The artists, however, were oblivious to the locals'

motives and just pleased to see more people. They chatted happily to one another, delighted, I think, to have their work hanging on an exhibition wall for once – albeit a low-key one – rather than stacked impotently against their studio walls. They wandered around admiring each other's work and being kind and complimentary. After a while their friends and family drifted in, excited for them. They started buying too, perhaps loyally, but who cares. And they didn't just buy their own relative's work, either; the love was shared, and before too long, at least half of the paintings had red stickers on them. The artists' smiles turned to beams. Hugh had thought through the accessibility on the day, and worked it all out with ramps and wide gangways to get to the loos. Whilst I was buzzing about introducing people and getting the little price list I'd printed from the table, I noticed he was always on hand to get someone a drink, or crouch down to wheelchair level for a proper chat. I blessed him for that.

Over the heads of the humming, excited throng – yes, I actually now had a throng – I saw Susie and Jane, chatting to one another in a corner. After a while, Jane ventured over and sought me out.

'She's lovely,' she breathed. Her eyes were shining and her cheeks were pink.

'Yes, I know.'

'Not grand at all.'

'No.'

'And sweetly nervous about doing your flowers. Not what I'd expected at *all*. She said she's never actually done a wedding before and I said I'd give her a hand, if she liked. She leapt at it. Is that OK?' She looked anxious.

'Of course, I'm thrilled!' Jane was very artistic and she'd be good at it. But I also knew we'd lanced the boil of me having a new friend and I was relieved.

Female friendships were very important, but when we were younger and bringing up children, any petty jealousies they engendered quickly disappeared, because we were too busy to care. But now that those of us who hadn't slogged to an office every day were freer, we fell back on those friendships and they became even more important. Mostly in a good way. I thought of the happy bands of women at Kaplinsky's. But occasionally silly jealousies crept back in, and loomed larger, because there was less to occupy one. It didn't happen with men, I knew.

And actually, Hugh didn't really have many friends, I realized, as I watched him pop a red sticker on a lovely watercolour by the door. Jane told me that Lance didn't, either. Or, at least, they did – and certainly had done when they were younger – but now, they couldn't be bothered. They were perfectly happy with the social lives their wives presented them with. They enjoyed the supper parties and holidays with friends, but I couldn't remember the last time I'd seen Hugh pick up the phone to have a chat with a mate. Or meet someone for lunch. He didn't play golf, or sail, or shoot. He read. And went to a few classical concerts in London when he was there. But he liked to go on his own, the better to appreciate the music. He was friendly, but self-contained. He'd happily go to a restaurant or a pub with a newspaper or a book, in a way that I never would. And I annoyed him, I knew, with my chatter sometimes. He was too kind to say, but I knew the glazed, abstracted look that would appear in his eyes if I told him my worries, or recounted my day with friends, shopping, or having lunch. Nothing really bothered him, or impinged on his relationship with Søren, Goethe, Sartre and the gang. So he'd probably be perfectly all right if I left him, I thought suddenly. Probably listen, his finger marking his place, then go back to *Fear and Trembling*, his favourite book. *Fear and Trembling*. Lordy.

I caught my breath, shocked that I'd even contemplated such a thing. Leaving him. But it was the thin end of the wedge, wasn't it? The contemplation. I glanced across and caught Hugh's eye as he handed Lance a beer. He smiled back at me. I turned away, my face burning. As luck would have it, Yanni and Larissa had just pulled up outside, and were coming through the barn doors together. I went to greet them, relieved at the distraction they afforded, hiding my shame with a smile. But I wondered too, as they came in beaming, if contemplation was indeed the thin end of the wedge, whether these two people, with their huge delighted smiles, glowing with their shared happiness, were the thick end? And if it wasn't, in fact, a really lovely thing?

18

Hugh and Sally obviously hadn't met Larissa before, but I'd decided it might be a good moment to introduce them, naturally checking it out with the siblings first.

'Yes, good idea,' Hugh had agreed, and I could tell he was relieved to have an awkward moment diluted by other people. Polly had also said on the phone that it was an excellent idea, much less formal, so I'd broached it with Sally a couple of days previously. I'd bumped into her in the drive as she'd been on her way to her car. She gave me a thin smile.

'Of course they should come.'

'No, but do you think it's a good idea?' I persisted. 'Or would you rather I didn't? Would you rather meet her quietly first?'

'Of course not. You always have such good ideas, Emma.'

She was still smiling but her eyes were glittering with something I couldn't quite place. But then, she'd turned away and walked to her car, so I couldn't investigate further, and when I'd repeated the conversation to Hugh, he'd looked perplexed.

'Well, she said yes, good idea. What are you going

on about, Emma?' He looked exasperated and before I could talk about tone, facial expressions, things he wouldn't understand anyway, he'd put his earphones in, the ones Nico had sent from America for his birthday, to resume his Mozart concerto, and returned to his book, so that both orally and visually I was no more. Before long, I thought, as I walked away, he'd take up smoking – something to do with his mouth, so that like the three wise monkeys he'd be completely incommunicado, and wouldn't have to reply to me at all.

And so here they were, Yanni and Larissa, making quite an entrance. Yanni was looking proud and exuberant and really rather splendid in a garish blue and white striped boating jacket and yellow shirt and was beaming as he basked in reflective glory. His particular glory was in a very short white dress, with brown legs, heels and an ankle chain. If Sally was taken aback, she didn't show it. She instantly went across with a wide smile to introduce herself with Hugh in her wake, although she'd had to tweak his arm as she'd passed to get him to fall in. There they stood, the four of them, in the middle of the room, smiling and chatting, Yanni's chest expanding so much I thought he might actually split his shirt. And although on the whole I thought this was still a good idea, I did wonder, as people glanced across, intrigued, if it wasn't a tiny bit public? Jane found my ear.

'Fresh from Magaluf?' she murmured.

I frowned. 'She's lovely, actually. A real breath of fresh air.'

'Just what Dad needs,' agreed Polly, who'd just arrived and come across to join us. 'I've never seen him look so happy. Oh, hi, Jane, how are you?'

They chatted on and I thought how Polly, with her violet eyes and friendly smile, could always be relied upon, not just to say the right thing, but think it too. Jane's cheeks were pink and I could tell she was embarrassed, wondering if Polly had overheard her remark. Well, serve her right, I thought, as I approached Lance. She shouldn't have said it.

Lance was on his own, as he so often was at social events, picking abstractedly at peanuts on the nibbles table. Wasn't it odd, I thought, as I engaged him in chatter about his daughters, his eyes clearing with relief as I did so, how even romantic heroes such as Lance had surely been, certainly in Jane's eyes, and in the eyes of many other young female undergraduates, eventually turned into the mundane? Or in this case the portly, slightly balding and a tiny bit sweaty, middle-aged man. Would Rory too? I wondered. Well, of course he would, eventually, and, don't forget, Lance had ten years on the rest of us. He was the future. But then, Rory's lean, tanned face and kind amber eyes rose in my mental retina, and somehow I couldn't imagine it. Instead, as Lance told me how my goddaughter, Cassie, was enjoying life in London, I imagined Rory in an olive grove in Umbria, standing high on a hill, an easel before him, painting the valley below. The beautiful undulating hills unfolded before him and nestled at the foot of the valley was the pink-roofed town of Orvieto, with its medieval cathedral, its terracotta houses, its cobbled streets – I'd obviously Google–Earthed the entire location. Although whether he'd be able to see the town from his olive grove was debatable. I imagined his farmhouse was well out-side the city walls, somewhere quite rural, but, nevertheless, he'd said ten minutes so –

'It's so funny, the nude, yes?' I turned to find Yanni beside me. As I abandoned my reverie his dancing eyes darted to the portrait at the far end of the room.

'Oh – d'you like it, Yanni? This is Lance, Jane's husband, by the way. My father-in-law, Yanni.'

As they shook hands I realized Yanni meant the rabbit tattoo, on the left buttock.

'The arse – it so large!'

'Oh, that!' I said as Lance laughed. The sitter had her back to us and was actually quite slim, but she had a very wide backside, a typical English pear shape, in fact, and so many nudes were idealized fig-ures of women; it was why I liked it.

'It's slightly the point, Yanni. She's got Ruben-esque proportions, which to be fair, most women have.'

'It's a warts-and-all approach, like Jenny Saville,' Lance put in helpfully.

'Oh it definitely warts and all, but I don't think it look like Jimmy Saville.' Yanni frowned. 'That too unkind.'

'No, no, Jenny –'

'And always you have the humour,' Yanni turned back to me with a grin. 'That light in your eyes, that feeling of joy, and it shows in your choice of artists here too – well done!' He swept his hand expressively around the room.

'Why – thank you, Yanni!' I was delighted. I'd tried not to be too heavy-handed with my curating, as I'd learned to call it, had kept the tone light, and as more and more red stickers went up – Hugh smiling over his shoulder at me as he added another one – I knew my instincts had been justified. And Hugh was genuinely thrilled for me, I realized in a sudden rush of love, tinged with guilt. I'd overheard him tell Polly and Kit that, no, he hadn't helped at all, I hadn't had help from anyone – just seemed to have a natural flair.

This was generous but not quite true, and I made sure I sought Sally out to thank her for all she'd done.

'Oh, but I didn't do a thing,' she insisted. 'As I told Teddy the other day, this is all you, Emma. You chose every single one of these pieces.'

'Well –'

'All I suggested, if you remember, were a couple of artists initially, but you went your own way and I have to concede, I was wrong. It's completely paid off.'

'Although one or two I think I might have over-priced,' I said doubtfully, 'which is why they're not selling. That ruin by the river, for instance, and possibly the collage by the door. And the nude, perhaps?'

Sally laughed. 'You're on your own with that one. She was never my cup of tea, but she's certainly a talking point. Maybe you should buy her yourself and put her in your bedroom!'

She laughed as she drifted away, but I was surprised, because as I recalled she'd encouraged me to take the nude, but perhaps I'd misremembered that. Perhaps she'd just encouraged me to consider the artist, whose two other works, a rustic scene by the door and a castle on a hill, were also expensive, but had sold quickly. He wasn't here today – the only painter who hadn't made it – but I determined to ring and tell him. He'd be thrilled.

After a while people drifted away with much thanks and congratulations; those who'd made purchases agreed they'd be back in three weeks' time, when the exhibition was over, to collect them, or else I'd deliver. I was pretty certain I wouldn't do a great deal of trade between now and then, we were so tucked away, but there were notices up in the village shop and the post office, so who knew. The hotel in town had also agreed to have a poster. When everyone had gone, Hugh, Sally and I were left alone to clear up. There wasn't much to be done, in fact; we'd only provided a glass of wine and a few bowls of peanuts, so it was just a case of putting all the hired glasses back in boxes and taking them back to Majestic, a couple of miles away, on the outskirts of town. Hugh loaded the car and I set off.

As I drove along both the boys rang, to see how it had gone. I put them on speaker phone, one after the other.

'Well done, Mum!' cried Nico enthusiastically down the line from New York. 'Sounds like it was a towering success!'

'Oh, I wouldn't say that,' I demurred, but I'd clocked my eyes shining in the rear-view mirror. 'But, as I say, I did sell ninety per cent of the stock.'

'Wow. That's amazing. Kaplinsky's will be taking notes!'

I laughed. 'I very much doubt it, but how are you, my love?' I asked, quickly changing the subject.

'In peak condition. And dying to introduce you to Tara. But I'm afraid it won't be for a bit longer; they want me to stay.'

'Oh? The bank? Not permanently?'

'No, but certainly for the next couple of years.'

'Couple of years!' I felt my eyes widen in shock.

'I know – but I thought maybe you and Dad

could come out in the autumn?' He sounded worried, and I knew it was concern for us missing him, not the other way round. I'd heard the excitement in his voice – being wanted by his firm, and staying on in a city he loved. I rallied immediately.

'Oh, well, at some point we definitely will, but Nico, if you're happy, and you've got a lovely girl, that's honestly all that matters. We don't need to see you to be happy too.'

'Thanks,' he said with relief, knowing it to be true but wanting to hear it, knowing that his father and I never put any pressure on them to see us; all we genuinely wanted was their happiness. They didn't need to prove it in the flesh.

'And I'll be back for the wedding, obviously. But it really will be a flying visit, I'm afraid, I'm up to here with work at the moment. I'll have to go back on the red eye. And Tara's in Seattle that week for a conference, so . . .'

'Honestly, Nico, I get it.' Tara was in corporate finance too, and flew regularly from state to state. 'And just to see you for forty-eight hours will be heaven.'

'Thanks, Mum. I'm dying to see you too. Give my love to Dad.'

I clicked the phone off, promising I would, but knowing too that he wouldn't ring Hugh. Have a chat himself. The two of them got on pretty well now, but they'd had their moments in the past. Mostly to do with the usual teenage problems: drinking and dabbling in drugs. Nico had been quite wild, but there'd been a shouty-crackers row when Nico was older, too. I'd worried it was to do with cocaine, which I knew some of his friends in the City used, but Nico had roared at Hugh that he was a hypocrite, and Hugh had never taken drugs, so maybe not. It had been a hot night in London, some years ago. I'd been upstairs and had come running down – it was so unlike my husband to raise his voice. But when I'd asked him about it, after Nico had slammed out, Hugh had just said he'd finally snapped at Nico's consumerism. Nico liked money and always had done. He always bought the best car, the best watch and the best clothes, which was anathema to Hugh. But then, Nico would mock his father's tatty jumpers, frayed slippers and old Volvo, saying that parsimony was awfully close to meanness. Nico also said there was something too studied and self-conscious about it; virtue signalling, he'd called it. They'd always come from slightly different planets. Better at a distance, and, these days, much better too when proximate, so they were fine, on the whole. And, as I say, it had only been that one major incident.

Teddy rang next, putting me on speaker so that Ella could hear too, thoughtful as ever; he was the peacemaker, always soothing if Nico got a bit hot. Always steady and temperate. Ella, it transpired, had been offered a job in Madrid, and they were debating whether or not to go.

'But how will you do that, darling? Be an accountant in London, from Spain?'

'Well, we've got a Madrid office so I'll work out of that if necessary, but, to be honest, practically everything I do is remote now, Mum. It doesn't really matter where I am. One effect of lockdown is that the world's opening up, paradoxically. But I'll be back once a month to the London office. It's only a two-hour commute – not as far, in fact, as if I lived where you are!'

I could tell the pair of them had already discussed it, weighed it up as an exciting possibility, as it surely was. Decided, from the sound of it. Even though my boys were grown, ridiculously, I still marvelled at their independence. We must have done something right, I thought, as I said goodbye and parked outside the wine shop. It was obviously wonderful for them to be living all round the world, with their partners. I deposited the glasses. So. Just me and Hugh, I thought, as I got back in the car. Just the two of us. I swallowed and my grip tightened inexplicably on the wheel as I drove off. I tried not to think about what had occurred to me earlier, about the fat end of the wedge. The happiness of Yanni and Larissa. Because that way madness lay. Instead, I reasoned that we could travel too, go to India, which we'd always wanted to visit. Maybe even

Australia. Yes, that would be lovely, I thought, trying not to think about the hideously long flight, or the intense heat when we got there. And always Hugh with the books under the arm. The panama hat. The pained expression at the cost of the hotel. Or, if I chattered too much, the glazed look in his eye. Reading, reading, reading. Still. Lovely. Deep breath.

On the way home, I passed the artist's house, the one who couldn't make it, but who'd sold two pictures out of three. I stared. It was a compact but beautiful Georgian rectory set back behind a beech hedge, but still visible from the lane. Sally had pointed it out to me once when we'd gone to the supermarket together. It was not the sort of house artists usually lived in, and I'd visited many; on the whole they were fairly unpretentious individuals who lived in modest cottages, but Sally told me the wife had inherited this, and was from a grand local family. On an impulse I stopped the car in the lane, reversed up and pulled into the drive. As I crunched up the gravel to the Queen Anne façade, I saw that there was a stable block too – quite a pad.

The front door, I realized, was open, as two large and friendly Labradors bounded down the steps. They barked loudly, bouncing around the car, but as I got out and stroked them they quivered with delight and one of them rolled over to have his tummy tickled. They were clearly the doorbell because a second later, as if by magic, an attractive, skinny blonde in tight black jeans and an old jumper whistled loudly as she came around the side of the house. She was trundling a wheelbarrow. The dogs abandoned me and ran to her.

'Don't worry, they'll lick you to death before they eat you!' she called in a friendly voice.

I laughed as she approached. As she came closer I saw that she was about ten years older than me and still beautiful; her navy blue eyes sparkled like a night sky. 'Can I help?'

'Actually I was looking for Adrian? The painter?'

'Oh, that's my husband. He'll be in his studio but he's engrossed at the moment, I'm afraid. Up to here in oils and turps. Can I take a message?'

'Well, just to say that I sold a couple of his paintings today. They were in my exhibition.'

'Oh! Oh, well, in that case come and tell him yourself. That's different, he'll be delighted!' She smiled broadly at me. 'Come and be the bearer of good news.'

She dumped her barrow and turned and I followed her trim backside and long legs around the side of the house, wondering if I could ever hope to look like her one day. Only with a serious crash diet.

'I'm Caroline, by the way.' She turned and flashed that grin again over her shoulder.

'Emma,' I responded, smiling.

We arrived at a pretty little brick and flint converted stable, with a gabled entrance. 'Adrian!' Caroline called, pushing open the stable door. In the distance, at the far end of what was a surprisingly light and bright studio, I glimpsed a figure with a brush, before an easel. 'You've got a visitor.'

'Tell them to fuck off!' boomed a well-bred, fruity voice.

'Really?' She turned and winked at me. 'Even if you've made a sale?'

There was a slight pause, then came a more breathless: 'Have I? Excellent! Was it to the Prado?'

'Sadly not,' I told him, as a tall, imposing man, who most definitely matched the fruity voice, a sort of good-looking and patrician Michael Heseltine type, came striding towards us. He was wearing an ancient blue jumper which was spattered with paint and the paintbrush was still in his hand, together with a palette in the other. As he put them on a table by the door, pale blue hooded eyes twinkled at me all the while under bushy brows – what Jane would call Come To Bed Eyes.

'I'm Emma,' I told him, 'from the Barn Gallery?' It was the first time I'd used its name and it sounded pretentious, somehow. Imposter syndrome, the children would say. Nonetheless I pressed on. 'My sister-in-law collected a few of your pictures for me. I hung them all, actually, and I've sold two. The castle on the hill and the woodland scene, with the deer in the distance.'

He stood over me and smiled down benevolently. 'Have you, by Jove. Clever old you! How completely splendid – well done! No one sells anything much around here, apart from that fucking poncy gallery down the road, and they refuse to take anything local. They're so up their own arses they can't see talent when it stares them in the face. Can I retire on the proceeds?'

'Only if you've got very frugal needs.'

'He hasn't,' warned Caroline. 'When he says retire, he means to Monaco, or somewhere similar. We're not talking slippers by the fire in Eastbourne.'

'Oh, I don't know. If you brought them to me every evening, my darling, together with my pipe and baccy, and sat on my lap, I might consider it.'

'Dream on!' She laughed as he pulled her towards him, squeezing her shoulders. She swatted him playfully and I thought what a jolly couple they were.

'But I'm afraid the nude didn't sell.'

'The nude?' He turned back to me frowning, confused.

'The one with the rabbit tattoo? That's still with us. But it looks great. I'd like to hang on to it, if that's OK, have another go? The exhibition's on for a couple of weeks.'

A chill seemed to descend on the proceedings: a

thin mist blown in from the east. Caroline moved away from her husband's side.

'Oh, you can hang on to that,' she snapped. Her eyes flashed with something other than merriment. 'We don't want that, do we, Adrian?' She turned to her husband. He was licking his lips nervously and had gone a bit pale. 'Or perhaps I'm wrong?' she demanded. 'Perhaps you do?'

19

'Oh ... well, I – I'm sorry, I –' I faltered in the silence, not knowing quite what to say. The conversation ground to a halt.

'Sally Petridis is your sister-in-law, I take it?' Caroline turned to me, her eyes still glittering.

'Yes, that's right.'

'Sally asked if she could collect a few paintings of mine,' Adrian broke in smoothly. 'I told her to help herself from anything in the barn. Caroline and I were in Mustique at the time. I knew she'd taken the castle and quite a few others, which she returned when you'd made your selection. I didn't realize she'd taken the nude.'

'I didn't realize it still existed!' Caroline snapped.

Adrian made a contrite face. 'So hard, my love, to destroy art.'

'But so easy to destroy so much else.' Another, horrible silence ensued. 'Sorry,' she turned to me abruptly, remembering her manners. 'This is absolutely nothing to do with you, I'm so sorry.' She swallowed, fought for composure. 'Adrian, why don't you settle up with Emma? I'm going back to the potting shed.' She sent me an apologetic look, but her eyes were full of something else, too: sadness and pain, I thought.

'Sorry about that,' muttered Adrian as she went.

'Don't worry.' I fumbled in my bag for my phone so I could record his bank details, murmuring something about sending across the money he'd made.

'The nude was not my wife.'

I glanced up from my bag. 'Oh.' I gazed at him as it dawned: the nude was not just a sitter, either. 'I see.'

No, *clearly* not the wife, I thought, blushing as he gave me his email. I don't think I'd imagined it was, but how stupid of me not to think the rest of it through. But why would I? Lots of artists painted nudes; it was a well-trodden path. I swallowed. 'Um, so . . . is it OK if I hang on to it?'

'Oh God, yes, please do,' he said hastily. 'As you can see, we don't want it back. I'm surprised Sally found it, actually. It was right at the back behind lots of canvases. I'd forgotten it was there. Anyway –' he came to – 'thank you so much for coming round. And if you'd like to refill your barn, do feel free to make a selection from any of my less – ahem – controversial works!' His mouth twitched as he swept his hand around the studio indicating the landscapes and still lifes and I couldn't help but smile. He was rather naughty. And very attractive, too. I had no doubt many women would not be impervious to his charms.

When I mentioned it to Sally later, she laughed.

'Oh, Adrian De Morgan is a terrible old rogue. It could be any number of women. Probably one of his floozies in London. It wasn't the only nude, incidentally. Despite what he told you, I found quite a few of them tucked away behind some innocent-looking landscapes. He's got a studio just off the Kings Road opposite the Chelsea Arts Club and I've heard he's seeing one of the young waitresses there. They're all art students and they often sit for elderly roués like him to earn a bit of dosh.'

'God. No wonder his wife was pissed off. I totally walked into that one.'

'My fault, I should have warned you. But I didn't know you were going round.'

'And to be honest, I wasn't. It was a spur-of-the moment thing. And it wasn't really about meeting the artist, either. I was attracted by the pretty house.'

'Another pretty face,' she said lightly. 'Amazing what looks can do, isn't it? Which is strange, really, when it's so superficial?'

I must stop thinking all her remarks were aimed at me, I thought, as she strolled languidly away. This was just the way Sally spoke. She'd always been coruscating about anyone who got anywhere in life through looks and charm, which I knew, in her book, included me. But I must stop taking it personally. I swallowed hard and went thoughtfully back to my barn.

*

Rory and I had obviously not intended to meet again, but fate kept deciding otherwise. The fact that it was accidental, for some reason, made it all the more shattering. Although some might say accidental on purpose, on my part. Because on some deep, subconscious level I knew I was asking Susie to act as florist with a desire to maintain contact with the family, even if Rory and I were not to be. I knew my desperate heart. The realization that I'd never see him again once he'd gone to Italy was too awful. I also knew that if the seeing was in my control – if Susie were to casually say, oh, Rory might be about today – that desperate heart might beat like a crazy thing, but I'd be able to talk myself down, tell myself to behave, to be calm and unemotional. Have time to collect myself. Nevertheless, my day would be made by just the sighting of him. I would feel that I could go on, that it would sustain me. See what a hopeless case I was? But turning a corner in his sister's house, when I'd gone to discuss table displays and vases, and coming across him, horizontal and feet up on a sofa, almost made me topple over with shock. Serves you right, some might say.

Susie and I had been in the flower room – doesn't everyone have one? – with the radio on. We'd been chatting merrily, discussing the options. The wedding was all of a sudden upon us, a matter of days away. It had surely crept up fast. One of the things up for debate was the idea that although it was lovely to have flowers running all the way down the middle of the trestle tables, people had to be able to see over them in order to speak. There was nothing worse than dodging a floral display just to get a word in. All of a sudden Susie remembered a series of pretty miniature jugs she had in the drawing room, pale blue and white, which she thought might be just perfect.

'I'll go and get them,' she told me, putting a huge soggy lump of Oasis back in the sink, when at that moment, her phone rang. She wiped her hands and pulled it out of her jeans pocket. 'Damn. It's Rupert,' she told me. 'I'd better take this, Emma. He's in Exeter today seeing our accountant, and he said I didn't have to go with him because it would be incredibly boring, but could I be at the end of the phone if he needed me.' She put the phone to her ear. 'Hang on a minute, darling.' She turned to me. 'They're in the drawing room,' she told me. 'Above the mantel, directly under the mirror. Go through the hall and straight ahead. Here – take a tray, there are loads of them.' She reached down and handed me one from under the sink.

I did as I was bidden and she turned, heading in the opposite direction to Rupert's office, walking and talking to him as she went.

I was slowly getting the hang of this huge house, but there were an awful lot of rooms off the hall.

Although she'd said straight ahead, did she mean straight ahead and left a bit, or straight ahead and right a bit? I dithered for a moment pondering the closed doors, uncertain, and then opened the one to the left. This was clearly not the drawing room however, unless one took that literally. A sea of drawings littered the floor: a mass of charcoal sketches. At the far end of the room, in the bay window, Rory was reclining on a chintz sofa, a pad of paper resting on his knees, a pencil in his hand. We stared at one another a long moment. As our eyes locked, it seemed to me the whole world paused.

'Emma.' He started up suddenly. Then he swung his long legs around and stood up quickly.

'God – s-so sorry –' I stuttered. 'I had no idea you were here.'

'No, me neither. I mean – I had no idea . . .'

'Didn't Susie say?'

He was going a bit pink and I could feel my blood rising too.

'Well, no, but she has loads of visitors. And she doesn't always know I'm here, to be honest. It's a bit of a home from home. I just arrive, find a room to sketch in and fail to leave.'

And why not? It was a huge place and Rupert and Susie were terribly relaxed. Why wouldn't her brother just wander in and out? But it had rendered me completely tongue-tied. It was, as ever, achingly lovely to see him.

'Like an artist in residence,' I joked lamely, for want of anything better to say.

'Yes, quite!' he agreed, overenthusiastically, as if I'd made a terrific joke. The tension between us remained palpable. 'And if I'm a bit stuck,' he went on rapidly, 'I quite often just paint the view.' But he wasn't gesturing out of the window with a sweep of his arm to indicate the glorious undulating parkland, as he might; he was quickly trying to retrieve the pieces of paper from the floor. I realized he'd tossed them around, possibly as he'd discarded them.

'Here – let me.' I crouched to help. It was something to do. A displacement activity.

'No, no – please don't.' There was an urgency to his voice that halted me and in that moment, he was across the room in a bound. He seized the piece of cartridge paper I was about to pick up, so that it shot out of my hand. I glanced up at him in surprise. 'Really, it's my mess,' he gabbled. 'And I'm a bit coy about my sketches, to be honest. Very much first drafts, first attempts, so –'

But I'd stooped and picked up another one. I stared. He hadn't been able to gather them quickly enough. It was of me, I realized. And another. And another. Picking them up slowly, I saw that they were all of me. The blood rose even higher in his cheeks.

'Caught red-handed, it would seem.' He scratched

the back of his head ruefully. He looked like a small boy. 'Beyond awkward. Would you fall for some story about doing a montage of all my sister's friends? Some sort of weird commission for her sixtieth birthday? Which is next month?'

I smiled gently. 'Ingenious, but no.' I knew I was looking at him tenderly but I just couldn't help it. He was in here, on his own, drawing pictures of me? An overweight, middle-aged mother of two grown-up sons? He'd idealized me, of course, in the drawings. In so many ways. Perhaps he always had done? I tried to lighten the atmosphere. 'You've taken about twenty years off me, you realize.'

'Twenty-eight, actually.'

My eyes widened as he flipped over the top paper of his collection which, I realized, concealed a photograph. Of me. And Hamish. And Susie. Taken, presumably, on a visit to Scotland. I'd never seen it before. The three of us were laughing as we looked up from dragging a boat up from the loch, on to the shingle beach. I was in the foreground, a huge smile on my face, the wind whipping my hair into wild curls. It must have been taken by Rory. I remembered the day very well, now that I saw the photo. Indeed, I could almost recall the exact moment that picture must have been taken, plus the heat generated whenever Rory and I dared to look at one another. He'd stolen that glance of ours with a camera this time. I took the photograph from his hand.

Hamish was grinning in the background, Susie was sticking her tongue out, but I was caught red-handed, just as I'd now caught him. I was gazing lovingly at Rory, the photographer, with wide eyes, in the full knowledge of what was occurring. I swallowed and handed it back to him.

'Accalty beach,' I murmured.

'Just after we'd come back from Jura.'

'Which we never actually reached. We turned back, when the weather turned bad.'

'Completely foul. That storm. And you didn't have a waterproof.'

So the two of us had sat huddled together under his huge yellow coat, as Hamish, the stronger rower, took us back in. We were behind Hamish in the prow as he rowed. I can see his strong broad back in his blue cagoule, pulling hard, rhythmically, on the oars. Susie wasn't in the boat, she'd run down from the house when she'd seen us from the kitchen window, perhaps a bit worried now that the weather had changed. She'd helped us to drag it in, out of the water. To this day, I remember the unbearable tension under that waterproof and our mutual, rigid determination not to look at one another. Touching sides was unavoidable though, sitting as close as we were. And despite the spray and the horizontal rain, I felt as though I was on fire. I remembered Hamish shouting over his shoulder that we'd be there soon, not long. Rory and I not answering. Unable to.

'Rory . . .' I mumbled miserably. I felt as though I might cry. 'As I said the other day, I can't . . .'

'I know. And I don't usually hark back like this, I promise. But we've all got our guilty secrets. And how was I to know you were going to come in here and –'

'Did you find them?' Susie's voice called out. She was coming through the hall, her quick footsteps echoing on the flagstones. 'So sorry about that. I had to find some papers for Rupert and – oh. You're in here.'

She stopped in the open doorway as she passed. Looked surprised.

'Yes, so stupid,' I said quickly. 'I got the wrong room.'

'And found me instead.' Rory grinned. He'd gathered up all his papers by now and was tucking them inside his sketch book, under his arm. 'But I'm going into the kitchen now, Suze, to raid your fridge. I'm starving. So you can flower-arrange in here all you like.'

'No, no, stay, we're after vases in the drawing room. We don't need to be in here at all, so don't feel you have to –'

But Rory had already gone. He brushed past us with a pained and troubled look on his face. A look, I realized, which hadn't escaped his sister. It was why she'd stopped mid-sentence. There was a silence. When he was out of earshot, her shoulders drooped. Her mouth too. She turned to me. 'Golly,' she said sadly. 'Isn't life complicated?'

I realized, in that moment, that she knew. Not that her brother had been in here drawing pictures of me, of that I'm sure she was oblivious, but she knew what was in his heart. She knew that both of her brothers had been in love with me. That one had died, very young, we all sincerely hoped as the result of a tragic accident. She also knew that Rory, her other brother, was quietly dying too. She could have hated me for it, but somehow I felt she didn't. I felt that she knew that love was messy and no one's fault. What she didn't know, was that I was dying too.

20

My mother arrived the day before the wedding. She drove herself down in her little blue Honda, her neatly packed bag on the back seat, her good navy suit fresh from the dry cleaners, hanging in the back. When I heard the car in the drive I went out to meet her, forcing my face into a bright smile. I told myself that it was lovely to see her, it had been so long. I'd rung, of course – I did so regularly, to keep in touch, but also to find out what Clem had wanted. Mum had just said something about getting a pass for the British Library, which Clem knew my mother was a member of, but I wasn't entirely convinced. That was a phone call, surely, not a lunch, but perhaps I was overreacting. It could easily be that two elderly, single women in London who liked their culture, also enjoyed each other's company. If so, I was delighted.

As her car door opened and she got out, dressed in a loose grey dress with large pockets and a long pendant, I realized she had lipstick on. She rarely wore make-up. I was startled – but instantly touched and pleased. She'd made an effort.

'Mum. How lovely to see you.' I went across and hugged her lightly.

'Careful.' She stepped backwards. 'It's linen. You're always in such a rush, Emma.' She smoothed her dress down.

'Sorry, I'm just pleased to see you.'

She didn't answer and reached into the back for her bag. 'You didn't tell me the A303 had roadworks at Stonehenge.'

'Oh, sorry, does it? I didn't know. There's a route round the back near the army base which –'

'I should have taken, yes. Instead I sat in traffic for an hour and a half.'

'Oh, sorry, Mum.' I took her bag.

'Never mind, I'm here now.' She looked at me properly and gave me a tight smile. 'How are you?'

'I'm really well.' I grinned, overextravagantly. 'How are you?'

'Oh, you know. Pleased to be out. It's quiet at home.'

'Yes, which is why I wanted you for at least a few days,' I said eagerly.

'Two. You want me to go on Sunday?'

'Well, no, go when you like, Mum, it's just –'

'The day after is bound to be a bit chaotic, yes, you said. So I'm here for three nights but only two full days.'

'Well, of course if you'd like to stay longer, do; it's just some of Teddy's friends might crash and –'

'No, no, two is fine. Let's leave it to the young.' She flashed me a tiny smile then looked around the garden critically. Her gaze settled on the pot of geraniums, brown and soggy by the back door. 'You can overwater geraniums, you know,' she said, as we went inside. My heart plummeted into my trainers.

The atmosphere changed, naturally, the moment Hugh walked into the room. It always did. My mother, despite my father's defection early on, was one of those women who looked around, and said: 'Where are the men?' And then sat up brightly when they appeared. And she was particularly enraptured by Hugh, in thrall to his brainpower and his lack of guile, which some might call charm. Hugh was honest to the point of bluntness. The fact that he often sat down to read, or to do the *Times* crossword in front of her, was terribly seductive as far as my mother was concerned. Plus the fact that he didn't talk much but when he did, he was measured, considered, so that people always looked up and took notice of what he was saying. I sometimes wondered if it was why I'd married Hugh, because he'd been such an unexpected hit with my mother. To some of my more garrulous, glamorous, some might say shallow, friends, I'd had to explain him, back in the day. Just as I'd had to explain them to him. But not my mother. She saw the light instantly. Her face would take on a strange, unnatural sheen when she spoke to him, so that I was almost able to imagine what she'd been like when she met my father.

Hugh sat down at the kitchen table opposite her and once the usual civilities about health and family were completed, they spoke of the current political situation at home. Then of Scottish devolution, and then of the war in Ukraine, the situation there. This was nothing new and I joined in as I made a tomato salad and arranged the cold meats. When they moved on to the finer points of the Brexit trade deal though, particularly paragraph twenty-four of the document they'd both read online, I fell silent. I considered myself intelligent and interested in all current affairs, up to a point. But surely this was not only pretty niche but also showing off, and slightly bad manners? A bit exclusive. A bit like me and another dressmaking friend discussing cutting towards or against the grain on certain silks, whilst a third party sat there mute. I smiled as I got to my feet and cleared the plates away. Oh yes, the whole of lunch. They were on to Somalia now, and the role of Al-Shabaab. I took the strawberries and meringues out of the fridge and set them on the table with a large bowl of cream. Neither of them commented on the home-made meringues as they served themselves and carried on. My mother helped herself to a second meringue.

'Ella's wearing a circle of lilies of the valley in her hair,' I said suddenly.

They both looked at me, startled.

'For the wedding,' I said.

Hugh smiled. 'Sometimes it's hard to sustain the momentum vis-à-vis the nuptials, darling.'

Oh, that was cruel. Particularly in front of my mother, who was giving me a patronizing look.

'Emma's feet have always strayed across to the sunny side of the street,' she said, as if I wasn't there, and just as Sally came in from the garden.

'Which is what I've always liked about her!' Sally said with a wide smile. 'Hello, Mrs Baker, how are you?'

I knew my cheeks were burning, and as my mother got up to say hello I flashed Sally a grateful smile, wishing she'd joined us for lunch, now. Unlike my husband, Sally was good at judging a situation and taking social cues, understanding why my mother exasperated me and not encouraging her. They hadn't met very often, but whenever they had and my mother started showing off, she'd been good at quietly slapping her down. And because Sally was bright, Mum got back in her basket and behaved.

'Years of dealing with my own tricky wicket,' she'd once said darkly when I'd thanked her. I remembered saying I'd much rather deal with Clem than my mother, and she'd said, 'No, you bloody wouldn't.' Quite vehemently.

When I showed my mother to her room I was able to ask her casually – with my back to her as I hung her suit in the wardrobe – where she and Clem had gone for lunch. And what else they'd chatted about? I made it light and conversational as if I'd just remembered.

She sighed. 'Oh, Emma, how you persist. Well, we went to the Cézanne exhibition at the Tate Modern, if you must know. We had a bite there, too. She wanted to know if I thought he was the founder of cubism, or if Léger was. Léger had a few pictures in the main gallery, so we went to have a look. We left undecided, actually.'

'Oh.' I was crushed, but relieved. Somehow I'd felt it must have been about me. My unseemly haste in occupying the house, perhaps. As ever, however, intellectual pursuits prevailed. I put a lavender bag on the suit hanger for her.

'She did also wonder if you and Hugh were happy down here.'

'Oh?' I turned.

'Well, Hugh particularly, I suppose. She thought he sounded a little low on the phone.' I stared at her, astonished. Hugh? Low? Since when had he betrayed emotion? And since when had Clem ever worried about her children? Was my mother making it up, being spiteful? I wasn't sure. 'Just because – you know – he's such a city type, isn't he?' she went on. 'Concerts, exhibitions, that sort of thing.'

'Yes, well obviously we discussed all of that!' I blurted out. 'And he still does go to concerts, every few weeks, when he's in the office. He was at Cadogan Hall last week, Mozart's something or other.'

'Well, quite. And perhaps he doesn't always contact his mother. Maybe there's a nose out of joint there.'

'Ah.' I gazed at her and, for once, our eyes communed. This was far more likely. Hugh in London not giving Clem a ring. I looked at her gratefully and she gave me a proper smile. A knowing look, too. I nearly ran across the room and hugged her, but managed to restrain myself, not wanting to spoil the moment by overdoing it. Instead I grinned happily back. This was how it was with my mother. Sometimes one went for miles over rocky, treacherous terrain thinking things would never ease up, and then every so often, a sunlit upland would appear. A little tranquil spot of reasonableness, affection even, which always took me by surprise.

Teddy and Ella arrived in the evening looking excited. There were huge congratulations and cries of 'Mr and Mrs Petridis!' Yes, already. Since we obviously weren't licensed to hold a wedding, they'd quietly got married in London. And, no, Hugh and I hadn't gone, because Ella's parents were still on their way over from America, and no one thought it was appropriate if we went and they didn't, so they'd just had two friends, as witnesses. And although I'd had a bit of a moment about that, after discussing it with Hugh, who understood immediately, I did too. And Teddy had sensibly emailed rather than telephoned, which gave us a chance to take it in. Later, Ella had rung to say that as far as she was concerned this was her wedding day, down here, the other just a formality, which had pleased me. So now here they were, married. Free from the worries of work and with a two-week honeymoon to look forward to. They looked relaxed and happy.

They greeted my mother warmly, and then Ella and I immediately started going over last-minute details for the weekend – including the flowers in her hair which Susie was forcing in her greenhouse. Just then Nico bounded in, fresh from a flight, a train and then a taxi purring out of the drive, and suddenly my world was complete. Having all my family in one house was rare these days, and having them in this one was a first. Hugh glowed too with pride and pleasure. He opened the champagne on the dot of six, jovially warning everyone not to go mad, as in 'first night on tour', to which everyone roared their disapproval. The boys practically downed their glasses in one. Nico planted his empty one firmly on his head for a refill, and declared it was like the Gobi Desert in here. He also told us there were two ways to fly the Atlantic: one was to drink heavily and arrive feeling dreadful, and the other was to drink nothing at all and still arrive feeling dreadful. He'd erroneously chosen the latter and was damn well going to make up for it now.

In contrast to Teddy, who was slightly built and

dark, like Hugh, Nico was tall, broad and blond with a high colour. He had a wide smile, and a loud, deep voice. I thought he had an irresistible easy charm, but he'd been a boisterous child, and Hugh still thought he was boisterous now. If someone had been throwing bread rolls in a restaurant as a teenager and generally behaving like a bit of a Hooray it would be Nico. And if there was a stag night that got slightly out of hand at a casino in Vegas, Nico could have been at the helm, a few years ago. Since he'd moved to America, however, and was working flat out, sometimes into the early hours, and had met Tara and bought a flat with her, he seemed to have settled down. And of course, he was growing up now: a grown man. The fact that his puppyish ways still shone out amongst his family the night before his brother's wedding was natural, and I could see Hugh smiling fondly as Nico ran us through an entirely fictitious best man's speech for his younger brother, majoring on Teddy's relationship with sheep, and on one ewe in particular, amidst howls of protest from the rest of us.

We were out in the garden by now, at the table on the terrace, and Sally was amongst us. She was bopping her nephew on the head with her napkin in mock indignation, and everyone at the supper table was boisterously tipsy, except, of course, my mother. But that didn't matter, because earlier on, both of the boys, and particularly Ella, had made polite enquiries and conversation, but as the evening progressed, she became slightly sidelined, sitting quietly by, listening. But she behaved, and after pudding, quietly absented herself before the cheese, to go and have a bath, entirely as it should be. She was nearly eighty, for heaven's sake; the pre-wedding festivities, and the world, could not revolve around her. With much standing up from the boys, and with Nico elaborately escorting her indoors to make her a Horlicks in the kitchen before she went up, she exited stage left, leaving the young to continue into the night. 'But not too late,' I warned, as I too left the table an hour or so later, 'we've got a busy day tomorrow.'

The day of the wedding had been scheduled to be bright and sunny, but the preceding few days had been overcast in the morning, and despite the weather man's optimistic predictions, this one followed suit. The morning held on to the cloud like a child stubbornly refusing to give up a soft grey blanket. Still, nothing could dampen Ella's spirits. She took one look at the heavy grey skies and told me it was miles better for the photographs than bright sunlight, and so long as it didn't tip with rain, who cares, and even then, apparently it was lucky. A wet knot was a tighter knot, they said in India.

Thank goodness we'd gone for the barn option, though, I thought, as I wandered down to check on the final seating plan. Lunch had always been scheduled in a pretty Raj-style tent, which, together with trestle tables and chairs, I'd ordered from a local company. At one stage, because she'd been to a friend's wedding, Ella had rung and said she'd thought just seats on the lawn for the actual marriage blessing, under a bower of flowers? Wouldn't that be pretty with the view? I'd wondered about the unpredictability of the English climate, not wanting to force my views, but apparently Teddy had voiced my silent opinion. So now the benches which we'd hired were all assembled, set out in rows on the well-swept barn floor, and everything was in place. I sat down on one in front of the little raised platform, where the actual ceremony – 'Such as it is,' my mother had murmured caustically – was taking place. Being profoundly religious, she'd naturally raised her eyebrows to me in private, but hadn't said anything publicly. The children, though, had caught the vibe, and explained that many weddings were conducted like this these days. She'd loyally kept her counsel, but couldn't resist wondering aloud if it was legal to hold such a ceremony? The children either ignored her or laughed, as if she'd made the most terrific joke, and it was how I wished I could be with her, too.

'Don't let her get to you, Mum,' Teddy had murmured as he saw my nostrils flare, the fire in my eyes. 'No one else minds.'

No. They didn't. She was irrelevant. Just an old lady. And I wondered if I was irrelevant to my boys. No, of course not, but not *as* relevant as Hugh's and my parents had been to us. Not as character-shaping, I didn't think. These days young people seem to shake the shackles of family much faster than we did, despite the current wisdom that children are infantilized for longer, perhaps because there is so much more going on now than when we were young. When we were their age our worlds were smaller; they consisted of our parents, a boyfriend, a handful of friends. Now there was the former, but hundreds of friends, courtesy of social media, and an ever-expanding world of work and opportunities. So we were treated on a need-to-know basis. More peripheral. Or maybe that was just sons? I couldn't speak for daughters.

'Mum?' Nico was beside me, bending down looking at me kindly. I realized I'd been sitting on the front bench in the barn clutching a table plan, staring into space.

'Sorry, darling.' I came to.

'I said, Grandpa and his girlfriend are here with the food, and also a lady called Susie with literally a truckload of flowers?'

'Oh! Yes.' I got to my feet. 'Come – I'll introduce you to Larissa. And Susie! She's a gem; you'll love her, too.'

*

It was still quite early in the morning, and the wedding wasn't until four. We had the whole day to prepare.

Larissa was already in the kitchen, unloading dishes from crates, which were making Ella and Teddy purr with pleasure.

'Ooh, is that the lentil and pepper salad? Amazing!' Ella was circling the table. 'Aubergines with – are these figs? I love figs!'

'These all Greek or Persian influence,' Larissa was telling Ella, as she spread her hands expressively over the half-prepared dishes and ingredients in colourful ceramic bowls and large platters on the table. 'Because your mother, Teddy, she tell me you both like that sort of influence and taste.'

'Oh, we love it!' Ella agreed, clasping her hands in delight. Ella was rather like my son, in that she knew exactly what she liked, but couldn't describe it. Her brief had been obscure: 'Sort of like that cook book with the lemon on the front? And not great slabs of meat or those funny small potatoes? And pretty, with lots of different colours, and modern?'

Larissa had known exactly what she meant, and gone was the woman Jane had recently described as being straight from Magaluf. Despite being dressed in skinny rolled-up jeans and a shirt tied at the waist showing a flat brown midriff, here was the successful businesswoman, who ran her own clothes shop pretty much single-handed, and who was now, with a little help from me, Ella and the boys, ready to produce lunch for fifty-odd without batting a false eyelash. Someone put some music on in the background – Ed Sheeran, I think – and suddenly, all was jolly, yet organized. Yanni, beaming with delight, walked around the table, his eyes shining. Every so often he nudged his grandsons and gestured to Larissa.

'See? My girlfriend, Larissa. Teddy – you see? Larissa. I marry her soon. Nico – look – my Larissa. Beautiful, no? And so talented.'

As the boys grinned and agreed, Larissa rolled her large brown eyes in apology at them. But as she reeled off a set of instructions about filo pastry being covered in damp tea towels and then to be stuffed with ricotta cheese, pine nuts and dates, before darting to the freezer to put her ice creams in to set, she flashed me a look to say she was grateful and happy to be here. I flashed her one back to say I was even more grateful and happy that she was. The looks that would be exchanged when Clem arrived back in her old house to find her here – although yes, of course, she had been warned – would not trouble me for the moment, I decided. The break-up of the marriage and the happy home had been all her doing, and according to Teddy, who'd had lunch with her in London, she was, if not relaxed, then sanguine about the situation. Sanguine, I thought nervously as I showed Larissa where the spices were in the larder. That could mean so many things with Clem, from arch looks to scathing remarks, but I was determined not to let it spoil my day. Instead, I darted out to the drive, where Nico and Sally were helping Susie unload her truck.

21

Susie was bending over her laden pick-up truck looking incredibly busy, but I noticed her hands were shaking slightly as she took out a box. She opened it nervously and presented it to me. It was Ella's bouquet.

'What d'you think?' she asked anxiously as we peered in. 'Is it OK?'

I gasped with delight. 'Oh, Susie, she'll love it! It's just completely perfect.'

It was. Loose and frothy and consisting mostly of something creamy, like cow parsley but no doubt more cultivated for longevity, with rosebuds and greenery and a tiny blue flower I couldn't identify. It was sitting in a bag of water but Susie instantly removed it and transferred it to a vase, then told me she wanted to hustle it to a dark place in the cool.

'The sitting room,' I told her. 'Nico will show you. Nico –' I turned to my son but she'd already gone, hurrying towards the house.

At that moment Rupert drew up in a Range Rover, with a horse box attached. He got out and greeted us cheerily, then went around to pull the ramp down, instructing us to follow. As we went round and gazed inside we saw that draped over the bars, which traditionally divided horses, were great ropes of flowers; they were similar to the ones in the bouquet, but were hanging in huge loops, to be draped about the barn, like bunting. The effect was breathtaking in its simplicity and Rupert's eyes were shining as Sally, Nico and I walked up the ramp to get a closer look.

'Oh!' Sally clasped her hands in joy as she spun around. '*So* pretty!' she breathed. 'Amazing!' And Sally didn't gush.

I couldn't utter a word I was so thrilled, and Rupert was almost speechless with pride. 'Isn't she clever? Don't you just love it?' He was hopping about from foot to foot like a delighted child, much as Yanni had been in the kitchen, and I just loved him for it. 'Susie's so nervous she hurried away while you came in to look, but I knew you'd love it.'

Ella had arrived, and as she walked up the ramp to join us, her eyes filled with tears. 'Oh, Emma,' she breathed. She turned and held my arm. 'It's going to be magical.'

It was. We carefully took the ropes out, then down to the barn in a convoy, then strung them around in great swags. The boys and Rupert were up on ladders, with Ella directing proceedings from below as they draped them over beams and around pictures. The effect was sensational. Susie had provided shepherd's crooks to form an entrance to the barn and showed the boys how to loop some more flower ropes through those. Two great milk churns from Rupert's farm stood sentry at the open barn doors, and both were bursting with the same creamy flowers flecked with blue and greenery. It truly was a bucolic idyll. As we clattered the ladders away and Susie filled the last of the tiny antique jugs with flowers and placed them on the pretty vintage cloths on the trestle tables, the whole barn suddenly flooded with light. The sun had finally decided to come out, and as the beams poured in full of dusty motes, everyone laughed with delight.

Ella fairly skipped away in her excitement, up to the house to try on the simple headdress Susie had given her, and to hold it against her dress. I followed. And, yes, of course I was nervous about the wedding dress, but she'd had fittings before, and had tried it on again last night, and loved it. I'd shown Hugh a few nights ago, when it was finally finished. He'd looked up from his book and said: 'Very nice.'

'It's Ella's vision, of course; her creation really,' I babbled nervously. I stroked the intricate French lace on the bodice. 'I just interpreted it.'

'Very nice,' he repeated, and went back to his book.

Well, of course, I'd made hundreds of dresses, I thought, taking it back upstairs and putting it away slowly in its plastic cover. But this one was special.

This one was for my beloved daughter-in-law, and I'd spent hours and hours hand-stitching that lace into place, and attaching the tiny pearls down the back – a hundred and forty of them in all – and he'd watched me, night after night, first in London, and then finishing it down here. Every evening I worked at it in my chair under the light by the fireplace, or at the table in the dining room with my machine. 'Very nice' didn't seem to cut it, really. I swallowed and directed Susie, who'd come in behind me, to Ella's room, so she could help her with her headdress.

As I went into the kitchen, I wondered then about what my mother had said. Was Hugh unhappy? Had I forced him to come down here, against his wishes? It had certainly been my idea, and I suppose I had pushed it through. But it was his family home, his heritage. And it was beautiful, surely. Enviable. But would I be happy to inherit my family home? Well, obviously not, I had terrible memories. Plus, I'd had so many; we'd moved a lot. Tiny terraced house after tiny terraced house, in ever-decreasing size. But . . . if mine had been as lovely as this, would I have wanted it? I couldn't answer that. Not with a clear conscience. Because who's to say if Hugh's memories were entirely happy? Instead, I went to the freezer to see if the ice creams had set.

People began to arrive an hour or so later, lots of gorgeous young people, most of whom I knew, and a few of whom were staying. Teddy showed them to their rooms. The girls were in floaty summer dresses with flowers and feathers in their hair, but no hats; the boys looked smart in jackets and ties, but no suits or morning coats. Hugh had got the latter out of his wardrobe yesterday, but Nico had had a quiet word about it not being the vibe, Dad. Since Teddy and Ella had wanted this to be the actual wedding, only Barnaby, Teddy's best and oldest friend, and Harriet, Ella's bridesmaid, had gone to the registry office last week. Both of them made a point of seeking me out quickly, and telling me it had been sweet, but casual, that the four of them had gone out to supper afterwards and had a plate of pasta, a bottle of wine. Lovely, but not even champagne, Harriet assured me, and she and Ella had gone straight from work, in their suits. And, no, no flowers. It had been a formality. This day, Ella had been very firm, was her actual wedding day.

Ella's parents, Peter and Pat – easy to remember – appeared, walking down the lawn together towards me. They were staying at a nearby hotel and were as smiley and amenable as their daughter, enthusing about everything they saw. Peter was small and grey with merry, twinkling eyes, and Pat was tall and angular, a terrific swimmer in her youth, apparently, with a hawk-like nose which swooped occasionally, and which I could easily imagine cutting through the water. She was the one with the charm and chatted away easily and excitedly, praising every-thing, whilst he twinkled away quietly beside her, like a little grey gem.

'He'll cry,' Pat warned me, when Ella appeared to greet her parents, still in her dressing gown but with her headdress on, and I'd thought she'd meant at the ceremony, but, sure enough, his eyes filled, and as Ella flew into their arms, a tear did indeed escape. I feared for their walk down the aisle together.

And then, of course, Clem rocked up. She was bound to make an entrance, and did indeed look magnificent. I'd quite forgotten how she was cap-able of that, and suddenly I was the teenage girlfriend again and she was the star. She'd stayed last night with a local friend – despite her hermitic existence down here she did have one or two – and had driven across in their edgy old Land Rover. Of course she had. As she wafted across the lawn towards us in a long, flowing, multicoloured patch-work silk coat, her hair swept back elegantly in a chignon, a floppy straw hat with a diamond brooch stuck firmly on the front by way of a flower, she looked elegant and commanding. Her blue eyes were soft, but I wasn't deceived. She was escorted by Sally, who'd seen her arrive, and I think we were both pleased to have Peter and Pat to introduce her to, to dilute the situation somewhat, and to force an air of polite chatter, rather than pointed remarks.

Out of the corner of my eye I saw that Larissa,

having organized the food as far as she was able, had changed, and was wearing, not a tiny skirt as I'd erroneously feared, but a floating linen dress the colour of pistachios, with a matching linen hat, no doubt all imported from Italy. She looked terrific, but not too obvious, and as she caught my eye there was an unmistakable hint of anxiety. I immediately took Clem's arm and walked her across – Sally, I was grateful to see, giving me a quick little nod of approval. Lance the boil early, I'd thought, and actually, without Yanni.

Clem was all charm and graciousness – indeed quite regal in demeanour – and Larissa, who looked for a moment as if she might curtsey, in fact I detected a little bob, was all deference. She exclaimed at her wonderful taste in dress, hat, house – acting as though it was still Clem's, which I thought was inspired – and grandchildren, and, of course, there was no arguing with that. So long as Clem was queen, and Larissa one of her subjects, all would be well. Larissa comprehended that in an instant. Yanni appeared looking a bit wide-eyed that all this had happened without him, but Clem, having greeted him in a perfunctory manner, then ignored him. She carried on talking to Larissa, telling her the best place in Italy to import her clothes, which Larissa pretended to be thrilled about – all ethically sourced, of course, Clem told her sternly – and the best place to buy fabric. On we went, nodding and smiling and agreeing the while, until Clem finally wafted away, to inspect her vegetable garden. It had gone to seed recently but I was so relieved to get that little interview over, I didn't even bother to intercept her. Yanni, Larissa and I exchanged relieved looks. Yanni mopped his brow theatrically behind Clem's stately back.

Time wore on: the bride disappeared to put her dress on – no hiding in her room for Ella; she'd wanted to greet her guests and parents the moment they arrived – helped by Harriet who was staying. Then Teddy went to change too. The ushers, a handful of Teddy's old school and university friends, with flowers in their lapels, took that as their sign, and went around encouraging people to file into the barn.

Aside from the few front benches, rows of chairs had been arranged. They were mostly from the house, but some were borrowed, and we all trooped in and took our seats, amidst much chatter and excitement. The young went to the back, and my mother, in her good navy blue, was escorted by Nico to the front row. There was a space beside her for Clem, then me and Hugh. Yanni and Larissa were in the row behind. Hugh and I took our seats and smiled across the aisle at Pat and Peter, who were with Mike, Ella's younger brother. There was a spare seat beside him for Ella's bridesmaid, Harriet, then Barnaby and Nico. As everyone marvelled at the beauty of the barn, I heard Yanni chuckle behind me. He tapped me on the shoulder and I turned.

'It so good, yes? You have it up there like an altarpiece!'

I turned back, following his shining dark eyes to the picture above the stage, where Teddy and Ella and the celebrant would stand. It struck me for the first time that maybe I should have moved the nude to a less central spot. That maybe it wasn't entirely appropriate. But it had been there so long, and we'd all grown so used to it, I hadn't really noticed it, if I'm honest. Like a tatty old chair that you don't really know has had its day until you go and stay with someone with immaculate furniture, then return and see it with new eyes.

I shrugged. 'It's fine, Yanni. It's a lovely painting and it's part of the fabric of the barn, now. I might even keep it. Buy it myself.'

He chuckled some more. 'That be even funnier. You should do that, Emma. I like to see what she thinks of that!'

Something about his words made me go cold. I whipped my head back to the painting and stared. The thick dark hair was piled on the head escaping in tendrils from a messy bun. The figure, pear shaped with slim shoulders and waist, had a very ample behind. My mind flew to the distinguished attractive artist, much older than his beautiful wife, the wife who'd looked so horrified when she'd realized I was talking about a picture of her husband's lover. Her husband's lover. Oh dear God. As Clem swept into the barn, having clearly decided to make a late entrance, her coat of many colours floating out behind her, and came down the aisle to take her place between Hugh and my mother, I shut my eyes tight. I felt my mouth go dry, my breathing become shallow, as I prayed for deliverance. To be anywhere, anywhere in the world, except at my darling son's wedding. That was what I asked for.

The chatter around me seemed other-worldly, as if it were happening in a parallel universe. My eyelids had gone into overdrive, flickering wildly with shock. Clem had taken her seat. I waited, paralysed with fear. In another instant, having ordered Hugh to swap places, she was beside me.

'What the hell d'you think you're up to?' she hissed. Her face, when I dared to look, was pale and terrifying.

I was almost too scared to speak. 'I didn't know,' I whispered eventually. 'I swear to God, Clem, I had no idea, until Yanni . . .' There was another terrifying silence and I realized I'd made it worse. I flicked my tongue over my lips. 'I took the painting in good faith, because I liked it,' I managed to croak.

'From Adrian De Morgan,' she hissed.

'Yes, from Adrian –'

'Who gave you no idea what you might be taking?'

276

'Well, I –' I stopped. I didn't take it. Well, I did, but I hadn't chosen it. Sally had. I caught my breath. Sally had selected it, and put it in front of me. But . . . did she know? Had she also been innocent of the identity of the sitter? My head swivelled around to find her. She was behind us, further along the row from her father, beside Polly and Kit, who she was chatting to. But not really chatting. She wasn't really gripped by Kit's conversation. She was doing it with her eyes metaphorically shut. Her actual gaze was on me, and as our eyes met, I saw at once that it was all there: the plot, the trap, the fall from grace – mine – and her mother in the net too. Gotcha. The pair of you. Now her eyes wondered what I'd do. Whether I'd give her away. Blab and say, Sally gave it to me, which might be even worse, I decided. Or take the blame myself, which of course, inevitably, I did. But even as I was telling Clem that it was all my fault, and I was completely to blame, and I was so sorry, an innocent but stupid mistake, I was wondering, with horror, at Sally. What had driven her to spoil my day like this? My special day? To spoil her mother's day, another special day? To elaborately trick us so? I'd even heard her tell her father, as he'd headed down to the barn earlier, to look, that, no, he mustn't go in; it was a surprise. The flowers, the decorations, were only to be viewed when we all sat down. Because even Yanni, diverted though he was, might have said something.

Might have taken me aside and said, 'It's funny, Emma, but she might not be amused, you know?'

And of course only Yanni would know. Only he would know that she had a rabbit tattoo on her bottom. Which Nico, yesterday, had told me, chuckling, probably meant the sitter went like one, too. That was the joke.

I told Clem this now – not the bit about the rabbit, obviously – but that no one in this congregation, apart from her ex-husband, would have any idea that it was her. No one at all. So, really, it wasn't a disaster. Even though I was truly sorry.

'*I* know,' she said, eyes flashing. '*I* know, and that is far more important than anything!' She gave me such a disgusted look that I felt my heart shrivel up and die like a scrunched old leaf.

Hugh was leaning forward and looking at me with confused eyes. 'What's going on?' he muttered, when, as Clem stood up and ordered him back to his seat, he took his place beside me. I had to tell him.

'It's her,' I muttered, nodding discreetly at the picture. What else could I do? Hugh was my husband. I had to tell him. How else to explain my pallor, my fearful look, his mother's terrifying demeanour?

Hugh followed my eyes. Then he went pale and I saw the shock and horror in his face. Here we all were, at our boy's wedding, staring at his naked mother. Our son was standing proudly beneath her, with our other son, his best man beside him, waiting for his bride.

'Idiot!' he spluttered furiously. This was huge for Hugh. He never got angry. Never. So now my day was over. Complete. Ruined. And later, I felt he could have got over his shock. A minute or two later, he could have patted my hand and said, 'It doesn't matter. So what, no one knows. Forget it, darling.' Some might, but not Hugh, apparently. He sat there in stony silence, as all around us bubbled the happy chatter of the young. And so we stared straight ahead, at Clem's large tattooed backside, because there was nowhere else to look. I felt tears gather under my eyelids. I blinked them away. The pianist, a friend of Ella's, was getting a little louder now, a bit more ceremonial, perhaps heralding the entrance of the bride. I blinked madly and took a few deep breaths.

But Ella's wasn't the first entrance to be made. The bride would be delayed a moment longer, because apparently – Rupert crept in to whisper to me – Susie was still helping her with her headdress. They'd be another minute. No, the first entrance was made by someone not on the guest list – Mrs Barlow, or Linda, from the village shop. She appeared in the barn doorway and coughed to make herself heard. I turned. She waved frantically and made huge eyes at me over the congregation's heads. At first I couldn't place her, out of context, but then I did.

I got to my feet. It must be something urgent for her to interrupt. I hastened towards her wondering, what now? A fair bit of me, though, was relieved to be escaping.

'Oh, I'm so glad I caught you,' she told me breathlessly when I reached her at the open doorway. She gripped my arm. 'Has it started?'

'No, not yet – the bride's still having her headdress arranged at the house.'

'Oh, I'm so glad. Only I was afraid he might have missed it.'

'Who?'

'Teddy's grandfather. He turned up at the shop a bit lost and I drove him down here. So he's not too late – good.'

'Yanni?' I frowned. 'He's already here.'

'No, no, not Mr Petridis. This gentleman.'

She turned. I followed her eyes. In the back drive, the other approach to the barn from the lane, was parked a grey Fiesta. The passenger door opened and a tall, elderly gentleman got out. As he walked slowly towards us, I knew immediately who it was. It was my father.

22

For a fraction of a second all motion was suspended as the world tilted. I stared, mesmerized. In another moment the horizon resumed the horizontal and movement commenced. The figure made progress towards me. He was an old man and therefore somewhat altered, but even though it had been very many years, it was so unmistakably him I felt my breath leave my body. Particularly tall and slim, and holding his head slightly to one side as if to reduce his height, his face was one I looked at daily in the mirror. It was also one I'd found in a drawer as a child in my mother's bedside table and scrutinized often.

'Good God,' I heard myself say faintly as he reached us.

'Hello, Emma.' His voice was soft and low.

Linda looked confused, if not confounded. Then she came to some sort of understanding. Backing away hurriedly, she made herself scarce, scurrying away to her car.

'Does Mum know you're here?' I felt overwhelmed by shock and my fingers were trembling. My voice seemed to be operating of its own volition.

'No. I didn't know if I'd make it.'

This sentence was complicated on so many levels. It suggested my mother either didn't know he was coming at all or, in some weird way, she did, but was unclear if he would turn up. I heard my voice ask him which it was, a strange, out-of-body experience.

'She asked me to come. We only communicate by letter, so I couldn't be sure she'd get mine saying that I would. Australian post can take a while.'

This sent further shock waves through me. My mother communicated with my father? He lived in Australia? But it was his voice that shook me. A cut-glass English accent. Not a hint of Australian twang, but not a hint of Estuary English either. The whole effect, together with the dark grey suit and discreet tie, was not of a down-market conman, a door-to-door salesman who'd been had up for thieving, but instead, this man – my father – appeared as erect as a Guards Officer. He had an unmistakably patrician air. Of course, looks can be deceptive. As he stood regarding me, his eyes were kind, warm and full of emotion. I felt something long suppressed and yearned for rise up within me, something suffocated and repressed for such an age began to seep into a great hole of sadness. It was a well of longing too great to be filled just like this, however – too wide, too deep. The pianist behind me was gaining in momentum and gravitas, pounding out 'The Arrival of the Queen of Sheba'. Out of the corner of my eye I saw Ella and Peter emerge from the house. Susie was scuttling along behind, arranging her veil, her dress, like Elizabeth Emanuel with Diana. They were coming towards us.

'You'd better come in,' I managed to mutter.

Inside the barn all the chairs were taken; we had exactly the right amount, except for mine at the front and – oh, look – there was one, right at the back. My father – *my father* – and I, exchanged a glance. He went towards it, with a smile from a friend of Ella's as she quickly removed her handbag before he sat down. Just a late guest.

I hurried to the front, my heart racing, and took my place beside Hugh, and next to my mother, who, clearly oblivious, was still peering myopically at the order of service. Hugh looked relieved to see me and raised his eyes enquiringly. I leaned in close.

'My father's appeared,' I whispered.

Hugh didn't startle easily, but he looked astonished. He drew his head back as if to give himself room to focus on me. 'Really?'

'Really. At the back.'

He didn't turn round – Hugh wouldn't – but he nodded, quietly digesting this.

We all got to our feet, as, to our left, Ella and Peter could be seen approaching the barn doors through the wild-flower meadow. They were processing via a mown path, under a bower of flowers.

In the rustle of everyone rising, I turned to my mother.

'He's here,' I told her softly.

She knew immediately what I meant. The eleventh hour, however, took her by surprise. There was a faint shock to the normally implacable features, but then her eyes gleamed. Not at me. She didn't look at me once. But straight ahead, into the distance.

I felt fury rise within me. How dare she? How dare she shock me like this? How dare she not tell me? But then Teddy, up on the stage, turned briefly, irresistibly, to glance at his dear girl, framed in the doorway with her father, looking radiant and beautiful, and suddenly, remarkably, nothing else mattered. Not Hugh and his lack of support, not Clem and the portrait, not Sally and her scheming, not my mother, not even Rory, always somewhere in my thoughts, and, extraordinarily, not even my long-lost father. Only Teddy, my darling boy, and his deep love and pride, his brother beaming broadly beside him, giving him a nudge and whispering that she looked amazing, as Ella came up the aisle. This was the here and now. The present. My real loved ones. Everything, and everyone else, was in the past. Distant, shabby, disfigured. Only this mattered. Teddy and Ella, Nico flashing back from America to be here, these were my true loves, and how strange that I didn't include Hugh. I glanced at him. His eyes were shining with proud delight, as we exchanged a smile.

The celebrant conducting the service was small, round and jolly, with bright beady eyes like currants in a bun, and a name to match – Bunty. She smiled broadly as Ella and her father, predictably damp-eyed, ascended the steps to the stage. The pianist stopped, a hush fell, and Bunty began to speak. She told us what an honour it was to be conducting this service, and what a pleasure it was to be gathered together in this beautiful rural setting, not a 'dearly beloved' or a 'thee' or 'thou' in sight.

If I'm honest, after that initial burst of love in my heart for my offspring, the ceremony itself – and certainly Bunty's address – was a bit of a blur, as I tried to recover from shock, I imagine. I sat there, in a kaleidoscope of thoughts, my heart racing. Until, that is, it came to the exchanging of the vows. They weren't the ones I was familiar with in a traditional service, but they were pretty similar, and the bits they'd both written about each other were so tender, and so heartfelt, it allowed me to cry properly, about so many things. I wasn't the only one, I thought, glancing about. Hugh passed me a hanky with a smile.

Then a friend of Teddy's sang. It was a rousing, popular song that all the young knew – Coldplay – and joined in the chorus, and I smiled and nodded along, trying to follow the words on the service sheet. Another friend – golly, where did all these talented children spring from? – played a fabulous trumpet solo, which switched key and tone, and suddenly became the Gloria. At that moment, Teddy and Ella turned and strode out, beaming delightedly as they came down the steps arm in arm, sweeping joyfully up the aisle, everyone throwing confetti as they passed.

Outside, in the sunshine, as we cheered and showered them with more rose petals, teenagers from the village, only too willing to earn some money, could be seen standing up on the terraced lawn by the house, ready to serve champagne. The guests drifted up there led by the bride and groom, and clustered around chatting, as the waiters passed through them with their trays. The sun was a little less radiant than it had been earlier, but it was warm and dry, which was all that mattered, and so what if dark clouds were gathering over the hills in the west?

In my peripheral vision I saw my parents approach one another. Neither was smiling as they talked quietly, but then, neither was particularly scowling, either, I decided. Forty years. Forty years since we'd seen hide or hair of him, and now here he was, at his grandson's wedding. Nico was giving my shoulders a squeeze and telling me what a fabulous service it had been and I quietly told him who was amongst us. He looked astonished.

'Shut up.' He turned and stared. 'How come?'

'Apparently Granny asked him.'

'And you had no idea?'

'None at all.'

'Shit. Do they keep in touch?'

'Nico, I have no idea.' We both watched silently as they continued to talk.

'Give them a moment and then go over. Get it done early.'

'You think?'

'Hundred per cent. In fact, I'll come with you. Then I can escort Granny off if she wants to catch her breath.'

'OK,' I breathed. Oh, I didn't need this. Not now. Not today. My fucking mother. Did she think I'd bounce into his arms? Cry 'Daddy!' after all these years? Or did she just not think about me at all, just herself? Yes, probably.

They seemed to be drying up a bit, looking at the ground, so Nico took my arm decisively and off we went. Nico had charm and he easily introduced himself. They shook hands, and then Nico said what a wonderful surprise and how amazing, and a cloud disappeared from my father's face. It was narrow and handsome. I'd been studying it closely.

'Well, I'm pleased. And thank you for saying so – it must be a terrific shock, too. I'm afraid I'm a Luddite when it comes to new technology and I had no one's landline either, otherwise I'd have telephoned ahead to say I was coming, but that I was going to be late. I planned to come a few days ago but my flight was cancelled.'

'Oh no, don't worry about that, we're all delighted. Teddy will be too, I'll tell him.'

'Yes, but maybe not now?' my father said quickly. 'Too much of a shock, I think. Let them have their moment.' We all glanced at Teddy and Ella who were on the upper lawn, moving amongst their friends in a shower of congratulations and happy chatter. It gave us a moment to think how to proceed. My mother took a small step backwards and Nico was on it in an instant.

'Granny will want to congratulate them, though,' he said with a wide smile, taking her arm. 'So I'll take her across.'

They exited smoothly, my mother very pale, I was pleased to see, and not even daring to look at me.

'So,' I said, taking a sip of my champagne – happily I had a full glass, 'How have you been?'

'Emma, I tried many times,' he said quietly, the sarcasm not lost. 'Many times, when you were young. But I was blocked every time.'

'Right. She didn't answer?'

'Not one letter. Or phone call, obviously. And you moved, again and again, according to the increasingly few friends we had in common. So I lost you completely.'

I thought back to the many houses we'd lived in. Every two years, every year, sometimes. Six months, once. Tiny rented terraced house after tiny rented terraced house. Mostly in London, but not always. And friends? My mother didn't have any. She was a recluse. Oh, she chatted to the people next door, in shops, in church, but it was polite, surface talk. For effect. She'd kept in touch with no one from her past. Deliberately, obviously.

'And she wouldn't accept any money, apart from the divorce settlement, and I tried, latterly, to send some. She never cashed my cheques. She was determined to cut all ties.'

'But there are ways. There are other avenues, these days.'

'Yes, so my children kept telling me, but the surnames were too common. Baker and Jones – they tried.'

Children. That rocked me. Punched the breath from my body. Brothers and sisters. I found I couldn't go there right now.

'What happened?' I found myself whispering instead, taking a huge gulp of champagne.

'You mean, all those years ago?'

'Yes.'

He sighed. 'Your mother and I fell in love after I met her at a party, that much you know?'

'No. I know nothing. Assume nothing.'

It was his turn to look shocked. 'Oh. OK.'

'Whose party?'

'My friend, Ralph Morgan-Pritchard. It was at his parents' house in Onslow Gardens. Your mother was waitressing.'

My mouth fell open. '*Waitressing?*'

'Yes.' He looked uncomfortable for a moment. 'Where she worked, at Aquascutum, she didn't get paid terribly well.'

'As a buyer.'

'No, as a seamstress.'

'Right.' All that I knew was wrong. All my knowledge.

'So anyway,' he swept on, alive to this, 'I fell for her immediately. She was very pretty. Very endearing. I asked her out. We had a happy time, and a year later we got married and had you. But . . . I became increasingly unhappy.'

'With her?'

'No, not with her, with my job. I was working in banking in the City, just as my father had done, and his father before him. And I loathed it. I wanted to start my own business, but your mother wouldn't hear of it.'

All around I was aware of youthful chatter and pretty dresses fluttering, and the day that this was, but actually, I wasn't needed. The canapés were circling beautifully, as was the champagne.

'You mean she wouldn't let you leave?'

'No. She'd married a banker, you see, in a suit, in

the City. And she was very proud. She was not going to give that up, or the money. So we rowed. Constantly. Every night, an argument, until I dreaded coming home.' My mouth went dry. I knew that feeling. Not wanting to go home. To my mother. 'But eventually, I did it. I just resigned. I thought, if I presented her with a fait accompli, she'd just accept it. Move on, support me.'

'But she didn't.'

'No. It just got worse. And obviously it was tough, the new life, at first.'

'You sold sandwiches.' I realized there was an accusatory tone to my voice. I wanted my mother to be right about something. 'Door to door.'

'Well, in a sense, yes. But in offices.'

'Right.' My internal vision switched from residential doorsteps to . . . 'Where?'

'In the West End, to begin with. I'd cook the chickens at home, get the freshest bread, salad, mayonnaise, and take them in a basket, still warm. They were delicious.' I realized Nico had drifted back, was listening. Had been listening.

'Like a start-up?' Nico said.

'Exactly. In those days, there were only reasonably ordinary sandwich bars, no Pret a Manger. A few Italian delis were good, but that was it. Your mother hated it, obviously. The house smelled of chicken and I was an embarrassment. She was ashamed of me. And it was a struggle for years, I admit. It was a real effort, no money. She wanted you to go to a private nursery, like our friends' children did, but I couldn't afford it. That was the final straw, I think.'

'She left you?' I was astonished.

'She chucked me out. Told me I could come back when I'd come to my senses. When I'd talked to my godfather about getting my job back, or at least something similar. Stockbroking, perhaps. I had connections.'

'Right. Where did you go?'

'To live? To married friends with a spare basement. They kindly didn't charge me. But it wasn't great. The basement kitchen was tiny and obviously full of chicken and food. I wasn't allowed to see much of you in those days, which killed me.'

I had a sudden familiar flashback that I had occasionally, of being in a playground at school. A man at the wire fencing on to the street.

'You came to watch me.'

'At playtime, yes. Until I was moved on. Your mother heard from the teachers.'

'But you didn't want a divorce?'

'No, I didn't. I hated the arguments but I thought she'd come round. And then I met someone.'

'Oh.'

'Drowning my sorrows in a bar in Earl's Court, doing my sums from the sandwich sales on the back of an envelope. An Australian girl, on her travels, working behind the bar, gave me a kind smile. We got chatting.'

'And?' asked Nico.

'And . . . we ended up seeing one another. She was lovely. Jody. She was renting a flat with girls nearby. In those days it was known as Kangaroo Valley and it was affordable. And they were out all day, nannying, so they didn't care about me using the kitchen. Jody and I saw a lot of each other. After a bit, I more or less moved in. And she helped me. Every morning I'd dash to the market for the salad and she'd go to the baker's as it opened, and then she'd quickly help me assemble the sandwiches before she went to work. It started to go like clockwork. After a bit she gave up the nannying and took the baskets to the offices instead of me. She lined them with red and white gingham . . .' He paused, looked a bit distant.

'Like Little Red Riding Hood,' I whispered.

He smiled. 'Sort of. And she was terribly pretty. So at twelve thirty in the City, just as the boys were getting peckish on the trading floor, a pretty girl would appear with a basketful of hot chicken sandwiches.'

'Irresistible,' breathed Nico.

'And then her flatmates left their au pair jobs and joined in. By then I could pay them more than they were earning. And they were charming, too.'

'And it could have been Mum, helping.' I swallowed. 'And her friends.'

'Yes.' He turned. 'It really could have been.' A light came to his eyes. 'And then we got a van. A green one with a logo. That was huge.'

A sparkle appeared in Nico's eyes too. 'So you could move faster?'

'Exactly. Take off from Long Acre to Leadenhall Market – or wherever. It was so exciting.' The gleam turned to a faraway look. 'We called ourselves Slice of Life.'

'Shit.' Nico looked astonished. 'Didn't that float?'

'Eventually, yes. Some years later. We sold it.'

I stared. 'And meanwhile, Mum . . . ?'

He turned to me. 'Well, yes. Eventually she came and found me. At my van, in Threadneedle Street, actually. I was just loading baskets for the girls, who luckily were already on the first run of the day, in Covent Garden.'

'And?'

'And she looked gorgeous. Terribly elegant. I remember the well-cut suit. I daresay she'd made it herself. And she had the grace to say it looked as if she'd been wrong. And that I was clearly, if not a success, on my way to making something of myself. And that she missed me. And that you missed me. And that she'd been a fool, and she'd like me to come back.'

Nico and I held our collective breath. 'So?' Nico asked eventually.

294

'So, I told her it was too late. That she hadn't supported me when I needed her, or believed in me. But more than that – because I had you, Emma, so I might have got over that hurt – no, much more than that, I told her I was in love with someone else. With Jody.'

'Right.' I nodded. 'Of course. Of course you were. Too much time . . .'

'I'd moved on.' He looked down at the grass. 'And I'm sorry for that. Very sorry.'

I swallowed. Shook my head. 'No. Don't be.'

'I'd have felt the same,' Nico said gruffly.

'So I never went back.'

'And me?' I said softly, glancing up.

'You I saw for as long as I was allowed. I hope you remember?' He looked at me anxiously.

'I do.' Trips to the zoo. The park. Patchily. I was very young. I remembered a sweet shop with jars of sherbet lemons. Just snapshots of things.

'But then came the court case.'

'Ah.' I jolted to attention. This I did know about. Vaguely. A theft of some sort. It had been alluded to once when I was young, but never explained.

'Someone in an office, a girl, said I stole her purse, when I was helping the girls deliver one day.'

'You didn't.'

'Of course I didn't.' He looked astounded. 'But she . . . she'd flirted before. And I hadn't responded.'

He shrugged awkwardly. 'Who knows how another person feels?' I regarded this man, still very good-looking. Something of a catch, back then, I'd imagine. 'Anyway, your mother was . . .' He lowered his voice. 'Vile. She appeared in court saying she couldn't swear I hadn't taken something from her mother's house, once.'

I felt my hand go to my mouth. 'A lie.'

'Complete. But it was enough. Your mother used the court case as an excuse to stop me seeing you. I appealed and got a court order, but she refused to open the door. Said I was unsavoury. It happens all the time, apparently. It doesn't matter what piece of official paper you've got in your hand.'

'So cruel,' I gasped.

He gave me a level look. 'Hell hath no fury.'

Nico looked down at the lawn. 'Shit,' he said softly.

'So when the whole thing had blown over – I just got a heavy fine, no sentence – Jody and I went to Australia. There didn't seem to be much point in staying if I couldn't see you, and we left the girls in charge of the London operation – well, the van. And then we did the same thing in Sydney, near her parents. Started up there.'

'Right.'

'Years later, the girl in the office had a breakdown, and admitted to her therapist that she'd made it up. The therapist went to the police. I flew back enraged, thinking I could surely get the authorities to do more, but your mother had started to move house, so I couldn't even find you. I came back quite a few times. Found a trail to Kent once, but never found you.'

'Yes, we lived in Maidstone for a bit. With a different name.' Two heads swung around in shock. I licked my lips. 'At school . . .' I went on softly, 'I was Emma Simpson. My mother told the teachers my father was looking for me and that he was . . . undesirable.' My father and Nico looked astonished. And then embarrassed. 'That only lasted a couple of years,' I said quickly, not adding – and I've never told anyone. 'When I was twelve, I became Baker again. We were in Essex then. Or Suffolk.'

'Oh, Emma.' It was said by my father with such sadness. Such regret. Such sorrow. Nico put an arm round my shoulders and held me tight. 'I'm so sorry.'

'She's been all right,' Nico said staunchly, looking at him directly. 'We've looked after her, always.' He gave my shoulders a jiggle to stop me crying, but it was too late, my eyes had filled and spilled. I was in trouble. I could hardly see, but I could just make out the house, the back door, not locked, but out of bounds today, with the Portaloo available. Making a gesture with flapping hands that I'd be fine, that I'd be back in a moment, and to continue with the party, I made for the back door. I avoided the crowded terraced lawn, skirting around it along the path. I hurried across the gravel and flew through the kitchen, locking myself in the loo. But not before I'd seen my mother, sitting perched at the kitchen table, in her good navy blue. Her face was ashen.

23

At length I emerged from the lavatory. I'd flushed the chain a couple of times to cover any nose-blowing, but actually, after the initial flood of tears, I hadn't sobbed; I was fine. And I'd had my bag with me so I'd touched up my make-up. That little ritual had calmed me down. Centred me. So that when I appeared, I felt shaken but steady. I sat down opposite her at the table. I didn't say a word. She could speak first.

'Emma, I'm so sorry.'

Not enough. Not enough. I waited.

'Obviously I've done some terrible things.'

'Vile.' I used the word my father had employed. Her mouth quivered in shock. She looked scared. 'Telling the court he'd stolen from your mother. Using it as an excuse to stop him seeing me.'

She hung her head in shame. 'I know. Awful. And Emma, I confess to all of that, daily.'

'On your knees?'

'Yes.'

'It's not enough,' I said with some violence. 'You didn't confess to *me*. You deprived me of a father, who looked for me, constantly. As I had obviously looked for him.' I remembered the fruitless searches on the computer, the dead ends. I'd even hired an agency once, but they told me what I knew. The lack of relatives and common surnames made it an impossible search. 'You deprived me of a man in my life. A nice man.' I felt myself begin to shake again. 'And then you produce him on a whim, on this day, my day, Teddy's wedding day.'

'He was a week late,' she whispered. 'His flight —'

'I know. But the lies, the deception, all these years.'

'I was so afraid.' She looked up at me, her eyes wet. 'So afraid after that girl confessed, that when my lie was revealed – my mother was dead by then so no one could ask her – they'd take you away. Your father and Jody. That he'd tell the authorities, and they'd put two and two together, say I was the unstable one, and the pair of them would be allowed to take you to Australia.' Her voice cracked. 'I'd lose you.'

I gave this some thought. 'I'm not sure that would have happened . . . access, obviously. But to live —'

'But it might,' she interrupted fiercely, clenching her fists on the table. 'It was a terrible, if remote possibility. I couldn't risk it.'

'And so you made it your life's mission to move us constantly, to be forever on the run, should he appear.'

She hung her head once more, a nearly white head, now, soft curls with a small pill-box navy hat.

So correct. So proper. So formal and . . . refined. Which I'd always secretly known, her background wasn't. My grandparents were both factory workers who'd died when I was young. That much I'd discovered. What a struggle, to conceal that. What a fight. For what? Me, obviously, tangibly – but for approval? She'd got it so wrong, purely to keep up appearances. To keep up with the Joneses – literally. My father's family. And every Sunday, there she'd be, in one gloomy Catholic church after another, with her rosary beads, in the darkness of the confessional, with another priest, mumbling the words, head lowered. Emerging with her quick, nervous gait, fiddling with her pearls, always worn to church, hurrying away from her sins. I wondered what the priest had thought as he gathered his Bible and emerged from his booth. Nothing, probably. Another sinner in the litany of many that day. But those really big sins. The terrible ones. Surely it was wrong not to say something – do something about it? Like the therapist did. What gave priests such a charter? Surely they could right those wrongs? I cleared my throat. I was ready to do this, now.

'I have siblings.'

She looked up. 'I know. Two boys.'

'Brothers,' I breathed, my eyes widening. How I would have loved those.

'Half-brothers.'

'Brothers,' I hissed furiously.

301

Again the head went down. 'Emma . . .' she said to her clenched hands, 'it is indeed a terrible thing I've done. Terrible things, I've done. But before I died . . . I wanted – I'd decided – to right it. Perhaps that was a mistake. Certainly the timing was terrible. But had I not made that decision, as I could so easily have done, would that have been better?' She raised her face, her eyes searching mine. 'Had I thought, we're so far down the track now, let it lie, would that have been preferable? You'd stopped searching years ago. Nico and Teddy would never bother to look, it's too distant, too past. Another country, as the quote goes.'

'They do things differently there,' I finished it.

She looked at me appealingly. 'Would it have been better to leave it alone?'

I considered this. 'No . . . but I wonder if you're doing it now for you, or me? As you say, before you die. Are you thinking of the relationship I might have with an elderly man, the brothers I needed so badly when I was young, now middle-aged – or your own relationship with God? On your day of reckoning, at the gates?'

This caused her breathing to become very shallow, very rapid. She licked her lips, nodding quickly, looking fearful. 'Yes. I admit, a bit. Of course.' Then she regarded me challengingly. 'But I could have done it on my death bed.'

God, this was so fucking *Brideshead*. I put my

head in my hands. Suddenly I felt defeated. Spent. There was no reckoning with this woman, with the demons that filled her head: the religion, the snobbery, presumably all learned from her parents who I'd never known, who'd died when I was three. Presumably she, in a way, couldn't help it either. It was who she was: who and what had moulded and defined her. Learned behaviour. From her very few stories, few possessions – crucifixes, her mother's Bible, the single strand of pearls – I'd formed a picture of my socially mobile grandparents who'd desperately wanted a better life for their only daughter. Didn't everyone want that, though, in their defence? And after all, I'd been so determined for my own background not to define me. But had it? I'd gone out with Hamish. I'd never have looked at Lance, as Jane, socially secure Jane, had done. And I'd married Hugh, from an equally established family – even Yanni was the son of a diplomat. And I'd thought I was the daughter of a sandwich seller. Yet so I was. So what did that say about me?

I lowered my head and massaged my temples feverishly with my fingertips, my thoughts whirring. Outside I could hear the little jazz quartet Ella had found locally in full swing. When I raised my head I saw, through the window, the pretty girls, the handsome boys, throwing back their heads, laughing, the flowers on pedestals. I had to go. At that moment Nico flew in. He took in the scene but it didn't deter him.

'Mum, the cake's about to be cut. The speeches.'

I was already on my feet. 'I'm coming.' I was. Out I flew. Or walked. Quite tall, actually, not anxious, not running, and it occurred to me that perversely I felt more in control than I ever had in my entire life. Because I knew now, you see. I knew who I was. I knew what was missing. And it all fitted into place. Before, there had been so much lacking. I felt complete. I knew it was what had been truly wanting in my life.

Hugh was on the outer circle of an ever-gathering crowd which was moving into the tent, his eyes searching for me. He looked relieved as I came across. Nico was behind us, firmly holding my mother's arm.

'Thank God. Are you all right, darling?' His eyes searched mine, concerned.

'Absolutely fine, honestly.' His face cleared; he knew it to be true.

'OK, cake in a mo, then speeches. Come on, up at the front.' He took my arm and muscled us through, but the young parted anyway, smiling, some girls darting a kiss on my cheek as we went to the cake table, the boys clapping Hugh's shoulder. I knew them all, loved them all. Darling Poppy, petite and blonde, always with her ready smile. Sam, Teddy's great friend from school, once chubby and bespectacled, now tall and handsome but still so funny.

Harriet, the bridesmaid, fussing briefly over Ella's dress as she and Teddy stood beaming beside one another, glowing with delight.

Hugh spoke, beautifully, as I knew he would, he'd rehearsed his speech to me before, then Teddy, amusingly – but so warmly, too, of Ella – and then Nico, hilariously. Mostly it involved his futile attempts to corrupt his more conventional, better-behaved brother, encouraging him to smoke, study less, drink more heavily. I caught sight of my father, at the back, laughing. Enjoying it. Learning a lot. All of it was perfect. The cake was then cut, a heavenly creation from Larissa: meringue, cream and raspberries, the top sprinkled with tiny blue edible flowers which Susie had given her. I'd spotted them together earlier, busy and whispering. The buffet table was laden with food, and everything could be eaten with a fork – Teddy and Ella hadn't wanted a formal sit-down affair – so although there were many chairs and tables dotted around the tent for those who wanted to perch, most people stayed standing and indeed, eventually, everybody drifted outside. The tent had been the wet-weather option and was muggy, and now that it was warm and dry, if not sunny, the lawn was preferable.

The photos were taken by a sweet friend of Ella's, a French girl, who darted about with her camera, whispering '*fromage*', which made everyone laugh. A few chairs were pulled out from the tent on to the

grass by Hugh, and I saw my mother and my father –
my parents – sitting talking quietly. I stared for a long
moment, then looked away. Over by the duck pond
I saw Larissa and Yanni on the Lutyens bench;
Yanni was encouraging Larissa to sit and eat, all his
hand gestures telling her the food was perfect, she
could do no more. At length I saw her sit and accept
the plate of food he'd got her with grace. Her eyes
still darted about though, watching as the young
devoured it with gusto – it was delicious – and then
as she ate, finally nodding, critically, yet approvingly.
Rupert and Susie joined them, dragging up chairs –
Yanni leaping to help – because I'd told the pair
very firmly they were not to go until they'd eaten,
that was the deal. They'd protested about their jeans
and T-shirts, but in this relaxed milieu, it couldn't
matter less, I'd told them, although I noticed they
made themselves scarce quite quickly, casting me a
grateful look as they deposited their plates. I shot an
even more grateful one back.

I was standing in a group of chattering young,
but was aware of Polly behind me talking to her
mother, who still looked furious. I overheard Polly
asking her what the matter was. Was it that Tom
hadn't come – he'd rung and apologized profusely,
farming being a full-time job – and Clem said, no,
it wasn't that. Polly persisted, but Clem was refusing to say, muttering something about a headache.
But instead of quaking as I normally would, I

actually felt quite angry. Oh, for God's sake, move on. No one knows it's you, Clem, and anyway, so bloody what? It's your own stupid fault for letting it be painted, and then not snapping it up, destroying it, if needs be. I even felt confident enough to turn around and flash her a quick glare before moving on to talk to Jane. Clem caught it and looked astonished. It was the first time, I realized, I'd ever astonished her. The first time I'd ever slapped her down, said – behave, at your grandson's wedding. It's not about you. What had given me that confidence? I wondered. Could it be that tall, distinguished-looking gentleman talking to Hugh, Teddy and Ella right now, Nico and my mother beside them? Had his presence made me ridiculously self-assured with Clem, my somewhat bullying, patronizing mother-in-law?

As I watched the group I realized Nico had abandoned his decision not to tell his brother. This was not a huge party and Teddy would naturally be intrigued to know who the stranger was. I pretended to fiddle with some flowers on a pedestal so I could watch the scene develop, but Jane had seen me make a move towards her and had peeled off from Lance to intercept me. She followed my eyes.

'Emma, who is that man?'

I swallowed. 'He's my father.'

She went very still. 'How come?'

I told her. As briefly as I could. It obviously took

a while, though. During which monologue the grandfather chatted to his new family.

'Christ. What a day to choose.'

'She didn't mean it to be today.' I realized I was defending my mother. 'His flight was cancelled last week.'

'Still, not to tell you.'

'She couldn't be sure he'd come.' Again, I came to her rescue.

'And how d'you feel?'

'Well, furious, obviously, that it's so late in the day. About forty years late.'

Jane made a face. 'I imagine she had her reasons.'

'Of course, but also, weirdly . . . I feel strangely OK. *Pleased* is beginning, just beginning, to creep into my internal vocabulary.'

She smiled and I saw her eyes well up. She took my hand and squeezed it but neither of us spoke. She knew me very well. Knew the pain, the loss, the sense of incompleteness. And the insecurity.

'He looks like you.'

'I know.'

'Can I meet him?'

'Of course.'

We moved towards the family group. A couple of friends were having to leave early, to catch a flight, and had also moved across to say their goodbyes. Ella turned to kiss them but Teddy saw me and, ever the enthusiast, sent his friend an apologetic look for his brevity, just clapping his shoulder, and bounded past him to envelop me in a hug.

'*So* pleased, Mum,' he whispered in my ear, holding me tight. Darling Teddy, always of the glass half full.

'Yes, I'm beginning to think that,' I whispered back.

He released me and held me at arm's length, his eyes searching mine. 'Of course. Of *course* better late than never.'

'Definitely,' Ella said coming across, her eyes shining with tears. 'And what a lovely man.'

'Isn't he?' I said, knowing my eyes were shining too, but not with tears – with pride, I realized. 'Isn't he nice?'

And he was where I came from. The other half of me. That was proud-making. Not just my reclusive, prim, slightly odd mother, who I always had to explain to friends – the occasional ones who met her. This charming, elegant, clever and, yes, OK, classy man, was my father. Who looked just like my friends' fathers. I realized I wanted to introduce him to Clem, to Yanni, to Polly and Kit – especially to Clem, I thought, as Jane, too overexcited to wait, had gone ahead to grab Nico, who willingly introduced her, as pleased as anyone to do so, I realized. And years ago, I had told both my children about a friend of mine, Martin, who was adopted, and who had, in his early twenties, and after a blissful upbringing with

309

adoptive parents, traced his birth mother, out of a gnawing desire for knowledge. For background and context. His search had led him to a slum just outside Naples, a tower block, where dustbins rolled in the wind, litter blew, needles were strewn on the ground, and mangy cats lurked. He'd climbed the outside staircase to the fifth floor and walked down a dank, smelly corridor. Behind a peeling apartment door came the sounds of angry voices; a large dog barked. Martin had turned away and gone home.

'Is that why you've given up?' the boys had asked, teenagers then. 'Because you're afraid of what you might find?'

'Of course.'

Their eyes had widened as they'd nodded. But they hadn't pushed it. And I'd wondered if, at their smart London schools, with their lovely friends, they had silently agreed, had not wanted me to push it either. Hadn't exactly warmed to the idea of welcoming grandparents and cousins from a totally different background, into their family. We're only human. And at that age we just want to fit in. At any age, maybe. Right now, however, I was pleased to see Hugh approach my father, together with his mother – stick that up your tattooed arse, Clementine Petridis – and was actually looking around for anyone else I might find who might meet him, before I obviously had hours and hours with him later, on my own.

I was aware of someone watching me. I turned. Sally. Her eyes darted away quickly, back to where she was fiddling with pieces of cake, putting a few slices on plates, with forks, a folded paper napkin beside them. Sally, who had decorated my barn so beguilingly, let us not forget. I exhaled a long breath. Then I put my empty glass down, raised my head, and marched across to her.

24

The couple with an imminent flight had intercepted me, however; they approached, smiling, wanting to say goodbye, to thank me for a fabulous party, exclaiming, enthusing. As they moved on, more guests approached. Most were going back to London. I chatted to them all, enjoying their company, their jokes, their banter, the girls rolling their eyes at having to drive their pissed boyfriends home, but one or two boys rolling their eyes at the girls who were even *more* pissed, so they were getting a taxi into town, to a B&B. I begged them to stay, even though we were full – Harriet and her boyfriend in one room, Barnaby in another, Teddy and Ella, Nico, my mother, of course – said I'd find room somehow, but they wouldn't, laughing and telling me that the Red Lion had always been an option. It became clear that quite a lot were staying there, having an evening session in the pub. I even wondered if Teddy and Ella might join them, and when I hastened to find them and ask, they looked relieved.

'But only if you really don't mind, Mum? We're super happy to stay, to have supper with the family and –'

'No, no, you must! I can't believe we hadn't thought that through – of course party on with your friends.'

'Well, it had never been the plan; it's all a bit impromptu – it always is with Barnaby at the helm –'

Teddy turned to grin at Barnaby who was making a helpless shrugging gesture, tie askew, eyes already a bit glazed, but clearly hoping Teddy had been given the green light. I laughed.

'Go. And take Nico with you. You're not flying to Greece till tomorrow; you could stay at the pub.'

'Exactly, they've taken the whole place. They had another wedding party there who cancelled at the last minute; the groom had an accident.'

'Oh, Lordy . . .'

'Well, quite. But it did slightly fall into place for us. Barnaby took the whole booking.'

I smiled. 'Perfect. Take your cases with you – and Harriet and Gus and whoever else was staying – Barnaby, obviously – and get a taxi to the station in the morning.'

We all hugged warmly. Ella whispered in my ear that it had been the best day ever and that she couldn't thank me enough, and then she flew upstairs to change into her going-away dress, a floaty Reformation number. Someone had tied tin cans to the back of our old Land Rover, which Susie had decorated with flowers, so first there was a bit of a charade as they pretended to go away – in fact, it was once around the fields – and we could even see them do the entire circuit, which made everyone cheer as they gathered to watch. Some people had missed the Land Rover taking off initially, however, so when they rumbled back in a cloud of dust everyone roared, 'Go again!' Off they sped once more, this time Ella tossing her bouquet, which she'd forgotten to throw, out of the window to Harriet, who caught it and everyone cheered again. My parents included, I realized. Both of them were laughing, caught up in the moment, and who could fail to be? Well, Clem could. Clem was amongst us, but on the fringes, a tight smile on her face, as Yanni shouted his approval to Harriet's long-term boyfriend, Gus, who looked sheepish but grinned broadly, admitting defeat.

Taxis began to arrive and the young dispersed, along with Ella's parents, who'd sensibly booked a quieter hotel at the other end of town. We'd invited them to stay but they'd been emphatic; even though Ella was in the house, and despite these less formal times, bridal parties should be separate. 'Trust me, you won't want us,' Pat had said firmly down the phone from the States. 'You've got enough on your plate as it is.' Yanni and Larissa drove off with Larissa at the wheel, but not before I'd thanked her effusively, insisting I should pay for more than just the ingredients, but she wouldn't have it; she maintained it was her wedding present. Polly and Kit went, having caught me earlier to say goodbye, and Jane and Lance were away too. I wandered down to the field with them where the cars were parked and stood at the fence to wave them off. Lance gave me an extravagant wave above the car roof as he took his jacket off, Jane blowing me a final kiss. Which was when I saw Sally again. And I'd been looking for her. She was darting forward into the meadow of parked cars from another gate to kiss Jane goodbye, and then they had quite a long and intense discussion. Finally, Jane got in the car where Lance was waiting, and Sally turned away. But not before she'd inadvertently caught my eye. I could tell she didn't mean to. She put her head down and hastened towards her cottage.

I was after her. I needed to do this now while I still had the nerve, and not some time later when I'd lost that edge, the one that was driving me on to be someone different, more sure of myself. Her footsteps were hurried and she didn't glance behind her as she went down the mown path to her cottage. The door was on the latch and she slipped in and almost shut it behind her – but my hand was in the jamb. I'm not sure whether she'd imagined she was alone, or had known I was behind her but thought she'd given me the slip. Either way her face fell when she turned and saw me.

'Sally. Could I have a word?'

'Could it wait? I've got a stonking headache. I just headed down here for some pills – too much champagne as usual!'

'It won't take a mo,' I said. I slid inside, not even offering to wait while she got the paracetamol. I knew it was a ruse. I shut the door behind us.

She walked casually to the other end of the room and was plumping a cushion, pills clearly forgotten. I joined her. 'Sally, why did you get me to take that naked picture of your mother?'

She glanced up from picking up another cushion. Dropped it and gave me a withering look. 'Oh, now, Emma. Come on. I did no such thing. I merely suggested Adrian was a good artist, which he is.'

'Not true. You gave me that specific painting. You even hung it yourself.'

'I gave you a collection of paintings.'

'Two others. All of which I took. You suggested three paintings from Adrian and I eagerly, gratefully, took them all. You watched me lap them up. And then you suggested Teddy and Ella got married in the barn. Under the portrait. And you don't deny you knew it was your mother?'

She sighed elaborately. Contrived to look weary. 'Dear God. What is this all about?'

'It's about you tricking me, Sally. It's about you laying a trap for me to fall into. A little unexploded bomb, which would go off at my son's wedding. Which it did, incidentally. She's furious. With me.'

'Actually you're wrong. I had no idea he painted her.'

'You're lying.'

She looked astonished. All her habitual, lazy condescension deserted her for a moment. It was a look I'd seen quite recently on someone else's face: her mother's. It was abject surprise at not holding the trump card, at not having superiority.

Suddenly her face turned to fury. 'All right,' she snapped. 'Maybe I did know. But if you were too stupid not to check out the provenance, not to go and see Adrian, ask who it was, just gormlessly watch me hang it there in pole position, to *imagine* you could set up some kind of an art gallery here, with no experience whatsoever – it was laughable. And the artists you *chose* were laughable too, all that realistic crap you took to ingratiate yourself with your new best friend –'

'That's not true!' I snapped. 'I liked their work!'

'Desperate to chummy up and be another do-gooder with your charitable tokenism, trying to be lady bountiful, the lady of the manor – the sort of stuff Mum scoffed at, incidentally; justifying privilege, she called it. You got that wrong –'

'Sally, this is me.' I was horrified, suddenly. 'Your friend. What are you – We go way back. What are you doing? What are you saying?' But she wasn't finished.

'Trying to occupy my mother's shoes –'

'I *never* tried to do that!'

'And, yes, we go way back.' She was shaking now, with anger. She was very pale. 'And you took everything from me then, just as you're taking everything

317

now. My family home, even my parents' bedroom for fuck's sake –'

'Sally –'

'But back then it was Hamish. Oh, you had to have him, didn't you? Even though you didn't really want him. Even though you were just passing the time until something better came along, and even though you knew he'd been my boyfriend and I loved him.' Tears had filled her eyes.

'Sally – you and Hamish . . .' I was astonished. 'It was so brief, so –'

'So what, Emma? So inconsequential? Just the one term, it hardly constitutes a relationship? And then he saw you. And fell in love with you – not that you cared. And then killed himself when he saw you carelessly fall for someone else. His brother. He drowned himself. You're careless, Emma. Because of the way you look, you think you can waft through life taking things that don't belong to you. Just because you're pretty and I'm not. You took Hamish, and you killed him. Then you took my brother. I invited you down here, and at that party, over there in that meadow, around the fire, you ensnared Hugh. I'm not sure you really wanted him either, because you were in love with someone else. But because he ticked all the right boxes, you thought you'd have him anyway. By then you'd taken Jane, my best friend. Oh, you've hung on to her all right. Really tight. So now you've got everything. And then, dear

Emma, dear, *charitable* Emma, out of the kindness of her heart, asks spinster Sally, poor, unmarried, unloved Sally, to take over the little cottage, in the grounds of her estate. Emma's estate. And everyone thinks she's fucking wonderful. But are you wonderful, Emma? Are you? Or are you at it again? Stealing things, like a magpie. Anything shiny that's not yours. Are you perching prettily on sculptures at Kaplinsky's taking other shiny men that don't belong to you? My boyfriend from Paris, perhaps? Did it even occur to you to wonder how I'd feel about that? And are you about to destroy someone else's life in the process, as you destroyed mine and Hamish's? My brother's, perhaps, with your careless ways?'

My legs, by now, had deserted me. I was sitting on the arm of her velvet sofa. I felt numb and cold as I stared up at her. Her face was deathly pale, but composed. Years of hatred, years of bitterness were there, and I was both devastated and flabbergasted. I'd never known. Never even suspected. She took a step closer.

'So did I plant a painting, of my equally careless, unloving mother – who was ashamed of me, incidentally, growing up, since I wasn't a beauty like her? Did I contrive for two electric shocks to go off at once? Yes, you're right, I did. Not in any formulated way, but when I saw the painting at Adrian's I thought, aha, I wonder. And, golly, it fell into place, didn't it? Worked beautifully. Not a huge retribution, I think you'll agree, in the scheme of things. When set against a lifetime of hurt. No one died. Hardly crime of the century. You had everything, Emma. You've always had everything. Charm, charisma, looks, an easy manner – and I had nothing. Yet you still took what little I had from me.'

She didn't move. She seemed rooted to the spot she was standing on. She didn't give an almighty sob and rush to her room in floods of tears as I might; she just stared down at me. Eventually I found my voice.

'Sally, you're wrong. *You* had everything. I was the one who had nothing.'

'Like what?'

'You had background. You had family. Money. Savoir faire. So did Jane. I arrived at university with nothing. I *had* to be charming, to make it work for me. I couldn't just exist, like you and Jane. I worked hard at the charm, the banter, to overcome my own insecurities.' Suddenly I was on my feet. 'I always felt in your shadow. Always felt I was running to catch up with my new friends, hiding my past, my home, my mother, my absent father –'

'No one cares about that sort of thing any more –'

'*I* care,' I whispered furiously. 'And *you* would care if you came from nowhere – if you didn't know where you belonged and were trying to, not just reinvent, but *invent* yourself. You didn't try hard enough, Sally,' I said sadly. 'You were lazy, because you were born with advantages. You were entitled. You acted entitled.'

Perhaps I shouldn't have said it, but I did. Because it was true. Sally would never hide a bad mood when we were younger, would never raise her game, never smile anyway. She was who she was, who she'd been born to be. Get on with it, everyone else, was her attitude. I'm going to be myself because I'm privileged, and I can afford to be. I saw some sort of recognition cross her eyes. There was a lot more I could say, but I didn't. I didn't say that not being blessed with beauty was a poor excuse. I didn't say that plenty of plainer girls had storming successes with their personal lives. I didn't tell her that if I came home from school in a bad mood my mother would make me go back up the road and come back with a smile on my face. She wouldn't understand. Clem would never do that. The Petridises could be who they wanted to be. Because there was no petty thief lurking in their midst, no conman, no restraining order.

I didn't say any of that to Sally. But I knew, with a heavy heart, that we could never be friends again. Too much had been said. And I was shocked and horrified, but strangely, just as a piece of a jigsaw had fallen into place in my life earlier, so another did now, with a horrible clunk. It did make sense of so much, over the years. So much of my tiptoeing around her, but not knowing what I was creeping over. What shards of broken dreams I instinctively avoided, but didn't know the true identity of, like sharp pieces of glass on the carpet you come across but don't recognize. I wondered if Jane knew, if she kept her counsel about both of us. Remained friends to both of us, but knew our raging insecurities and, in her sweet way, tried to reconcile and juggle both of us. I suspected she did.

And what of Sally now, what more vengeance might she take? What would she do with that piece of information she'd spat out, that dart in my eye about Rory and me sitting in the gallery garden. It wasn't such a surprise. I knew she'd been in the deli opposite, had seen the Kaplinsky's box. I had obviously wondered. And I hadn't disregarded her seeing us. Would she tell Hugh? I thought not. Her shoulders had sagged now in her silk Rixo dress, and she was turning away. Going towards the stairs. She looked old and tired. Much, I suspected, as I looked old and tired. Two hormonal old women finally locking horns after all these years. Now spent.

I turned too and made for the front door. But as Sally went upstairs to her room and shut the door behind her, I heard another distinctive click, which I'd heard before in this house. Another door closing. A familiar one. It was the entrance Sally and I usually used to this cottage, the back door to the kitchen, together with a cheery 'yoo hoo!'

I moved to the window and glanced out. Someone was hurrying away along the path, but they'd gone. I couldn't see who it was. I went into the little galley kitchen at the back of the house. There was a mug of tea on the side, untouched. But there was a smudge of bright magenta lipstick on the rim. I'd know it anywhere. It was Clem's.

25

So Clem had been in here, listening, all this time. Of course she was staying here, I realized. In Sally's cottage. No room at the inn, up at the house, with Teddy's friends, and indeed she'd suggested this arrangement. It had suited everyone, frankly. To have the slightly prickly pair down here. What had she made of all that, I wondered? Everything she'd overheard?

As I left, I saw I was about to find out. Far from hurrying away, as I'd assumed she would, when I turned the corner of the mown path which led back to the marquee – only the boys and girls from the village remaining, moving back and forth into the tent for empty glasses – Clem was sitting on the bench by the pond. She was watching as I approached. It was almost as if she was waiting for me. So this was interesting. Because she would not be aware that I had recognized her lipstick. That I knew she'd overheard. And she'd scurried away quickly enough not to be seen, just a rustle in the undergrowth. She'd think she had the upper hand.

I tried, frantically, to remember exactly what had been said: the painting, obviously, which she now knew was her daughter's doing. Not ideal, but it did put me in the clear. And perhaps Sally saying she felt unloved because her mother had expected a beauty, and had been disappointed, was not a disaster either. It might be good for Clem to know. She would have her own views on whether I, with what Sally called my careless ways, my magpie eye, or Clem herself, with her obvious disappointment in Sally, had wrecked her daughter's life. Or, indeed, if neither of us were responsible. If Sally just hadn't taken enough responsibility for her own actions, had harboured too much bitterness. But what of the other detail? Sally hadn't mentioned Rory's name, had rather obscurely referred to me sitting on sculptures with an ex of hers. I felt it was oblique enough to be confusing to Clem, certainly now, in the immediate aftermath, and without the benefit of more forensic reflection. Although Sally had asked if I was about to wreck her brother's life too. What would Clem make of that? My heart began to beat right up in the base of my throat as I got closer. I plastered on a smile and Clem crossed her legs and smiled too, but it didn't reach her eyes. Her back was to the marquee and on an impulse I raised my hand.

'Coming, Gemma!' I called above her head to a waitress, as if I'd been summoned.

Gemma turned in surprise, gave me a wave, and carried on.

'Must give them a steer,' I explained, flashing a

smile to Clem as I made to go past, but she wasn't having it.

'Oh, they'll manage,' she said, darting out a hand to catch my wrist. She patted the space on the bench beside her with her other hand. 'Come. Sit a minute with your old mother-in-law. Take a moment.'

Terror beat in every vein; every pore on my body seemed to open wide and gush forth. I hesitated, but her eyes were like narrow slivers of steel. I sat. Obediently. What else could I do? Being side by side at least had the benefit of not looking at each other, but on the flip side, our view was of Sally's cottage. The scene of so much recent drama. I swallowed and waited.

'Lovely wedding,' she said smoothly.

'Wasn't it?' I agreed, not fooled for one minute. 'I'm glad you enjoyed it, Clem.'

'Well. Not all of it, obviously.'

'No. I know. And I've apologized for that.' You old witch. You absolutely know that was not my fault.

'You'll have it removed?'

'I'll have it destroyed.'

She looked taken aback. Pulled her patchwork coat around her knees in an uncharacteristically prim manner. 'Oh. Well. No need to do that. Tell you what, I'll dispose of it. I'll take it.'

You bet she would. It was actually a very good picture, a very flattering, beautiful portrait, albeit with an ample behind, of a stunning woman in her younger days, with a tiny waist and tumbling dark hair. Clem would not want to see that go up in flames. I could even imagine her hanging it in her Shoreditch flat, puffing on a long, thin cigar as her bohemian friends admired it.

'Clem, darling, what a stunning nude!'

'That? Oh, you know. I picked it up, somewhere.' A secret smile to herself as she poured the drinks, eyes ostentatiously averted, so they'd all know. Ah. Clem. The beauty. Painted by an admirer. A lover. Back in the day. She'd love it.

'OK,' I said lightly. I made to get up. 'If you put the seat down in your car I'm sure it will fit in the back. I'll ask Nico to pop it in.'

'Yes. Or Hugh.'

I looked at her. 'Yes. Or Hugh.'

She gave me a narrow look. 'How is Hugh?'

Breathe. Deeply. 'Hugh's fine.' I gave a little laugh. 'I mean, obviously he's fine, we've just had the best day of our lives. In fact, he's in heaven, like me.'

'Yes. Of course.' Even Clem seemed to wrestle with herself as to whether or not to shove me off my stratospheric cloud, but what came next was unexpected. 'Classical music really is his great love, isn't it?'

I was surprised. 'Yes. It is.'

'Mahler, Strauss – all the gang, as he used to call them. His bedroom used to hum with all those records or tapes he had. Does he still play it here?'

'Music? Of course. All the time. But mostly through his clever ear things Nico got him for Christmas.'

'Ah yes. A private pleasure. The best sort.' I looked at her. What was she up to? 'And his concerts, in London –'

'Hello, you two!' My mother suddenly appeared beside us. She looked bright, perky even – something she rarely did.

'Hello, Mum,' I said warmly as she sat down beside Clem, who was in the middle of the bench now. I leaned forward and smiled around my mother-in-law at her. 'You've had a good day.'

'Oh yes. And I hope I didn't ruin yours?'

'Not a bit of it.'

Clem was looking put out. Struggling with herself again. Too much was not about her, suddenly: *her* son, *her* family, the Petridis clan.

'Yes, a wonderful surprise. Your father appearing,' she said politely, and I watched as she wracked her brains for a way to steer us back, conversationally.

'Where is he now?' I asked my mother, before she could.

'Gone back to his hotel. We're having dinner there later. He wanted to shower and change and give Jody a ring – she'll just be waking up. Tell her it went well. Tell her it's fine.'

I gazed at her. Begone, Clementine Petridis. I just want to talk to my mum. Tell her I'm proud of her. That it is so much better to be late than never.

'He thought the two of you could have lunch tomorrow,' my mother went on. 'I said I'd float the idea with you first. No rush if you wanted more time, he said; no need to –'

'No, I'd like that. Please tell him yes.'

My mother and I both rose as one. If Clem wouldn't go, we would. This was an intensely private moment. Mum reached for my hand and I took it. In some small corner of my mind it occurred to me to wonder why she'd sought me out when I'd been with Clem, but we were on our way now, back to the house, arm in arm, which was a first. In my whole life, we'd never linked arms. We chattered quietly about this man, David, my father, tentatively, sometimes, painfully, wistfully, but that didn't matter.

'When is she going?' my mother asked me later. We were in the kitchen and she was slipping into a jacket, getting ready to go into town. I'd ordered a taxi for her.

'Clem? Tomorrow. Early, I think.'

'And she's not going with you tonight?'

Ella's parents had texted from their hotel to say that since Hugh and I were now on our own: *The young having bomb burst!* 😊 *How about joining us for supper? There's a nice Italian down the road from our hotel.* I'd run off to find Hugh and we'd accepted eagerly, not wanting the day to end, wanting to pore over every detail of the wedding, our joint, glorious day. We could relive the flowers, the speeches, the young people, and get to know Pat and Peter better. I turned to Hugh now, who'd just come in from paying the boys and girls. He was still looking happy and flushed from the day as he shrugged on a linen jacket.

'You haven't asked them along, have you?' I asked him. 'Clem and Sally?' God, the horror.

'Absolutely not,' he said firmly. 'We don't want them. This is our day, a happy day.' It was the first time I think I'd ever heard him say anything remotely derogatory about his family.

A car drew up outside. 'Come on,' he said suddenly, 'let's all get in your mum's taxi. I'm far too pissed to drive. And we'll get one back.'

I hurriedly grabbed my bag and my jacket and out we all flew, like naughty children. A happy band, it occurred to me in surprise, as Hugh got in the front with the driver, and Mum and I climbed in the back.

And a happy evening it was too, as, having dropped Mum off at my father's hotel, we went on for supper with Pat and Peter at the Italian, where Pat and I relived every moment of the day. The flowers – I told her all about Susie. The dress – she enthused madly about my work. She'd known I'd made it but her eyes popped out of her head as she marvelled at the intricate needlework, enlarging photos on her phone, poring over them with me. I'd been far too preoccupied to take any so was delighted to see them. The food – 'That cake!' she exclaimed. 'Who made it? Larissa again?' Pat wanted to know every detail, and I was so willing to forget the bits that hadn't made the day so fine, so dandy, that I was more than happy to have a girly chat about everything else. Hugh and Peter, meanwhile, extolled the virtues of the English sparkling wine we'd served, and its merits over French champagne.

Eventually, we moved on to my father, who, of course, they'd heard had arrived. Ella had pointed him out. As the men broke off their wine chat to listen, I found myself telling them his story, which I'd yet to tell Hugh, and which of course was private, but, in a way, not. It was fact. And these people were my daughter-in-law's parents, not just anyone – extended family, really. Everyone here had my back. There was a silence when I'd finished. Hugh was gazing at me. Only then did I wonder if I should have told him privately, but there was no disapproval in his eyes. Only a sadness, I think, for what I'd never had, what had been taken away. He put his hand over mine on the table and Pat sweetly reached out and squeezed my arm, but I didn't cry. I didn't feel sad, you see, as I think they did, recalling their own happy childhoods perhaps, with their fathers around. I felt very pleased to have finally got there. To have caught up. It had been a long race, but I'd made it in the end.

'He looks very fit,' Peter said thoughtfully.

I turned to him gratefully. 'Doesn't he? Not an old, old man.'

What we meant was it looked as if we'd have a good few years together. And no one said Australia's a long way. It was all too immediate to get practical. Let's just absorb. Let it sink in.

'He's here for a couple of weeks, though,' I said with pleasure. That much I had gleaned from my mother. 'Staying in London, at Claridge's.'

Why had I said that? I don't know; I couldn't resist it, I suppose. But I made a mental note not to do what the Petridises had done so often to me. Paraded their credentials. Pat, however, was sweetly enthusiastic.

'Oh my, that's pretty grand, isn't it? He must be quite a guy.'

'Yes,' I said happily. 'Yes, I think he is.'

And why resist it, actually? Surely everyone on *Who Do You Think You Are?* would rather find Henry VIII at the end of their family tree, and not the workhouse? Certainly not a thief. Or a conman. Which is what I'd thought all my life. It was the one thing I knew I'd struggle with forgiving my mother for, but I knew I must. Who was it said to forgive was divine? Probably Jesus. And there she was again, Mum, in the confessional, with her rosary. I sighed. I had to do it. Had to forgive her. I knew I sort of had, already.

We walked Peter and Pat back to their hotel, said goodbye fondly, and prepared to look for a taxi home. We dithered for a moment, wondering whether to text my mother, see if she was ready to go too, but then decided not to interrupt them. Besides, it was only ten o'clock. I'd got my phone out of my bag, however, just to check she hadn't already texted. I hadn't looked at it all day, for obvious reasons, and now I realized there was a message from Rory. My heart began to quicken ridiculously. I glanced around. Hugh was inside Peter and Pat's hotel now, asking the receptionist to arrange a taxi. I read it.

Greetings from Orvieto. Thinking of you all today, and hoping you are all having the happiest of days.

This time tears did spring. So kind. So like him. Not some pointed message just to me, reminding me, on a family day, about our relationship, but a message for my whole family, who were my happiness. A message I could frankly have shown to anyone. A message from an old friend abroad. And yet it was full of love. I slid the phone quickly back in my pocket as Hugh approached. In fact, he jumped the last few steps from the hotel in a joyful, uninhibited manner.

'OK?' I smiled.

'Yep. He's got us one, it's right here.' He pointed to a dark grey Audi parked at the kerb. Hugh ushered me in, and we drove away.

My mother arrived back an hour later. I'd thought

of waiting up for her but had decided this was her own private time, to mull over what had been said, and that I'd let her go to bed quietly, with her thoughts. So I just turned over in bed and went back to sleep.

The following morning I realized we were out of milk. The bread was pretty scant too, so I went into town. I was so glad I did, because as I came out of Waitrose, I nearly ran over the bride and groom. There they were on the pavement, very hung-over, and trying to summon a taxi on their phones to take them to the station, and on to London and Heathrow. Nico and Barnaby came panting up behind them dragging bags on wheels and looking dreadfully dishevelled and red-eyed.

'Oh, you are so disorganized!' I cried, delighted, as they piled in the car. I ferried them all in an indispensable-mother-however-old-you-are kind of way to the station. I was thrilled to see them, and accepted their thanks and hugs and kisses as we got there in time – two miles outside town, incidentally – to catch their train to London. Nico was on a midday flight to New York, and Teddy and Ella to Greece. How lucky, I thought, as I drove slowly home, to have run out of milk. How gorgeous it had been to have those final moments with them. And how lucky indeed, I thought, slowing right down, to see Clem's car, complete with painting in the back, pulling out of the drive. She was glancing the other way and didn't see me, thankfully. She drove off in the opposite direction.

Excellent, I thought, exhaling. I hadn't even realized I'd been holding my breath. She's gone. My mother would be leaving soon too, but actually I was less delighted than I would normally be about that. A bit of me wished she was hanging around, so I could discuss my lunch with my father with her. But maybe not. Maybe that, too, was private.

I was surprised to see her looking less than happy, though, when I went up to her room to check on her. She seemed to be waiting for me, almost. Agitated. Packed and ready to go, her small black bag by the door. The bed was stripped and neatly covered with the bedcover, towels and sheets no doubt already in the laundry.

'What's wrong?' I crossed the room and turned her round to face me; she'd been staring out of the window, twisting her hanky. 'Didn't it go well last night?' I was suddenly alarmed.

'No, no, so well,' she reassured me quickly, touching my arm. 'The best of evenings. Everything shared and forgiven and forgotten and talked about as you both will today, I hope. I so definitely did the right thing and I'm delighted. As David is too. He's a fine man, always was. And if you can only forgive me –'

'Yes, yes, I can, Mum, I've said that. But what's wrong? You're looking so pale.'

'It's Clem.'

'Clem?' I felt furious. I glanced out of the window in the wake of her car which Mum must have seen leave. 'What's she said?'

'It's what she's about to say that's the problem. What she tried to say yesterday, in the garden. What she told me in London, when she asked to meet me for lunch. Yes, we talked art for five minutes, but we mostly talked – or she did – about Hugh.'

'Hugh? Oh – yes, she wondered if he was happy in the country, you said. If he missed London.'

'Yes, his concerts.'

I thought back. Clem had mentioned his music yesterday. I shook my head, bemused. 'Mum . . . ?'

'Emma, Hugh has been having an affair. For a long time. Many years, in fact. With a violinist. They go to concerts together every few weeks. Stay the night.'

I stared at her. 'No. That's not true.' I went very still; it was as if I'd been petrified. I gazed at my mother uncomprehendingly.

'It is true, Emma.' She led me gently away from the window to the bed. Sat me down. I felt very cold. 'They met at a concert, years ago. Then just started going to them together, apparently. Arranging to meet in the foyer. Nothing more. But it grew.'

All the saliva had left my mouth. It was extraordinarily dry. 'Where is he?' I whispered.

'Taking the glasses from the wedding back to Majestic.'

My brain wouldn't process this. Like a little mouse it scurried around picking up pieces here and there. Hugh. At the office. Every few weeks. Taking in a concert while he was there. Staying at his club. It didn't compute.

'Who is she?'

'I don't know. Clem discovered because one of her arty friends knows her. Or knows her father. Who's a sculptor. It came out.' I nodded, trying to absorb this. Trying to imagine it. 'Clem met me for lunch that day because she wanted me to tell you.'

'Why?' I turned.

'Exactly, why. That's what I said. She said it was unfair that you didn't know, that she was furious with Hugh. But I didn't believe her. I said if she was so furious why didn't she confront Hugh? Tell him to pack it in? She pretended to look scared, which we know she's not, and said she couldn't possibly do that. Interfere. Hugh would be furious.'

'Hugh's never furious,' I said mechanically. My hands were freezing. I felt shrivelled. As if someone had reached in with both hands and wrung out my heart until it was dry. But it was the deception, actually. The treachery. Hugh. Yes, he was private, secretive even sometimes, but this level of deception? It was shattering. And he didn't even like sex that much. Or did he? My heart began to beat. I whipped my tongue over my lips. 'And you're telling me because . . .'

337

'She would have anyway. I knew that. She kept hanging on, this morning. Or Sally would. One of them. The bitches.'

I looked at her. Yes. It was far better I heard it from her. My mother. I reached out and took her hand. She squeezed it gently. We sat there together in silence for quite some time. Was I shocked? Yes, of course. But Hugh had never really let me in. This was probably the happiest day – or yesterday was – that we'd had since our own wedding day.

At length we heard a car. My husband returning from Majestic. The engine stopped. A car door closed quietly. Hugh never slammed anything, unlike me. Never ran. Everything was controlled and quiet. Just like his affair. His *affair*. Fuck. What was she like? I wondered. A violinist. Controlled and quiet too, perhaps. No shrieks of laughter in bed. I gulped.

We heard movement downstairs. The kettle whistled on the Aga. It stopped as Hugh took it off to make coffee. Soon he'd be wondering where we were. Or perhaps not? Perhaps, relishing the quiet house, he was even now taking a book, and his earphones, to sit in solitude under the apple tree at the bottom of the garden. A quiet man. An honourable man. Or so I'd thought.

I stood up. My mother rose too. We hugged, gently. I walked her downstairs to the front hall. At the bottom, she turned.

'Emma, I'm sorry . . .'

338

'No, don't be. You had to. Otherwise Clem would have, and that would have been far worse. I'll be in touch very soon.'

She nodded sadly. Knowing that she wouldn't say goodbye to Hugh, I walked her to her car. We hugged again quietly in the drive and in the distance I saw Hugh's panama hat, under the tree, on the lower lawn. If he heard the car door open and shut, he didn't leap to his feet, didn't dash over to say goodbye, but I think he did hear, because the brim of his hat tilted upwards.

My mother got in and with a last squeeze of my hand through the window – goodness, we'd done a lot of touching these last few days – she drove away.

26

Because I'm the sort of person I am, and not the sort of person I'd like to be, I went straight down the garden to talk to Hugh. In retrospect I could at least have made a cup of coffee, eased my dry mouth, gathered my thoughts, ruminated over what I might say, but I didn't. I marched around the side of the house, down the steps from the terrace to the lawn, took hold of the garden chair beside him, swung it around and sat down opposite him. It had the advantage of at least being an upright iron chair, rather than the old-fashioned deckchair he favoured; it gave me a bit of height. I regarded him a moment as he finished his paragraph as I knew he would: middle-aged, grey, slim, immaculate as ever in a pressed blue shirt and putty-coloured chinos, a punctilious, fastidious man. He looked up, finally. Gave me an enquiring look.

'My mother tells me you're having an affair.'

Hugh didn't shock easily but this did take him by surprise. Two spots of colour, not bright, but pink enough, rose to his cheeks; he blanched slightly.

'Your mother?'

'Yes. Clem was told by a friend and she told her. Is it true?'

He took a deep breath. Sighed. The same sigh I might get if I suggested going on a skiing holiday.

'Well, I don't really know what constitutes an affair these days,' he said carefully.

'Come on, Hugh, don't be an arse. Do you love her?' I never spoke to my husband like this. He couldn't abide coarse language. He looked startled.

'To quote a prince, whatever love is.'

Christ. Pathetic. 'Hugh, he was pilloried for that.'

'He was. And yet . . . we're not all the same. Perhaps he meant it? Perhaps it wasn't an evasive, slippery tactic. Perhaps he didn't really know. Never had.' He wrestled with the truth. 'Yes,' he said finally. 'I suppose I do love her. But I love you too.' For the first time fear entered his eyes.

'Great. Deep joy.'

'It's not . . .' Finally he put his book aside. On the grass. A first. He sat up. 'It's not as you imagine.'

'You mean you don't have sex?'

'No. Not any more.' He had the grace – no, not the grace, the shame – to look sheepish.

'But you did,' I hissed murderously. 'You did have sex, with someone other than me!' Fury consumed me. 'And you love her. Shit. Fucking hell, Hugh, you've been living a total lie!'

'Emma –' He reached out for my hand. I snatched

it away, realized it was trembling. 'Emma, I implore you. Please listen. It never felt like that; it was the music, you see.'

'The *music*.' I stared at him incredulously.

'We became so enraptured, both felt the same. It was how we always met, you see, at concerts. How we originally met, sitting next to each other at a Brahms recital. A wonderful evening, his third symphony, in the Cadogan Hall. We just turned to each other at the end, two strangers, and our faces were on fire. "Spellbinding," she said, as we stood and applauded. I roared, "I'll never forget it."' Hugh roared? That shook me more than anything. I simply couldn't imagine it. 'And she –'

'She?' I interrupted. 'Her name, Hugh.'

He moistened his lips. 'Virginia. Is not a demonstrative person either. But in the heat of the moment, I asked if she'd like a drink in the bar afterwards; she seemed to be alone. To talk about – you know, the music.'

'Ah yes. The music.'

He caught my tone. 'Yes, really, that was all. To share the pleasure.'

'And one pleasure led to another?'

'No. No, of course not.' He looked shocked.

'Oh golly, am I leaping ahead? Silly me. It's just I've been told it's an affair. Back to the bar.'

'Well, after that, we just obviously recognized one another in the foyer now and again. The concerts are regular, as you know.' I didn't speak. 'And – and we sat next to each other. And, yes, we would have a drink afterwards. Discuss the piece. She – Virginia – is a violinist.'

'So I gather.'

'And then . . . well, then . . .' Finally he struggled with the truth. Looked ashamed.

'How long until you had sex with her?'

He shrugged miserably. 'About a year? Eighteen months, maybe. And only . . . about once a year.'

It was my turn to be shocked. 'Once a year?'

'Virginia . . . she doesn't, you know . . . And I – well.'

'Neither of you are into sex,' I breathed.

'No. But it was the companionship, the music. The shared love.'

'You had companionship at home.'

'Yes, but . . . oh, Emma, you know what I mean. She understood every note, every cadence, it was a shared passion. We talked about every nuance of phrasing, every . . . Don't make it hard.'

'Don't make it hard?' I repeated incredulously. 'Why not, Hugh, why not? I've just been told that for the last however many years of my life, I've been living a lie. That the man I was married to was not the man I thought! How many, Hugh? How many years?'

He looked at me, scared now. And I felt scared too. Wondered if I could take it. I went very cold.

'Twenty,' he muttered.

I stared at him, horrified, then pushed my chair back, shrinking away from him. Twenty years. The children were – what? Two and four. Pushchairs. Nursery school. Moving into our new house. Hugh and I painting the kitchen together, the radio on, laughing, joking. I felt sick. The treachery almost threatened to overwhelm me. And yet he didn't see it like that, I could tell. Yes, he was ashamed, particularly now it was being articulated, but I had the feeling, at the time, even now, he thought it was sort of OK. I asked him if I was correct, if he somehow thought it was sort of acceptable behaviour. I didn't recognize my voice. It was strained, peculiar.

'Because – because it was in essence about something you weren't remotely interested in,' he stuttered, 'and to me it was my whole life, I suppose – I suppose, Emma, I did feel I was entitled to it. Entitled to share and enjoy my passion with someone else. Can you understand that?'

I struggled to be fair. Hugh was an intellectual. He had a very different brain to me. 'Up to a point, yes. And had you told me about her, said you met up for concerts, I might have been all right with it.'

'Would you?' He pounced, instantly. 'Or would you have wanted to be introduced? Ask her to dinner? Get involved. Have lunch with her?'

I was startled. He meant – I'd want to share. And

he so badly wanted her – or her conversation – for himself. I tried to be even-handed, to understand.

'Ye-ess,' I said slowly. 'I might. But would that have mattered? Wouldn't that have been normal?'

'Normal for you.'

But not for him. And it struck me, very forcefully, that we were so very different. Not for the first time, obviously. But this was more revelatory than anything we'd ever come across in our long history. A light had been shone on our very humanity, our polarity. A deep chasm lay between us. I breathed deeply. Swallowed. Felt my nails digging into my hand.

'Tell me a bit about her.'

He sat forward and pushed his glasses up his nose. There was a silence while he formulated his thoughts. Then he started to speak quietly. 'She was widowed young. Two children. She's a bit older than me.'

I stared. Older. 'Pretty?'

'You wouldn't think so.'

Something frivolous and shallow relaxed inside me. A bit.

'But you do?'

'Well, I . . .' He floundered for a moment, then looked me straight in the eye. 'To be honest, it's not something I think about when I'm with her.'

He liked her mind. It was a meeting of minds.

And I was well aware I couldn't do that for Hugh. Meet him on that level. But it had never mattered. We complemented each other, everyone said so. And lots of brainy people had less intellectual partners. And I was no fool. I was creative. Just not fiercely academic. But did it work? Did *we* work? I stared at him hunched forward, hands clasped, in his deck-chair. Up to a point, yes. And if I'm honest, I'd always thought he was rather lucky to have me. Which isn't a very nice thing to think. But he'd always been . . .

'I'm a bit of a cold fish, aren't I?'

I blinked. 'A bit. I was just thinking that. But I felt I warmed you up.'

'You did. Do.'

'And you toned me down.'

'Yes.'

We sat, for a few moments, in contemplative silence.

'Nico knows,' he said suddenly.

I gazed, horrified.

'Has known for years,' he swept on hastily, know-ing this was the worst news. My children. My own particular passion. Not music, my boys. 'He found out when he was about fifteen. A friend at school saw us together at a concert. Or his parents did. He confronted me.'

I jolted in my chair as if I'd received an electric shock. I remembered that terrible row, which I hadn't understood at the time. The teenage Nico, the rebellion thereafter. How hurt he must have been.

'Jesus, Hugh,' I breathed. There were no words.

'But I told him exactly what it was, a friendship.'

'I hope you lied,' I hissed.

'I did – a platonic relationship, I told him.' He was pleading now, with his eyes, and Hugh didn't plead. His mouth looked sticky and white at the corners. 'I said you wouldn't understand –'

'You blamed me!'

'Well, no, just . . .' His hands were so tightly clasped they were mottled red and white.

'You fucked him up!'

'No – no, I didn't. Nico would always have dyed his hair, bunked off lessons, had an earring, you know that. And I swore it was just a friendship, but one I wanted to keep to myself, just as I've told you now. Even at fifteen he sort of understood. Knew there were things he didn't want to share with Teddy, perhaps. But I did lie to him. Told him I'd never see her again. And somehow . . .'

'You got away with it.'

He looked abashed. 'Yes. I didn't, in fact, go to concerts for about three months.'

'But then you did.'

'Yes.'

There was a silence.

'And the very few times, you – you know. Or so

you tell me . . . ?' I steeled myself. He realized what I was asking. What I wanted to know.

'Oh.' He nodded quickly. Looked down at the lawn. 'At her house. Very few times,' he repeated quietly, looking at me beseechingly. 'Really, Emma.'

I could sort of believe this. They might have performed this ritual just to prove they were human, but then gone back to Brahms. Or Mozart. Or Liszt. All the gang.

'And now . . . ?'

'Oh God, no. Not for years,' he said hastily.

Perish the thought. And I thought of all the times I'd suggested a weekend away, a trip to Paris, gone on the internet to google somewhere, to rekindle that side of our relationship. Less so, now. I'd sort of given up. It was something of a relief to know he wasn't getting it elsewhere. That he hadn't gone off me, physically. He just wasn't interested. Weirdly, because again, that's the sort of person I am, I asked:

'Do you have a picture?'

'Of Virginia?'

'Yes.'

Actually I could tell this didn't surprise him. Mine is a very visual intelligence. He reached for his phone. He flipped through, and handed it to me. I stared at the photo. The woman who was looking at me had a scrubbed, plain face: slim, but with a heavy jaw. Her grey, unhighlighted hair was drawn back from her forehead with an Alice band. She looked embarrassed to be photographed and wore what looked like an M&S sensible shirt. I handed it back, stunned. Right.

'Hugh, are you even aware of the effort I make? Of the clothes I wear, the make-up I put on, the flowers in the house, the new cushions, furnishings?'

'Of course; it always looks lovely. *You* always look lovely.'

It was mechanical, though. Hugh could live in a cave. With his books. His music. With Virginia.

He looked at me earnestly, with kindness. Pity, almost. 'I'd never leave you, Emma.'

I stared at him. Rage bubbled within me. It came to the surface and spilled over in an almighty torrent. 'No,' I roared. 'But I might leave you!'

I got to my feet, knocking my chair over backwards. My fists were clenched and knowing that I badly wanted to slap him, to knock his oh-so-intelligent glasses flying off his nose, to shock some life into that pale, clever face, I shot him a furious look, then turned and ran back to the house.

27

She would be called Virginia, wouldn't she, I thought as I drove off to meet my father a couple of hours later. Not Ginnie, even. Virginia. Virgin Virginia. Or almost. Two children. Did they know? I wondered. Did Teddy? Probably not. What was there to know? Two people had enjoyed a friendship, a love of music, had done the business a few times just to cement things, just to show willing, show there were no hard feelings – Jesus. I swept a despairing hand over my face as I drove down the lanes.

I'd calmed down a bit in my bedroom: stared out of the window for a long time, sitting on the side of the bed. The marital bed. Although it had been Clem and Yanni's bed too. The one back in London was more ours. The one we'd slept in together, side by side, for nearly all of our married life. Whilst Hugh lay beside me with a secret. But didn't I have a secret too? No, not then. Now, though . . . ? I shook my head to clear it. This wasn't about me, right now; this was about Hugh. *His* deception. *His* other life. Christ – I'd never for one moment thought he was capable of having one. I thought I was the one who dreamed of other vistas occasionally – well, quite a lot actually. The one who had to pull herself together, remind herself she was a lucky girl, with Hugh Petridis, one of the great Petridises, beside her, and then to pass the travel agent in town, look at a poster of a cluster of little white villas, and wonder what Malta was like. Gozo, for a long weekend?

And yet, all the time, Hugh was . . . no, I decided. Not fantasizing about Virginia. I knew it wasn't like that. But no doubt going online and looking up concerts, wondering if they would enjoy Elgar at St Martin-in-the-Fields. Or Liszt at the Barbican? Texting her. Did he text her? He must have done. And, no, of course I never looked, checked his phone. Yes, we left our emails up, but I never scrolled through them. As I say, I had no inkling, so why would I? And yet . . . everyone said, and indeed every romantic novel I'd ever read – quite a few, incidentally – they insisted you'd know, if your partner was leading a double life. But I categorically didn't know. Perhaps because, for twenty years – *twenty years* – it had *been* our life. Our normal life. I had one half of Hugh, and she had the other.

I'd always felt he wasn't quite with me. But if I'm honest . . . even for the few years before he'd met her, I'd felt it. Hugh was not a man to give himself entirely to anyone. In a way, that had been a bit of an attraction, a challenge. But now I wondered if it was because there was nothing really to give. I considered this sadly. Was that it? Was it all he'd got?

I breathed out a long, shaky breath and looked at myself in the rear-view mirror. A middle-aged woman who'd had a nasty shock, who'd very recently heard of her husband's infidelity, and who, almost in the same instance, was driving to meet her estranged father. A father she hadn't known existed. A couple of fairly large hammer blows, surely, by anyone's standards. And yet . . . if I was being brutally honest with myself, now that the shock had sunk in, on both counts, husband and father, I didn't feel myself to be wrung out like a damp towel. I felt . . . OK. And I wasn't quite sure why. On my father's count, I believed it was because he was so much more than I'd ever hoped he'd be. And because some terrible fear, of a disreputable, drunken rogue, maybe someone coming begging for money in his final years, the only reason he was seeking me out – oh, I have a vivid imagination – had been dispelled. I swung the car into the forecourt of the hotel and parked. Sat there for a moment. On Hugh's count . . . I was still horrified, obviously. Shocked. But yet again, it was that jigsaw of my life. The missing piece. Something – not consciously, but subconsciously – had never added up. It was as if I'd jammed in a bit of sky, which didn't quite fit. But now the right piece had been found, on the floor, under the table, and it did. The finished picture wasn't terribly attractive, but nonetheless it was complete. It made sense.

I got out and shut the door. Stood there for a moment. It occurred to me that of course Hugh wouldn't leave me; he had everything he wanted. He had a woman in both camps. One who complemented his cold nature – oh yes, I made free with that word now, no euphemisms like 'reserved' or 'distant'; after all, I'd heard it from his own lips – and one who satisfied his intellect, and was extremely similar to him. I wondered what they did when they weren't talking about music. Sit in silence and commune mutely? Hugh liked silence. Communicate on some higher level? Disgust rose within me at the lofty nature he'd somehow suggested this liaison possessed. But then I sighed and locked the door. This was not something I could comprehend in the space of one morning. It would have to be digested at length.

My father was on the terrace around the back of the hotel overlooking beautiful parkland with rolling hills beyond. He was sitting at a small round table, a waiter hovering at a distance. His shirt was buttercup yellow, his linen jacket, pale biscuit, and his pressed trousers were bright blue, the colour of the sky. Young colours, all of them – not old browns and fawns.

'Ah!' He got to his feet eagerly at my approach. Rubbed his hands together, eyes bright. 'Champagne?'

I laughed, despite myself. 'Yes, why not? How lovely.'

I surely needed a drink, and could always leave the car here, I thought. I deliberately hadn't drunk much yesterday, to keep a cool head, but now, I wanted that surge of alcohol and those cold, clear bubbles to the brain. My father looked at the wine list the waiter was showing him and I marvelled at his knowledge, his questioning of the grape variety: the Pinot Noir, a good one, he thought. All things I would have loved. But it was the kindness and the apprehension in his eyes when the waiter had gone that I knew I'd really missed. The slight nerves as he took my hands in his and told me once again how happy he was to have found me, and how truly sad he was that it hadn't happened before. How bereft his life had been, without his daughter. And I was secretly glad that he didn't have another daughter. That I had always been the only one. I said exactly the same things with a huge lump in my throat. About what an enormous hole there had always been in my life, and how happy I was to have at last found him. And both of us cried a bit. And held each other. When we'd swallowed, blown our noses and laughed through the tears, the champagne arrived. It was cold and crystal clear. God, it was good. We laughed some more as it hit the spot. I thought of that programme, where they find long-lost relatives, and then they sit drinking each other in, eyes damp. Often in a hotel garden. So now I was in *Who Do You Think You Are?* and *Long Lost Family*.

And because, as we know, I'm quite literal, and visual, and possibly a bit shallow, in that moment, I actually saw myself starring in that programme with Davina McCall in it, who was waving happily at me from her car. I almost wanted to tell him.

'How was Mum, last night?' I asked instead, wiping a last happy tear away. 'How did it go?'

'Remarkably well. No bitterness, no recriminations and a lot of understanding – on both sides, actually. She had a point of view, however much it contrasted with mine back then, and we were so young. Too young, really, and too inexperienced, to sort our feelings out. We were married at twenty-one, don't forget. And she was bitterly ashamed, of what she'd deprived you of. Deprived both of us of.'

I nodded. 'A lot of people would say it's unforgivable.'

He gave me a thoughtful look. 'But you . . . ?'

I shook my head. 'No. I do forgive her. Now I know why. Know more. And the thing is . . .' I hesitated. 'She tortured herself her whole life with the guilt; I see that now. It was why she was difficult, I think. Why she was so cold, so critical. One might suppose she'd shower me with love and affection, but she didn't. Or . . . that's not true. I always knew I was loved, but she didn't show it.'

'Because to show love is to make oneself vulnerable, perhaps.'

'Perhaps.' I thought of Hugh, who'd never been

demonstrative. Meaning I'd gone from one chilly person to the next. Hugh, who'd gone away to school at seven and hated it. And I suspected that he too, like my mother, had vowed never to be that vulnerable again. Not consciously, but a shell had irrevocably formed. It was why we'd never sent the boys away. Kept them in London. I'd never said as much to him, but it was my reason for doing so. So they didn't turn out like Hugh. With their emotions cauterized. I told my father this now. He nodded, understanding. My grandparents, he told me, had done things differently with him. He'd gone to boarding school at thirteen, but after a local day school. And of course, in Australia, it was entirely different. So with his boys . . . He broke off.

'Can I see them?' I asked eagerly. 'Do you have pictures?'

He did. Of course he did. He reached eagerly in his jacket pocket for an envelope, opened it, and handed me a photo. It was of a middle-aged man. He was blond, broad, tanned and smiling, wearing a blue T-shirt and shorts, a glass of wine in hand.

'Tommy,' he told me gently.

I stared. Extraordinary. My brother. Then he handed me another. And I got a shock. I glanced up.

'Oh my God.'

'I know.'

I stared down again. This man was so like me. Slim, dark, the same high cheekbones and distinctive almond-shaped eyes. I felt my mouth fall open as I drank him in.

'Banjo.'

I looked up and laughed. 'Banjo!'

'It's quite a common name in Australia.' He laughed too. 'Jody chose it.'

He handed me another photo, of an elderly, smiling, maternal-looking woman, with her arms around both her boys. A gracefully faded blonde; I saw Tommy in her. Then another of Jody, my father, the two boys, and two pretty blonde women – their wives, I was told, Mandy and Sarah – and an assortment of teenage, or grown-up grandchildren. The entire family, plus a couple of golden retrievers, were standing on the lawn in shorts, laughing into the camera. My father, also in shorts, still had the barbecue tongs in his hand. This was when my eyes filled up and spilled on to my dress. However much I wiped the tears away, I couldn't stop them falling. My father came around and sat beside me, holding my shoulders, knowing what I wouldn't say. About what I hadn't had. Barbecues on the lawn. Easy, lazy days. No. Just me and my difficult mother. Seventeen different houses in all. In increasingly run-down parts of London. All those schools. I made friends easily, eager to be liked, but never for long. Because after a year – we were gone. We'd moved on. And all so that this happy family couldn't find me. I fought valiantly with myself as I stared at the photo. Might

I have been tempted to go? To Australia? To my family? When I'd been old enough to choose, say at fourteen? I couldn't in all conscience answer that. I could see why she'd turned to God, my mother. And I daresay my father could too. All those prayers. Please Lord, don't let it happen. Don't let them take her. Don't let me lose my child. There was no need to articulate any of it. He knew.

I wiped my eyes, nodded to show I was all right. Then I lined up all the photos on the table in front of me. I couldn't take my eyes off them. Couldn't get enough. I stared at them, all in a row. Then I shuffled them quietly back together, put them in the envelope and handed them back. There was only so much a person could take in one instance. But my father pushed them back to me, across the table.

'For you. For later.'

I smiled. Wiped my face again and nodded. I put them in my bag. I'd brought some photos of my own, for him. I took them out. One of each of the boys separately, and then the two of them together: Teddy and Nico with their arms around each other. There was one of me on my own that Teddy had taken, and, of course, Teddy and Ella on their engagement. There was also one of the whole family, but for some reason I kept that back. My father noticed.

'There isn't one of you and Hugh together?'

'There is . . . but . . .' I sighed. Handed it over.

'You didn't want to?'

'No, it's just . . .' I hesitated. 'Something happened. This morning.'

He smiled. 'Bit of a domestic? Weddings are often very fraught, very emotional. I wouldn't read too much into it. All sorts of things can surface. I remember when the boys got married, Jody and I argued over nothing.'

I looked at him. It was the sort of reassuring advice I'd missed. He wasn't accurate in this case, how could he be? But I knew I could have talked to him about a lot of things, as I couldn't to my mother. She'd always shut down any sort of intimate conversation. But it hadn't been a domestic, this morning, a tiff. It was . . . I swallowed, took a deep breath, and then somehow, found myself telling him about it. About the conversation I'd had not two hours ago with my husband. Which was extraordinary, really, when you came to think about it. But on the other hand . . . who else? Who else would be so firmly in my corner, not judge me? Not judge either party. It obviously took quite a long time because I had to explain Hugh. Give him some background. Explain why it wasn't really as shocking as it seemed, given the man. And given what I hadn't been able to provide him with. I found myself couching it like that. As if I might be to blame, excusing my husband. There was a long silence. Eventually, he spoke.

'Are you being generous in your lack of condemnation of Hugh because you yourself have found the marriage lacking? Have wondered if he's been enough for you, on an emotional level?'

I felt myself flushing. Did he know? Suspect? Well, he was my father, of course I could tell him.

'Yes,' I said simply.

'And is anyone capable of filling that void?'

And so I told him about Rory. And about Hamish. Which meant I basically had to tell him my life story. The Petridises were all there. Sally featured. It all came tumbling out. But mostly, it was about Rory and me, and our own guilt. Not so different to my mother's really, in its enormity. Worse, perhaps, because in her narrative, no one had died.

He nodded. 'So, is that why you've deprived yourselves of one another?'

'Well, I've . . . I've put – us – in a box, always. In a cupboard. Marked it "forbidden". As he has too, I suspect.'

'But now you don't have to.'

This was something I hadn't dared think about. That Hugh's private life somehow made it permissible for me to have mine. My breathing became rather shallow. Rapid. I let Rory's dear face flit into my consciousness for a matter of seconds, then away. That way madness lay.

'Do you have a picture?'

I looked shocked. 'Of Rory?' There, I'd said his name.

'Yes, of course.'

I'd been about to deride the very idea, but realized it was the same question I'd asked Hugh, not two hours ago. A request for visual information. Like father, like daughter. And right at the bottom of my purse, I did have a photo. I knew I did. It had always been there. There were others, of course, for cover: one of Jane, the boys, Sally, the Petridis family, Hugh and I – six photos in all. But one, a group shot, on a Scottish beach, was of Hamish, Rory, Susie and me. And, no, Hugh would never look. Not in a million years. And even if he did, he wouldn't mind. I showed my father. Pointed Rory out.

'Many years ago.'

He nodded. Looked at it for a while longer, then handed it back to me. 'And now?'

'Sorry?'

'Where is he now?'

'At his house, in Italy.'

'Alone?'

'Well . . . yes.'

'And does he still love you?'

I swallowed. 'He does.'

We regarded each other a long moment. His soft gaze didn't leave mine. It didn't challenge me, but it held me.

'Such an upheaval!' I blurted out at last. It sounded as if I were considering changing the carpets.

He gave a small shrug. 'Life can be.' My breathing became rapid again. He gave another shrug. 'But that's living.'

'Hugh. The boys . . .'

'Emma, I'm not recommending anything. But I can see what lies in your heart. And the boys are grown men. You've done a very good job there. But maybe the time for doing a good job is over. And you can't make a career out of love. It's too important.'

My shoulders relaxed a little and I reached for my drink. Its clear coldness filled my mouth with surprisingly few bubbles. But then I remembered someone telling me quality champagne didn't have much fizz. Hugh, perhaps. I looked beyond my father, taking in the view of the emerald-green hills rising up from the valley floor; they were freckled with creamy sheep. In the foreground, a few deer grazed peacefully in the parkland below. As I gazed, I realized in that moment, that whatever I decided to do, whatever happened in the future, sitting here, on this sunny terrace, drinking champagne and talking to my father thus, in the most confidential, candid way imaginable, was one of the most pleasurable moments of my life. The best moment of my life.

28

When I got back to the house, Hugh was nowhere to be seen. The kitchen was clean and tidy – he'd washed up – and the sitting room looked orderly too; even the cushions had been plumped. I went down the garden to see if he was still there. He wasn't. The deckchair was empty and the one I'd swung around and then knocked over as I'd run into the house was still on its back. The lawn looked like an empty stage. I went to the barn and realized someone – presumably Hugh – had cleared up in here, too. All the chairs had been removed, the flowers, the fairy lights; it was as if nothing had ever taken place. No joyous wedding, just a barn, with some paintings, for when it served as an occasional art gallery. Except, of course, the portrait was missing. I went across and gazed up at the empty space above the stage, just a solitary nail remaining. Thank God. I shivered. I realized I wanted every trace of her, Clem, removed. Be gone. I heard quick footsteps behind me. Sally came into the barn. She'd clearly been watching out for me. She looked anxious.

'Sorry about all that, yesterday, Emma. I totally lost the plot.'

I shook my head. 'Don't be sorry.' I felt my eyes harden. 'It needed saying.'

She gave a nervous laugh. 'Well, it was all a load of old bollocks, really. Just overemotional crap after a long day and a lot to drink. You've been very good to me. Very kind.'

There was something in her eyes that I'd seen recently in Hugh's: a pleading. Fear even. And they both knew I was a very soft touch. A pushover, in fact. But even pushovers have their saturation point and I'd reached mine. These two Petridises with their secrets: Sally's about how she really felt about me, and Hugh with his. They thought they could just gloss over it and I'd be fine, roll with the punches. After all, I'd spent my life keeping the peace, mending fences between the Petridises, my boys sometimes, or with their father – it was what I and many other mothers spent our lives doing. But both Sally and Hugh had crossed a line. It occurred to me, for a moment, to do as they would do: to keep my secret loathing to myself, to pretend all was indeed fine, but that made me feel sick.

'As I say, it needed saying. I'll talk to Hugh and see what's to be done.'

That shocked her. I saw it flash across her face that I might be about to upset the applecart. Ask her to leave. She remembered what her mother had told her and her own eyes hardened. Then switched to one of faux concern. Her voice became low and confidential.

'Emma, I need to talk to you about Hugh. It will upset you, I'm afraid, and no doubt he won't want me to tell you, but we've been friends a long time and I feel I should. We're sisters, after all.'

'Virginia? Oh yes, I know all about that. Excuse me, Sally, I'm afraid I can't bear to be in your company a moment longer.'

I moved past her and went across to where, happily and conveniently for me, by way of a distraction, a lorry was trundling its way into the field, with a flatbed trailer on the back. The marquee men had arrived to dismantle and remove the tent. I went across and had a word with Rufus, the boss, realizing I was perfectly calm. Rufus was a local chap and I knew him a bit; he was genuinely interested in how the day had gone – had it been a success? I gladly talked him through it as his army of boys removed the hessian matting and relaxed the guy ropes. We chewed the fat for quite a long while and I wondered if Sally was watching. When the tent was ready to come down, Rufus and I went inside and removed the last of the tables, a few pedestals belonging to Susie, and some flowers from the central pole. As I came out I saw Sally, still hovering around the barn. I knew she'd be flabbergasted. This was a side of me she'd never seen before – ordinarily I'd be rushing to put things right – and I wondered what she'd do.

Twenty minutes later, the marquee was on the back of the lorry and I was waving them out of the far gate. As I shut it behind them, my phone rang. I took it out of my pocket. Ah. Of course. It was Jane. That's what Sally would do. I ignored it, turned it off. Jane, another mediator by nature, appealed to by Sally to make me see reason, not to throw everything away, and, more particularly, her, Sally, out of the cottage. Oh, they wanted to push me to the limit, these Petridises, but they nevertheless wanted me to keep the show on the road, to keep needing them, not to be the one to walk away. I could read them all. I knew them so well, you see. And what *was* I going to do? Was I really going to walk away from all of this and run to Rory in Italy? Live amongst the olive groves and the cypress trees and forget my family? I stood for a moment on my lawn, just before reaching the house, swaying slightly in my trainers. I turned and gazed back at the view. In the distance the hills were just beginning to brown off, to turn to a heavenly shade of gold. A bright red combine was trundling about them, spewing dust. More proximately, where the garden ran down to the meadows, everything was blooming, synchronized perfectly, of course, to come out for the wedding: the roses, cabbage white and fragrant, the floppy new hydrangeas I'd found in the market and which I'd planted myself in an avenue for

Ella and her father to walk through, nodded at me, smiling. I'd almost broken my back planting those. Everywhere bees hummed amongst the lavender, and the pretty bantams – Silkies, with feathered feet – pecked attractively in the bushes. I'd seen myself feeding those chickens with my grandchildren. Oh, how I wanted those. And I knew Ella wanted to get going; she'd told me so. I had everything ready for them: the baskets to collect the eggs; I even knew where the swing was going, hanging from the walnut tree on ropes, not a metal one. I had it all planned.

I walked slowly up to the house. Hugh would want me to stay, I knew that, from all the tidying up he'd done. That was the message. He wasn't about to throw in the towel. Wouldn't want to disrupt the status quo. Quite what his suggestion would be as to how we were to proceed I didn't know, but I didn't really care; I wasn't interested. I knew I had to make my own mind up. It came to me, as I shut the back door behind me – and I was rather shocked to realize it – that it was quite possible I'd stay. It rocked me on my heels a moment. But stay on my own terms. And I'd need to decide what those terms were. This was a long twenty-five-year-old marriage. But it wasn't about the marriage, I thought sadly. It wasn't about Hugh and me. It was the other beating hearts, and the yet-to-be beating hearts. Those were the ones that would make me reconsider.

As I took a clean tea towel from the drawer to

replace the one Hugh had used to distraction yet still folded damply on the Aga rail, I realized I'd missed a note on the draining board.

Gone to take the flowers to the church. x

I stared. It was something I'd said I'd do today, and Hugh had just smiled. Smirked, actually. I don't know why. I often didn't know why. Maybe I was amusing, with my good works? Let's not forget what Sally had said about justifying privilege. Perhaps I amused the Petridises? And a kiss. On a quick note like that? Never. He was trying. I wondered if I should. Mechanically, I went back to the site of the marquee. The vases and pedestals had been put in a cluster on a table, and Hugh had put Susie's set of tiny blue jugs on a tray, outside the barn. I collected everything, took them all up to the house to wash them thoroughly, then transported them to the back of my car. I shut the boot. Functioning on automatic was what was called for at the moment, I decided. As Churchill had said, keep buggering on. I got in the car, put it into gear, and drove off to Susie's house. I knew I wasn't up to seeing anyone, but I'd already decided I'd leave them in her flower room, or her greenhouse, and text her to say I'd returned everything.

As I drove up her back drive, the one her friends used, I realized her little blue Audi was missing from the yard. Then I remembered her saying they were going to Dorset for a few days, to stay with friends.

Excellent. I relaxed. So the flower room was not possible, as the house would be locked, but I'd leave them in the greenhouse. Or actually, no, in the shed, by the back door, closer to where she'd want them.

As I opened the door to the shed, I heard women's voices, laughing. I turned, surprised. Through the boot-room window, inside the house, three or four women were laughing at something another woman had said. We all saw each other at the same moment and looked startled. I went across. Who on earth . . . inside an empty house?

A smart woman in a blue suit opened the back door.

'Hello.' She smiled pleasantly. 'I'm from English Heritage. Doing a tour.'

'Oh!' I relaxed. I knew Susie and Rupert did this sort of thing, or rather allowed others to. 'We should really do it ourselves,' Susie confided, 'and we used to, but we've become rather bored with our own voices showing off our house.'

'Oh, in that case, I'll leave these inside, if I may?' I gestured to my collection of china in the back of the car and explained about the wedding, Susie's vases, the flower room.

'Of course!' She opened the back door wide and I carried them all in. I went into the little scullery, while the women carried on. One vase was still a bit green inside so I was able to wash it properly at the sink and then put them all back in the cupboards where they belonged. As I arranged them neatly I listened to the tour guide explaining the history of these back rooms, the below stairs servants area, as it had been once. And actually, she was good. It was fascinating. Apparently the house had been requisitioned in the First World War and this had then been the ops room. The battle of somewhere famous, which I couldn't quite catch, had been planned from here. I turned from the sink to listen to her explaining about the bells on the wall, how they'd historically been used to summon each maid or footman, but then later, each radio operator. She saw me listening and smiled.

'Join us, if you like? We're about to go into the West Wing, which is fascinating. Then upstairs.'

'Oh no, I . . .' I paused. It was soothing, listening to her bring the history of this house alive. It was – not taking me out of myself, exactly, there was too much in my head, to do that – but helping.

'OK.' I nodded. Smiled. 'Thank you. Just for ten minutes. I won't go upstairs.'

That would be weird, I decided, traipsing around my new friend's bedrooms. But I knew there had been a fire in the West Wing, and Susie had told me it was quite a story. The bravery of the maids and servants in the seventeenth century, who would not let it burn, who were up all night, working with their much-loved employers, Rupert's ancestors. Passing buckets in a long chain, the footmen up with the master of the house on the roof, risking their lives, all stripped to the waist, all in it together, as it burned. And so I joined the small group of women who smiled inclusively at me, and we went across the main hall into a side of the house I'd never been. Mary, the tour guide, showed us one panelled room after another, explaining the painstaking restoration. She pointed out the paintings that had been saved, brought out in another long line of servants: the Stubbs, the Reynolds. Precious carpets that had been rolled up. It reminded me of Windsor Castle, the pictures I'd seen as that burned. On she went, opening one interconnecting room door after another.

'And because of the light, this next room is the art room, where years ago, the owner's brother, an aspiring artist, painted the view and – oh.'

She stopped. As she opened the door, Rory turned from standing at an easel, brush in hand.

'As this owner's brother still does!' he said with a grin. Then he saw me. At the back. He looked astonished, as I did too. As our mouths fell open, uncomprehendingly, our eyes locked. I was stunned – but also, quickly, horrified. Rory. Here? Not in Italy. And – and what must he think? This was surely my Elizabeth Bennett moment, snooping around Pemberley.

'Rory, I –'

He didn't say anything, just stared at me transfixed. The women stared too, absolutely gripped.

This was far more interesting than the guided tour, and it was all playing out before them. A dozen pairs of eyes gleamed excitedly, glancing from me – blushing furiously and stammering – back to this handsome man, in paint-spattered jeans, a crumpled white shirt hanging loose, tatty canvas shoes, rumpled dark hair, tanned, slightly lined too, but oh-so attractive. The air seemed to seize up with excitement.

I found my voice. 'I – I came to – to return Susie's vases. And – and to . . .'

'We'll leave you,' the tour guide said smoothly, much to the evident chagrin of her group. 'I'm so sorry, I had no idea anyone was here. Mrs Alexander said the house was –'

'Yes, they're away. But I'm her brother. I'm staying here.'

'Ah, of course. Excuse us.'

She ferried her troop out. The women's eyes were still round and some even looked back over their shoulders, as Mary encouraged them to proceed to the next room, and look at the incredible view. The door shut behind them.

'An incredible view indeed,' Rory said softly, and I realized he meant me. Fierce exultation surged within me but I beat it down. My pulse seemed to be throbbing in my fingertips. I gulped.

'Rory, what must you think? So much has happened to me and I found that small slice of normality soothing. I can't really explain it any more than that. I just – I just joined in.'

'Why not? I've done the same myself, years ago. With Rupert at the helm. It is fascinating. The fire.'

There were a few moments of silence. I saw a tiny feather float to the floor.

'I thought you were in Italy?'

Rory dipped his brush in a small well of turpentine on his palette. He wiped it thoughtfully on a rag. Then he turned back to face me.

'I didn't go. Not sure why. I think I didn't want to be so far away. But I thought it was unfair to tell you. I decided to paint here. Swore Susie to secrecy. And as you can see, it worked. I've built up quite a body of work.' He gestured to the canvases scattered around the walls of the room. They were all similar views to the one from the tall window, of the parkland beyond, the golden hills in the distance. All were breathtaking – one or two still wet, it seemed.

'It often does work that way for me,' he went on. 'Bursts of creativity coincide with times of high emotion. Crisis, even. The paint flows.'

I nodded. 'And . . . you didn't think it was fair, because . . . ?'

'Oh. Too much pressure. Too much – hey, guess what, I'm still hanging around. Don't forget me. Too . . . needy, I guess.'

He looked down. Frowned. This handsome, charming man, needy? I caught my breath. But he was right. Not about the needy bit, but about the proximity. It would have unsettled me. Upset my big day.

'Thank you.'

He looked up, his eyes accepting my thanks.

'And the day was . . . ?' he asked kindly, his eyes warm.

I felt my face clear. I believe I even smiled. 'Everything I hoped it would be. Fabulous. But . . . eventful. My father turned up.'

He looked astonished. 'In a good way?'

'As it turned out, yes. But it was quite a shaker. There were other shakers too . . . have been, other shakers.'

He nodded. His brown eyes were soft, not expecting anything.

'Do you want to talk about them?'

'Yes.' I nodded. 'I do. But not right now. I'm still getting my head round it. Them. But in short, well, in short – although there's nothing short about it – Hugh's having an affair.' Even as I articulated it, it rocked me anew. 'Has been having an affair, for many years. Twenty. A love affair, rather than a – you know. Physical one.'

His eyes widened in surprise. He nodded. 'A bit like us.'

It was my turn to be surprised. 'Oh – well. A bit more physical than that. I mean . . . we haven't seen each other, have we, or –'

'No, but we've been in each other's hearts. At least, you've been in mine.'

It seemed to me all breath had left my body. Just my beating heart remained.

'You've been in mine too, Rory.'

We stood there, facing one another, in the painting room. It was as if we were waiting, the pair of us, to see what would happen. Where this would take us.

'I'll go now,' I said at length, drawing my eyes away from his. I looked at my shoes. 'So much to – you know.'

'Digest.'

'Yes.' I looked up, thanking him for that. Because of course I was giving up so much more than he was. Or at least, would be giving up. It would be so much harder to extricate myself. If indeed he wanted me to? His eyes told me that he did. But I knew, in my heart, that despite it beating wildly, and despite this highly charged moment, my greatest love – my family, my sons, those little girls running around the orchard collecting apples, boys in shorts with fishing nets in the pond, Hugh showing them how to scoop beneath the lilies and the weeds – that was still there too. Despite the incredible view from here. And Hugh loved me, I knew. I didn't doubt that. It was just that grown-up love, married love, could be very many things. It could be complicated. There could be grey areas. Nothing at all, in time, and with age, was black and white. Even if it had been when you were twenty. Back then, at that age, there were only two hearts involved. Now there were so many more. Accommodating romantic love in late middle age was not straightforward. Sometimes it just had to fit in, whenever and wherever it could. Where there was time or space. So, no, it wasn't straightforward. I didn't know what I'd do. I turned and left the room.

Epilogue

Six months later I was fastening my seat belt, putting my paperback away in my handbag, and tilting my seat into the upright position. Rory was beside me. We'd taken the plane from Peretola airport in Florence. I'd thought about staying with Hugh, but not for any protracted length of time, if I'm honest. I'd spent a few weeks walking in the hills around the house, watching the harvest come in, the wheat being loaded into lorries, with the dog beside me for company, but not Hugh. I didn't really consult Hugh. In fact, not at all. I was just thinking. Thinking, thinking, thinking. And thinking had convinced me I couldn't stay with him. Because after all, he hadn't considered me. Not once. Too much had happened under my nose for too long, whatever he might say about it simply being a meeting of minds: a gap in his intellectual life that needed filling, a musical relationship – crap, he'd been having an affair. A love affair. And it was the deception that hurt. All those times he'd come in late from the Wigmore Hall, or St Martin-in-the-Fields, and I'd say, 'Had a good evening, darling?' And he'd say, 'The best.' His eyes shining, like a little boy. Or he'd say, 'A fabulous night!' But the expression I remembered most often was: 'The best.' It was so unlike Hugh. And I used to glow with pleasure for him. Well, now we knew why. Now we knew why his eyes were on fire. What a great cover. And how convenient to have a wife who liked him to have his own interests, his own cultural pursuits, who glowed too, for him.

And what had she thought of me, Virginia? Had they discussed me? During their suppers, which he'd always told me he had alone – so hungry, he'd say, after a long concert. 'I take a book.' Nothing unusual about that, being Hugh. And he'd always leave the house with a book, always remember it. Had she said, 'What's she like?' And had he sighed and said, 'So different to you. A homemaker. I'm not sure she understands this side of me.' And would they smile complicitly over the candle?

A homemaker. He'd called me that once, when I'd jokingly asked him to describe me, in one of what he called my 'silly talk' moments, in bed.

'Go on, Hugh,' I'd said, nudging him, hoping for a spot of playfulness. 'What am I?'

When he'd replied without hesitation, I'd been surprised. Wasn't that a slightly derogatory term? But then I'd been defensive.

'Yes, you're right, I am. Because somebody has to be. Otherwise there isn't one. It doesn't just happen,

378

you know. Without someone making one, it's just a house.'

I wouldn't say it had shut him up, but he'd looked thoughtful. Perhaps he'd thought – yes, I do need both of them. And how long had he imagined he'd get away with it? Those candlelit suppers with Virginia, in different venues presumably, to cover their tracks. I'd almost run back in from my walk that day in the hills, from the harvest, the dog at my heels. I marched, certainly, back up the valley, up the garden, and burst into his study, where he was at his desk, reading a manuscript.

'How long would it have carried on?' I blurted.

He'd looked up, startled. Then he'd looked ashamed. And then, because he was an honest man, or so I'd liked to think, he'd answered truthfully.

'Well . . . forever, I suppose.' He blinked at me behind his glasses.

'Forever. *Forever*. So – so, what, when one of us died, you, perhaps, and there we all were at the funeral, some strange woman might appear? Who's that? we'd all wonder. And then we'd discover. Oh, it's Dad's – or Grandpa's – mistress. Like some – some French grandee, de Gaulle. Didn't that happen at his graveside?'

Hugh shook his head in wonder. 'Your imagination . . .'

'Yes, my imagination, Hugh. Because it's all I've

got. Because without you filling in the gaps for me, without you even writing me a letter or something, and since it seems you can't bring yourself to speak, can't communicate like a normal human being, that is what I'm reduced to. What I imagine.'

Our evenings, the only time we spent together, with me sewing, him reading, were excruciating. The television was on low in the corner, but neither of us was watching: just a third wheel. And all the time I thought he might look up from his book, and say, 'The thing is, Emma, I've always loved you more.' Not just 'as well', as he'd said previously. Regard me earnestly and say, 'We've created so much between us, look at what we've got. Let's not throw it away.' But he never did. And no way was I initiating that conversation. No way. Would it have made a difference? I don't know. But it would have been nice to hear it.

'I'm leaving you,' I told him, still in my wellington boots in the study, the dog panting beside me, then, sensing the mood, slinking under Hugh's desk to her basket. 'Even if you won't say it, I will. We have loved each other, but now we love other people. Our boys will be fine, because we'll still be here for them, as parents.'

And do you know, he didn't even ask. Didn't say – who are you in love with? He didn't even look that shaken. A bit. But not devastated. Did he know? Or, more likely, being Hugh, did he think it indecorous to ask? Too nosy. Too . . . personal. Yes, that was it. *Christ.* I felt sick. Always, I'd had to cajole him to say the magic words. Never would he talk about feelings, or anything intimate. If I really pushed I might get: 'Well, we're here, together, so obviously we love each other.' Or obviously not. Or at least, not enough. For me.

He conceded my decision with a small nod and a pained expression. And that is how our marriage ended. With that small inclination of Hugh's head, at his desk, in the study. Like a headmaster, I thought. I, on the other hand, ran from the room, flew upstairs and flung myself face down on the bed, sobbing. And, no, he didn't come after me. At length I got up, blew my nose and washed my face. Extraordinarily, I felt better. Exhausted, but better. I'd crossed a line, you see. Made a decision.

The following day I rang the boys. I knew Hugh would be hopeless, just say, 'Your mother and I have decided to part.' And I wanted them to hear it properly, from me. But Hugh's long affair I would have to leave to him to explain, if he wanted to. Nico was not that surprised, funnily enough. He asked me if it was because of what he'd found out, years ago, and incidentally, he told me, Teddy knew too. I had to sit down abruptly on the side of the bed, at that. I told him yes, in a way, it was. But also, I'd fallen in love too. I wanted to tell the truth. Nico did ask with whom, and I told him. Told him the whole story. We were on the phone for well over an hour that night. The same with Teddy.

Obviously it was shattering for everyone. I'm not saying it was easy, not by any stretch of the imagination, but the boys were adults. They had their own lives, their own partners, and would soon have their own families. They understood about love, whereas younger children didn't. Not that sort of love. There's never a good time to part, as parents, but perhaps this was better than most. They both wanted to know how Dad was, if he was – they didn't say distraught, they knew better than that, but – OK? Upset? I told them about the pained expression. But not in a bitter, sarcastic way. Just that he'd asked no questions. 'Oh,' they both said quietly.

Six months had gone by since then, and now, here I was, sitting on this flight, and I knew they'd both accepted the situation. Or come to an understanding, perhaps. Which was a relief. And got on with their lives. In quite major ways. Nico was engaged to Tara, and Ella was pregnant, we'd just heard. Back then, though, after speaking to the boys, having made my decision, I'd left the house and gone to London for a bit. For a transition period. A friend had lent me a place. It was Jane's aunt, actually. The same flat we'd had years ago, in Sydney Street. Jane came and saw me there. We'd talked and talked, which helped. She understood. Then, from there, I'd gone to Italy, where Rory was already in situ. He'd said he'd thought it better for me to be alone in London, to think things through, with no pressure from him. And he was going to paint, he told me. And I was to join him if I could. But only if I wanted to. Well, I did.

He was waiting for me at the airport in Florence, and when I saw him, I understood why a friend of mine, a photographer, said she could stand at airports all day with her camera. We just ran. I didn't think I would, but Rory ducked under the barrier as soon as he saw me, and I hobbled towards him in my heels which I'd changed into on the plane, dragging my bag. We cannoned into each other. Clung on. Snap, snap, went the camera.

After that we'd driven to his house, which was some distance from Florence, right up in the hills. And it was everything I'd imagined it to be. Perched on a hill just outside Orvieto – a beautiful city, with an amazing cathedral striped black and white like a zebra – we approached it via a dusty road. The road became a dark lane which plunged down, through trees clustered in the valley. The lane was long and secluded and soon became a track, which suddenly climbed. Over ruts and potholes we inched upwards, a wild boar crossing once, and all the time the heady scent of pine needles filled the air. When the trees finally cleared, something magical happened. There, up on the pimple of the hill, was an old stone farmhouse covered in creeper, and in the low afternoon light, the leaves shimmered like so many shifting mirrors. Long and low, the house was just two stories, because, Rory explained, it had been a cattle barn once. The hay had been stored up on the first floor, whilst the cows slumbered below. The walls, therefore, were of the thickest stone to keep cool in the summer, and warm in the winter. It was flanked by another hill, and approached via tall, thin cypress trees, but not in a formal avenue, just dotted about, mixed in with an olive grove. Rory told me he'd planted an orchard too, with figs, and apricots. He pointed to the left and I saw the young trees with guards. There was no pool, he said, but next spring he might put one in. What did I think? Obviously I saw small children in armbands running around. I smiled and said, 'I'd love that.'

We got out and he led me around, holding hands all the while. Hugh and I never held hands. And I hate to keep harking back to him, to keep comparing him, because I know he was a different man, with different ways of loving, but I had needs too, and I like holding hands. Always have done.

We went upstairs and Rory showed me where he slept. It was a large, airy room at the far end of the corridor, the walls the colour of faded plaster. It had windows on three sides. One looked down the front to the olive grove and the forest, one to the hills behind tinged with blue mist now, and one, right down the valley to Orvieto, just beginning to wink its lights in the gathering dusk. I leaned out. The restaurants were gearing up for supper, Rory told me, leaning out with me. It was still taken outside on these balmy autumn nights. Not too remote, then, this house, I thought. Not too isolated. Ten minutes, he told me, even though I hadn't asked. That was all it took, to get to the bustling city.

'I'll have to learn Italian,' I told him, drawing my head back in.

'You will.' He laughed.

'*Come lo sto facendo?*' I said, raising my eyebrows. Or how am I doing?

He roared with delight. '*È fantastico!*' he replied.

Because obviously, what had I been doing all this time? After I'd made my decision, and started tying up my life in London?

Although naturally, there'd been quite a bit of tying up to do. Dinners with Teddy and Ella, lots of talking. More talking on the phone with Nico. And the Petridises. Yanni I'd gone to see, in his cottage by the sea. He'd sat and listened, Larissa beside him. Then he'd risen: opened his arms expansively. I'd walked into them.

'But of course,' he'd said hoarsely in my ear, his voice cracking with emotion. 'Choose life. Of course you must, Emma. Look at me? Eh? Look at Yanni. Forced into living, by Clem. But best decision of my life!' He stood back and held me at arm's length, his eyes damp.

'You say that even though he's yours? Hugh?'

'He is mine, and I love him dearly.' He placed his hand on his heart. 'But we both know he's Clem's. Is Clem,' he told me sadly.

I heaved up a great sigh from my shoes, as he did too. It was full of regret, but relief, too. Larissa, sitting by quietly, reached up and squeezed my hand.

And then I went to see Clem. In London. But I bottled it at the last minute. I rang her from the car, instead, outside in the road.

'Yes, I know, I got a letter from Hugh.'

More than I did, I almost said, but I didn't.

'Apparently you've reached the end of your relationship.'

'Helped along by you, Clem. Thank you for that. I mean it. And please thank Sally, too.'

She was silent. Shocked. Not the ending she'd envisaged. But then, endings rarely are as one imagines they will be, are they?

'Well . . . I suppose I should wish you luck,' she said coldly.

I didn't reply. And I didn't ring Sally, either. I'd talked to Jane, who understood, and said she'd tell her. If I'm honest, I didn't want to see or hear from those two Petridis women again, which is odd, when you think how much they'd influenced me. How I'd copied them. Back when I'd felt – well. Less sure of myself.

The house in the country, the Pink House, was

sold, the boys told me. It went quite quickly. It transpired no one wanted it, in the end. And Hugh also came to London, and again, bought quickly. But weirdly, not with Virginia. Instead he bought a flat down the road from her, in Chiswick. It turned out they wanted to be together, but not live together. To keep their own independence and space. Which some older people do, Teddy told me. Nothing odd about that, Mum. But it was to me. To me it was downright extraordinary. If you loved someone, surely you wanted to be with them? Teddy hesitated, then agreed.

'But we're all different,' he finished sagely. Dad's different, he meant. Amen to that.

My mother was delighted for me. Now that she'd made her peace with her past, she'd thrown herself into the church, but not in a quiet, private way like before – in a community-minded way. She organized church fetes, became a warden, did the flowers, was in the choir. For a woman who was used to doing nothing except brooding and ruminating, she was busy. And she would come out to stay with us, she promised. Of course she would. And I'd be back and forth to London, to a small flat I'd buy, once the divorce settlement was final. She was coming out in November, as it happened. Rory said it would still be warm then, a pleasant month for her to visit.

I'll put her in here, I thought, as we left the main bedroom and Rory showed me the other bedrooms. This blue one, at the opposite end, over-looking the orchard, with the figs and the apricots.

We clattered back down the wooden staircase – no carpets, I noticed, just rugs – and I admired all his paintings on the walls. He took me to his studio. It was at the back of the house, a large north-facing room. The only room with that crucial light. All around the walls were stacked his paintings, and I spotted a poster too, for an exhibition, in town, in Orvieto. I exclaimed when I saw his name; he shrugged.

'No big deal. I mean, I'm a local artist. They almost have to have me.'

'They absolutely don't. Is it still on?' I crouched to read the dates.

'Just. Tonight's the last night.'

Obviously I wanted to go. And after a quick shower we gathered our things and prepared to set off. To have supper there too. As I came out of the bathroom, he was waiting, in the bedroom. He looked a bit apprehensive. A bit . . . nervous.

'What is it?' I asked quickly.

'No regrets?' he asked, in a slightly hoarse voice. 'Now that . . . you know. You're here? It doesn't feel strange?'

I loved that he'd asked. That he'd been astute enough to realize that once completely discon-nected, once well and truly untethered from my life, I might wobble, slightly. I gazed into his dark, honest eyes, with no guile, no deceit, and took his face firmly in my hands. I kissed him squarely on the lips.

'None at all,' I told him gently.

We smiled at one another and as our smiles became grins we seized our things – his keys, my bag – and headed downstairs and off, into the night.

And night was falling yet again as, two months later, having tucked my paperback in my bag and deposited my glasses in there too, Rory closing his Kindle beside me, we came in to land. The stewardess came round, smiling and checking our belts. I looked out of the plane window at the clouds as we made our descent. Rory, in the window seat, pointed out the runway lights. I smiled. This journey had been his idea, which I considered a supreme act of love. As we touched down on the tarmac with a shudder, we didn't speak, but we held hands. Then it took us another hour to get through passports and customs, baggage. When we finally emerged through Arrivals, our trolley laden with luggage, I stopped, for a moment, to take a deep breath. Rory put a hand on my arm to steady me, to alert me, perhaps. But there was no need. I'd already seen them. There, at the barrier, at Sydney airport, was my father. Tall, lean and eager-looking, with a familiar-looking fair-haired woman in a pink floral dress beside him, smiling. They were flanked by two tall boys. Men. My brothers. I gasped. Couldn't speak.

But they could. They couldn't contain it. They shouted, arms shooting up in the air.

'Emma!' they roared.

And then I flew. And, as it turned out, they were duckers and divers too, like my new husband. They both dipped under the barrier and sprinted towards me, and we collapsed, laughing and crying, the three of us, in each other's arms. Snap, snap, went the camera. Snap, snap.

Acknowledgements

With grateful thanks to Harriet for allowing me to weave a storyline around Daily Bread, the brainchild of a dear friend, her late husband Tim Roupell.

Book Club Questions

1. What do you think the pink house represents within the novel? In what ways do you feel the author uses location to portray her characters' journeys?
2. In what ways do you think the theme of art is an important one in the novel?
3. Consider the female friendships in the novel. To what extent did you feel these friendships withstand the events of each woman's personal life?
4. The novel contains themes of fresh starts and new beginnings. To what extent do you think these help or hinder the characters?
5. The novel opens with a divorce. What observations did you have of long-term relationships and marriage within the novel?
6. In the novel, Hugh asks, 'Why does everything have to have a happy ending, Emma? Or at least, not a happy ending, but a neat little tie-up?' In what ways do you feel this is reflective of the novel's ending?
7. In what ways do the tragedies of certain characters' pasts affect their futures?
8. Consider the theme of parenting in the novel, e.g. Emma's raising of her two sons, her reflections of Hugh's upbringing. Do you feel Emma's own parenting is influenced by the families she sees around her?